WALK WITH THE DEVIL

Tom Foote

WALK WITH THE DEVIL

Tom Foote

DUFOUR EDITIONS

First published in the United States of America, 2013
by Dufour Editions Inc., Chester Springs, Pennsylvania 19425

ISBN 978-0-8023-1353-9

Cover Image: © Stephanie Swartz | Dreamstime.com

Library of Congress Cataloging-in-Publication Data

Foote, Tom, 1935-
  Walk with the devil / Tom Foote.
    pages cm.
  ISBN 978-0-8023-1353-9 (pbk.) -- ISBN 0-8023-1353-1 (pbk.)
  1. Fathers--Fiction. 2. Revenge--Fiction. 3. Drug traffic--Fiction. I. Title.
  PR6056.O59W35 2013
  823'.914--dc23
                                                    2013004476

Printed and bound in the United States of America

To Hilary for her constant encouragement.

My grateful thanks to Liam Cullinane
for giving me an invaluable insight into
the French Foreign Legion.

And everlasting thanks to Nancy Thompson
for her wisdom and guidance.

"I've a rendezvous with Death,
At midnight in some flaming town
When Spring trips North again this year,
And I, to my pledged word am true,
I shall not fail that rendezvous."
                                    —*Alan Seeger*

PROLOGUE

Someone coughed nervously at the rear of the room and a chair scraped on the hardwood floor, then a hushed silence fell over those assembled there. Judge Albert Murphy straightened his wig before switching his reading glasses for those with which he could view the packed courtroom. The black-rimmed spectacles with bottle-thick lenses magnified the judge's pale face, transforming his bony features into those of a predatory bird. His eyes swept across a sea of expectancy. Had there been capital punishment on the statute books, Ryder thought morosely, Murphy would be known as a hanging judge.

The judge opened his blue-white lips and spoke in a voice that was unexpectedly resonant and powerful, his words crashing like waves over the silenced courtroom and reverberating back from its paneled walls.

"Robert James Ryder, you have been tried and found guilty of murder on two counts. The sentence of this court, over which I do not have any discretion, is that you serve a life sentence on each count to run concurrently. However, I must recommend that you not serve less than twenty-five years. Is there anything further you wish to say?"

Ryder raised his eyes and fixed the judge in an icy stare. The beginnings of a smile flickered at the corners of his mouth, then instantly disappeared. But during the moment that it was there, the scar that stretched from above his right ear to the corner of his jaw lost some of its vividness. "Thank you, your Honor," he said quietly. His ramrod-straight figure relaxed into what might have been an imperceptible bow, causing a strand of hair to fall lightly over his forehead. "What is done is done. I have no regrets."

Judge Murphy's pale features fused into angry lines. "Take him away," he snapped.

Ryder felt a light touch on his shoulder. He turned to allow himself to be handcuffed and was led away from the court. As he stepped down from the dock his eyes met those of a woman seated far back in the public gallery. Dressed in black, she looked older than he remembered her and although he had been aware of her presence during most of the trial, this was the first time that he had looked at her directly. In that brief instant of contact his eyes lost their bleakness, becoming soft, so that their color changed to one that was as luminescent as a tropic sea. He smiled at her then. It was a smile of reassurance.

Too fearful to smile, her lips simply tightened into a thin line. She showed no further sign of recognition as she watched him being escorted from the room. But he knew she understood.

Detective Inspector William Brophy stepped outside into rapidly fading daylight. He lit a cigarette and turned up his coat collar against a gust of rain-laden wind that caused a shiver to run through him, bringing thoughts of his mother, long dead. He remembered her saying that such shivers were caused by someone stepping on one's grave.

His companion turned to him. "Well, that's that, Bill," he said. "Ryder's going to be an old man when he gets out, if he makes it." There was satisfaction in his voice.

Brophy inhaled deeply. "Another judge might have given the bastard a medal." His voice sounded oddly bitter, and lines of regret edged the corner of his mouth.

"Christ! You're not now saying that he didn't do it? The evidence was all there. We even had a confession for God's sake! We proved it beyond question."

Brophy scanned the homeward bound Dublin traffic with little interest. Eventually when he spoke, his voice sounded hollow. "Oh! He did it all right, and maybe a few more besides. No doubt about that. Our friend Ryder deserved to be sent down. But it's the way he did it, out in the open, knowing what was coming, as though he didn't give a shit about being caught." He threw away his half-finished cigarette, watching its sparks as the wind flicked it down the steps onto the pavement. "You know, it's difficult to imagine that in a month he accomplished what we and the entire squad have failed to do in twelve years. No. Ryder did all of us a favor, that's the irony of it." He glanced up at a western sky that was heavy with dark mountains of cumulus cloud that threatened to bring rain even as far as the coast of Wales before morning. He blinked his eyes. "Sometimes," he said, "Our justice system leaves a taste in my mouth. Like drinking piss."

Brophy had a far-away look in his eyes as he buttoned up his coat and turned to descend the steps. "Anyway, its over now. Have a nice weekend, Colm. I'll see you on Monday. It should be quiet now for a while, so enjoy the rest. Just remember that next time we won't have Ryder to do the job for us." He paused on the top step. Turning, he smiled. "The only thing I'm glad about is that he is no longer our responsibility. Someone else has to keep him inside. I don't envy them that for one minute."

ONE

The undertaker's mortuary was less forbidding than the exterior had suggested. It smelled clean and the scent of flowers dispelled that of death.

Rob Ryder stood staring into the open coffin and drew in his breath. He had seen death on young faces before but never on a face such as this. In spite of the ministrations of the undertakers, the young man's face was pale, gaunt and lacking tissue, with the bone structure striving to break through a stretched parchment of skin. Thin hands protruded from frayed jacket sleeves, clasping a set of rosary beads that wound in snake-like spirals through fingers that appeared to be sculptured from porcelain. He tried to envisage the body itself, and shuddered. It was an impossible thought, and an agonizing one.

He heard a movement behind him and turned to see a rag-tag group of scarecrows congregating in the doorway as though reluctant to step inside. They finally straggled in as a group. One, bolder then the rest, summoned the courage to speak when they drew closer.

"Are you his Dad?"

The youth extended his hand in greeting but Ryder ignored it, looking instead at the young man's gaunt features, noticing hands that shook as though unseen marionette wires controlled them. "Yes I am," he replied curtly.

"I thought that," the youth said, avoiding Ryder's gaze. "The undertaker said you would be coming; I was the one that found your phone number for him. It was in Mark's wallet. My name's Billy." He drew back his hand and looked around at the others who were hanging back. "We were his friends."

Emboldened by Billy's words, the group moved around the coffin to peer inside. One of them, a girl, wore a shapeless dress that reached to the top of black boots that were laced with string. She clutched a shawl tightly about her shoulders. Suddenly, she started to cry. Sobbing noisily, her shoulders shaking.

Billy looked at Ryder with colorless eyes. "Sheila was Mark's girl," he said.

Ryder's jaw tightened. They all stared at him as if they expected him to say something that might change everything, but he made no reply. His tanned features seemed chiseled from stone, and the scar running down the side of his face had a jagged newness to it that frightened them. His pale blue eyes glared; only the hard set to his jaw spoke of emotion inside him. His dark blue suit looked new, as though he had bought it just for this. White shirt cuffs bared massive hands with skin the color of burnt mahogany. He transmitted power and barely concealed anger. Silence gripped the youths and they gaped.

Angrily, Ryder slammed the lid of the coffin down over the skeleton that had once been his son, a son whom he hadn't seen since the boy was six years old. In June, he would have been twenty-one.

The hollow thud of the falling lid penetrated into another room and the undertaker swept in on cushioned soles. "Screw it down!" Ryder's voice thundered in the room. The girl swayed on her feet. Seeking support, she clutched the arm of one of the others.

"Are you expecting anyone else, Mr. Ryder?" The undertaker's voice came as an obsequious croak, barely breaking the silence that had descended on the room.

"No. Load him up and let's get it over with."

Billy flinched at the words. He glanced nervously at the others as though seeking their approval before speaking.

"We'd all like to go to the cemetery, to see him off, proper like," he said.

Ryder swept them with a distasteful gaze. "Suit your-selves." He led the way outside and walked quickly towards a waiting taxi. The driver got out, holding the door open for him. Ryder swiveled, one foot inside the car. "I want to talk to you before I leave Ireland. After the funeral, where can I find you?"

Sheila scribbled an address on the back of an old envelope that she took from a knitted handbag. "We're all at the same place," she sniffed. "It's in Rathmines on the top floor. Mark used to live there as well." She started to cry again. A bubble of moisture formed on her nostril, then lengthened into a trickle that joined with her tears.

Ryder accepted the proffered piece of paper. "Thank you," he said. His voice was more gentle. He climbed into the taxi and was driven off through the open gates after the hearse.

Nestling at the foot of the Dublin Mountains, the grave-yard at Bohernabreena, even in sunshine, looked desolate. There were few houses nearby to break the sweep of farm fields edging the surrounding hills. To Ryder the place looked nothing more than a dumping ground to take the over-spill from other cemeteries closer to Dublin that were now filled. He climbed out of the taxi and told the driver to wait.

To his surprise, a priest was waiting at the gates. One of Mark's friends must have summoned him, Ryder realized. The need for a priest had never occurred to him; you buried your dead and that was the end of it, he thought. He had done it many times.

The coffin was as light as he expected it to be; he could have lifted it on his own without the aid of the others. Instead, he had to shoulder it unsteadily through the gates; one end awkwardly higher than the other. He adjusted his pace to avoid stepping on the heels of those in front, almost stumbling as out of the corner of his eye he glimpsed a black Jaguar saloon gliding to a halt behind his waiting taxi.

The open grave gaped black against the early spring grass as they lowered the casket onto waiting trestles. Ryder spread his feet and clasped his big hands behind his back. As if from a great distance, he heard the priest intoning prayers, followed by muttered responses from the others. Nearby, a small terrier dog strayed over to cock his leg against a convenient headstone and relieved himself in short yellow bursts.

A man and a woman walked uncertainly towards the group, taking up a position off to one side. Ryder looked up at the woman across the open grave. She was over-dressed in a sable fur coat that glistened in the weak sunshine. Her companion wore a wool overcoat cut short above the knees, below which showed impeccably creased trousers and soft black Gucci loafers.

Imelda was heavier than the last time he had seen her, fifteen years ago, but she was still striking in a blowsy sort of way. Her lips were petulant and down turned, as though she could smell something offensive. His eyes met those of her companion. He'd only seen the man once before and hardly recognized him, but he knew it was Peter, the man she had left him for. Both of them reeked of money, the sort that was easy to come by. Their presence only served to tighten a growing knot of apprehension in Ryder's stomach.

Just for an instant the years rolled away. He visualized Mark grinning in delight astride a pedal car that he had bought him for his sixth birthday. Ryder had come home from Germany unexpectedly, just to bring the present; Imelda had refused to move to Germany when his battalion was sent there. To live in a private soldier's married quarter was too much of a strain on her personal image, so she had remained behind in Aldershot.

Minutes later in mid-afternoon, he had dragged Imelda screaming out of their bed - his bed, a bed that he had found her in with this man at whom he now stared with mounting dislike. The last time Ryder had seen him, Webster had been naked and white faced, his hands fluttering in a futile effort to hide his erection. Now he looked more like a flashy, handsome

spiv with a propensity for high living that suited Imelda better
than the role of a soldier's wife. Instead of beating Webster to
a pulp that day, he had simply walked out and never gone
back. The divorce had been an un-contested formality that
had shocked him with its speed and finality. It marked a turning point in his life.

Ryder continued to stare at Webster. The man looked a little older, but not much. His figure was as sparse and bony as
Ryder vaguely remembered. Webster's brown eyes glared
back at him. He still had the same self-satisfied curl to his
mouth. His sleek black hair was oiled, and had yet to show a
hint of grey. Life had been good to Peter, Ryder saw. For an
instant he wondered what sort of life Mark had with this man
after he had left. Webster had replaced him. Had they learned
to love one another, as a father and son? Somehow he
doubted it.

Webster finally looked away towards the distant hills.
Ryder could tell that he was uncomfortable. It was obvious
that Webster was shocked to find him here. Ryder's eyes
returned to the coffin as he realized that he had not brought
flowers. He had meant to, but in the rush to get here he had
forgotten. He felt a sudden rush of failure.

At that moment, as if sensing that nobody had much interest in what he was saying, the priest ended abruptly. Carefully
the coffin was lowered into its place in the clay. Two gravedig-
gers spat on their hands and began shoveling earth swiftly
into the hole. They seemed eager to be done with it, as
though neither of them could remember a funeral with so few
mourners. Perhaps they would remember this one for a long
time because of that, Ryder thought.

At the first thud of soil on cheap wood, Ryder turned
away. It was over. He could go now. He handed money to the
priest and the workmen, and then turning his back, started to
walk quickly towards the gate.

His taxi driver, seeing him coming, glanced at the meter
and started his engine. The driver was smiling. Ryder could
almost read his thoughts. With a fare like his, there would be

no need to work tonight. Instead, he could have a good night out in the pub and to hell with the begrudgers. The driver looked pleased, flashing him a smile as he drew near.

An angry clack of high heels on the concrete path behind him warned Ryder before he heard the words. "Robert, wait! I want to talk to you about Mark."

Imelda's voice still held the self-centered whine that he had learned to hate. Ryder turned abruptly and faced her. He could see Peter hanging back near the grave, wiping a smudge of mud from his camel overcoat. "I don't think there is anything to talk about, Imelda," he said stiffly.

He fought to prevent anger spilling into his voice but he knew she could sense his impatience to be gone. She glared at him, her face coloring with rising anger. "We haven't seen him for years either, you know. What about his affairs, who's taking care of them? I'm pretty sure you're not. You never had any bloody interest in him."

Close up, she looked fatter, he thought with some satisfaction. The lines were showing and he could see that the caked on camouflage only worked in the distance. There were no signs of tears. Their absence did not surprise him. His voice, as before, was cold. "If you're here for the pickings you've wasted your time, but there may be a few bills if you're interested." Ryder spoke savagely to her, "Your son - my son - was a fucking junkie! He had nothing and now he's dead! There's nothing left of us. Nothing to talk about."

She was close now; close enough to take in the scar on his face. She sneered, revealing expensively capped teeth. "What happened to your damned face? Still playing soldiers, I suppose?"

Ryder moved away, quickening his step. He knew she was goading him. Nothing had changed. He reached for the taxi door and plunged into the back seat, slamming the door shut.

She spat at him in hatred through the open window.

"Go back to London suburbia Imelda," he said. He glanced at Peter coming through the gate, "And take that walking clothes horse with you, you deserve each other."

There was still enough daylight as he approached the house to prepare himself for what he knew he would find inside. Ryder checked the scrawled address and peered at the number nailed to a door that hung open on suspect hinges. He paused on the steps and looked down on the overgrown front garden leading to the busy street. It was full of litter. A dead place, where even the weeds struggled to survive amongst a collection of trash bins and a rusty bicycle that lay chained to the derelict iron railings, as though it had been there since the beginning of time.

Inside the hall, a baby carriage rested at the foot of the stairs. From somewhere higher up in the gloom he could hear a child wailing. Voices from elsewhere in the back of the house were raised in argument. He could smell urine, unwashed bodies, boiled cabbage. He spat as he passed a pay phone that hung from a tangle of wires where it had been wrenched from the wall, then began to climb the stairs, wanting to get it over with.

Ryder raised his fist and hammered on the only door on the top floor. He heard shuffling footsteps from inside and the door swung open. Sheila peered at him in the half-light. She didn't smile. "Come in," she said. There was resignation in her voice. "I thought it might be you. No one else bothers to knock."

She led him to a Formica topped table near the window and gestured towards a clutter of cheap plastic chairs, "Sit down, if you like."

Ryder took a seat and looked around the room. It was difficult to see clearly as evening crept in. A handful of candles wavered in the slight breeze from the open window providing light. The sound of traffic blared from the street outside and he could hear a clock ticking somewhere in the darkness. A greasy stove littered with dishes and a collection of empty tins stood in one corner. There was a rustle from one of the mattresses strewn around the floor and Billy emerged from the shadows, a cloth tourniquet dangling from his upper left arm, a hypodermic syringe hanging from the fingers of his lifeless left hand. His face was white, his eyes glowing.

Ryder lit a cigarette and settled his frame more comfortably. "Don't you have electricity here?"

Billy carelessly dropped the syringe onto the table. "Yeah," he answered, "It's on a meter, but it's just run out."

Ryder closed his eyes for a second. "Where's the rest of them?"

Sheila pulled her shawl closer about her shoulders as though she felt a sudden chill in the room. "They've gone out. They didn't want to see you. You scared them."

Ryder smiled and pulled on his cigarette. He glanced around the room again, trying to imagine what sort of life went on here. "Is this where he lived?"

Sheila nodded. "Yes. Four of us share." She pushed a plastic bag across the table. "Just a few of Mark's things that you might like to have," she said in a whisper. "Some tapes that he liked, a few photographs - stuff like that."

Billy shifted uneasily on his chair. "Mark told us you were a soldier, is that right?"

Ryder's fingers traced the scar on the side of his face. "Yes, that's correct." He leaned forward and tried to read the youth's eyes, whose pupils were sharpened to steel points. "How did he die? Was it AIDS?"

Billy looked away.

Sheila coughed and started to sniffle.

"I'm asking you two a fucking question! Answer it!" His voice boomed.

"No, he didn't." It was the girl, her voice barely audible. "Mark was HIV positive but - but he didn't have AIDS. I'm the same. He overdosed. It happens sometimes." Her voice was distant, sounding hollow, as though she was no longer in the room.

Billy stared blankly at some unseen spot on the floor between his feet. "Mark was a dealer as well as a user," he muttered. "He probably got some bad stuff. It could just as easily have been one of us."

"Where did he get the heroin from? Who supplied him?"
Ryder reached out and touched the girl's bony hand lightly.
"Tell me. I want to know."

Sheila shivered and looked away from him, but her eyes
kept coming back to his scarred face. "I don't know, that's the
truth. He would never tell me."

"What about you, Billy? You were close to him too."
Ryder fumbled in his pocket and pulled out a bundle of notes.
"There's two hundred quid here, enough to buy you two a fix
and get the electricity back on."

Billy's eyes were greedy. "I don't know either," he lied.

Ryder moved with the fluidity of a cat, soundlessly, and
with the same graceful purpose. With one hand he reached
across the table and gripped Billy's throat, drawing him
upwards as he rose to his feet. His chair skidded away behind
him as Billy's eyes bulged, his feet barely touching the floor.
Then Ryder applied pressure cutting off the blood supply.
"You have three seconds, you little fuck, then your neck
breaks!" Billy's eyes rolled wildly as oxygen was cut off from
his brain, his battered runners scrabbling at the floor. Ryder
relaxed his grip and slammed him back on the chair. He
could hear Sheila sobbing. "It was a man called Hennessy -
Flicker Hennessy," Billy choked.

"That's better. Now we're getting somewhere." Ryder
retrieved his chair and sat down. He lit another cigarette. "I'm
not saying that I want to, but if I did, where would I find this
Hennessy guy? What does he look like?"

Billy fought to regain his breath, his eyes awash with fear.
"I don't know what he looks like," he gasped. "That's the hon-
est-to-God truth, Mr. Ryder. I swear it on my mother's grave.
All I know is that Mark used to meet him in a club down on
Leeson Street. A place called the Mandarin. I swear to God I
don't know anything else."

Sheila stopped sobbing. Her face was ashen, her eyes wild.
"He's telling the truth. I swear it. Mark would never tell us.
He was too frightened."

Ryder got to his feet and scattered the money on the table. "I just wanted to know, that's all. I think I have a right to that much." Picking up the package of tapes, he walked to the door without another word.

He thudded down the darkened stairs glad to be leaving the miserable place. He went outside into a night that blanketed the city, where only the streetlights added some semblance of long lost charm to the faded Georgian buildings. He looked back at the building just once, before purposefully striding into the crowd moving up towards the pubs of Rathmines, he had an early flight in the morning and he needed to find a place for the night. There was no need to stay any longer.

Two

Ryder woke to the sound of marching feet drumming on the tarmac outside the single window to his room. Earlier, a bugle had disturbed him briefly when reveille sounded at six, but he had rolled over on his bed and had immediately gone back to sleep. Officially he was still on the sick list and would not have to resume normal duties until after his meeting with Colonel Marchand later that day. It was a meeting that he was not looking forward to. There was too much at stake. Whether to go or to stay was not a decision he wanted to rush into.

He lit a cigarette, a Gauloise, and inhaled slowly. It felt good to be back. There was a harsh but comforting warmth in these familiar surroundings. He knew that when he drew the curtains there would be sunshine outside, soon to become blistering hot until noon stilled the thud of marching boots. Then the parade ground would be empty, and the tricolor of France would stop fluttering fitfully and wait for wind that would surely arrive from the sea in the afternoon.

This was home, such as it was; at least for the present. For the moment he could forget the brooding skies of Ireland and the reason he had gone there; to bury a son that he did not know. He sat up and stubbed the thought out, grinding it with the remains of his cigarette into a metal ashtray.

He looked about the familiar room. It was small, perhaps nine feet by six. Ryder had never bothered to measure it.

It contained his bed, a small writing table, and a metal chair. As an NCO, he also enjoyed the luxury of a private shower and a washbasin. A small fitted wardrobe held his clothes, all of which were pressed with knife-blade creases. Covering the tiled floor was one of his few private possessions, a rattan mat that he had brought back from Mayotte in the Indian Ocean. Except for a small television and a DVD player that stood on the table it was his sole luxury, adding a vestige of warmth and individuality to what was otherwise a monastic cell. Because of his rank he could have chosen to live off base in far more comfort in Calvi, but the harshness of the barracks suited him better and he felt protected by it. The accumulation of possessions had never concerned him.

He showered first, and then shaved, studying himself for a moment in the mirror. The blond hair that had re-grown in hospital was now gone, and his skull, recently shaved back to a fine stubble, picked up the light, so that it looked pale against the rest of his skin.

Turning his head sideways, his fingers traced the scar that glowed red like a new crescent moon, stretching from his ear to the point of his chin. It was healing well he thought. Soon it would be a memory, just another badge of honor to add to the list already etched on his body. The top of his right ear was missing where the scar started; half an inch of it had been severed by the blow that had opened his face to the bone. He frowned at his reflection in the mirror. The man who had swung that rusted machete would never do so again. Disemboweled by his own blade, a five-point-six millimeter hard jacket drilled with precision through the centre of his forehead for good measure, he had long since joined his ancestors in the dust and filth of Eyl.

It had been a short but brutal action, and one that would be denied by the politicians if it failed. For it was an assassination, pure and simple. Legionnaires were expendable and that coupled with the cloud of their anonymity suited such actions. Inserted at night by a French naval vessel that lay offshore, they had surrounded the house where three warlords that controlled most of the piracy were meeting. In just a few noise filled minutes his CRAP team had left the Somalis dead, but they had been forced to fight their way back to the boats.

In that malodorous street, the blood of his unknown assailant had formed a dried up river bed darker than the dust, to become a feeding ground where flies gorged themselves until their bloated bellies could take no more. But Ryder had failed to see the concrete block hurtling like a meteor out of the sky. Seconds later the missile had smashed his collar bone, driving him to his knees. A .50 caliber heavy machine gun had instantly opened up in retaliation, shattering the frail rooftop parapet behind which the thrower sheltered. Ryder remembered the scream of the gunner - "Et ta soeur!" It echoed now in his mind, filling him with pride in this fraternity of men that was his family, a family that protected him when he was in need, every member staunch and committed, only lacking in tenderness. True to the traditions of the Legion, he took pride in knowing he had returned with his dead and wounded and none were left behind, nor did the raid feature in any news bulletin or newspaper report.

He opened his wardrobe and reached for his black red-topped kepi displayed with crossed red epaulettes. Round and hard edged, its gold chinstrap and the seven-flamed grenade crest of La Légion Étrangère reflected the sunlight that spilled from the window. There was a trace of reverence in the way he placed the hat on the desk, and then donned a uniform shirt and trousers. Knotting his dark green tie, he placed his kepi square on his head. Before leaving the room he checked himself in a mirror. With just a minor adjustment to the parachutist's wings worn on his right breast, he was ready for the world outside - his world - a monastic world of fighting men.

The words of a French marching song echoed faintly through the open window as he left the room. "We are the damned of all the world, the wounded of all the wars, we cannot forget a woman, we have pain in our hearts, we walk with the devil . . ."

Colonel Bertrande Marchand stared implacably across his desk and waited for a moment before speaking. He did not smile. He rarely did so but beneath his shaggy black eyebrows that held flecks of silver hair, his brown eyes roved over Ryder, registering brief approval.

Ryder saluted. Removing his kepi, he stood rigidly at attention waiting for Marchand to speak. An overhead fan whispered, its blades stirring the air so that he could feel it on the back of his neck. He noticed a box of cigars on top of the neatly arranged desk. White Owl. A knowing smile flickered at the corners of his mouth. They were the ones that the Americans' smoked. The battalion had intercepted a whole container of them in Djibouti before flying back to Corsica.

Selecting a file from a desk drawer, Marchand placed it unopened on the top of the desk. He looked up and studied Ryder for a moment. Speaking in French, his voice was heavy and as thick as molasses. "Good to have you back, Sergeant. Your wounds have healed?"

Ryder inclined his head. "My shoulder is still a bit stiff, but I guess it will work itself out. The hospital physiotherapist was an animal, but very effective."

Marchand nodded. "Good. The battalion goes on exercise in three day's time and we need you back by then. On Friday the CRAP unit flies to Guyana for jungle survival training and you will go with them under the command of Lieutenant Arvans. However that's not really what I wanted to see you about."

Ryder felt uncomfortable under the intensity of Marchand's gaze but his eyes did not waver. He knew why Marchand wanted to talk to him. His contract was due to expire soon. He had hoped for more time to think it over. Almost fifteen year's service in the Legion had given him all he needed, but now he was no longer sure if he wanted to remain. He wasn't even certain if he was young enough anymore. Especially in the CRAP, a specialist Pathfinder unit. He smiled inwardly. CRAP was the abbreviation for Commando de Renseignement et d'Action en Profondeur. The French regular army had recently dropped the abbreviation for obvious reasons, but the Legion was perverse enough to retain it. The humor inside him evaporated. Twenty-three eventful years of soldering in two different armies had taken its toll, and now every time he jumped, he knew pain would follow as inevitably as the sunrise.

"You have a decision to make," said Marchand.

"I haven't made it yet," Ryder replied.

The edges of Marchand's mouth drooped in disapproval. He spoke quietly, carefully choosing each word. "You need the Legion, Sergeant. Without it, you are nothing, and the Legion needs NCO's like you. I'm your commanding officer, but I am also your brother. We are the same, you and I. We are magnificent dogs of war honed from back street mongrels. But outside, you will be a mongrel again, a cur. You will have no family to protect you. Have you thought of that? If not, you should."

Oddly, Marchand's words did not seem excessively theatrical. Ryder had served under him for a long time, long enough to trust and respect him. He was a fine officer, fair to his men, but demanding too. Marchand was one of the most committed officers to graduate from the St-Cyr French military academy. He saw his service in the Legion as the highest form of honor. He was a throwback, a medieval knight who viewed every battle as a crusade.

"I need a little more time. A week or two to think about it."

"I understand."

Ryder knew that he didn't understand at all. To Marchand, the Legion was all black and white. There were no grey areas. Visiting Dublin had disturbed Ryder more than he wanted to admit, but he couldn't tell Marchand about that. The Legion didn't approve of leave being taken outside France, but with EEC barriers now withdrawn, things had changed. A passport was no longer a necessity, and a return ticket with an identity card had enabled him to slip away easily.

Marchand fixed him in another penetrating stare, his voice harsh. "You had a few days vacation after you left the hospital?"

Ryder did not flinch. "Yes," he lied easily, "I went to Paris for a few days."

Marchand came close to smiling as his eyes warmed. "Paris? Are the girls still as lovely as ever?"

"Nothing ever changes in Paris," Ryder's face betrayed nothing. Momentarily, his eyes shifted to three photographs arranged in black frames on the wall behind Marchand's head. One was of the Ali Khan. The second, that of Cole Porter, and the third, Alan Seeger, the American poet who died in the Legion. All three were part of the Legion myth that all recruits were subservient to. The words written by Seeger flitted into Ryder's mind. "I've a rendezvous with death, at midnight in some flaming town, when spring trips north again this year. And I, to my pledged word am true, I shall not fail that rendezvous."

"Very well. I expect your decision when you return from Guyana." Marchand paused for a moment and flicked through the folder on his desk, his face pensive. "Your team performed well in Eyl. You are a fine soldier, Ryder. You would have been decorated for your courage and resourcefulness during that operation if it were not so clandestine, but, if you sign on for another five years, I can promise you a promotion to Sergent-Chef. Think carefully my friend. You gave your body to the Legion. In return, we will protect you from yourself. That is our contract."

Marchand closed the folder and replaced it in a drawer. The meeting was over.

"Thank you, Sir." Ryder donned his kepi, saluted, and left the room.

As he crossed the parade ground he could hear the throb of idling helicopter engines coming from behind the infirmary where he could hear NCO's barking orders above the whine of turbines. He walked over, and from a shaded corner, watched a company of recruits loading up into the waiting Puma helicopters for their first jump. It brought back his own inauguration into the REP - a test of nerve in which failure meant a return to the infantry. Their faces were also young and too concerned to show fear at the prospect. Those that made it in the requisite time would be taking their first step out onto the razor's edge of the 2nd REP. Afterwards they would face six drops before being allocated to one of four Companies in the regiment.

At that moment Ryder envied their youth. To his surprise, he found himself thinking of Mark, something that he had rarely done before. Except for an occasional exchange of short notes or e-mails they had not communicated. Now, he saw his son's waxen face lined by self-abuse, so different from these faces that were full of expectancy and fear of the unknown. But their fear would go in time and their features would harden as they were transformed into men, men whose adventures in life all lay ahead of them. Bitterness welled inside Ryder, producing a strange sadness that forced him to consider what might have been. The rotor blades thrashed and he turned away abruptly as dust swirled and blotted out the pale faces staring in the open doors.

THREE

The Right Honorable Richard Critchley left the House of Lords and climbed into a maroon taxi as a flurry of sleet swept the street. Nearby, a group of Japanese tourists scurried for shelter, their cameras flapping uselessly. "Winston's Club," he snapped. "And be quick about it!"

The taxi driver responded by pulling out into a stream of traffic, sandwiching himself between a red double-decker bus and another taxi. He glanced in his rear-view mirror at his passenger's flushed face. Critchley noted the questioning eyes in the mirror and pulled up the collar of his blue Crombie overcoat. Gratefully he sank into a corner, placing his furled umbrella on the seat beside him as the car slowly navigated Parliament Square. He could hardly conceal his fury, and his hands shook with the effort of controlling his emotions. Underpinning his rage was fear. Hadn't his father always warned him that he was approaching the end of the road? Now he knew that it was true. Five minutes ago he had learned that the old man was no longer bluffing. "Richard," he had heard him thunder, "I don't give a damn who you owe the money to. This time you can stand on your own two feet for a change. You are nothing but a drunkard and a waster. Except for your allowance - which I can do nothing about, thanks to your Grandfather - not a penny piece more! Damn it, boy! We have only just recovered from that dreadful business with Air Commodore Howard's wife!"

Critchley gagged on the thought of it. He heard again, the slam of an oaken door echoing down the wide hallway as he stood shaking outside. The bastard, he fumed, the absolute bloody bastard! All over a measly twelve thousand quid! But it was twelve thousand that he did not have. It might as well have been a million. By midnight tonight, he had promised Webster. He sagged in the seat, frantically searching for a solution. In desperation he scanned the crowded pavements, searching for some familiar face that might offer a way out.

As the taxi neared Piccadilly Circus, Critchley rapped sharply on the glass partition. "You can let me off here," he growled. The driver pulled sullenly into the curb. "Thought you wanted to go to Winston's?" he whined.

"I've changed my mind," snapped Critchley. "I'll walk the rest of the way." He handed the driver a ten-pound note. "Keep the change."

The driver's demeanor brightened. "Thanks Guv! Don't forget your brolly!"

Critchley glared at him and slammed the cab door. He crossed the street and entered Old Bond Street. Halfway up the street, as the clouds rolled away, wintry sunshine picked out a polished brass plate, the sole indication that Winston's Club even existed. It marked a narrow fronted building squashed alongside The Romantica Club, which discreetly advertised the services of hostess dancers every night, seven days a week. Doors open at eleven thirty the sign outside announced. One was a twenty-first century bastard child alongside the quiet understated elegance of the other, he thought.

Inside, Critchley handed his overcoat and umbrella to a dapper porter whose be-medaled chest spoke of a grander uniform than the one he now wore.

"Good morning, Mr. Critchley."

"Any messages for me, George?"

George scanned his pigeonholes, each with its individual brass member's nameplate. "Sorry, Sir. I almost forgot. A Mr. Webster telephoned." He selected a folded slip of paper and handed it to Critchley.

Critchley scowled, accepting the message without opening it. He could visualize the contents and experienced a sudden tightening of his stomach muscles. "Thank you, George. I'll be in the reading room, perhaps I'll take lunch later."

"Very good, Sir. The head waiter mentioned that the veal is excellent today."

Critchley nodded glumly. With his appetite fast disappearing, he moved towards a pair of double doors leading into the reading room. Inside, all was quiet except for the crackle of logs burning in a large open fireplace. There were no voices to break the silence, and except for the occasional rustle of a newspaper from one of the winged high back leather armchairs, the room seemed empty. It was a somber but friendly room of large proportions, full of familiar objects. At this moment, it signified sanctuary and a modicum of normality for him from what was an increasingly stressful day.

He crossed the room to a secluded corner and selected a chair close to a Georgian window that overlooked the street. He could hear the sigh of muted traffic filtering through the spotless glass windowpanes, and from the far side of the room a clock ticked ominously.

He switched on a shaded reading light before opening the folded piece of paper. The writing was in the porter's schoolboyish handwriting. "Mr. Webster wishes to remind you," he read, "that you have an appointment with him tonight. Around midnight would be convenient."

Just nineteen words. To Critchley, they spelt ruin. The room suddenly felt cold and cheerless, closing in around him. The outside world had breached his refuge's ramparts. He felt that his narrow world was fragmenting under the pressure. Perhaps he could sell the car? No. What would he get for a six year old Porsche? Maybe the bank would...shit! No, he owed them as well.

Angrily, Critchley screwed up the piece of paper in his fist. He failed to hear a soft footfall on the Indian carpet. "Good morning, Sir!" He looked up, recognizing Albert Gibson, the Club Secretary.

Albert looked ill at ease in his black jacket and formal striped morning trousers. His features looked as pale as his dove-grey silk tie.

"Morning, Bertie." Critchley tried to sound cheerful. "What can I do for you?"

"Might I sit down, Sir? It's rather a delicate matter. I wouldn't want to cause any embarrassment."

Gibson didn't wait for Critchley's response but sank into an armchair. He leaned forward and whispered, "Its - ah - the matter of your account, Sir...your mess bill to be precise. I have to bring it to your attention. I'm sure you understand."

Gibson glanced around nervously. No one seemed to have overheard him and he relaxed a little, but a bead of perspiration still gleamed on his forehead. Critchley could tell that he hated this sort of thing, and for an instant he felt sorry for the man. Critchley sighed and reached into his inside jacket pocket for his checkbook. "Get on with it for God's sake, man," he snapped. "How much?"

Gibson looked relieved. He gave a polite cough, covering his mouth delicately with a mottled hand. "Well, Sir, including your membership..." he lowered his voice even further. "Fifteen hundred in all."

Critchley filled out the check. With a flourish, he handed it to Gibson. Regaining some of his hauteur, he said, "I don't appreciate being hounded like this, Bertie, especially over such a paltry amount. No one would."

Gibson pocketed the check with tangible relief. "Of course not, Sir. The committee of Governors...you understand? It's not like the old days, not like that at all. Times change don't they, Sir?" He rose quickly to his feet, not waiting for a reply.

Critchley frowned. "Do me a favor, Bertie?"

"What's that, Sir?"

"Hold onto the check until the end of the month."

"Of course, Sir." Gibson smiled and glided away.

Critchley slumped into his chair and stared into space, his stomach a knot of apprehension.

FOUR

Peter Webster arrived at the Club Marbella much earlier than usual and long before the croupiers checked in for the night's entertainment. He had a lot on his mind. To add to his worries Imelda was up to her usual tricks again. Now she wanted a new car. Tomorrow it would be something else, but today it was a Volkswagen Golf. Fed up with her whining and an ensuing violent argument, he had fled from his house in Hampstead two hours earlier than normal. He had to find his way through a drizzle of rain that blanketed London, slowing the late evening traffic to a crawl. However his early departure had allowed him to avoid a bad accident at Hyde Park Corner, which was now adding to the traffic chaos spreading down Oxford Street and all the way into Regents Street.

He parked his car and went inside. Only Willie, the head barman, was there before him already polishing glasses in preparation for a busy night. Willie looked up when Webster came into the gaming room. "One of the ice machines is acting up again, Mr. Webster. It's the third time in a week," he moaned.

Webster shed his raincoat and shook off the raindrops. His lips tightened. "Okay, Willie, I'll see to it; I'll order a new one tomorrow."

"Mr. Phillips is waiting for you in your office; if you ask me, he doesn't look too happy."

"I didn't ask you, Willie!" Webster snapped. Scowling, he crossed the room and walked towards the staircase that led to his office. Crossing the floor, he glanced up at his tinted office window, but he couldn't see anyone inside. The window overlooked the gaming tables and allowed him to privately study the actions of the punters below it without being seen. It was his spyglass into another world, a world over which he held a semblance of power that sometimes he could turn to his advantage. Either by way of a little judicious blackmail or just by rubbing shoulders with the rich and powerful, tidbits of information could be gleaned that sometimes proved useful and rewarding.

He took the stairs two at a time and went into his office. Sid Phillips occupied his leather chair in a proprietary manner and was seated behind his desk. He had a champagne bucket by his side and was smoking a Havana cigar. "Evening, Peter." He said. "I hoped you would be early." He picked up the bottle. "Drop of bubbly?"

Webster contained his annoyance. "Thanks, Sid. I'll take a glass," He noticed a pile of ledgers lying on the desk. "I see you have been going through the books." He hid any hint of disapproval in his voice. Phillips did own the bloody place, he reminded himself. The bastard had every right to go through the books if he wanted to. Besides, Webster thought smugly, the books would reveal no irregularities. He was far to smart for that.

Phillips puffed on his cigar and opened a ledger. He ran his index finger down a neat column of figures. "I notice we have a couple of debtors this week?"

Webster frowned and sipped from his glass. "Two," he said. "Sheikh Aziz is an old customer and he always settles before he leaves London. Thirty thou' is fuck all to him," he snorted. "Christ! If you owned that many oil wells in the Gulf, would you worry? I've seen him drop a quarter of a million in one night before now!" Webster gave a short laugh. "No, Sid. You don't have to worry about the Sheikh!"

"What about this guy, Critchley?" Phillips persisted.

He raised his bleary eyes and peered across the desk. He saw Webster's frown deepen. "He's different eh?"

Webster shrugged. "He's always been good for it in the past. You know who his old man is? Lord Critchley. Chairman of half the bloody companies in the country."

"But you're not sure, Peter? Be honest."

Webster did not like being put on the spot, especially by Sid Phillips. Phillips was a hard man, one with a lot of even harder friends. He knew too, that the gaming club was only a front for Phillips. It was a place to wash money that wouldn't bear too much scrutiny. "I've put him under pressure, Sid. He'll pay up tonight."

"And if he doesn't?" Phillips poured himself another glass of champagne and watched the bubbles sizzle. He picked up the glass and twirled it speculatively. On his little finger a heavy gold ring inset with a cluster of small diamonds flamed with light.

"Have I ever let you down before? Leave it with me, Sid."

"Very well." Phillips closed the ledger. He changed the subject abruptly. "I've been talking to a few friends about expanding."

Webster looked at Phillips with renewed interest. "Another club?"

"Nah!" Phillips gestured towards the window through which they could see the floor below, where croupiers were now setting up their tables. "There's more out there than gambling, mate – know what I mean? Most of our punters like a little snort now and then. There's a ready market just waiting to be exploited. The secret is tapping into it without getting our fingers burnt. There's a shortage of quality stuff and whenever there's a shortage there's a lot of money to be made. A ten-year old kid could work that one out."

Webster crossed his legs. He felt a momentary flash of panic. "I hope you're not thinking of getting mixed up with the Colombians," he said quietly.

Philips stared at him for a moment as if he were trying to make up his mind about something. "Escobar's been gone a long time now. The Colombians have lost their grip. There's a whole bunch of new players on the scene, Peru, Bolivia, Guatemala, and the Mexicans are all in the frame."

He tapped his finger on a folded copy of the *Daily Telegraph* that lay on the desk. "The Yanks are making life hell for them and that's in spite of the cartel pumping more than six million dollars into election funds over there. Some of them are smart enough to look towards Europe and London's crying out for the stuff, Peter. Christ! I've been eying the street price, no matter what is happening elsewhere, it's holding its own over here. We're not too late to make a bundle if we get in quick."

Webster gave a disdainful sniff. He had a handy sideline going himself, admittedly on a very small scale, but enough to make staying in a job with lousy hours worthwhile, and for a moment he wondered if Phillips knew about that and was leading him into a minefield. "I wouldn't trust any of them," he managed lamely. "You never could rely on those South American bastards."

"There's more in life than coke, mate." Phillips stubbed out the butt of his cigar. He shifted his chair to look through the window again. Downstairs, Lilly, one of the waitresses, had changed into her short skirt and was preparing her tray. She bent over and her black stocking tops showed against a flash of creamy white thigh. "Nice legs!" Phillips observed. "Have you had a go at that yet, Peter? I wouldn't blame you if you did!" He twirled in his chair and laughed coarsely, then his face became serious again. "Forget the South Americans for a minute, a few of the lads have come up with a scheme in the Far East. There's a pot of money in it and some of it could be yours."

"You're talking heroin, Sid. That's junk food. Fuck! My wife had a kid that died from that stuff. We buried him only a few weeks ago."

"Yeah, you told me about that. Sorry."

Webster shrugged. "No skin off my nose, the kid was hers from her first marriage." He picked thoughtfully at a spot on his chin, "He was always a pain in my arse." Webster inspected his fingernail. "I suppose you've thought about the Chinese in all of this. You'll have to buck the Triads if you get into the South East Asia trade."

"Ever hear of the Tai Huen Chai?"

"No, what the hell is that?"

Sid seemed pleased that he knew something Webster didn't. "It's the Big Circle gang. They're running Amsterdam now. They're probably the toughest Chinese Triad in the business; but more important, they're ambitious. They want in. To the UK, and that's where we come in to it. They need us as much as we need them."

Webster shuddered. Phillips was finally off his rocker as far as he was concerned. "Our Asian friends over here won't like that," he said flatly. He thought about it for a while. "Have you ever seen a Chinese gang war, Sid? Close up, I mean. Even a small scale one? Christ! Look what happened over in Soho last year with the restaurants! It attracted the cops like flies to a fresh shit! You won't be able to breathe if you stir up those bastards!"

Phillips stayed silent for a moment, watching the first trickle of customers gathering in the room below. He looked at his watch. "Nearly eleven," he said eventually. "Another glass before I go?" He drained the bottle in their two glasses and dropped it back into the ice bucket. "This French plonk is a bit overrated if you ask me, too gassy. Give me the Aussie stuff any day, or better still, a good pint of Newcastle brown."

Webster knew that Phillips had not finished. He waited patiently and when Phillips spoke, it was not what he expected to hear.

"How familiar are you with Ireland, Peter?" Phillips bit the end off a fresh cigar and spat into a wastebasket beside the desk.

"Not much. It's where Imelda's kid died, in Dublin. We went over for the little sod's funeral. I couldn't wait to get out of there. Bloody end of the earth it was, all yahooing and diddly-do music. Full of Mick's getting themselves pissed up!"

"Takes all sorts, Peter my lad." Phillips lit his cigar and blew a cloud of smoke towards the ceiling. "The Irish are okay. Think about it, we wouldn't have any motorways without 'em. No bloody Channel tunnel neither!"

Webster said nothing. He hated all foreigners. If they weren't honest-to-God Anglo-Saxon, they were no good in his eyes, but he refrained from saying that to Phillips. He knew that Sid had made his money years before in Beirut and was convinced he was part Arab, although he knew that Phillips' passport documented his birthplace as Gateshead.

"I need a front man in Ireland, Peter, to get this show up and running. Someone that won't excite any attention."

Webster felt a sense of momentary panic. "I don't know the scene over there, Sid," he said. "You'd want to be careful though, they've got terrorists over there who'd be only too happy to give you a private war. Especially now that they have nothing better to do."

Phillips scowled. "I wasn't thinking of using locals," he said. "I need someone legit, no record or anything like that, someone to put a face on it."

"I hope you're not looking at me."

Phillips chuckled. "Relax, mate," he said. "You're too close for comfort." He dotted the ash of his cigar into an ashtray. "Anyway, I need a gent for this – a country type – know what I mean? All tweeds and waxed jackets! That's what brought me here tonight. I thought you might come up with some ideas."

Webster felt relieved, he got up and walked over to the window and stood watching the scene downstairs. He could smell money in this, lots of it. Maybe Imelda wouldn't have to wait long for a new car after all. "Well, if you're determined to get into this, Sid," he responded slowly. "I'm really not sure you are doing the right thing; it needs to be some body that owes us, someone that we can control. Someone who won't fuck it up."

"Exactly." Phillips picked up his overcoat from one of the office chairs and folded it over his arm. "What about that bloke Critchley?"

"Forget him, Sid. He's a shit!"

"Tell me about him anyway. What's his background?"

"Like I told you, Sid. His old man has a seat in the House of Lords, the usual crap, chairman of this and that, but the son is a cretin. Take my word for it. He's never worked. He plays polo now and again – the usual bullshit. Drives a Porsche, wears good suits, and belongs to the right gentleman's club. Smooth, though, and well educated. Eton or Harrow wouldn't surprise me. About five eight in height, thirty-five years old, never married but had plenty of girl friends. Until lately, that is." Webster sniggered.

"What does that mean?" Phillips showed renewed interest.

Webster thought for a moment. "Well, there was a rumble going around that he was caught fucking some Air Commodore's wife. In those circles you do it, but woe betide you if you ever get caught. Critchley obviously did, and they dropped him once the word got out. Apart from that, I'd guess he is short of the readies right now. He owes us a bundle and that's probably the tip of the iceberg."

Phillips narrowed his eyes. He stuffed his cigar into the corner of his mouth and pulled on his overcoat. "I have a gut feeling that Critchley's in trouble, big trouble. Sound him out, Peter. I'd go so far as to write off what he owes us, and that's just for openers." He walked stiffly towards the door and paused as he opened it, "Be careful what you say to him, tell him nothing, you understand?"

"I'll handle it, Sid. But I still think you are making a big mistake with this guy."

"Just do it!" Phillips closed the door behind him.

Peter Webster remained standing at the window for some time watching the increasing activity on the floor below. He could see Sid Phillips smiling and waving to acquaintances as he crossed towards the exit. Greed overtook him then as his thoughts intensified on how to maximize the possibilities he had been presented with.

Richard Critchley glanced at his watch, it was almost quarter to twelve and the rain had stopped, leaving the pavements wet and greasy. He took a deep breath. Climbing the steps from the street, he pushed open the door.

"Good evening, Sir!" The bouncer wearing a black evening jacket tried to look welcoming but only succeeded in looking more like a Hollywood thug. "It's quiet tonight, Sir," he offered as Critchley deposited his coat with the hatcheck girl in the foyer. "Perhaps it will pick up now that it has stopped raining."

Critchley managed a non-committal grunt.

Holding open the door leading to the gaming floor, the bouncer gave him a gap-toothed smile. "Good luck," he said.

Critchley surveyed the tables, recognizing faces here and there, nodding occasionally when he made eye contact with someone he knew. Just for an instant he felt that familiar surge of excitement that came from the click of chips on baize covered tables, but it left him almost immediately as he remembered why he was here. He felt suddenly dispirited and exposed. He strode across the room trying to avoid looking up at the smoke glass window above him, where he knew Webster waited. He collected a drink at the bar before tackling the stairs, his stomach fluttering as he knocked on Webster's office door.

"Come in, Richard. You're right on time. I like that. Timeliness is a virtue."

Webster made it sound as though he was glad to see him as he flicked a speck of dust from the sleeve of his dinner jacket before seating himself at his desk. "Please sit down," he said. He adjusted his white shirt cuffs, and then placed his fingertips together so that they formed a protective cathedral before his face. "We obviously no longer have a problem, otherwise you would not be here." His voice was deceptively smooth.

Critchley placed his drink on the desk and lit a cigarette as he took a seat.

His mouth felt dry and he had to make a conscious effort to control a nervous shake in his hands. He risked a sip from his glass. "I need a little more time," he began hesitantly.

"Time is not on your side, old boy, nor on mine either." Webster's eyes narrowed as the creases on his forehead heralded a frown of disapproval.

"All I need, Peter, is another twenty-four hours, surely that's not too much to ask." Critchley faltered. "I've been a good customer for years."

Webster stared at him, recognizing the look of a human being under siege. His eyes gleamed. Adjusting a heavy gold signet ring on his right index finger, he leaned forward across the desk that separated them and coldly slapped Critchley a backhanded blow across the face.

Critchley touched the corner of his mouth where a trickle of blood oozed slowly. He withdrew his hand and stared wordlessly at the red smear on his fingertips.

"That was simply a reminder to talk sense," Webster said icily, sitting back in his chair. "I don't represent the Social Security. All I have to do is to make one call and you will end up tomorrow morning in a concrete pylon supporting a flyover!"

Critchley contemplated the blood on his fingers. His first reaction was to launch himself across the desk and hurl Webster through the window. He would be more than a match for Webster if it came to it he thought, but he knew there would be repercussions. If he wanted to die, he'd be choosing a quick way to go about it. He realized he had got himself into this, now he needed a way out. He threw his car keys on the desk. "Take the Porsche," he snapped. "I don't have the money, Peter, not right now that is." Critchley felt defeated.

"Stuff the car! It's not enough!"

"I understand, but..."

"There ain't no but's about it, mate, and you don't fucking understand anything!" There was a vicious ring to Webster's voice. "You're an over-privileged shit that understands nothing anymore." He threw his hands in the air, "Christ! I don't believe this! You're a bloody stereotype that I thought had gone out with the charge of the Light Brigade!" Webster strode furiously to the window and gazed balefully at the gamblers on the lower floor. He turned suddenly from the window and faced Critchley and when he spoke his voice rose to an angry shout. "Klosters and all that shit is over and done with, Critchley! You and the likes of you are fucking dinosaurs. Your status doesn't mean shit here. Only your money does. It's time to pay up or suffer the consequences."

"I can't give you what I don't have at the moment. I just need a bit more time that's all."

"There isn't any fucking time, Critchley. Get that into your head." Webster walked slowly back from the window. His voice became quiet. "You're just going to have to earn it the hard way."

"What does that mean?"

Webster sat down and glared across the desk. "Something you've never done before," he sneered. "Work! That's what it means." He gave Critchley a crooked smile. "It means that you are going to work for me, lad, until the debt is paid." He leaned forward. "I'll bet you didn't expect it to be so easy, did you?"

Critchley's mouth opened but he said nothing. Instead, he listened attentively while Webster explained what he wanted of him.

FIVE

The Transall C-160 fled down the runway like some wounded bird and only at the very limits did its engines thrust it into the air. Fighting for height, it left Cayenne shimmering behind in a cloud of burnt fuel before banking in a sweeping turn over the sea.

Fifteen minutes later, as the engines settled into a monotonous roar, Ryder unclipped his seat belt and stood up to peer out of a small window. Far below, ringed by a sapphire sea, Devil's Island lay innocent and purged of it's hideous past. "Ile du Diable!" he shouted, beckoning to Corporal Klein seated opposite to him. "Take a look, Klein," he roared. "That's where you might have ended up if you weren't seduced by the Legion!" He laughed loudly. Klein managed only an angry scowl.

Those within earshot laughed too. Even though it was an unwritten rule in the Legion that one never asked questions of a man's past, it was common knowledge that Hans Klein lived in some fear that one day he would be released from the service and have to face whatever had brought him there.

Still climbing, the aircraft nosed into clear blue sky, away from a distant wad of feathery clouds that lay over the Tumuk Humak Mountains. Ryder turned away from the window as the low scrub below gave way to a mattress of green jungle that stretched like algae into the far distance. He checked his container and ran his eyes over the twenty men seated closest to him. They looked as relaxed as a group of businessmen commuting to the office. After all, this was a routine exercise for which they were well prepared. The difference was that they carried weapons instead of briefcases, and each man had folded and carefully packed his own parachute shortly before take off. He thought about the drop. It wouldn't be easy; he knew that. It involved the insertion of the team into a small jungle clearing, followed by an arduous twenty-five mile slog in four man patrols to the Approuague river. After that, they would travel down river in Zodiac boats to a Legion base at Regina. It sounded simple but he knew from past experience that it would not be a picnic. The Legion did not give free lunches; he had the scars to prove it.

Some of the men were dozing already, amongst them and part of his own team, two Vietnamese and a huge Zulu warrior from KwaZulu-Natal Province. The African was lost in shadows towards the front of the plane.

Ryder could only guess at how a Zulu had come to join the REP. His nickname was Sinbad. In Somalia, Sinbad had referred to the Somalies as brothers, but there was no brotherly love that first time in Mogadishu when, following the American withdrawal, the REP was sent in to support the Pakistanis. Even though that was years ago when he was still new to the Legion, he started to ache when he thought of that mess. The United Nations was toothless, he thought. Over-burdened by bureaucracy and populated by faceless people whose major decision for the day was what to eat for dinner. And the Americans - Jesus! They should never have got sucked into the cauldron of Somalia. While they paused on the beaches before CNN television cameras to write their impossible rules of engagement, in contrast, the Legion had marched off their planes at Mogadishu airport in swaying slow march singing "Contre les Viets – Fighting the Vietnamese." Ryder was proud of that. They had made it known that this was their desert; just as all the others had been theirs. Their message was simple; nobody messed with the Legion and if they did so it was at their peril. Left to their own devices, Ryder was confident they could have cleaned the place up and destroyed the arsenals of hidden weapons, but the bureaucrats, in fear of civilian casualties, had shackled them. Unacceptable collateral damage, they had said. Now the warlords had rested, grown fat again and had re-taken the damned place.

The arrival of the jumpmaster interrupted his reverie. "Five minutes to the DZ!" he roared.

Organized chaos reigned for the next three minutes as men, weighed down by equipment, struggled to their feet and shuffled towards the rear cargo door.

With two minutes to go, the Dispatcher pressed a button on a control panel and the rear door hissed as hydraulic pistons lowered it into a launching ramp. Ryder watched the Dispatcher go out on to the ramp speaking quietly into a microphone head-set to the pilot on the last seconds of the approach. On his word they would jump. They depended on him to hit the DZ accurately.

Ryder shuffled out onto the ramp as a red light flashed, he could hear the clank of equipment and shuffling boots behind him as the others closed up to take their places beside him. At thirteen thousand feet, the thick green jungle below showed only as a layer of moss with no sign of a gap anywhere. He glanced at the men standing beside him, took a deep breath and steeled himself.

Ryder left the ramp like a swimmer leaving a diving board and suddenly he was out of the plane. The familiar feeling in his stomach was strangely pleasurable as the slipstream caught him and he went into a controlled free fall. For a full minute he soared downwards, exulting in a feeling of freedom. It intoxicated him, as he knew it would. It had since his very first jump.

At three thousand feet Ryder pulled his ripcord and four seconds later felt the reassuring tug on his harness as the canopy deployed itself overhead. Instantly he was floating in the private world of a Para as he flicked release catches to lower his equipment container below his feet in readiness for landing. He looked up. Around him he could see the others floating gently downwards, their sky blue parachutes melding in a cloudless sky. He concentrated on a small clearing, probably left behind by a landslide in the jungle, just a little bit forward and to the left of his boots. Pulling hard on the lift web, he lined himself up. Far away he could see smoke rising from the forest where a river glistened as it took a snaking passage through the green carpet that was already taking on distinctive shapes.

Ryder steered himself into the wind so that his forward speed fell to zero just as his boots touched the ground, it was a soft textbook landing, seconds later he was gathering his chute as the thud of others landing surrounded him.

Within minutes, as the rest of the men gathered and unpacked their equipment, Ryder realized that two were missing. He got to his feet, his eyes scanning the clearing. It was strangely quiet except for the receding drone of the aircraft carrying Arvans and his group towards the second drop zone. "Where's Corporal Klein and that bloody Zulu of mine!" He bellowed.

Someone in the group answered. "They both overshot, boss. I saw them going into the trees, east of us."

"It's just as well this is a bloody exercise and not a war zone," Ryder growled ominously. "If they're not here in an hour, I'll take my lads and bring 'em in. The rest of you get on with it but leave me a radio operator. We'll try to catch up with you at the river." He sat down and watched the small group disappearing into the jungle. Soon they were swallowed up and the noise of their progress faded. Ryder rolled onto his back and stared at the sky. The heat was intense and the surrounding jungle smoldered under the onslaught of the sun. Silence had descended on the clearing, and then life suddenly returned as if by magic, and the air became filled by strange animal sounds mixed with the incessant buzz of insects. He relaxed and lit a cigarette. Exhaling, he watched a smoke ring forming in the still air and studied a huge yellow and black butterfly hovering near it. As the ring widened, the insect fluttered in and out of it, as if investigating a new phenomenon.

Forty-five minutes passed with still no sign of the missing men. Ryder felt frustration tugging at him. He could wait no longer. He looked across to where the radio operator lay supine on the ground. "Van Delden," he called. "Wake up! You stay here with the radio. Chen, Joby, you two come with me!" Without a word the two Vietnamese shed their heavy packs and followed him into the brush.

The three made good time, following a shallow stream and stopping every now and then to listen. Then the stream bed narrowed abruptly allowing the foliage to close in overhead, and then the sunlight flickered out as though an unseen blind had been drawn. Beneath the covering of trees it was humid and strangely quiet and whatever creatures inhabited the trees fell into watchful silence as they approached. The splash of every footfall increased the silence, isolating them in a world filled by unseen eyes.

A sudden sound reached them. Ryder raised his arm and they waited, listening. Somewhere off to their left they heard it again; there was no mistaking the swishing crack of a machete as it cleared a way in the tangled undergrowth. The sound got louder until finally Sinbad stumbled into the stream ahead of them cursing to keep his balance as his boots skidded on the rotten branches of a fallen tree.

Ryder drew in his breath to contain his anger. Draped across the African's shoulder lay Corporal Klein. One brawny arm supported Klein's body; the other swung the heavy machete as though it was a toothpick. Across Sinbad's sweat-stained chest hung his FAMAS assault rifle. His clothing was ripped and bloodstained and a wide grin of recognition spread across his face as he splashed towards them.

"Where the fuck were you!" Ryder roared. "And what the hell's wrong with Klein?"

The Zulu's grin only broadened as though Ryder's anger pleased him in some way. Sinbad sank to his knees and gently lowered the German to the ground between the curving roots of a rotting tree. "Klein had a bad landing, boss. He's fucked up bad."

Ryder could see that Klein was conscious but obviously in extreme pain with shock lines etching his features. Klein said nothing as he bent on one knee and cut away what remained of the German's right trouser leg, unprepared for such a frightful wound. The flesh was ripped open from his calf to the top of his thigh where a jagged piece of bamboo lay lodged in a hole that seemed to extend into his groin. Ryder drew in his breath. "Jesus Christ! Someone get me a medical kit before the bastard bleeds to death!"

Ryder worked quickly; a Guyanan jungle was no place to suffer a wound like this. He injected Klein with a shot of morphine, pinned the folds of torn flesh as best he could, dumped a tin of Quik-clot powder on the wound, applied a field dressing and applied hand pressure to stem the blood flow. Once he knew the morphine was taking hold, he extracted the sliver of broken bamboo and bound up the wound with a second field dressing. By the time he had finished, Klein had passed out. "Pick him up," he ordered. "Get him back to the DZ and we'll call in a chopper to lift him out."

Between them they carried Klein back to the Drop Zone, where Van Delden was still dozing beside his radio set. They were three hours behind schedule and darkness was not far off.

"Van Delden! Get off your fucking arse and get on the radio. Order in a chopper. We've got to get Klein out of here!" Ryder was in a brutal mood. If he did decide to remain in the Legion, all chances of his promised promotion were fading with every minute. Marchand was fair and wouldn't hold him accountable for Klein's misfortune, but Lieutenant Arvans might. What should have been a straightforward exercise was turning into a nightmare.

The Dutch radio operator crouched over his set making repeated calls. "Zulu Fox-Trot this is Alpha Victor, how do you read? Over!" The radio simply hissed steadily without response. "Zulu Foxtrot this is Alpha Victor, do you copy? Over!" Van Delden fiddled with the controls. "Nothing, Sarge! I've tried VHF to the other squad, but that was too much of a long shot. The set's working, I'm pretty sure of that, we just seem to be in a bad spot for HF. Perhaps later, when it gets dark."

Ryder made no reply. He knew that radio transmissions from deep in the jungle could be hit and miss at the best of times. Perhaps later they would have more luck when they reached higher ground. Right now Klein was his main concern. He knelt to check his field dressing again before ordering the men to move. Klein was conscious again, and although his bandages were blood stained right through to the outer layer, the compress appeared to have stemmed the blood flow. "How are you doing, Hans? Feel like taking a walk?" Ryder smiled reassuringly.

"Good, Sarge. You've done a good job." Klein grinned, making light of it, but he had listened to their failed attempts to bring in a helicopter. He tried to peer down at his leg, but stretching to do so brought on instant pain and his face clouded. "Looks like you might be carrying me for a while." There was edginess in his voice. Beads of perspiration bubbled on his forehead and his face had an unhealthy waxy looking sheen.

"Just relax, Hans. Whatever it takes, we'll get you out of here, so just hang in there." Ryder got to his feet. He knew from the way Klein closed his eyes that the German realized that his problems had only just begun.

"Sinbad! You and Chen make up a stretcher, we'll move out as soon as you get that done."

As they abandoned the clearing, roosting birds fought for their places overhead in the treetops and from away in the distance came the drone of an unknown aircraft. Ryder glanced at his watch, it was hardly their own returning to Cayenne and was certainly too far away for them to attract its attention. He glanced up at the sky just before the trees closed in around them but could see nothing.

At dawn, as the jungle woke to face another day, Ryder calculated that his small group, hampered by Klein, had only covered a painful three miles, even though he had pushed them to their limits to make up time. By now, he knew that the other patrols were far ahead and unconcernedly thrusting on towards the river.

The stream bed they had followed for the last two hours now petered out. Faced with rising ground that was covered in dense undergrowth, Ryder called another rest halt to attend to the injured German and prepare him for what lay ahead. The others collapsed thankfully onto the peat moss of the jungle floor and huddled over their ration packs.

Klein had spent an uncomfortable pain-riddled night on his make shift stretcher, but not once had he complained. Nor did he now, as Ryder gently loosened the dressing on his leg. He opened his eyes and his skin shone with perspiration as Ryder began his inspection of the wound.

Gently, Ryder removed the last layer of dressing. The skin felt clammy and cold and that was not normal, not in this heat. The wound looked swollen and edged with purple. Ryder leaned closer sniffing suspiciously. Putrefaction came quickly in the morass of a South American jungle, he knew. As he expected there was already a bad odor. He swatted away a cloud of flies that had settled to gorge themselves on the blood stained bandages.

"How do you feel, Hans?"

"I'm fine, Sarge." Klein grimaced and his body stiffened as Ryder's fingers probed the wound higher up in his thigh. They were the words of a man who was anything but fine and his eyes showed it. There was fear in them.

"I think I'll give you another shot of juice and maybe a tetanus shot too. How do you like the sound of that?" Ryder laughed dryly, making light of it. "You must be getting to like the stuff by now, eh!"

"Keep it up and I'll be a junkie by the time you get me out of here, it's good stuff!" The German managed a weak smile.

Ryder's face clouded. He remembered the open coffin in Dublin and what lay inside it. His son might have believed it was good stuff too, on the night that it killed him. He pushed the thought aside and concentrated on making Klein as comfortable as possible, but as he applied a fresh field dressing, he noticed Klein's testicles had swollen abnormally and had taken on an unhealthy bluish color. Again he prodded the wound higher up in the groin and sweat broke out on Klein's face, but the German stifled any cry of pain. The wound had looked clean initially, but it was deteriorating rapidly. Ryder knew that the man needed a hospital immediately; he didn't want to think what tomorrow would bring. "I'll get you some grub." He said tersely, moving away. Klein nodded and closed his eyes.

Ryder returned with a mug of chocolate and some cheese. He managed to force some of it into Klein until the German gagged on it after a few sips, raising his hand in protest. At that Ryder became impatient. "Get it down you, Klein, for Christ's sake! You're going to need it for what's ahead. With food and water you can survive, but without it you're fucked! It's make your mind up time, buddy. We have to tackle that escarpment before dark." His voice lost its edge. "It's going to be a bitch, but after that it's all down hill."

Klein gave him a dejected look but attempted to drink more of the hot chocolate. Ryder could see that the morphine was already taking effect as Klein's features relaxed, reflecting the lightheaded euphoria that comes as pain subsides. Ryder waited long enough for Klein to drift off into his own private fairyland that held him with soft cocoon-like fingers, and then he roused the others.

With Sinbad leading the way out in front, hacking a path through the tangled web of vines and bamboo, they lifted the stretcher and stumbled upwards over ground that was treacherous with lichen-covered rotting vegetation. Every yard took its toll.

Evening brought silence to the jungle as they reached the top of the escarpment. Underfoot, the ground felt firm as though the soil was thin, even though the overhanging foliage of the trees had hardly thinned in the last few hundred feet.

Wearily, Ryder lowered his pack to the ground and eased away the cloth of his shirt where it stuck to open lacerations from the straps. The savageness of the climb had blunted any sharpness in his thoughts. He had cursed and cajoled the others forcing them to the limits of their endurance, fighting for every uphill yard, but now close to collapse himself, he only wanted to sink into the damp ground and let the jungle do what it would.

Only Sinbad and the two Vietnamese still seemed to have any residue of strength left. Studying them, Ryder doubted that their legs could feel as weak as his own. Their youth enabled them to make lighter work of a forty-kilo pack and their weapons. Perhaps, he thought sadly, it was just another in the growing list of reasons he had for not renewing his contract. Even though he was fitter than any man he knew of his age, how could he hope to compete and lead men such as these?

He rolled onto his back. Overhead, the green canopy appeared more yellow now, shot with red shards from the sinking sun; soon it would be dark. For several minutes he out-stared a small white-faced monkey until the creature bared its evil looking yellow fangs in anger and swung off to the security of a farther tree. There, it hung upside down and continued to study the intruders from a safe distance, occasionally gibbering fitful insults.

Van Delden brought his rifle to his shoulder and thumbed off the safety catch. Taking aim, he squeezed the trigger. The monkey dropped instantly with a thud to the ground as the sounds of the single shot echoed back from the nearby jungle, a strange silence followed. "Dinner is served," Van Delden announced as he walked over to the small bundle of fur lying on the jungle floor.

Ryder closed his eyes, willing the pain that wracked his body to subside. Opening his eyes again he saw the Dutchman returning with the monkey. It was mostly black, he saw, only the innocence of its small white face spoiled by lips peeled back over yellow teeth clenched in the grimace of death. Out of death comes life, he thought slowly. The meat might put some life back into Klein too.

Van Delden threw the carcass at the feet of the two Vietnamese Legionnaires. "You two can cook it!" His laugh had a contentious ring to it.

It was his contemptuous way that he said it that irritated Ryder. "Shove it, Cloggie!" he snarled. Van Delden shot him a dangerous look, "Fuck you, Ryder!" He snapped in return. Ryder knew that Van Delden was a loner; morose and known for his savage temper and like most men in the section he had picked up a nickname. Inevitably, his was Cloggie. It was obvious he didn't like it. That was too bad, Ryder thought. Ever since the drop, the big Dutchman had been a thorn in his side and he constantly shirked his stint on the stretcher. Ryder knew that part of his reluctance in that respect was due to the obvious enmity that existed between himself and Klein. The Dutch Legionnaire never lost an opportunity to remind Klein of the German occupation of Holland during the last World War. Ryder didn't like that either. Politics was the same as religion, he believed, something not to be discussed. There was no room in a CRAP team for a man carrying grudges or who was unwilling to pull his weight. Whatever the reason, he could not afford to keep him, he decided. "You're going on report when we get back to Calvi," he announced. "I've had enough of your bullshit, Van Delden."

The Dutchman gave him a smoldering look. "You have to get back there yourself first," he muttered.

Ryder ignored the implied threat. He lit a cigarette and watched shadows forming around them. He harbored a certain amount of sympathy for the Dutchman if the truth were known. He'd heard rumors that Van Delden was Jewish and that his grandparents had died in Dachau. He could understand that memories like those died slowly and that at times Klein epitomized the Nazi storm trooper of yesterday. Sometimes Corporal Klein could be unnecessarily hard and demanding and he too had few friends. The difference, Ryder mused, was that Klein had been tested in action and unlike the Dutchman, he had proved himself.

As the Vietnamese set about skinning the monkey, darkness came with a swiftness that surprised them. It was instan-
taneous, as though someone had thrown an electrical circuit
breaker. One minute Ryder was studying the shapes of yel-
low-green leaves above him and the next, all was black noth-
ingness. Then came the patter of rain that instantly became
ferocious, rattling down in blobs of water heavy enough to
penetrate a grave. That thought immediately brought back
Mark again, plunging him into a sense of black self-pity.
Lately, he had begun to torture himself with wandering flash-
backs and thoughts of what might have been if things were
different. What if he had stayed married to Imelda? He had
loved her once, had he not? What if he had given up soldiering? What if...if...if. Christ! Lately it was always if. He rolled
on to his side willing the thoughts to go away, fighting off
hunger pangs as he watched the fire blaze and spit angrily
when raindrops found it. In the light of its flickering flames he
could see the faces of Joby and Chen, giggling and chattering
excitedly as they dropped chunks of monkey meat into a collection of simmering mess tins. Sinbad, too, was a dark hulk
by the fireside, snoring loudly with his head on his pack. To
one side, Van Delden squatted, alone as usual, watching the
food being prepared with hungry eyes.

Joby passed around the stew and they ate in silence. To his
surprise, Ryder found the spicy food tasty and his strength
was returning. He wiped his mouth with the back of his hand
and belched.

Sinbad gave a short laugh. "Good, boss?"

"Not bad, Sinbad, not bad at all." Ryder found himself
smiling for the first time that day. His stomach no longer
ached and his weariness seemed to be evaporating. Klein had
eaten too, and the food had brought color back into his
cheeks. Ryder relaxed, allowing his muscles to unwind as he
listened to the drone of a mosquito closing in before raising
an ineffectual hand as it landed on his neck. Again his
thoughts were back at the funeral and his visit with Mark's
friends in Dublin, but this time he felt glad to be where he

was, and not back in the midst of their miserable lives. The heat and pestilence of a South American jungle was better than that, far better, he told himself. His eyes closed. Maybe Colonel Marchand was right after all. At least the Legion protected him. He was safe here with his brothers.

Ryder awoke just before dawn. It was still dark, but the Vietnamese already had a fire lit and were roasting what looked like meat on long bamboo skewers. Whatever it was, it smelt delicious; but then nearby, he caught sight of the bloody remnants of a snake's skin. Sphinx-like, Sinbad was sitting up watching them too. Van Delden was nowhere to be seen.

Ryder felt rested, but he knew instinctively that the pain would return as soon as he moved. He lay for a few minutes longer, almost at peace with the world. Having the Vietnamese in his section certainly paid off when it came down to cooking, he thought. The scent of coffee bubbling in a blackened mess tin at the edge of the fire reached him. Yes, he thought, those two Viets were worth a dozen Van Deldens. He got unsteadily to his feet, aware that his whole body ached and his stomach felt empty and bilious. He hoped it was not from the monkey meat the night before. He relieved himself and went over to take a look at Klein. The German was awake, but his eyes looked even more sunken in his skull, his pale features lined by fatigue. "Did you sleep, Hans?"

"Not much." Klein's voice was weak and barely audible. "That fucker, Van Delden was snoring like a pig!"

Ryder made no response, turning his attention to Klein's leg. "Leave it, Sarge. Sinbad already took care of it."

Ryder studied him carefully. He could see that the German was in a bad way; there was no doubt that his condition had deteriorated overnight. His chances of survival were slipping away and Ryder knew that he was going to have to force the pace. If yesterday was bad, today promised to be hell. "Are you ready to go on, Hans? I'm going to up the pace to get you out of here."

"The leg's fucked, Sarge. Sinbad told me it's infected. There's poison in it now." Klein moistened his lips with the tip of his tongue. "But I'm ready whenever you are. There's no point in lying around in this fucking jungle."

Ryder returned and joined the others squatting around the fire. Joby handed him a skewer and he chewed hungrily on the white, greasy meat, washing it down with strong black coffee that tasted of wood smoke. "Sinbad," he said. "See if you can get Klein to eat some of this shit!"

The African licked the grease from his fingers, picked up a skewer of meat, and wandered over to where Klein lay. Ryder watched the German trying to eat. He could tell that Klein knew the score. If he didn't eat, he would not survive what lay ahead. Unable to chew, Klein swallowed whole chunks of meat simply to get it down. The effort seemed to exhaust him.

Van Delden reappeared then, buckling up his trousers just as a torrential shower of rain fell vertically, clattering like spent shot through the covering leaves of the trees. The deluge lasted for only a few minutes, drenching them and quenching the cooking fire. An artillery roll of thunder clapped directly overhead, and just as suddenly, the rain stopped as shafts of sunlight broke through like veins of liquid gold high in the trees. The ground steamed as though it was about to boil and a macaw shrieked bringing the jungle alive to face another day.

Ryder studied his map for a moment longer. They still had twelve miles to the river and another thirty down it, before they would be out of this mess, "Okay," he said, "Let's get on with it. Move out!"

By midday Ryder estimated they had covered five miles. The going had been savage. Twice, Klein had been pitched from his bamboo stretcher, but he never voiced a word of complaint. His foot was now twice its normal size and his pain was unimaginable, but Ryder had only one syringe of morphine left, and he was saving that for when the German could take no more.

Now, faced with a rock face that fell like a sheet of burnished steel to the tops of trees one hundred feet below, Ryder called a halt. Somewhere below them in the far distance lay the river, but even binoculars revealed no break in the green swathe that shimmered in the noontime heat below them. He turned yet again to the Vietnamese. "Chen," he ordered quietly, "Make a recce. See if you can find an easy way down this bloody cliff. Joby, you take a look in the opposite direction. We'll rest up here for an hour."

Sinbad, still looking surprisingly fresh as though he had been out for a morning walk, dumped his pack and shed his webbing. He hunkered down on his haunches and commenced re-sharpening his machete on a flat-topped boulder with an hypnotic swishing sound.

To Ryder's great surprise Van Delden set up the radio without being ordered to, holding a pair of headphones to his ear as he fiddled with the controls. "Good thinking, Cloggie! Try anywhere, the fucking base, anywhere will do! Maybe you can pick up one of the other patrols. They have to be down by the river by now." But five minutes later the radio still hissed in defiance and there was no response to repeated calls.

Ryder broke open biscuits and meat paste from his ration pack and tried to get some food into Klein but the pace since dawn had taken its toll, and the German seemed to have fallen into a semi-coma. His face had taken on an unnatural greenish tinge and his mouth worked uncontrollably with no sound coming from his lips. When Ryder removed the dressings from his leg, the limb resembled some monstrous bloated melon. It had swollen to twice its size and was yellow in color, shot with purple. The wounds were even more hideous and suppurating. Klein's testicles had swollen unrecognizably. Ryder prodded Klein's thigh tentatively with his finger. The skin felt hard, like an over-inflated football. Only a low groan of agony escaped from Klein's lips. The smell from the wound was abominable and if it wasn't gangrenous already it was not far off it. Grimly he renewed the dressings realizing that without hospital treatment it was only a matter of time now before the German would die.

Ryder glanced across at Van Delden who seemed to have given up on his radio. "Cloggie, keep trying that bloody radio." He tossed over his map. "Broadcast the grid position, maybe the transmitter is working and it's just our receiver that's fucked!"

The big Dutchman opened his mouth to protest.

"Just get on with it!" The edge in Ryder's angry voice silenced him. Sullenly, Van Delden crouched again over the radio, repeatedly calling and giving their position.

Ryder sat and removed his boots. His feet were painful and swollen and his socks were just filthy tatters clinging wetly to the puffy white flesh. The smell made him want to puke. "Fuck this fucking jungle!" he thought. Athlete's foot was all he needed to add to his misery. Angrily he shook talc over his feet, filled his boots with the stuff and threw the empty tin into his pack.

Shortly afterwards, Chen returned with the good news that he had found a way down 500 yards away. "There's a rock ledge about sixty feet below; we can rappel down to it. After that it's all jungle again." Ryder had the uneasy feeling from the way he said it that their difficulties were far from over. "Okay," he announced. "On your feet! Lets get on with it!"

It took them two hours to lower Klein on his stretcher down on to the ledge and by the time they had reached the jungle floor he was screaming in agony. Ryder unceremoniously stabbed the remaining morphine injection into him so that his screams gradually became a string of incoherent obscenities as the drug took hold.

The rest of the day was a sweat ridden blur as the small group hacked their way onwards through an almost impenetrable tangle of heavy undergrowth until in the early evening, they stumbled unexpectedly onto a narrow jungle trail that looked well used.

Ryder consulted his map but the trail did not appear to be marked, but wherever it led to, it indicated a settlement of some kind, maybe even medical help. It also seemed to lead in the general direction of the river. "Okay! Rest up! One hour!" Gratefully he sank down at the edge of the path and closed his eyes. His last conscious thought was how old he felt.

Sinbad woke him exactly an hour later. To Ryder, it seemed more like five minutes. His entire body continued to flash warning signals to his brain. He was not even sure that his legs would support him if he stood up. He forced himself into a sitting position and inserted his arms through the straps of his pack, feeling a trickle of blood as the webbing re-opened the sores on his shoulders. Struggling to his feet, he swayed for a moment uncertainly; his eyes, blurred with tiredness, were slow to focus. "Move out!" he ordered hoarsely. In a stumbling gait he led the way into the growing darkness of the forest.

On the morning of the third day the bedraggled and exhausted group blundered into a clearing on the banks of a muddy tributary where a bank of mist lay in thin fronds over the water. They came upon it so suddenly that Ryder barely had time to take in the collection of silent brown faces of the inhabitants gathering around them in a tight curious knot. There were no smiles, he noticed, only sullen watchful stares. Not everyone was happy to see Legionnaires, he realized. Their reputation had preceded them. Noticeably, their women folk remained hidden in the dark security of the scattering of huts that rested on stilts over the ground.

Slowly, Ryder's eyes focused on the scene and his brain started to register; the clearing was a tiny area hacked from the jungle that extended tentative fingers in an unceasing effort to reclaim it. The entire compound was rubbish strewn and malodorous. In the centre a shallow ditch carried sewage and other debris down to the riverbank where a cluster of grey pigs foraged noisily in the mud. There was an air of hostility about the place that Ryder couldn't quite define and he became instantly alert. Furtively, he ran a hand over his MP5 sub-machine gun and flicked off the safety catch. His action did not go unnoticed and the group of villagers immediately pulled back, making way for them.

Then, as quickly as it had arisen, the tension seemed to evaporate with the arrival of Sinbad. Excitedly, the villagers clustered around the huge African in wonderment. A small boy nervously reached out to touch him as though he half expected the Zulu to disappear in a puff of smoke. Sinbad grinned and hoisted the struggling child onto his broad shoulders and immediately, the sullen suspicion of the villagers gave way to gap-toothed smiles and a buzz of excitement. Ryder relaxed and engaged the safety catch before swinging his weapon over his shoulder. As they rid themselves of equipment, food was produced and thrust upon them. They gorged themselves on bananas and some strange fruit not unlike avocado.

With his strength returning Ryder squatted in the dust and produced his map. An elderly toothless man, who seemed to command the respect of the others, stared at it blankly. He screwed up his pockmarked face and nodded vacantly, now and then showing the blackened stub of the only tooth left in his lower jaw. It was obvious the map meant nothing to him. Finally resorting to sign language and using a stick to trace outlines in the trodden dirt of the compound elicited a response that the map had failed to produce. Ryder knew now that they were close to the Approuague river, perhaps only a kilometer or two from their rendezvous with the boats.

Then in response to a call from the headman, two diminutive women emerged from a nearby hut and carried Klein inside on his stretcher, Ryder followed. He could see that the German was in a state alternating between delirium and semi-consciousness and he remained oblivious to the two women clucking noisily as they removed the mess of bandages on his leg. One of the women went outside only to reappear a few minutes later with a handful of green leaves and a bowl containing something not unlike cold porridge. She warmed the bowl for a moment in the ashes of a fire and then smeared handfuls of the contents over the festering gashes in Klein's leg.

Ryder went outside and lit a cigarette. In the centre of the clearing he could see Van Delden working on the radio, which continued to hiss its defiance. Then without warning, the heavy thud-thud of a helicopter engine penetrated the jungle clearing as the machine approached, flying low as it followed the winding path of the river. It came around a bend like some giant green and black moth less than half a kilometre away, skimming the water with its rotors kicking up a fine spray on the muddy surface, the down draught from its blades lashing the fringe of the jungle that lined the river banks where black clouds of shrieking birds took to the air.

Wearily, Ryder exploded a smoke grenade in the clearing and as if by magic, the terrified villagers fled into the surrounding jungle leaving them alone.

The chopper rose higher to survey the landing site, circling once before making its approach. Someone waved from an open door in the fuselage and after a moment's hesitation the machine swooped down and settled in a cloud of fine dust, sending the pigs squealing in panic along the river edge. A swirl of grey ash from a burnt out fire rose into the air and hung there in an opaque cloud as the rotors slowed. Through the ash Ryder could see the natives filtering back with wonderment on their faces.

Without a word the tattered group loaded Klein inside the helicopter. A Marine crewman jumped out. His eyes sought out Ryder's badges of rank that now barely showed on the remnants of his camouflage shirt. "We picked up your last radio call," he announced, "But obviously you couldn't receive our transmissions. The rest of your mob are already on their way down river and your orders are to force march, a boat is waiting for you a mile south of here." He sniffed as though he couldn't care less what happened to them and climbed back inside the aircraft, but as the roar of the engines built up he leaned from the door and shouted, "You're on your way home as soon as you reach Regina."

Ryder grinned. If they were going home so soon, before their training stint was over, something must have come up. At the same time, he thought, there could be no great urgency; otherwise they would not have to make their way out by boat. "That's fine by me, friend. You just take care of my boy. His leg is fucked – enjoy the smell of it!"

The crewman spoke into a microphone and the engine note rose into shrill whine, the fuselage shuddering in the first second of lift off. Dust swirled and Ryder ducked away from the spinning rotors as the aircraft lifted hesitantly from the ground.

In less than a minute it became a black dot climbing higher over the trees, speeding away in a Westerly direction. As the dust settled, Ryder kicked Van Delden awake. "Saddle up!" He shouted, "You bastards still have to earn your pay!"

Cayenne offered little after a fast journey by high-speed Zodiac down the Approuague River followed by a helicopter lift out of Regina. They were all exhausted and there was only a brief respite for a decent meal – the first in five days – cold beer, wine, and a chance to wash away the filth and blood that caked their bodies. The flight home that night would be a time to sleep.

Evening brought a sunset that hung over the nearby jungle in a blood red mist as Ryder's unit boarded a charter aircraft to take them back to Corsica. If Lieutenant Arvans knew why they were returning to their Mediterranean base so soon, he was saying nothing. Arvans seemed content to leave that until later. Ryder felt far too tired and worn out to think about it. All that mattered was that it saved him from another fifteen days of punishment in the jungle that he could see from the windows of the plane as the noise from the engines built up to a throbbing roar. His eyes closed and he was asleep before the wheels left the ground.

Six

Richard Critchley turned the key and his powerful BMW came to life. The engine throbbed silkily as the ramp of the ferry dropped down to reveal a square of sunlight. Still unused to the new leather upholstery, he ran his left hand over the surface of the passenger seat, luxuriating in the feel of it while he waited for the order to move.

First off the ferry, he left it with a satisfying squeal of wide tires on the polished metal ramp, and then thudded onto concrete, following the signs that led to the green lights of the customs exit. The sunshine surprised him. Didn't everyone say that it always rained in Ireland? He could hardly credit how good he felt. Webster was fast becoming a bad memory. At the exit gate, a disinterested customs officer waved him on impatiently as he slowed the car. He passed through into a street edged by ugly warehouses. Welcome to Rosslare, a sign read as he negotiated a sharp right hand turn.

Critchley drove out of the town at a casual pace, following the road up into the rolling Wexford hills. On each side the fields sported new green shoots of corn, their stalks bobbing and dancing in unison as they played in a light easterly breeze that came in from the sea. He switched on the radio and listened to an unfamiliar newscaster giving details of some new EEC ruling that promised untold riches to those farmers who volunteered to grow less, and let their fields lie fallow.

Used to the bustle and anonymity of London, the whole

idea of such discussions sounded alien to Critchley and just
for a moment he wished he was back in London, where the
talk was not of crops and farm animals, but about finance, the
theatre, reviews of the best restaurants, and places where one
should be seen. He shuddered. To have remained in London
was just not possible, not while he owed Webster and Phillips.
Had he stayed, he would probably be part of some unnamed
motorway extension by now. No, he told himself, he had to
look on the bright side. He was alive. He had money, and his
new job could not be simpler.

His Porsche had been repossessed by the bank a week ago
and the last time he had seen Webster was when Peter was
writing the cheque for the BMW. "There you are mate," Peter
had said with a sly smile, "Now you have a set of wheels that
should charm the knickers off those Irish colleens!"

Webster had laughed at Critchley's discomfiture. Critchley
just saw it as the final confirmation of his banishment to a
country that he knew little about, and for which he cared
even less. He had not had any contact with Sid Phillips before
he left, but he knew that Webster was not orchestrating this on
his own. Phillips was the real paymaster out there on the side
lines. Whatever his motives were, they were still a mystery.

The road ahead now turned into a shaded area of fine
beech trees that hung out over it, momentarily blotting out
the sunlight. On the right hand side Critchley passed the gates
of an unknown estate, barely noticing stone pillars topped by
heraldic birds. He was driving too fast to see clearly but
caught a quick glimpse up a winding gravel drive where
pheasants strutted unafraid.

Soon afterwards he joined a wider road heavy with traffic
heading in the same direction, all following the signs to Cork.
He turned up the radio as the announcer introduced *Music
for Middlebrows* and reclined his seat.

It was late evening when Critchley finally pulled to a halt
outside Acton's Hotel in Kinsale. The sun had only just disappeared behind the rooftops clustered on the hill above the

harbor where he could see a small Dutch coaster unloading at the commercial quay. He stood for a while taking in the view. On the far side of the harbor, high on the wooded hills that swept down to the water, he could see the red glow of the setting sun reflected in the windows of a hideous concrete jungle of apartments that defied any rational planning laws. Further away, rows of older houses clung to low cliffs near the water's edge. In all, it was a pleasant sight, one that was much better than he had expected and as if to lend a general holiday atmosphere to the place, a number of yachts setting colorful spinnakers were rounding a point on the opposite side heading in the direction of the marina.

Critchley stubbed out a small cigar that he had just lit and extracted his two suitcases from the trunk before making his way inside the hotel. In the reception hall an aroma of food wafted from the open dining room doors and he caught a glimpse of crisp white linen. The chink of cutlery reminding him that he had not eaten since breakfast.

Facing him, a receptionist smiled warmly, encouraging his approach. "Good evening, Sir. Can I help you?"

"Good evening," he replied. "My name is Richard Critchley; I believe I have a reservation."

"Yes, of course, Mr. Critchley, we've been expecting you." She flashed another smile. "Perhaps you would sign the register." She pushed a blank form and a pen towards him. "You are in room 20, overlooking the harbor. Your room has a lovely view. Will it be cash or credit, Mr. Critchley?" Her tone was warm and genuine.

"Credit card." Critchley liked her already. "American Express," he added. Maybe Ireland was not such a bad place after all, he thought. He noticed that she did not wear make up. With skin like hers it wasn't necessary. No perfume either; only the faintest trace of soap lingered in the air as she leant forward to hand him his key.

"I'll have your bags sent up," she said, her eyes dropping to his ring-less left hand. She smiled again. "Welcome to Acton's. I hope you will enjoy your stay with us, Mr. Critchley."

"I'm sure I will," he replied.

He caught her looking at him again as he walked towards the lift. Good looking, he thought. Personable too! The soft lilt of her accent stayed with him for the rest of the evening. Things were certainly looking up.

"A house is it?" Matthew Brennan leaned back in his vinyl covered office chair and swiveled it towards a steel filing cabinet where he tugged at a drawer grandly marked *Desirable Residences.*

The drawer squeaked with irritation. Brennan grinned. "Must put a drop of oil on that someday," he remarked. He selected a manila folder and turned back to the desk.

"Yes, a house. Preferably not a bungalow," Critchley added. "Something secluded and substantial you understand."

Critchley was not sure that Brennan understood at all. His eyes took in the disarray of the auctioneer's poky office. It was a cluttered room that hadn't seen paint in years; its walls may once have been pink, but they were now a dull nicotine brown. Papers were strewn everywhere and in one corner, a grubby looking fax machine sat on a low shelf that sagged under the weight of a collection of old newspapers. Elsewhere, a lopsided oak bookcase defying gravity, and risked disgorging it's contents onto the floor.

"Is it to rent, or to buy?" Brennan's foxy eyebrows loomed over his eyes like a hedge that needed clipping.

"That's really immaterial, providing it meets all of my requirements." Critchley was about to add that cost was not a problem, but reading Brennan's face, he omitted it. "It must have its own foreshore," he added as an afterthought. "Preferably with sheltered water for a mooring."

Brennan raised his eyes. "You're not looking for much are you!" He smiled disarmingly. "Not that it's impossible you understand," he added hurriedly. "Kinsale has developed into something of a yachting capital in recent years, and everything is possible, given time." He rummaged in the folder with thick hairy fingers as if he was searching in a kitchen trash bucket for something discarded in error.

Critchley felt his patience ebbing. "I don't have much time," he snapped impatiently. "If you can't help me, I'll go elsewhere."

"Oh now, I didn't say that, did I?" Brennan selected a well-thumbed sheaf of paper from the folder. "Clonbar House," he announced triumphantly. "Now that might suit you nicely." He showed his teeth in what was meant to be a reassuring smile. "Might be made for you actually. Rolling parkland, secluded bay, total privacy. A gem, just the ticket!" He handed Critchley the papers.

Ten acres of bewitching grounds, Critchley read. Five bedrooms, lounge, study, dining room, kitchen. Small walled orchard and outbuildings suitable for stables. And at the very bottom in smudged print, "in need of some re-decoration. Priced to sell at 350,000 Euros." Critchley wondered just how long this particular gem had been on the market.

"When can I see it?"

Brennan looked taken aback for a moment, but he quickly recovered. "Right away," he replied. "I have the keys. The owner is a psychiatrist in Alberta, Canada, and very eager to sell. I think he would respond to an offer close to the asking price."

"I'm sure he would." Critchley replied dryly. "Let's go shall we?"

Situated only 10 miles from Kinsale, Clonbar House surprised Critchley. They approached the entrance from a narrow unmarked lane that led off the main road to Clonakilty. He noticed with satisfaction that it was the sort of lane that would not warrant a second glance by anyone passing by on the main road. It was something else that Webster had ordered him to look out for.

At the entrance a pair of rusted iron gates hung open, suspended drunkenly from pillars built of cut granite. Inside them lay a curving driveway well bestowed with weeds. The house itself still lay hidden behind a low hill and was not visible from the entrance. Another plus, he thought.

As he drove through the gates, Brennan expounded on the beauty of the place. "This property is a gem," he said. "You'll not find another like it." Critchley was beginning to wonder if the auctioneer had any other word in his vocabulary besides "gem."

"A veritable gem, Mr. Critchley," Brennan repeated, swerving the car to avoid a pair of deceptive potholes that lay like tank traps in the drive. He brought the car to a halt as they crested the hill and looked down on the house. "Now," he said, "Isn't that a view? I'll vouch there's nothing like it in England."

Critchley opened his door and stepped out of the car. He took a deep breath. The air was fresh and salty, with just enough breeze to sway the branches of nearby beech trees. Then he heard the click of the driver's door as Brennan joined him. Below them, the drive curved away through a grassy paddock towards a grey stone house partially hidden in a small copse of trees. At the back of the house he could see a walled orchard where the first buds of pale pink blossom showed, and behind that the slate roofs of the outbuildings.

In front of the house, a barely discernible path led across a field to a gap in the cliffs. Directly below them, was a cove where Critchley could see small waves breaking on the outlying rocks at the narrow entrance and beyond that, the sea shimmering like a sheet of glass. He noted that there were no neighboring houses.

Brennan gave a slight cough beside him. "A gem, Mr. Critchley! Well worth the asking price I should say, wouldn't you?"

Critchley made no reply. He allowed his eyes to search the countryside. Only a few cows moved in the fields. He had to admit that it seemed just the sort of place that Sid Phillips had told him to find. Far in the distance, perhaps three miles away, he could see what looked like a farm house with a tractor crawling slowly up a narrow lane that wound its way in the direction of the main road. It really looked ideal. "How deep is the water in the bay?"

Brennan looked confused. "I don't know," he said finally. "But I'm sure we can find out, I take it you want to keep a boat there? It should be plenty deep enough for that."

"Depends on the size of the boat," Critchley replied with some sarcasm.

"I suppose so. I don't know much about boats." Brennan sounded faintly annoyed.

Critchley smiled. "Let's go down to the house shall we?" He said, turning on his heel. "I'll walk. You bring the car."

As he came nearer, Critchley could see that what had once been a fine lawn with flower beds in front of the house was now totally overgrown. Nettles and briars fought each other for space and the building looked more neglected than it had from the distance. To add to the apparent decay, a number of slates were missing from the roof, and a scatter of tattered crows circling in protest overhead suggested they had been disturbed from their homes in the chimneys.

When he reached the house, Brennan was waiting at the top of a flight of steps leading to the front door, looking anxious, but still eager to please. "Lovely place, don't you agree?"

Critchley scowled and mounted the steps, biting his tongue to refrain from saying that he thought it was a gem. The front door was already open. Inside, the hall was dark and musty smelling. At the far end, a broad flight of wooden stairs faced Critchley. He noted carved oak balusters, and overhead, a high ceiling with patches of peeling paint.

Brennan opened a door on the left and sudden sunlight flooded the hall. "This is the lounge," he announced proudly. "A really fine room, don't you think?" He led the way inside and his voice echoed around the empty room. "Excellent proportions. Ideal for entertaining, if you have that in mind, Mr. Critchley."

Sunlight from two large casement windows overlooking the sea flooded the room, revealing a deep layer of dust on an ornate Victorian mantelpiece. Critchley stared at a large stain on the ceiling.

Brennan coughed nervously. "That's been fixed. A burst pipe last winter. A spot of paint will do wonders."

Critchley grimaced. The place was a dump, but he had to admit that it had potential. Whatever Sid Phillips and Webster were up to, it was just what they had asked him to find, and the price was far less than they had indicated they were prepared to pay. Already his mind was working overtime. Maybe there was an opportunity here to divert some of the money into his own pockets, especially if Brennan was the type of man he suspected him to be. The secret, he thought, was not to show too much interest. "It needs a hell of a lot of work," he commented.

"Purely cosmetic, Mr. Critchley. They don't build houses like this anymore, I assure you." Brennan led the way across the hall and showed him into a similarly spacious dining room. The room had the remnants of once fine velvet curtains on the windows and even boasted a glass chandelier in the centre of its ceiling but the light did not work when Critchley tried the switch.

"Probably a fuse gone," remarked Brennan. He diverted Critchley's attention away from the chandelier. "There's a serving hatch over there in the corner opening into the kitchen. A very useful arrangement, quite unusual these days." His voice sought approval that was not forthcoming.

At the end of the hall Brennan showed Critchley through a dark doorway that led into a large kitchen with a quarry-tile floor, a range of cupboards and a modern stainless steel sink that seemed slightly out of place.

Brennan ran his hand over the top of a Stanley range. "Brand new," he said appreciatively. "The owner had it fitted when we had the problem with the burst pipe." He made an expansive sweep with one arm. "You don't get kitchens this large anymore. There's a walk in larder too, big enough to convert into a utility room."

Critchley arched his eyebrows and the auctioneer fell into uncomfortable silence as he led the way upstairs.

The bedrooms were all large and entered from a wide landing at the top of the stairs. Brennan steered him into a draughty barn of a bathroom containing a vintage bathtub that showed rust stains at one end where a tap dripped slowly.

"If that tap had dripped like that last winter," Brennan said. "We wouldn't have had a burst pipe!" He chuckled.

Critchley rewarded him with a thin smile and led the way downstairs to the front door. After a brief inspection of the outbuildings at the rear of the house, he wearily sank into the frayed front seat of Brennan's Ford.

They drove back to Kinsale mostly in silence. Now and then, Brennan slowed the car and pointed out places of interest. Critchley only nodded absentmindedly, making it plain that he couldn't care less. But when Brennan suggested stopping for a drink in a quiet pub on the outskirts of the town, Critchley didn't demur. Seated in an alcove facing the bar, he sipped his whiskey appreciatively and waited for the auctioneer to open the conversation. He didn't have long to wait.

"Your health, Mr. Critchley!" Brennan raised his glass and sipped tentatively at his drink. "Business in Ireland, Mr. Critchley, is best conducted over a social drink. It's a civilized practice, don't you agree?"

Critchley nodded sagely.

"It's a fine house that's for sure," Brennan probed.

"It needs a lot of repair," Critchley replied after a moment's thought. He made it sound as though he was very unsure. "The cost would be substantial."

Brennan hesitated for a moment. "I have a brother-in-law who is a builder, and he does excellent work. I'm sure something could be arranged with him that would not be out of sight."

The auctioneer shifted uneasily on his seat. Warily he said in a half whisper, "For instance, VAT can be conveniently hidden when cash is involved." He lent forward in a conspiratorial manner. "I presume of course, that a cash transaction is what you had in mind?"

It was the question Critchley was waiting for. "It would be cash," he replied guardedly.

Brennan looked pleased. "Another drink?"

"Thank you. Perhaps a little ice in it this time?"

Critchley watched Brennan walk over to the bar where he cracked a joke with the barman. The auctioneer was a big bulky man with powerful shoulders, perhaps over six feet tall with a thick red neck that strained at the collar of his shirt. His hair was red and curly and beginning to thin on top, but was thick, like fleece, over his ears. His suit hung on him like a threadbare sack. Like all auctioneers he seemed well known, taking time to ensure that he was favorably looked upon, something very necessary in his line of business, Critchley decided. Politicians shared the same knack, he thought. Of one thing he was sure; Matthew Brennan could not be trusted. It took one con man to recognize another. Critchley smiled at the thought.

Brennan returned with the drinks and placed them on the table. "Cheers!" he said picking up a glass.

Critchley raised his own glass in a salute. "I won't waste your time, Brennan. I'll offer you two hundred grand, not a penny more, but the paperwork shows two hundred and fifty."

Brennan appeared startled by the suggestion, but only for an instant. "I don't think I could agree to that, it's not a legal transaction." His eyes were wary now, sizing up his adversary.

Critchley leaned forwards, elbows on the table. "Fuck the legalities," he snapped. He sat back, staring coldly at the auctioneer. "You can take it or leave it," he said firmly. He picked up his glass and swallowed a mouthful of whiskey with an air of finality. "You know," he said, smiling, "This Irish is not half bad. I've always been a Scotch drinker myself, but upon my word, I think I'll change!"

Brennan studied him cautiously for a moment. Critchley could read greed in his eyes. Eventually Brennan spoke. "What's in it for me?"

"Ten grand," Critchley replied. "Plus your commission, plus a cut for the solicitor. I assume you know one that is not averse to making a few bob!"

Brennan nodded slowly. "Perhaps," he said. "There's a man up in Tralee who once tied himself in with some Dutch speculator. There was a bit of a stink at the time, but I think it's blown over and he's still in business. Of course, you're assuming that my client will accept your offer. He might, and he might not."

Critchley's lips curled into a sneer. "You know bloody well that he will. How long have you had that bloody dump on your books? Five years? More?"

Brennan sipped his drink. "You are obviously representing a third party, or you wouldn't be suggesting an arrangement like this."

Critchley hesitated for a moment. For a brief instant he thought of Webster and Phillips back in London, but London now seemed a long way away and the stab of worry dissipated. "I represent an English property company," he said finally. "There's time enough to go into the details later, when we get to the paperwork." He shot a quizzical look at the auctioneer. "Have we got a deal?"

"We have," said Brennan slowly, "but I want to see fifteen grand, not ten."

"Twelve," Critchley shot back. He stood up to leave. "Not a cent more!"

Brennan smiled slyly and put out his hand. "We have a deal Mr. Critchley. All things being equal, that is."

Later that night Critchley telephoned Webster at the club in London. "Bingo!" He said when Webster answered his call.

The voice at the other end of the line was indistinct, but Webster sounded pleased. "That was quick," he heard Webster say. "You've done a good job mate. What kind of money are we talking about?"

Critchley smirked. "Two hundred and fifty, in Euros," he said smugly.

"Euro's you say! As cheap as that? Blimey! We should all move over and live there!" Webster sounded genuinely impressed. "Run with it, mate. Let me know when you get it agreed." The phone clicked to a dead line.

Critchley replaced the receiver and undressed for bed. Things were certainly looking up. He would go out and take another look at Clonbar House tomorrow.

SEVEN

"He hasn't lost any time has he?" There was surprise in Sid Phillips' voice. He swiveled his chair to face Peter Webster. "What time did he call?"

"About an hour ago, just before eleven."

There was an awkward silence while Phillips mulled the news over in his mind. Webster watched him twiddle a heavy gold ring round and round on his finger with his thumb. It was a sure sign of Phillips' discontent. Webster was amused, maybe Sid should consider getting himself a set of those worry beads; he'd seen other Arabs with them. He stifled a smile, only yesterday one of the punters had confirmed that Sid was Lebanese and not native English as he liked to pretend. His informant should know, Webster thought. The man claimed to know Phillips from the old days when Beirut had been the pearl of the Middle East

Phillips bit the end from a cigar and spat it into a waste paper basket beside the desk. He lit his cigar slowly, twirling it now and then to ensure it was evenly lit. "I want you to make sure we can trust this bastard, Peter. There's a lot at stake. Eventually we're going to have to tell him, and we don't want him blabbing his mouth off over there."

Webster felt a growing sense of irritation. They'd been over this so many times already. "It was your idea to use the bastard as a front, Sid. He's a greedy little sod, but he's desperate to get himself out of the fire." He paused and cracked his knuckles noisily, knowing that the action infuriated Phillips. "Besides," he went on, "Critchley is scared, scared shitless, I made sure of that."

"Maybe you should go over and mark his card again," Phillips retorted coldly.

Webster made no immediate reply but walked over to the window where he stood for a moment, assessing the crowd milling about below in the gaming room. It was busy tonight, he thought. It was much better than earlier in the week. Now that the Arabs were back in town, the girls would do well tonight. He could already see several of them looking pleased with themselves. "I don't think so," he said slowly, "It's too early. Let him get the place organized first, then I'll go over before we sign up for anything. It could fall through, remember. He said the owner was in Canada and has yet to agree to the sale."

"Maybe you're right. Perhaps I'm rushing things. But it pays to be careful. Critchley isn't one of us, know what I mean?"

Webster frowned. "You said you wanted a gent, Sid. Those were your exact words. I got you what you wanted, although I tried to warn you. Now you don't like it." He threw up his hands in a gesture of impatience. "For Christ's sake, Sid! He knows nothing. We can always get rid of him if it doesn't work out." Webster walked over to a drinks cabinet and poured himself a vodka. "Drink?"

"No thanks." Phillips heaved his bulk out of his chair. "I'm going to have an early night and sleep on it. Take no notice of me; I have a lot of balls in the air at the moment. I have to go to Amsterdam in the morning to meet with the Chinese."

Startled, Webster swallowed his drink too fast. The vodka hit his throat and he spluttered. He dabbed his mouth with his handkerchief and put down his glass. His mind was racing. Why hadn't Phillips taken his advice and kept the Chinese out of this? As he started to speak, Phillips cut him off.

"I know what you're thinking, Peter. How many times have I got to tell you that we can't operate in the Far East without them? For fuck's sake drop it, will you!"

Webster glared at Phillips. "You're the boss," he snapped. "It's your fucking money."

Phillips exhaled a cloud of cigar smoke and grinned. "Too fuckin' right mate! It's my bankroll. Talking about money, Critchley seems to have picked up a bargain. I thought we'd have to go at least double that."

Webster brightened. "To be quite honest, so did I. Obviously the Paddy's don't know what it's like to buy a place in London!" He shrugged. "If the worst comes to the worst, it looks as if he's found you a nice little retirement pad."

Phillips glared and straightened his tie. "I'm not ready for retirement, mate. You'd best remember that." He walked towards the door. "I'm going home. I'll talk to you when I get back, probably Thursday. Meanwhile, keep tabs on Critchley." He walked out without another word, slamming the door behind him.

Webster settled himself into his swivel chair. It annoyed him that the leather was still warm, but he knew that Phillips only sat in it to needle him, to show who was in charge. Through the window Webster watched him crossing the floor below, noticing that Phillips walked with a peculiarly rolling gait. He recalled someone telling him once that Sid had been a ship's steward long before he'd moved on to better things. Better things all right, Webster thought. Like a bloody mansion out in West Byfleet and a Rolls to cruise around in. Webster had spent little time in Sid's house, but had seen enough on those occasions to be pierced with pangs of jealousy. One day, he thought, he would have the same.

It came to him then that he should put in the effort to see that Phillips was successful in his scheme. If Sid made it big on this one, so would he. Without Phillips he had nothing.

EIGHT

The Regiment's Corsican barracks seemed like a palace to Ryder after the stark confines of Cayenne with its sulfurous heat. Calvi had an air of permanence about it that was lacking in the Guyana base, which still clung to the faded remnants of Colonial unreality. French Guyana was a relic of the past, he thought. Just a memory of imperialism long since gone. For just an instant, he wondered if perhaps the Legion was the same.

During the long flight home, his fellow members of the CRAP unit had talked little. Training exercises in the Legion were rigorous and physically demanding, sapping the energy of even the toughest of them. The Legion promised little, and gave even less. They were expendable and were all aware of it so they had slept on the plane in case tomorrow would not allow them to do so, nevertheless, throughout the flight an air of expectancy hovered. Each man on board had known that they were not being recalled without some very good reason.

In spite of his physical exhaustion, Ryder had slept only sporadically during the first few hours of the flight. Although his body ached and screamed out for rest, his mind would not permit it. The more he had tried to evade his thoughts, the more savagely they attacked him. It was becoming increasingly difficult for him to rid himself of his own private ghost.

So many times, Mark's wasted face came and shimmered before him and would not let go. In his dreams, when he did sleep, Mark would come again, stealing stealthily into his mind with soft footsteps. Sometimes, he would appear as a young child, fit and healthy with smiling features, just as Ryder remembered him, but at other times the vision was an aged skeletal ghoul that taunted and mocked him. That face was a grinning skull, where once, Ryder saw serpents coiling from black, empty eye sockets. He felt such despair at these times that Ryder wondered if he was suffering from Le Cafard, that mythical black beetle that he had heard invaded the minds of Legionnaires at times of stress.

Now as he lay on his bed in the familiar surroundings of his room, he willed the thoughts to go and tried to concentrate on the briefing only one hour away. Some of the men were already betting that they were going back to Chad but others argued ominously that the odds were on Afghanistan. There was some sense in the latter prediction. The Taliban, although weakened, remained unbowed and coalition troops continued to suffer a depressing number of casualties. Only a week before, two more Legionnaires had been killed in Kapisa province. France, alone, was becoming increasingly impatient and frustrated by the rules of engagement. When that patience ran out, the tight leash on the Legion would be the first to be released.

Of one thing Ryder was certain. 2REP was coming to full alert and making ready to move, and he sensed that this time something big was in the offing. Too many planes had been landing and taking off from Calvi airport all day. Even now, as evening shadows chased themselves across the parade ground, he could hear the steady drone of engines in the sky.

He stared at the ceiling and wondered what Klein was doing now. There had been no time to see him before they left Guyana. Together with an Italian from another patrol who had been bitten by a snake, he had been left behind in a military hospital in Cayenne. Ryder doubted if Klein would keep his leg, if so, his days in the Legion were numbered. He closed his eyes and sleep came quickly. This time, no ghosts haunted his dreams.

Colonel Marchand strode quickly to a central table at one end of the briefing room, silencing the babble of speculation and rumor. Dressed in combat fatigues, his swarthy features were serious and his mouth was set in a grim line. With his usual sense of theatre, he paused to dramatically survey the rows of expectant faces before him.

Ryder stood rigidly to attention with the others, waiting for the order to sit. He wished Marchand would get on with it; he felt drained.

Marchand motioned for them to be seated. When there was silence, he cleared his throat. "2REP is honored to be chosen again," he began. Ryder groaned inwardly. Marchand was determined to take the long route, he thought. But despite his frustration, the adrenaline started to pump in his veins and he could not shake off a growing sense of excitement. Whatever was coming was serious, but maybe it was what he needed to purge himself, he thought. Maybe action would cure him. He crossed his legs, listening intently.

"Once again we have been selected to mount an operation into Somalia!" The pride in Marchand's voice echoed hollowly around the room, hanging in the air for an interminable second.

"Not again." The man sitting next to Ryder groaned.

Ryder heard someone cough uneasily at the back of the room. Probably some jerk wondering where the hell Somalia is, he thought. Judging from the look on Marchand's face, whoever he was, he would know soon enough.

Marchand swiveled round and pulled down a roller wall map showing the Horn of Africa. Picking up a wooden pointer, he stabbed it at the map, circling the borders of Somalia with its tip. "Somalia is bordered by Kenya and Ethiopia and to the North lies Djibouti, which as some of you know is to all intents and purposes ours as the 1st REC is stationed there, and it will be the headquarters base for the entire operation." He turned and faced them. "Some of you have served in this part of Africa before, so you will understand the swiftness of developments in this area. In fact a number of you were on our last little fling in Eyl not so long ago. This operation is bigger and as on the last occasion in 1992, Mogadishu will be our objective."

Marchand cleared his throat again. "You may also be aware that famine is sweeping across Somalia at this time and hundreds of thousands of starving refugees are making their way on foot into Mogadishu and over the borders of neighboring countries. Both the World Food Organization and the UN are trying to get food supplies into the country but the local Islamic insurgents are preventing this and refusing any offers of aid. They are renewing their attacks on forces of the Somali Federal Government and peacekeeping troops of the African Union are under increasing threat. These are largely Ugandan troops who we have trained and our purpose is to support them in their efforts to regain control of the situation.

Marchand paused to sip from a glass of water, allowing his words to sink in. "As before," he continued proudly, "Only the Legion can stabilize the situation, and I am glad to say that this time, the Americans are reluctant to become involved and it is a purely French initiative." A smile flickered unexpectedly on Marchand's face that generated a chorus of titters around the room. His eyes twinkled. "This time there will be no television cameras to announce our coming!"

Ryder grinned at a grizzled Legion Sergeant from Pittsburgh who had served with the US Special Forces. The American sitting across the aisle from him smiled and raised one finger enigmatically.

Marchand, serious again, continued ponderously. "Over the next four days, eight hundred men will fly into Djibouti Armored support will be provided by units of the Régiment Étranger de Cavalerie. By lucky coincidence Units of 1REC and 13 DBLE have been on exercise in the area for the past week and are already in position to support the operation."

A ripple went around the room as Marchand sipped from his water glass. "Any questions so far?" he queried

No one spoke. Ryder squirmed uneasily in his chair and uncrossed his legs. He didn't need reminding of the atrocities he had witnessed in Africa the last time. But he knew Marchand far too well. The Colonel was building up to something else and he had yet to mention the role of the REP. Whatever it was, excitement now showed on Marchand's face, and if it excited Marchand, it promised to be spectacular.

Marchand faced them again, drawing himself up to his full height, his eyes gleaming. "Yesterday," he said, "The U.N. reported that a breakaway Al Qaeda group of the Al Shabab led by a Mohamed Deid stormed the airport in Mogadishu and arrested five religious missionaries and an unknown number of Aid workers. These people are being held hostage at the airport - three of them are French nationals. It is feared that the French Ambassador and his First Secretary from Djibouti are among them. There are reports that suicide bombers were used in the initial assault and that a large number of casualties ensued. African Union troops have been forced to withdraw from the airport perimeter."

Here it comes, thought Ryder. Despite himself, he felt elated and sat forwards in his chair.

Marchand tensed himself. "Deid is demanding five million dollars in return for their release," he announced flatly.

Ryder released his breath. It was the loudest sound in the room. Kolwezi all over again, he thought. He knew that the raid on Kolwezi in 1978 had gone down in the annals of the Legion. It had been 2REP then too, also operating out of Corsica. They had saved the lives of two thousand hostages for the cost of five dead and twenty-five wounded Legionnaires. In that action they killed two hundred and fifty Katangan rebels and captured one hundred and sixty three. It won 2REP worldwide admiration.

"Mes amis," Marchand said slowly. "CRAP teams, under the command of Lieutenant Arvans, will lead an assault on Mogadishu airport to free these hostages. This operation is code named Operation Cougar and will be launched forty-eight hours from now."

Marchand paused, allowing the tension and the buzz in the room to subside. "The operation will be a high altitude parachute drop under cover of darkness. You all know what this means, you've practiced it often enough. A second larger unit under my command will follow the first wave to secure the runway and clear any booby traps. Reinforcements from 1st REC and 13DBLE will be flown in once the airport is under our control, their objective will be to stabilize the area so that humanitarian supplies can be administered. They will also secure the K50 airport 32 miles from Mogadishu in the coming days."

Ryder tried to breathe, but his chest felt suddenly constricted. A stand off HAHO jump with the aircraft remaining in friendly air space was not for the uninitiated. For survival at a low rate of descent, it required oxygen helmets and thermal gear, and meticulous navigation, he thought numbly. Vaguely, as if from a distance, he heard disjointed words relating to terrain, ground temperature, expected wind strength and direction, and the likelihood of cloud cover over the target. At least, he thought, this gave him more time to make up his mind. Marchand would now be far too busy to even think of the approaching deadline for his contract. Ryder paid full attention again only when Lieutenant Arvans took Marchand's place, and in clipped tones, started outlining the strategy for the raid and the weapons to be used.

Arvans stopped to pour himself a glass of water. Sipping it, he touched the track pad of a laptop computer and the display on the wall behind him revealed a low altitude photograph of Mogadishu Airport showing abandoned trucks littering the runway.

He picked up Marchand's discarded pointer and calmly began describing the target layout. "Here," he said, pointing at the roof of the terminal building, "Is the control tower. If you study it carefully, you will notice anti-aircraft weapons placed here and here, on either side of the tower. It is imperative that these are taken out before the second wave arrives over the target area. The safety of the hostages depends on speed and surprise and we cannot rule out the further threat of suicide bombers, it is kill or be killed!" Arvans ran his pointer along the length of the runway that was fringed by the waters of the Indian Ocean. "The runway is paved and roughly two miles in length. These trucks that you can see appear to be abandoned to prevent aircraft from landing, it is possible that they are booby-trapped. Again, I must emphasize that their clearance is essential if we are to be flown out at the end of the operation and to permit the insertion of reinforcements."

At this point, Marchand interjected. "You are expected to take the airport within three hours of the landing. Three Transall's will bring you and the hostages out at dawn. For that to happen, immediate clearance of the runway by the second unit is essential after the initial assault." Marchand nodded to Arvans. "Please carry on," he said quietly.

"Thank you, Colonel." Arvans selected another slide. "Flight time to the DZ will be a little over five and a half hours with mid-air refueling taking place over Chad. Release will be from twenty two thousand feet at 0100 local time. You can expect moderately strong northerly winds of up to twenty knots that are ideal for our purpose, but there is a risk of isolated thunderstorms and possibly some lightening during the final approach. The second wave will make a conventional jump from 800 feet two hours later."

Lieutenant Arvans droned on and Ryder looked about him. If there was fear in the room, he couldn't detect it.

It was late when he finally left the briefing room after going over the details of the assault with his own CRAP team. The entire briefing had been conducted in a very matter of fact way as though they were simply gearing up for another exercise. Pointedly, no mention of expected casualties was made, either by Arvans or later by Marchand, during his summing up.

As he walked slowly back to his quarters, Ryder picked up the rumble of trucks out on the highway already hauling equipment to Calvi airport. On the far side of the parade ground lights still glowed in the foyer and Ryder heard the sound of voices raised in song. First, the haunting words of "Kamaraden" floated eerily on the night air, and then, as he changed direction and walked towards it, came the words of "Kepi Blanc."

The Legion was girding itself for war, and just as generations of Legionnaires had done before them, they did so in song, drawing courage from their jealously guarded mystique, the legacy of those who had fallen for France. How many would still sing tomorrow, he wondered.

Ryder watched a line of men snaking out on the runway towards the waiting aircraft. He had slept until dawn came too soon, ushering in a day of frantic preparation. It seemed like a blur of activity; briefings, weapons checks, the myriad tasks to prepare men for action. Check, re-check and check again. Their lives depended on it. This was not another tedious exercise; in a short few hours blood would be spilled and no one planned on it being theirs.

He ground out his cigarette under his boot and shouldered his pack so as not to disturb the hardened scabs that still covered his shoulders. The effort was useless; he already felt a trickle of blood inside his shirt.

He strode towards the shadows of other men loaded down with equipment who were waiting to board the plane. Corporal Perez, who had replaced Klein, was waiting for him underneath the black bulk of the Transall. Across his shoulders he carried an ERYX rocket launcher. As the lightest man in the team, Perez had to carry a heavier load than the others to achieve an even distribution of weight during the jump. Perez seemed an unlikely name for an Australian with freckled skin who looked as if he would be far more at home with a surfboard on his shoulders than with an anti-tank missile launcher. Above him, Ryder could see the faces of the pilots lit by cockpit lights as they started their pre-flight checks. He grinned at Perez. "All set Digger?"

"Rarin' to go, Sarge." Perez stuck out his hand and Ryder clasped it warmly.

"Good to have you with us, mate!" Ryder had worked with the Australian before. He liked him and respected his ability. He could not have gotten a better replacement for Corporal Klein.

Perez hefted his pack and moved towards the ramp leading up into the black belly of the plane. "By the way," he said, "I heard a few minutes ago that Klein lost his leg. They're flying him back to Marseilles."

Ryder sucked in his breath. "It was his own fucking fault. That Zulu of mine jumped with him and missed the DZ as well. He was lucky he didn't end up in the same shit!" He shouldered his MP5 and followed Perez up the ramp.

Inside the aircraft, men struggled to settle themselves, jostling for space among their equipment. Weapons clattered as they hit the metal floor, and the smell of stale sweat permeated the hold. Someone farted and a chorus of obscenities blistered the air. Ryder found a seat by an exit door and strapped himself in. Perez sat opposite, facing him, his eyes on the jumpmaster forcing his way down the central aisle to make last minute checks.

Then the ramp came up and seconds later the big engines coughed one by one and burst into life, drowning all sound inside the fuselage. The plane lurched as the brakes were released, and then it trundled forwards down the taxi-way towards a line of guidance lights that edged the runway like a string of white pearls.

At the end of the tarmac, Ryder braced himself for the familiar forwards rush as the aircraft poised itself. His mouth felt unusually dry and for a strange moment he experienced a craving for an ice cream. He felt suddenly uncertain and apprehensive. He wondered if others felt the same. He thought again of Klein, wondering whether they had taken the leg off above, or below the knee. What the hell did it matter anyway, he thought bitterly. Either way, Klein was finished. There was nothing for him in the Legion anymore. He was a piece of scrap destined for a junkyard. As Ryder shook his head, the plane thundered down the runway and launched itself out over the sea.

At cruising altitude the clouds fell away revealing the moon as a pale orb in a blue sky tinged with red from the setting sun. Ryder unbuckled his seat belt and stood up to study it silently through a nearby window. All its shadows were in relief; it looked closer and bigger than he had ever seen it before. It resembled a round white oasis of peace out on a wing tip where a red light flashed its silent warning.

He noticed that his reflection in the window was that of a stranger. The face staring back at him had bags under the eyes and looked old and unfamiliar. It was unsettling and he turned away quickly. Settling back in his canvas seat, he tried to concentrate on nothing other than the mission, but his mind was a jumble of thoughts. Further up the aisle, Ryder could see Joby and Chen with their heads together chattering in Vietnamese and laughing. Nothing ever seemed to concern those two, he'd noticed. They were no more disturbed than two schoolboys on an outing to a football match. He stared at them moodily, wishing he was more like them. He had been once, he recalled, but those days seemed to have deserted him.

Angrily he got up and wandered down the plane looking for something to do. He passed Van Delden, who had already blackened his face and was lovingly stripping his MP5. The Dutchman had his eyes closed while his fingers delicately caressed and reassembled each part of the gun. The ecstatic look on his face suggested he might be stroking a woman's body.

Ryder frowned; there had been no time to get rid of Van Delden. Now he would have to watch him carefully; he was the weak link in the chain. If the Dutchman had a score to settle with him, this action could well present him with an opportunity.

Sinbad sat next to Van Delden silently stropping his combat knife on a strip of leather. The blade hissed like a snake. Sinbad's deep-set almond eyes smoldered, his mind clearly some-where else. Sinbad looked up at him and smiled. "Yes, boss?"

"You stick right behind me tonight, Sinbad. I want you on my tail leaving the plane. No fuck-ups. Savvy?"

Sinbad grinned. "Sure boss." He went back to honing his blade.

The Zulu had plenty to smile about, thought Ryder. As the biggest and heaviest in the team, Sinbad would only have his knife and his weapons with him when he jumped. All his other gear would be distributed amongst the others.

Many of the men were trying to sleep but Ryder knew it was a sham. Mixed with the smell of sweat and oiled machin-ery was the palpable scent of fear and uncertainty. It was the perfume of war. He wandered back to his own seat and closed his eyes, but sleep would not come and the ghost returned with a swiftness that dismayed him. Mark swayed before him in a misty cloud, but for once, he was smiling and seemed to be reaching out to touch him. Ryder groaned and opened his eyes and the specter retreated. He fixed his eyes on Perez slumped in his seat opposite to him and tried to concentrate on the mission. Had he forgotten anything? Night vision goggles? Rations? A fine time to be worrying, he thought, as out of the corner of his eye he saw Lieutenant Arvans approaching.

Arvans was of deceptively slight build with features that reminded Ryder of a wizened child. His ears were far too big for his domed skull and stuck out like fungus on a tree trunk. With three year's service in the CRAP team already behind him, Arvans was bucking for promotion, having built up a reputation of ruthlessness. He was a cold and calculating offi-cer who seldom saw good in anyone. He was prone to take chances, and the men both feared and hated him.

"You've heard about Corporal Klein I suppose, Sergeant?"

"Yes sir, just before we took off."

"Most unfortunate, Klein was a good soldier." There was a hint of insincerity in Arvans' voice that annoyed Ryder. "There is a message for all of us in his misfortune," he continued.

Ryder narrowed his eyes. "What do you mean?"

"He misjudged the DZ. I intend to make sure that it doesn't happen this time. I'd like you to guarantee it Sergeant. Make sure those men get out on time, and on target."

Ryder shrugged. "Whatever you say, Sir. But I suspect it was a wind sheer. The Zulu missed as well."

"Your loyalty to your men is admirable, Sergeant, but I doubt that very much. There was very little wind. You know as well as I do that they fucked up." Arvans looked away and peered out of the window. "Libya," he said in a whisper.

"What was that?"

"I said, Libya." Arvans nodded at the window. "Down there, the oil wells."

Ryder stood up and craned his neck. He could see fires burning far below, coming from the waste gasses of the desert oil fields. The cloud had cleared away and stars showed in the sky all the way as far as the darker line of the horizon.

Arvans stepped closer and looked at him coldly. "No mistakes tonight, Sergeant. Timing is vital for a successful HAHO jump. You know that as well as I do." Arvans pushed his face closer and his eyes rested for an instant on Ryder's stripes. There was a whiff of garlic on his breath. "I am relying on you." He left the implied threat hanging in the air and melted away to the front of the plane.

Ryder watched his disappearing form, inwardly seething with resentment. What the fuck did Arvans think he was, some kind of dummy recruit? A zero, for Christ's sake! Jesus, he'd done more high altitude jumps than Arvans had seen breakfasts! Angrily, Ryder picked up his weapon and started to strip it. He ejected the ammunition clip and for the tenth time reloaded the bullets, counting them as he did so. Twenty-seven, twenty-eight...twenty-nine. He always loaded one less than the magazine would hold to ensure that the spring mechanism would have extra tension to avoid jamming. He methodically worked his way through the rest of his kit. By the time he had finished, he was perspiring heavily in his thermal clothing and his skin itched.

An hour later the aircraft slowed to carry out in-flight refueling over Chad. Ryder looked out of the window. He could clearly see the lights of a city showing as faint dots on the tip of the horizon. Someone said it was Khartoum, but he doubted it. Below, all was blackness as Africa slept. The Dark Continent was living up to its name.

Nearing the borders of Ethiopia soon afterwards the inside of the plane became a scene of feverish activity as each man checked his oxygen equipment, double checking that nothing would be left behind. Ryder smeared battle paint onto his face, blacking it to transform himself into a predator like all the others. It was almost time to do the business.

The aircraft reached a height of 13,000 feet and oxygen masks went on. Cold now penetrated the skin of the aircraft, and every movement became an exhausting effort. The dispatcher moved down the aircraft showing a square card, H-60. He held up a second card and Ryder quickly jotted down the Northerly wind direction with a wind speed of 30 miles per hour. Then he worked his way up the plane to brief his team on the jump sequence. One hour to go.

NINE

High over the Somali desert, with two minutes to go, the dispatcher moved quietly into position holding a card marked, H-2. A minute later, he opened the side door, sliding it open so that cold black rarefied night air swept in, chilling them to the bone in an instant. Loaded down with equipment, some of the smaller men were already having difficulty breathing.

A red light flashed. Ryder shuffled into position. Tensing himself in the open door, he tried to breathe normally to relieve the constriction in his chest. He glanced over his shoulder and motioned impatiently for Sinbad to close up. Success would depend on them going through that door with one second spacing. Ryder moved closer and the muffled roar from the engines penetrated through his helmet as he looked into the shapeless black sky. It reminded him of a grave. Sweet Jesus, not now, he thought. Stilling his fear, he braced himself and summoned up the aggression needed to punch himself through the opening. Then suddenly he was out in the whirling slipstream with a dreadful roaring sound in his ears.

Icy cold ate into him, leaving pain so intense that his bones felt as though they would explode. The temperature was minus forty-five degrees Celsius but it felt worse as frost formed over his goggles and facemask. He tried to relax so that he could stabilize his trajectory and maneuver himself into the imaginary cone for the forty-mile glide into Mogadishu.

He glanced at his chest-held instruments. On course, altitude 21,500 feet. Ryder breathed rhythmically.

Ryder briefly wondered what waited for him below. Death? Death could solve so many of his problems, he thought. If his chute didn't open he wouldn't even feel it when he hit. Three seconds! Shit! He'd been out of the plane nearly four seconds now - time to pull! He jerked his ripcord and felt the ram-air canopy explode above him. Relief flooded through him as he glided in a slow trajectory towards the unseen Drop Zone. He looked up. He could see a few stars and the soft haze of the moon hidden behind a layer of altocumulus cloud. There was no sign of the others but he knew they were watching the dull glow of a luminescent panel on his chute. Soon they would group, forming up into a tight wedge for the landing.

At 17,000 feet he glanced at his GPS receiver to check a programmed way point and adjusted his chute to take advantage of a wind shear, gaining distance in an effortless curve. Everything was as they had predicted but still there was nothing but infinite blackness below.

Ryder checked the clock on his panel again. He was now forty minutes out of the aircraft and still gliding! His altimeter read 10,000 feet and he shed his oxygen mask as the bottle emptied. There should be lights by now, he thought. He felt as if he was falling into an abyss. Finally it became warmer as the heat of the land reached up to touch him and he fancied he saw the light of a fire far below in the distance.

Five minutes before landing he sensed someone near to him just overhead and he knew the others were with him and the sheer joy of knowing he was not alone became overpowering. The wind from his descent whipped away the tears forming in his eyes.

Three minutes later he saw the lights of a truck moving slowly below him and some distance off to the left, then saw a flickering cluster of lights directly in front of him. It had to be the terminal building. He made an adjustment and steered towards it. Lowering his pack he steeled himself. The earth was close now; close enough for him to smell it. He floated in as lightly as a leaf falling from a tree until his boots touched soft sand. Christ, he was down! He scrambled to his feet as his parachute collapsed into a limp mass. Quickly he unpacked his night vision goggles and slipped them on. He could clearly make out the start of the runway, and then he heard a series of dull thumps as the others glided in around him. He was aware of vague shapes silently gathering equipment, keeping low and running for the storm culvert that they knew to be over on the left of the runway.

Quickly and silently two four-man teams gathered, breathing heavily as they shed their thermal clothing and non-essential supplies. It took almost twenty minutes to redistribute their weapons and ammunition, and a few seconds on the radio to raise Captain Arvans with his group at the north end of the target. Arvans wasted no time. "Advance!" was his single word to all five teams.

With Perez close beside him, Ryder sped away. The only sound behind him was the soft pad of feet hitting the concrete. His heart pumped and sweat started to trickle down his back. Mark was nowhere now. Had he rid himself of Le Cafard? Was it purely a fake - a myth? Far away a dog barked. Others, that seemed much closer, picked up the warning and repeated it. Had they been scented? Ryder sped on waiting for gunfire to lance the night, expecting at any moment to be revealed by a searchlight, already tensing himself for imagined bullets ripping mercilessly through his body.

Perez had taken up a position behind him covering the flank. Ryder slowed and warily circled the dark outline of an abandoned truck, on guard against a challenge that didn't come. Seconds later, he saw a shadowy movement ahead of him and he stopped, dropping silently to the ground. He glanced back. All the others were down, waiting for his signal. Ryder raised his eyes slowly willing the shadow to move. Had he imagined it? No! There came the flare of a match as a cigarette was lit directly ahead of him near the outline of a second truck. There were no voices.

Only one man was there, probably smoking to stay awake. Ryder heard a cough as the sentry cleared his throat noisily. Suddenly, the man moved away from the black bulk of the truck and became distinct in his night vision goggles.

Ryder inclined his head. Perez was lying prone close to him. Ryder crossed two fingers. Perez nodded and passed the signal down the line.

An instant later, a marksman specializing in night combat wormed his way alongside Ryder. The sentry was still standing, a darker patch against the skyline. The sniper raised his FR F2 and took careful aim through his sight. For an interminable second Ryder watched the white spot of the laser settle on the back of the sentry's head, then came an imperceptible plopping sound as the sniper squeezed the trigger twice, pumping off two shots. There was no muzzle flash and the shadow crumpled into a dark heap on the runway.

Up and running again, Ryder paused only to check the body. From just below the man's left ear a slow trickle of blood dripped to the concrete forming an oily pool. Ryder began to move forwards in a crouching run. Behind him the others fanned out to take up their planned assault positions. One team of four broke off to circle away with the rocket launchers.

The terminal was close now; showing as a rectangle of white concrete that even in darkness looked bruised and run down. Above the second floor windows, a low blue parapet surrounded a flat observation roof directly underneath the control tower. Only a dim light showed inside the all-round windows of the tower and there was no sign of movement inside. On the parking apron in front of the building a Daallo Airlines aircraft sat. Its undercarriage looked damaged and the nose was smoke blackened.

Ryder dropped to one knee in the shadows of a fuel truck and sniffed the night air suspiciously. A vague sense of unease crept up on him. He couldn't yet make out the anti-aircraft guns that were supposed to be up on the roof, but he could see a sign with peeling blue paint. *Aden Abdulle International*

Airport, it said. *Welcome to Mogadishu*. Somewhere behind those windows were the hostages, but nothing moved, even behind those windows that showed lights. He moved swiftly across the apron and took up a position against the wall of the building. His breathing felt ragged and he wished he hadn't smoked so much before boarding the plane. One by one, other Legionnaires flitted quickly across the open space and took up positions along the wall.

Silently, Ryder circled right and began to approach a doorway. He was almost there when the door suddenly opened and a pool of light spilled out onto the greasy tarmac. Ryder froze and brought his weapon to his shoulder, thumbing it to full automatic.

A man dressed in camouflage fatigue trousers and a red tee shirt stepped from the door into the pool of light. Without looking around he unzipped his trousers and turned, exposing his back to them, and began to relieve himself up against the wall of the building.

Ryder hugged the concrete wall of the building and motioned with one hand without taking his eyes off the man for an instant. Silently, the sniper knelt beside him and raised his weapon. They were so close that they could hear the splash of urine against the wall. Ryder held his breath and watched the white spot of the laser beam move lazily onto the back of the African's head.

Thuck!

The insurgent pitched face forwards and slid down the wall into the pool of urine. Ryder crept forward and halted to one side of the open door. The Somali terrorist lay with his legs showing in the rectangle of light coming from the room within. Ryder noticed that he was barefoot. There was surprisingly very little blood, but it was obvious that he was dead. Perez moved closer, poised to fling himself through the open door.

Something scraped on the balcony directly overhead and Ryder froze, gluing himself to the wall. A voice from above him called out. Ryder stiffened. Anyone looking over the parapet had to see the body lying in the full beam of the light. Mother of Jesus! Whoever you are, don't look down, he prayed. His breath rasped, sounding unnaturally loud in his ears. There came a scraping noise like a belt buckle on concrete. Someone was leaning over the edge, he realized. Ryder waited for gunfire, steeling himself for the agony of bullets tearing his body apart. Nothing. Only footsteps fading away on the roof as his heart pounded like a trip hammer inside his chest.

Why the fuck wasn't the power cut yet, Ryder wondered wildly. What the hell were the other teams doing? He brought up his MP5 and went over the threshold in a running crouch into the room.

Perez flitted in behind him. They found themselves in an office with another door facing them. The room was full of scattered papers, and ransacked drawers were strewn around the floor. Near a rifled filing cabinet, a Kalashnikov rifle was propped against the wall and there was a stained mattress on the floor in one corner where the dead man outside had obviously been sleeping.

The door facing them had a small glass window in its centre. Peering through it, Ryder could see into a baggage retrieval area where a rusted carousel lay in silent misery. Nothing moved. The vast room looked deserted, and looted baggage lay strewn in miserable piles. Ryder didn't hesitate. He slipped inside like a wraith followed by the others who took up positions at each side of the exit doors. Ryder thought back to the briefings. If the information was right, the arrivals area lay beyond the doors, an open concourse with a broad staircase leading to the second story. Somewhere up there were the hostages. They were seconds away from their objective, and still the lights had not gone out. Ryder swore. Arvans and his larger group should have already been in position; and as yet, there had been no shots fired.

Suddenly, the lights went out and immediately muffled gunfire erupted from somewhere outside. It seemed to come from further down the approach road, away from the front of the building. The air instantly became filled with the sounds of automatic fire, and then Ryder heard the shriek of a missile followed by a violent explosion. Through the windows overlooking the tarmac he could see tracers lancing across the runway and then came the dull crump of exploding mortar shells in the distance. Shouts reached them from somewhere up on the roof as the sky filled with exploding anti-aircraft shells. They were compromised.

"Go! Go!" Ryder roared the words as he snapped down his night vision goggles and burst through the exit doors. Once through, he whirled towards the staircase. The others followed right on his heels, fanning out to cover the area. He tried to see which one was Van Delden and failed.

A rocket shrieked past the windows that overlooked the car park and exploded somewhere up on the roof. One of the anti-aircraft guns that had been hammering away overhead fell silent and Ryder could hear wounded men screaming.

Confident that Arvans and his men were gaining control outside, Ryder raced for the stairs, taking them two at a time. The balcony at the top appeared deserted. He was less than halfway up when a door at the end of the check-in counter burst open and a Kalashnikov chattered, filling the lower concourse with whining bullets. Ryder saw one of the Vietnamese, he wasn't sure which, go down, his legs flailing wildly in the first withering burst of gunfire. Sinbad shouted a warning and lobbed a frag grenade down the room where it exploded inside the doorway, filling that end of the concourse with flying shards of glass and shrapnel. The Kalashnikov fell silent as Sinbad went in for the clean up.

Ryder moved like a machine, his legs pumping swiftly upwards. His head felt clear, concentrated on the kill. He risked a glance behind him looking for Van Delden and saw him poised at the bottom of the stairs. A man dressed only in soiled underwear appeared suddenly at the top of the stairs. He was unarmed and had a startled fearful look on his face. The whiteness of his terrified eyes was mesmerizing but Ryder hardly slowed his pace. Give no quarter, Marchand had said.

He opened up on the run, so close he could not miss. The air was heavy with the acrid scent of spent ammunition and he felt his gun grow hot as his empty cartridges clinked down the stairs, but his silencer drowned any sound. The man went down like a deflated balloon, spraying blood where a line of closely spaced bullets stitched a jagged tear in his belly.

A grenade came rolling across the floor at the very top of the stairs. It rattled down the steps as Ryder bounded past it to reach the upper level. Half way down it exploded and he heard screaming as Van Delden fell.

Perez raced level with him and lobbed a stun grenade down the corridor where it exploded, filling the air with sulfurous smoke. Outside, the night sky was full of tracers as gunners opened up in panic from all sides of the airfield. Heavy machine gun fire swept the front of the building and the arrival's area became filled with flying glass as windows shattered inwards. An anti-aircraft gun was still in action up on the roof firing, wildly at shadows in the sky. Then another missile lanced into the parapet and practically the entire wall facing Ryder at the front of the building disintegrated and tumbled inwards.

Ryder moved into the corridor and kicked open the first door that he came to. Empty! He moved on to the next as Sinbad booted it open with such violence that it shattered off its hinges. Through the smoke and dust Ryder saw frightened faces. His eyes swept the room. On the bed, camouflage clothing and a man bringing a weapon to bear. He squeezed the trigger and released two close range body shots. The man crumpled against the wall, his Kalashnikov spinning from his lifeless fingers. A woman sat up in the bed screaming in terror as he kicked her violently out of his way.

Ryder whirled back through the door. On down the interminable corridor, his killer instinct consumed him with its ferocity, driving him on. He and Perez worked through the rooms on the left, Sinbad and Joby those on the right. So it was Chen; the thought barely registered. Nothing mattered to him now except the mission. His own safety became secondary. Mark was nothing, not even a flicker in his memory.

As he ran he slipped in another ammunition clip, his MP5 red hot in his hands. A burst of automatic fire came out of the smoke from an open door, plaster burst out of the wall of the corridor and he saw Perez reeling as his blood gushed in a torrent from a head wound. A Kalashnikov rifle came skidding out on the floor and a naked man appeared in front of Ryder as if by magic. He had his hands up and was shaking in fear, babbling incoherent sounds of submission. Ryder dropped him with a close three round burst that blew out his chest. Then he bounded through a smoke-wreathed door that sagged open. A black man appeared in front of him clasping a child to his chest. Ryder instinctively fired on automatic in a short savage burst. It was then he saw it; the white clerical collar of a priest. One of the hostages! Jesus! He had shot him! The man crumpled and the child rolled way across the floor in a bloody bundle of rags. He saw white faces then, hugging the floor in terror. "Out! Out!" He roared the words at them, prodding them savagely. A woman screamed hysterically as he dragged her to her feet and thrust her violently towards the door. The wall facing him disintegrated into dust, and flying mortar filled the room, then came the shriek of shrapnel and he felt blood pouring down his neck even though he felt no pain. As the dust cleared, through a gaping hole in the wall, he could see running figures on the runway. Men sprinted in terror away from the building, throwing down their weapons in panic, as controlled bursts from a light machine gun picked them off one by one.

Flames were now curling out from one end of the terminal building, sending licking tongues of fire towards a nearby fuel tanker. The truck exploded seconds later and flame swept in a molten flow across the concrete.

Away in the fetid sprawl of Mogadishu, guns were opening up in indiscriminate mayhem, exploding star shells into the first hint of dawn's light. Through it all came the measured roar of aircraft engines. Seconds later, parachutes from the second wave began to float down like so many tiny mushrooms through the flak and tracer trails.

Further down the corridor, Sinbad and Joby flitted from room to room mopping up. Showing no quarter, they went about their deadly business in silence. All resistance faded and the inside of the building became strangely quiet except for the moans of the wounded.

As quickly as it had begun it was over. Ryder found himself downstairs in the arrival's area. A strange lethargy overtook him. Flames bled from an office at the back of the check-in desks throwing flickering light on a scene of complete destruction. He wound a field dressing around his neck stemming the flow of blood and stared blankly at the pathetic group of hostages huddled together in the rubble. Twenty sets of frightened eyes staring back at him in disbelief. Van Delden lay behind them. "Which one of you is the French Ambassador?"

"I am." A tall grey haired man tried to stand, but his legs buckled and he sat down again hurriedly.

"Relax! We'll have you out of here very soon."

The Ambassador just stared at him in wordless disbelief.

A nun dressed in a ripped habit detached herself from the group and knelt beside the Dutchman trying to stem the blood flowing from the stump of his leg. The other hostages clustered closer together. Ryder replaced an ammunition clip and lit a cigarette with shaking hands. Gratefully, he dragged in the smoke, allowing the pent-up excitement that came in the heat of battle to wither and ebb like a receding tide. He saw Joby and Sinbad coming down the stairs lugging Perez between them. Chen lay dead a few feet away.

Silently, Joby went down on his knees and cradled his friend in his arms. His eyes shone wetly and he made small cooing sounds. Sinbad came then and gently laid Perez in the dust and broken glass on the floor, tending to him with bloodied hands. He smiled grimly. "He's copped it," he said quietly. "Perez is dead."

From somewhere outside came the sporadic sounds of renewed small arms fire. Then the single crump of a heavy caliber artillery shell exploding in the far distance. Ryder nodded slowly. He felt tired and deflated, sickened by the smell of blood. He glanced at his watch. Christ! He had lost track of time. He could hardly credit how easy it had been. The lack of resistance was almost unbelievable, but then, they had planned it that way. There had been no warning of their coming.

Colonel Marchand suddenly strode through a yawning opening that had once been the front of the building, his boots stirring up small puffs of dust from the rubble littering the floor. In comparison to the rest of them he looked neat and well dressed, as though he had just strode off the parade ground back in Calvi.

"Well-done, Sergeant," Marchand said hoarsely. "Your lads have done an excellent job." He looked coldly at the bedraggled group of hostages. "Unfortunately, I'm sorry to say that Lieutenant Arvans was killed. He ran into heavy resistance from a mortar unit a kilometre down the road." Marchand paused and glanced at the bodies of the dead Legionnaires. "What's your butcher's bill here?"

Ryder's eyes flickered. "Two dead, including Corporal Perez. Van Delden is seriously wounded; he got his foot blown off."

Marchand seemed relieved. "Not bad," he said in a quiet voice. "We'll have a full debriefing later."

Ryder half expected one of Marchand's rare smiles but it didn't come. Just then a young woman dressed in shorts and a tattered check shirt got unsteadily to her feet from amongst the hostages. Her eyes were wild. "Butchers!" she screamed hysterically. "You and your butcher's bill! You killed a priest and a child!" She collapsed and started to sob uncontrollably, tears streaking small rivers in the dirt on her face.

Marchand stared at her for a moment, his lips set in a cruel line. His eyes swept over her and he turned away contemptuously. "Sergeant Ryder, get these people to the rear of the building and have them ready to move as soon as the planes arrive." With that, Marchand turned on his heel and went back out the way he came.

Ryder watched him go and ground out his cigarette. He turned to the Zulu. "Sinbad, get these people into the baggage area. Joby, you watch the road. See if you can get a medic for Van Delden." He didn't wait for an answer but went back upstairs.

Two Legionnaires had moved half a dozen wounded Somali insurgents onto the balcony and were attending to them. The corridor was slippery with congealed black pools of blood. He stepped over them gingerly. He checked each room and counted twenty-five bodies, all of them Somalis, including the priest and the child. He knew there were two more out on the runway. Twenty-nine in all, and that was only the first count. Undoubtedly there would be more when the final tally was made.

Wearily, Ryder climbed the second flight of stairs and went out onto the roof. The control tower was a blazing wreck. Only a smoking hole remained where one of the anti-aircraft guns had stood. At one end of the roof the second gun leaned drunkenly over the shattered parapet. He found three more bodies and turned them over with his boot. One of them groaned and opened his eyes. The soldier was young, perhaps only fifteen or so. His chest had been blown open and blood pumped steadily, making a sucking noise through the remnants of his singed smock. The wounded boy's eyes flickered. Ryder read death in them. Quietly, without feeling, he placed the muzzle of his MP5 against the boy's temple and squeezed the trigger. As he released it he suddenly felt sick to the pit of his stomach and Mark came again then, dancing on spindly legs of bone like some contorted marionette, just as the first pale tips of dawn fingered the sky, the drone of aircraft engines ushering in a new day.

TEN

Outside the Golden Dragon restaurant, Amsterdam was vibrant. Even a grey foggy evening failed to dull the fresh green shoots on the trees that lined the city's waterways. But inside, seated in a small private dining room, Sid Phillips felt ill at ease and trapped by the confining walls. Tentatively sipping his rice wine, he studied the two Kung brothers seated opposite to him as he pushed away his empty plate.

Phillips gave a grunt of appreciation. "That was a delicious meal," he said eventually, dabbing at his mouth with a white linen napkin.

"A little more fried rice, Mr. Phillips, perhaps some prawns - or a morsel of duck?"

"No thank you, that was excellent – probably the best that I have ever tasted and I've always been very partial to Chinese food. My wife says that it is the most healthy way to cook, but unfortunately, we English find it difficult to go without our roast beef and steak pies," Phillips folded his napkin carefully and placed it on the table, arranging it precisely beside his empty plate. He took out his cigar case and offered it towards the two men seated opposite to him. "Perhaps you would care for one?"

The two men shook their heads in unison as the older one replied. "No thank you. We don't smoke."

Phillips sighed. "A good cigar is one of my great pleasures in life, especially after such a superb dinner."

Mo Kung inclined his head in an imperceptible bow. "Thank you," he said, "Your words are most kind." He clicked his fingers and a waiter entered their room to clear away the dishes. When he had gone, the elder brother placed his hands flat on the table and studied his manicured nails for a moment. "We have told you much about ourselves, Mr. Philips," he said eventually. "It is an indication of our esteem, that we have been so frank in describing our organization and its goals." He looked searchingly at Phillips. "No matter what the outcome, we expect, or rather, we demand, that you respect the confidential nature of this meeting. Is that clearly understood?"

Phillips nodded quickly. "Of course," he said in a low voice. "That goes without saying." His eyes wandered to a silk tapestry depicting a golden dragon decorating the far wall.

Mo Kung sipped from a delicate porcelain cup and returned it to its saucer. "Much of our business is legitimate." he said. "For instance, we are the largest European importers of frozen fish and dried flowers from South America. We also have a profitable enterprise importing a variety of goods from the Far East. All of this enables us to move large sums of money at will. In addition, it allows us to transport other merchandise transparently. Recently, however, we have suffered setbacks in our ability to ship our products into England. Your venture in Ireland is of interest to us. There are too many eyes watching the Channel and the North Sea routes now. It would seem that you have something that we want, and we have something that you want."

Phillips quietly drew on his cigar and exhaled a blue cloud of smoke as he regarded the two men facing him. They looked like businessmen, he thought. Their tailored suits suggested bankers perhaps. Certainly they did not look like the leaders of the Tai Huen Chai, the most murderous Kwon triad ever to put down roots in Europe. They had natural poise and were skilled negotiators and since his arrival they had treated him with the utmost courtesy, as though he was a visiting *taipan*.

He held a mouthful of smoke for a second longer, then he exhaled it and raised his eyes to peer through the opaque cloud that drifted over the table. "I've given careful thought to your proposal," he said cautiously. "A million is a lot of money up front. I'm prepared to go in at half immediately, with the other half after our first delivery. I am already investing heavily in the Irish operation; you can look on that as a gesture of good will."

Mo Kung glanced at his brother and received a look of disapproval. "You are wasting our time, Mr. Phillips," he commented coldly. "We are an effective business organization with all the resources that are needed to control European distribution. We have offered you a franchise in that business." His sallow features relaxed into a faint smile showing even white teeth. "Rather like an agreement with McDonald's or a Southern Fried chicken chain. The money is secondary, purely a measure of your commitment. I regret that perhaps we have overestimated your ability to be an effective partner in our operation."

There was an air of finality in Kung's words and Phillips felt a bead of perspiration forming on his forehead. "Look," he said, "Let's not be hasty. A million up front is not to be sneezed at. I need to be sure. I have to be convinced that you can provide the merchandise on a regular basis."

"Please allow me to show you something, Mr. Phillips." Mo Kung led him to a small window that overlooked the street and drew back the curtains.

It had grown dark since Phillips had entered the restaurant, but the streetlights showed a steady throng of people moving up and down, some stepping cautiously around small puddles of water that lingered after a recent shower of rain.

"The building that you see on the corner is the main police station," Kung pointed with his finger, "The one with the brightest lights, Mr. Phillips. Most of those people that you see down there in the street are dealing in drugs. Heroin, cocaine, marijuana, amphetamines; you name it. Anything is available down there, and I challenge you to point out a single policeman." Kung pulled back the curtains and returned to his seat at the table.

Mo Kung smiled as Phillips returned to the table. "Why do you think there are no policemen down there, Mr. Phillips? It is because we control this situation so well that the police no longer believe that they can prohibit the flow of drugs. A number of Dutch politicians already favor removing the prohibition on drugs. It will be many years before you will see such an enlightened approach in England, don't you think?"

The elder brother leaned forwards resting his elbows on the table. His eyes narrowed in his fleshy face. "World wide, the value of this merchandise is conservatively estimated to be worth five hundred billion dollars per year and only seven billion of that finds its way back to Cali in Colombia." He paused and sipped his tea. "There are no borders in Europe any longer, and Eastern Europe is opening up. There are five million existing customers for hard drugs in the EEC alone, and that number is growing."

Mo Kung did not miss the flash of greed in Phillips' eyes. He continued to speak softly, choosing his words to maximize their effect. "We believe that twenty to thirty million people have a requirement for hashish and marijuana alone. I confidently expect that there is three hundred and fifty million pounds worth of business to be done in the UK, but at present, England is in a mess with twelve un-coordinated families squabbling over pennies."

The elder Kung paused for a moment and stared into the middle distance. "If you can organize those people into an efficient unit with reliable lines of distribution, your investment will become ludicrous in comparison to the profit margin. We have investigated you carefully, and until now we felt satisfied that you could be a suitable partner for our future expansion. You need to understand that effective money laundering is critical to the success of our business. Your casino and the club circuit in the North of England form an ideal conduit. Other than controlling the UK market, we have no designs on taking over your territory. You have our word on that."

Phillips swallowed hard. The bastards had done their homework thoroughly. He knew Kung was only speaking the truth; a million was chicken feed. "Very well." Resignation slightly dulled his voice. "One million it is. How do you wish the transfer to be made?"

The younger brother, Liung, finally spoke. It was the first time he had done so. He was the smaller of the two and his voice had an oddly child like ring to it as though it had yet to break. "A cash deposit to our Zurich bank will suffice. We will place the first order on the Far East as soon as we have confirmation of that. Our ability to deliver is beyond reproach. There are thirty-five thousand ships using Rotterdam port annually. Those ships carry more than four million containers in and out of the port every year. No authority in the world could be expected to scrutinize that volume of traffic."

Phillips nodded firmly and Mo Kung extended his hand. "Be assured, Mr. Phillips, that we have all the necessary con tacts to ensure a successful outcome to our venture. I might add, with the minimum risk to us."

"I'm glad to hear that." Phillips tried to relax his shoulders to relieve a knot of tension forming in his neck muscles. "I have already conducted preliminary discussions and have reached broad agreement with London, Manchester, and Liverpool. Only Glasgow and the North East still need to say yes, but once I can assure their supply, they will row in with us."

Liung Kung managed a cold smile. "You need have no concern regarding supplies; we will provide you with what ever you need. Your biggest problem will be spending your money from now on!"

Phillips studied the tip of his cigar for a moment. He toyed with the idea of saying nothing more, then thought better of it. "There are one or two minor difficulties to overcome," he began.

Liung Kung stirred in his seat and frowned. "You are talking of course, about the group that controls Newcastle and

Glasgow. We know about Henry Dawson. It may not be possible to agree it with him. He's a bit of a mad dog, not at all suitable for our purpose."

Phillips was visibly startled. They already knew. "Dawson is out of it!" he spluttered. "He's doing fifteen years for armed robbery. Stephen Bergman is the man now, he controls most of the pubs and clubs on the Tyne."

Mo Kung poured himself a glass of rice wine and passed the jug across the table to Phillips. "You are wrong, Mr. Phillips," he said quietly. "On the contrary, Dawson is issuing orders from inside and he still controls half of the Newcastle gangs. Have you heard of a man called Patrick Gill?"

"Yeah, I know Gill, he broke out of prison two years ago and nothing has been heard of him since." Phillips felt uncomfortable; the room seemed to be suddenly unbearably hot and he felt a need for fresh air.

There was a touch of ironic satisfaction in Mo Kung's voice when he spoke. "Gill is a valued member of our organization. He runs our Spanish office. It is his opinion, that Bergman is the man to encourage. It will be necessary to neutralize Dawson in the interest of harmony. We have no need for mad dogs, as Liung so aptly describes him. That should be your first task when you return to England. Can you do that?"

Phillips loosened his tie and popped the top button of his shirt. He was conscious of two sets of eyes fixed on him. "Of course," he said.

Liung Kung smiled. "I'm glad that we understand each other," he lilted. "We are making progress. Afterwards you should ensure that Mr. Bergman fully understands the changing nature of our business. At the moment the demand in the North East is for amphetamines and Ecstasy. That is all very well, but we need to steer that demand into more lucrative channels, and that should be one of his first priorities."

Phillips nodded. "I understand," he replied.

"What can you tell us about Glasgow Mr. Phillips?" Mo Kung's eyes were questioning. "That is an area in which our information may not be fully complete."

Phillips brought his cigar back to life. "There are four families involved; two of them are not a problem. Michael Battersby and Tommy Haddon are both eager to get involved; they understand the need for a national supply network. Harry Gilmore and Frank Holroyd control the other two. Gilmore knocked off Holroyd's older brother a few years ago, Frank's father won't let him forget it. To be honest it's a worse situation than in Newcastle."

"What do you suggest? You must have thought about it."

The squeak of the younger Kung's voice was becoming increasingly irritating. Phillips resisted a desire to punch him in the mouth. "I've told you already, I'm working on it," he growled defensively. "I'm going to talk to both of them when I get back. If that doesn't work..." He shrugged. "Then we have to take another route."

"The same as in Newcastle," Liung Kung prompted quietly.

"Yes, if that's what it takes." Phillips was angry now. Not used to being cornered in a defensive position, his face flushed hotly.

The older Chinese moved quickly to defuse the tension. "That is most reassuring. Liung, I think we can rely on Mr. Phillips to take care of these problems, especially now that he fully understands our concerns." He extracted a neatly folded sheaf of papers from his jacket pocket and handed them to Phillips. "You will need to complete one of these for each of your employees, Mr. Phillips."

Phillips glanced at the uppermost sheet of paper. It was marked with a logo of a tiger's head and the words South East Asia Enterprises. "What the hell are these?"

Mo Kung gave a short laugh. "Pure formalities, Mr. Phillips. They are employment contracts. As I already explained, we are a business enterprise and like all such corporations, we value our employees. For instance, you will find exact details of our benefits scheme to provide financial protection for each member's family if he or she should - how can I phrase it - suffer loss of employment for any reason!"

Phillips was speechless. He noticed that the younger brother was smiling for the first time.

"Please complete them at your leisure, Mr. Phillips." Mo Kung got to his feet and stretched. He was a big man for a Chinese, dwarfing his younger brother when he too, stood up. "I think we have talked enough for one evening, perhaps now is the time to show you something of Amsterdam. Later I will tell you how the first delivery of merchandise will be organized."

Phillips stuffed the papers into his pocket and followed the brothers out into the main restaurant, where the noise of other diners and warm aromatic spice laden air assailed him. He was committed now, he realized, whether he had signed a contract or not. Those papers burning a hole in his pocket sought complete details of every member of each signer's family. Phillips was certain that those details were required for more reasons than to manage a benefits package. They made it clear that there was no turning back.

ELEVEN

Richard Critchley dissected his kipper without enthusiasm. There was something disconcerting about looking into the empty eye sockets of a long-dead fish at nine in the morning, especially when a surfeit of wine the night before removed any appetite for breakfast, and he wished they would learn to remove the heads from the damned things before serving them on a plate. He buttered a slice of toast and propped a copy of the *Irish Times* against his coffee pot before searching the front page for some news of London. There was nothing and it only served to deepen his sense of despondency.

On page three there was a graphic photograph of the aftermath of a weekend disturbance in Frankland prison. Part of its roof devoid of tiles and a gentle wisp of smoke still curled from its barred windows. A terse report said that a convict named Henry Dawson had been found dead with his throat slashed after the prison authorities regained control.

Critchley folded the paper in annoyance. Kinsale was becoming a drag, he thought. He longed for sight of his old haunts, and the clink of chips on baize tables instead of the morbid whine of half-tuned fiddles and thudding bodhrans.

Critchley had just ordered more coffee when Matthew Brennan strode into the hotel dining room and joined him at his table. The auctioneer looked unusually pleased with himself.

"Morning, Mr.Critchley! I've got good news for you." Brennan sat down and helped himself to coffee.

"I hope so. It's taken you long enough." Critchley glared at the auctioneer, disgusted by the man's appearance and bad manners. Brennan's shirt collar looked grubby and the man looked as though he had slept in his clothes. He needed a haircut too, Critchley noticed. In addition, Brennan had cut his chin shaving and a blob of pink toilet paper bobbled on his face when he spoke.

Spotting a passing waitress, Critchley caught her eye and pushed his plate nearer the edge of the table. "Please remove this dammed fish. I think it's trying to hypnotize me!"

The waitress smiled politely. "Of course, Mr. Critchley. Didn't you like it? Perhaps I can get you something else?"

"More coffee, I think. Strong coffee. I've got a headache this morning."

"Overdoing it last night were you?" Brennan grinned.

"None of your bloody business, Brennan." Critchley snapped. His stomach churned and his headache intensified, becoming a band of steel that screwed itself tightly around his temples. "So what do you have to tell me?"

Brennan accidentally slopped some coffee into his saucer and when he raised the cup to his lips, it dripped, leaving a trail of brown spots on the white linen tablecloth. "A fax came in overnight from Canada. My client has accepted your offer."

"Good. I thought he might." Critchley's tone was acid, lacking enthusiasm. "What's our next move?"

"Preparation of contracts. I'm going up to Tralee today to talk to the solicitor. I don't suppose you would like to come along for the drive?"

"Not particularly." Critchley fought off another wave of nausea. The thoughts of spending hours cooped up in a car with Brennan only served to heighten his misery. "I thought I might go out and take another look round the house. Could you leave me the keys?"

"Sure." Brennan pulled a bunch of keys from his pocket and dropped them on the table.

Critchley glanced through a nearby window wishing Brennan would just go and leave him in peace. Outside, sunshine sparkled on the waters of the harbor across the road from the hotel, speckling its surface with a thousand signaling mirrors. Only a single fleecy cloud hovered in a clear sky, promising a fine day. He turned his head to focus on the auctioneer, studying him for a moment with heightening distaste. "I'm relying on you to handle this correctly, Brennan. I hope that there are not going to be problems?"

Brennan shook his shaggy head. "None that I am aware of. I've already spoken to our man on the telephone and he knows what we are looking for. You're in luck, too, because the seller has authorized me to nominate a solicitor to act for him. We'll use the same man in Tralee. He'll draw up two sets of contracts, one for Canada, and one for your people in London."

"What about signatures? How do we handle those?"

Brennan shrugged and lowered his voice, "We'll have to forge them. It shouldn't be difficult." He studied Critchley for a moment. "By the way, do you want me to arrange for my brother-in-law to put in an estimate for repairs?"

Critchley hesitated for a moment. There was merit in keeping this whole business as close as possible between himself and Brennan. Tight was the right word, with no unnecessary complications. "Yes," he said. "Let's do that. I'll go out with him and instruct him on what I need."

"Fine. I'll get him to meet you out there later today." Brennan buttered a slice of dried up toast and popped it into his mouth, chewing noisily. "I'll have him phone you to set up a time." He rinsed his mouth with cold coffee and wiped his lips on the back of his hand. "What about your boss in London, is he going to want to use a solicitor over there?"

"No. I spoke to him yesterday. He's happy for me to deal with a local man here."

"He must trust you," Brennan commented wryly.

"Save the sarcasm," snapped Critchley. "Just get on with it. I want to get this tied up quickly. The sooner it's finished with, the better I would like it."

Brennan heaved his bulk out of his chair and brushed some crumbs off his shiny navy-blue jacket. "That's it then," he said, tugging at the waistband of his trousers. "I'll be in touch."

"I look forward to that," Critchley watched the auctioneer disappear into the lobby. Even the thoughts of the extra cash that was coming his way failed to dispel his feeling of gloom, and his headache worsened, taking on a throbbing resonance that made him want to scream.

Matthew Brennan's brother-in-law, Harry Meadows, was an ox-like, ruddy-faced man whose cement-stained jeans hung in baggy folds, exposing his hairy buttocks every time he bent to inspect something, or to take a measurement with a tape measure that took on the size of a penny piece in his gnarled hands.

Whereas Brennan had consistently used the word "gem" when extolling the virtues of Clonbar House, Harry clicked his tongue mournfully as Critchley led him from room to room. Meadows tut-tutted ominously as he surveyed the bathroom where the tap dripped at the end of the bath. "Plumbing," he said eventually, rolling the word in his mouth as though it was a succulent boiled sweet. "That's the major problem, Mr. Critchley. That, and the electrics. Yes indeed, plumbing and complete rewiring before it even gets a lick of paint." He pressed his foot on a loose floorboard and was rewarded with a suspicious creak.

Critchley's head throbbed. He wished he had a drink to steady his nerves. "How much?" he asked wearily. "What's the bottom line, and how long will it take? That's all that interests me."

"Round figures?"

"Yes! For God's sake! Round figures, and no bloody VAT!"

Meadows straightened up after fiddling unsuccessfully with the dripping tap and hitched up his sagging trousers. "Probably about twelve by the time we have the decorating done." He rolled his eyes. "I suppose you're in a hurry. Everyone is, these days."

Critchley eyed him fiercely. "Yes, I am in a hurry, and no to twelve thousand. I'll give you ten, and you bill me for twelve."

Meadows stroked the grey stubble on his chin for a moment. "Very well," he said. "I'll start next week. It should take a month, no longer than that. If I don't find anything worse than I've seen, I may finish it sooner."

Critchley felt relieved. The black economy was alive and well in the Emerald Isle. The whole country seemed willing to work a scam, but it suited him perfectly. "That's fine, Mr. Meadows." he said. "I'll see you on Monday."

Meadows smiled and gave Critchley a wink. "Matthew told me you were a gentleman."

Critchley made no reply and led the way down stairs. He stood for a few minutes on the front steps watching Meadows rattle away up over the hill in his battered pick-up truck. Slowly his headache receded as the warmth of the sun sought him out, making him feel better than he had all day.

He was about to lock the front door when he heard the sound of an approaching car. It inched over the brow of the hill as though it was unsure of itself. Then it speeded up and came to a halt at the bottom of the steps. Critchley felt a shock wave hit his stomach as the door of the taxi opened and Peter Webster stepped out. "Afternoon, mate!" With a broad grin Webster paid off the driver and climbed the steps. "Took me a while to track you down. They told me in the hotel that I might find you out here."

Critchley's headache returned instantly and his mouth felt suddenly dry. "What the hell are you doing here?"

Webster's grin faded. "Don't tell me you're not pleased to see me. Sid sent me over to see what you are up to. I flew into Cork this morning." He belched loudly. "Whatever you might say about the Irish, they give you a decent breakfast on the plane." He turned and faced the sea. "Nice view, if you're into that sort of thing."

Critchley nodded towards the door. "Come in and see what you are buying."

Webster looked about him with the air of a man who had just detected a bad smell. "Bit of a dump," he sniffed, his voice echoing hollowly around the empty room.

Critchley smiled wickedly. "A gem, old boy! Spot of paint here and there, a few pipes to fix and it will be a jewel. Let me show you around."

"Don't bother, I've seen enough." Webster went to a window and looked out. "You did well enough. It's what Sid wanted. Have you found out how deep that bay is?"

"Yes. I had a local fisherman check it out the other day. He says there's twelve feet in it at low water and he's offered to lay a mooring in the deepest part if I want, but if you ask me, you'd be better off to keep a boat down in the marina, if you intend to have one. It's easier to get at and a lot safer. That's what the fisherman told me anyway," Critchley finished lamely.

Webster turned away from the window and glanced up at the stained ceiling. "Get him to lay the mooring, and while you're at it, reserve a berth in the marina as well. Sid wants it all done quick. We're in a hurry. While we're on that subject, Sid told me you knew a bit about boats. He said that he heard you had done time in the Navy. Is that right?"

Critchley flushed, it reminded him of another episode in his life that he preferred to forget and it was yet another failure that his father often liked to remind him of. After a few disastrous years spent in Harrow his father had actually been pleased for once when he squeezed a place in the Royal Navy, but it hadn't lasted for long. Nothing in his life ever had. He scuffed at the dust on the floor with the toe of his shoe and said nothing.

"I asked you a fucking question!" Webster shouted.

Critchley shrugged. "Not exactly. I didn't finish Dartmouth. I was a midshipman, that was all!"

"You mean you got yourself thrown out, you little shit! Webster sneered.

Critchley stared at him. It was plain that Webster enjoyed

trying to make him feel small. The crap he had to put up with over money, he thought. And from a low class guttersnipe like this! With difficulty, he controlled his rising anger and remained silent.

"What I'm really trying to establish, is that you know how to handle a boat," Webster continued. "Navigation and all that. You understand?"

"I suppose so, I've done a bit of sailing since then as well." Critchley's eyes narrowed. "Look, isn't it time you told me what is going on? I mean, how long do you expect me to hang around this place?"

Webster didn't answer at first. A faint smile hovered for a moment on his lips and then faded as he straightened his tie, pulling the knot tighter at his throat. "For the moment, we want you to stay here. Get the place sorted out, be the gent, enjoy yourself. Christ! We're going to give you a bloody yacht! You can swan around living the high life. Later on, you will be able to take the odd jaunt to London if you want, but for the moment, just do as I fucking tell you!" There was an edge to his voice and the room seemed suddenly cold as the sunlight streaming through the windows retreated behind a cloud.

"That's not good enough," Critchley snapped. "I want to know what I'm getting myself into."

Webster stepped forward and grasped him by his lapels, slamming him back against the wall so that the breath exploded from him and his head snapped backwards violently. A shower of loose plaster flaked away from the wall and clattered to the floor. "You owe us, mate. Big time. Don't you forget it. You're getting paid well to be here." He released Critchley and dusted flecks of plaster off his shoulders.

Webster stepped back. When he spoke, his voice was more conciliatory. "Play your cards right, and you'll come away just fine. Otherwise, you'll get a wooden overcoat. Savvy?"

Critchley nodded. He was angry with himself for stirring Webster up. He could smell money, lots of it. That was good enough for now. In the meantime, he had to learn how to deal with these people. "Sorry," he said. "I'll shut up and do it your way."

"You'd better. Now be a good boy, and show me around Kinsale. You can buy me dinner, and I want you to sign a contract before I go back to London. I'm getting the last flight from Cork tonight."

TWELVE

Ryder slowly opened his eyes and watched dappled sunlight flicker across the ceiling to form mottled patches on the plaster. For a moment he wondered what day it was. Then he remembered. It was his last day as a soldier; his last day in the bosom of a family that had cradled and nourished him for fifteen years, a family to which he had returned love and fidelity, one that he had shed his blood for. Today, however, he would leave it. Today, he would step out into a world that he no longer knew. The thought startled him, and frightened him.

Ryder got up and ran hot water into the washbasin, splashing it with both hands onto his face to wake himself. He looked into the mirror and smeared shaving soap onto the stubble on his chin, noticing for the first time that his beard held traces of grey. He shaved slowly, carefully avoiding the hard scab that covered the wound on his neck. He prodded the scar gently with one finger. The medics had done a good job on the plane coming home from Somalia. Despite being sore to touch, it had healed quickly. Now he wore a jagged sliver of shrapnel on a cord around his neck, a souvenir to remind him that his luck had almost run out. This latest near miss had helped him to make up his mind not to renew his contract. So had the memories that still refused to go away. Memories of Mark. Memories of old campaigns and more recent memories of Somalia, which brought with them the smell of gunpowder and blood, and the vision of a child that had not lived because of him. It was the child that had done it, that, along with the boy on the roof of Mogadishu airport. It had convinced him that he finally could live without the savagery.

It did not take long for him to pack his few private possessions. Most of his bulkier things, like his television, he had already disposed of and in a fit of drunken sentimentality, and he had given his rattan mat to Sinbad.

He made a last minute check of the room where in a bottom drawer he discovered a forgotten combat knife and a prismatic compass, two of the spoils of war. He dropped them into his bag and in a dark recess of his wardrobe he came across the plastic bag containing the tapes that Mark's girlfriend had given him before he left Dublin. He had never listened to them. He was about to drop the bag into the waste bin when he thought better of it and threw it into his kit bag with the rest of his things. Then he turned his back on what had been his home.

Outside, the asphalt of the parade ground shimmered in noontime heat, sending up hot air that distorted the shape of the buildings on its far side. The vast expanse of the parade ground was deserted, but he could hear the crackle of far off gunfire coming from the firing range. It served to remind him that without him, nothing would change.

Ryder left the ferry from Bastian in Marseilles and went straight to the military hospital. One last task remained before he took military transport to Aubagne for his discharge, and that was to call and see Corporal Klein who had recently returned from Guyana. He found Klein sitting up in bed in his hospital ward. He had lost weight and his cheekbones protruded under tightened skin. Ryder hesitated as their eyes met. They had never been close friends, and he wondered why he felt that he owed Klein a visit before he left.

Klein's eyes roamed over Ryder's dress uniform and came to rest on his parachutist's wings. His mouth tightened into a thin line.

Ryder sat down on the edge of the bed, turning his eyes away from the flat section on the counterpane where Klein's leg should have been. "I brought you a few fags, Klein. I'm going to have a shot at giving them up." He smiled. "Again."

Klein looked wary, almost hostile. "Thanks," he said after a moment's silence. "I heard you were leaving. Is today your last day?"

Ryder nodded. "I'm off to Aubagne for my discharge."

"What are you going to do outside, got any plans?"

Ryder looked away. "I don't know yet," he said. "I'll find something. I'm going to London for a start. What about you?"

Klein snorted. "I'm waiting for a new leg."

Ryder unconsciously shifted his weight to the edge of the bed. Klein laughed bitterly. "It's okay, Ryder. The old one isn't there any more." There was resentment in Klein's voice and his forced smile faded, leaving small lines of self-pity on the corners of his mouth.

Ryder looked uncomfortable and lowered his eyes. There was an awkward silence between them while he shuffled his feet, trying to think what he should say.

Klein coughed and struggled with his pillows. "I should thank you," he said. "You did your best. Thanks to you, I've still got my manhood. I might not have got out at all if it was up to the others. That bloody Dutchman would have left me to rot and you're damn lucky he didn't put a bullet in you down in Somalia."

Ryder shrugged. "Well, he didn't, and if it's any concilia-tion, he's in the same boat now. He got a foot blown off in Mogadishu."

"I know. Sinbad told me." Klein coughed and spat phlegm into a bowl on his bedside locker. "The bastard is here, did you know that? In another ward, thank God!" Klein pulled himself further up in the bed and rested his head on the iron frame. "I was sorry to hear about Chen though. He wasn't a bad guy. Did you know that he and Jody used to share their women?"

Ryder chuckled. "No, I didn't know that, but it doesn't sur-prise me. Those two were close. I sometimes wondered if they were queer."

Klein gave a harsh laugh. "They weren't queer, far from it. They often used to go down to Calvi to the Dolce Vita and work a deal with the whores. Two for the price of one! That way they reckoned they'd be able to save a bit to get themselves back to Vietnam when they got out." He gave Ryder a searching look. "I heard you had it easy on the Mogadishu raid. Sinbad gave me a call and said they didn't put up much of a fight."

Ryder looked away again. He didn't want to be reminded of it. The blood bath of Mogadishu was still too vivid in his mind and it was some time before he spoke. "They didn't expect us to react so quickly, I guess." He shrugged his shoulders. "We did a quick job - you know the score - in and out fast." He paused for a moment. "Anyway, I didn't come here to talk about it."

Klein reached under the bedclothes with one hand and scratched at the stump of his leg. "It itches," he said quietly. "Sometimes I even think it's still there and I want to scratch the big toe." A small shiver ran through him and his face became suddenly pale.

"You'll be okay when they fit a new one." Ryder had little faith in his own words and he knew by the look on Klein's face that the German didn't accept them either. He tried to change the subject, looking for a way out. "You haven't told me. What you are going to do yourself after you are discharged?"

Klein frowned. "I have no real plans, but my brother has a garage in Hamburg. He's doing well by all accounts. I might go there for a while until I sort myself out." His eyes looked wistful. "Were you ever in Hamburg, Ryder? It's a great town. Everything you could want is in Hamburg."

Ryder shook his head. "I've never been there, but I've heard of it. At least you have a place to go. I've got nothing."

"No woman waiting on the outside?"

"You must be kidding." Ryder thought for a moment. "I was married once, a long time ago. It didn't work out. I was too busy jumping out of planes and she couldn't take the waiting, not knowing when I was coming home, that sort of shit. I didn't see it coming until it was too late and she fucked off with someone else."

Ryder felt uncomfortable as he ran out of words. He had never discussed his past with anyone. Klein wasn't even a close friend, and it surprised him that he had given so much away.

"Women are like that." Klein gave him a look of despair. "Fuck! I could do with a smoke! Open that carton will you?"

Ryder moved the box further out of reach. "You're just going to have to wait, pal."

Klein smiled weakly. "Maybe you should go back to Africa. There's plenty of jobs down there, I'm told. You remember that Rhodesian who left last year, the one that said there was no such place as Zimbabwe? Only Rhodesia, he used to say."

"You mean Williams?"

"Yeah, that's the guy. I heard he's running a show down in the Congo. He's a bloody Colonel or something with a South African mob. You should go and talk to him. With your experience, he might make you a General!" Klein chuckled. "Imagine that, General bloody Ryder!" He caught the hard glint in Ryder's eyes. "Well, it's worth a try at least."

Ryder stirred and glanced at his watch. "No," he said firmly. "My days of soldiering are over. I've had enough. If I wanted more, I'd stay in the Legion, especially now that there's a rumble that the REP will go into Afghanistan. That could be one hell of a firefight and it's thanks to the Yanks all over again, just like in Somalia. Their campaign is bogged down and they want to get out. It'll be down to the squaddies to sort out the shit, just as always." His eyes glazed momentarily. "Anyway, I think I've done my share of killing for France, Klein."

Klein made no reply. He reached over to take a pad and a pencil from the top of his bedside locker, scribbled an address and ripped off the page. "Take this," he said. "It's my brother's address in Hamburg. If ever you fancy a few beers, you'll know where to find me."

"Thanks Klein, you never know." Ryder glanced at the scrawled address before putting it in his jacket pocket. "Is Klein your real name?"

"No, but I'm keeping it. What about yours?

"Ryder was always my real name. I had nothing to hide and never made a secret of being in the Legion." He extended his hand as he stood up to leave. "Good luck, mate!"

"Yeah! Good luck, Ryder!" Klein shook hands and slid further down in the bed. It was a defensive movement, one that reminded Ryder of a snail withdrawing into its shell. He squared his shoulders and strode from the ward. He knew Klein was watching him, he did not look back.

THIRTEEN

The unfinished building that would eventually become a twelve-story tower block of offices had reached its eighth floor, but even at that level it dwarfed what little remained of the old warehouses that once had been home to ships of the General Steam Navigation Company. Since the days of sail, those once-proud little steamers had graced the muddy waters of the Thames and nuzzled the quay walls directly beneath Tower Bridge in the heart of London, but now only their ghosts came when the damp river fogs beckoned them home.

Ryder paused from his exertions and fought off a sudden craving for a cigarette. Looking down, he could see fronds of early morning mist lazily drifting over the brown waters of the river under the arches of the bridge. Although it was still early, the bridge was already jammed with City bound commuters, hurrying like so many ants towards the city where financiers and manipulators controlled the destinies of others over optic communication lines that spanned the globe. Perhaps some were the same speculators who were thrusting this latest pinnacle to their success into the city skyline. It was all new to Ryder and he hated it already.

From the corner of his eye he saw the jib of the crane swinging towards him, moving across a uniformly grey sky. Gone were the blue skies of Corsica and its gentle Mediterranean breezes. Here, the north had not yet yielded to summer. The construction site was a cheerless place, buffeted by a

wind that stirred off the river, carrying moisture that lay in
pools on the half-finished concrete of the eighth floor. Carefully, Ryder directed the battered skip of dripping cement as
it swung over his head. When it was in position, he released
its clasps, sending its load cascading into a steel reinforced
cavity like so much grey porridge. His job was a bit like that
of a dentist, he thought moodily. He wondered if filling teeth
was just as boring.

For three days now, he had worked on the site, glad
enough of the job, doing the work that he was told to do by a
burly foreman whose gruff tones still carried the lilt of distant
Connemara hills. Patrick Hughes was the foreman's name,
and he had already made it obvious that he preferred to
employ his own countrymen. From the way he spoke, it was
clear that he had only hired Ryder under sufferance. With the
amount of new construction in the city, it was becoming
harder to pick and choose; good men were in demand, and
companies took good care to keep them on.

The rest of the gang that Hughes held court over were a
mixed bunch, mostly Irish, but some Scots, whom Hughes
seemed able to get along with. Apart from them, there was
only one Nigerian, who was rumored to be an illegal immi-
grant, and as such, put up with Hughes' bullying like a dog
thankful for any scraps that came its way.

To Ryder, the melting pot of laborers had similarities that
reminded him of the Legion, although it lacked the Legion's
cohesiveness. The spirit was dead in these people, possibly
with the exception of the Irish who stuck together, drank
together, and sang together. He noticed that they seemed to
find sustenance mouthing the mournful dirges that bound
them together and which provided nourishment to their roots.
But these men were not soldiers, the only kind of men Ryder
understood.

The crane towering over the building swung again on its
spindly steel legs, this time carrying a load of wooden shut-
tering suspended on the hook at the end of its cable. High
up, the white face of the crane driver was visible in his cab.

Ryder smiled to himself. What happened, he wondered, when the man up there needed to take a piss? Surely he wouldn't clamber all the way down that ladder? No, he thought. He probably pissed into a bottle, or maybe he did it out through the window. He chuckled, resolving to ask him when he came down.

The load swung lower over Ryder's head, and he became aware of someone shouting above the racket of jackhammers and all the other noises that surrounded him. The voice was angry, coming from the far side. "Don't just stand there, ya feckin' eegit - unhook the feckin' thing!"

Ryder glared across at Hughes who was waving his arms like a madman, trying to attract his attention. "Get fucked Paddy!" He roared out the words without thinking, instantly knowing that it was a mistake.

Hughes bounded across the dividing space, nimbly jumping over the debris of construction material. His face was flushed in fury, and the vast expanse of his beer-belly strained at the buttons of his check shirt. Despite the belly, he was a powerful man, with a broad torso set on legs that suggested the strength of a rogue elephant. He was ominously close now. "Who the fuck are ye calling a Paddy, ye useless bastard!" he screamed.

Ryder tensed, feeling his muscles contract into hardness. His pale blue eyes turned to steel. "Back off, Hughes!" he countered. His voice was hard.

Hughes didn't stop, but came at him without a moment's hesitation. Ryder ducked away from the first murderous blow of his iron fist and delivered an open-handed killer chop to Hughes' neck as the foreman plunged past him. Then, he lashed out a reflexive muay-thai roundhouse kick to the kidneys that laid Hughes flat on his face on the concrete floor.

A lesser man would have died from that kick, but the Irishman was tough enough to survive, although he could not take the brief scuffle further. He rolled over onto his back and tried to sit up, but the effort of doing so was too much. His eyes reflected the stabbing pain that lanced through his abdomen. When he spoke, it was with difficulty. "That's it, Ryder, you're fired. Collect your fucking wages and get your arse off this site! Don't bother looking for another job. I'll see to it that you never work on another site again." Hughes relapsed into a fit of coughing.

Ryder looked down at him. "That's fine by me, mate," he said quietly. "I didn't really like the job anyway." He spat onto the concrete floor close to Hughes' boot.

For a few brief seconds Hughes looked into eyes that seemed to change from steel grey to the palest blue. It was like watching traffic lights go from red to green. In that instant, Hughes knew that he was lucky to be alive.

Ryder looked up. The crane driver was already halfway down his ladder taking the rungs two at a time. Others were gathering on the far side of the floor and approaching in a group. One of them wielded an iron bar, another, a sledge-hammer. Hughes sat up and waved them away. He fought off another fit of coughing. "Get out of here, Ryder, while you can, and don't come back. Not if you know what's good for you, that is." His chest heaved as he fought for his breath, a strange rasping sound coming from his throat.

It was just before the evening rush hour and the subway at Piccadilly Circus was not yet too crowded when Ryder changed trains on his way home to a small bed-sit that he had rented in Hammersmith. He had wasted the rest of the day in a futile search for another job, scouring the city for work. Anywhere that he had seen a crane or heard the sounds of building work he had enquired, but no one was hiring. Maybe Hughes had already spread the word, although he doubted that. Everywhere he went he had been met by an uncompromising shake of the head, but he was not unduly worried. He had three day's pay in his pocket, and the 15,000 that he accrued over the last fifteen years had been trans-ferred from a savings bank in Marseilles. The amount had surprised him, and it spoke of the way he had served his con-tracts. It was the result of a decade and a half of dedication to one of the oldest professions in the world, a profession as old as that of prostitution, but not so profitable.

Entering a tiled tunnel that led in a sweeping curve towards the escalators, he passed a bearded young man with dreadlocks of matted hair that tumbled to his shoulders as he strummed a guitar. His tune was unrecognizable, and the sound discordant. At the man's feet lay a cardboard box containing a scattering of loose change. Ryder passed him by without slowing his pace, and then he thought of Mark. He retraced his steps and threw a handful of coins into the box. The young man didn't pause, but his eyes reflected a flash of appreciation before the glazed look came down like a window blind. Ryder shivered and turned away. He could smell the flowers in the mortuary as though he were standing amongst them.

Around the next bend in the tunnel, a soft wind carried the heat of electric trains that assailed his nostrils with a pungent odor as he drew nearer to the next platform level. In the background he heard the distant rumble of a train pulling to a halt followed by the sounds of automatic doors sliding back on their stops. Next he saw a crowd gathering at the bottom of an escalator leading to the street.

Halfway along, standing next to a doorway that was marked as a toilet, stood a girl in a short clinging black skirt that barely covered the tops of her skinny legs. She wore a bomber-style furry jacket and spiked red shoes that looked several sizes too large for her. Over one shoulder she carried a tasseled string bag. He noticed that she was studying him as he drew nearer, her eyes appraising. She stepped away from the wall, moving in such a way that he could see the nipples of her small breasts poking against the thin material of a white tee shirt that she wore beneath her open jacket. She was not wearing a bra, and was doing her best to conjure up the suggestion of a pout that was meant to look sexy, but only served to make her pale features look thinner than they already were. Something about her was familiar, but he couldn't think what it was, and concentrated on avoiding her outstretched hand.

Perhaps it was the defeated way in which her shoulders sagged that suggested she already knew the outcome, but her eyes showed it too. Set deep in the pallor of her face, they reflected failure.

He was close now; close enough to pick up a trace of cheap perfume. Her lips, overdone with crimson lipstick, curved into a smile that was meant to be seductive, but came across as mechanical, without warmth or welcome. She glanced nervously over her shoulder towards a small group of people that had entered the tunnel and were now walking towards them. Then she looked back again, satisfied that none was a policeman, and stepped directly into his path.

"Looking for a good time sweetheart?" she said.

Even though her words were half expected, Ryder slowed his pace. Something about her voice startled him, triggering a lost memory. He searched her face for an answer.

She raised one hand and tweaked at a nipple, caressing her breast so that it jiggled when she released it. Her tongue flickered across her upper lip. "Wanna fuck me?"

Sudden recognition exploded in Ryder's brain and he stopped directly in front of her. "You're Mark's girlfriend, right?" He found himself saying the words without thinking and his stomach felt empty as he watched her smile fade.

She clutched at the straps of her shoulder bag. "Yes." Her voice was almost a whisper. "Mark was my boyfriend, but he died." She peered at Ryder. It was a short-sighted look as though she was having difficulty focusing her eyes. "I know you from somewhere, don't I? Maybe you fucked me once, is that it?"

Ryder reached out and took her hand. Turning it gently he pushed up the sleeve of her jacket so that he could see the underside of her arm. The tell tale needle pricks were every-where, and higher up they had become a festering sore. One was fresher than the others, pink with a tiny speck of blood at its centre. "What's your name," he asked.

"Sheila," she said. "But if you don't like it, it doesn't matter. You can call me something else if you like." Her tone changed and became wheedling. "I give good head, baby. You want some of that?"

A group of office workers funneled into the tunnel and moved towards them, their eyes averted. He released her hand and it flopped to her side as though there was no strength left in her arm. He breathed out slowly. "I'm Mark's father," he said eventually. "I met you at his funeral in Dublin."

The girl stiffened. Her attempt to be suggestive evaporated, and she instantly looked what she really was, a discarded waif, part of the flotsam of the world. All pretence of seduction fell away.

"Please," she said, "Go away, I don't want to talk about that." The girl sagged back against the tiled tunnel wall and looked in desperation at the small knot of people now passing. It was as though she expected someone to rescue her. Somewhere a door banged and a uniformed policeman appeared briefly at the end of the tunnel. Only visible for an instant, he did not look down towards them as he hurried towards an escalator, but Ryder could see that the girl was shaken. The uniform had made her so nervous that her frail hands shook.

"It's time for you to go, unless you want to do business." she said. Her eyes were beseeching, and then her voice went up an octave as she tried to fight off rising anger. "Just fuck off and leave me alone for Christ's sake! I need to earn some money, and you're not helping any by cramping my style!"

Ryder shrugged and his eyes hardened. "Suit yourself!" he snapped. Then, without thinking, he pulled a crumpled twenty-pound note from the pocket of his jeans and thrust it into her hand. "Get yourself some food," he said, more gently this time.

The girl stared numbly at the money resting in the palm of her hand. "Thanks," she muttered.

For a moment Ryder thought that she was about to cry, but she didn't. A small shudder rippled across her scrawny shoulders, but it evaporated instantly.

"You remember Billy? The guy that you met when you called to the flat in Rathmines?"

Ryder had been about to walk away but he paused, waiting for her to go on.

"He's dead too," she said in a flat voice. "They're all dead now."

"How old are you, Sheila?"

"Twenty-one, and a bit." Her features froze. "You wouldn't think it, would you? I look like shit, I know. Feel like it, too. You know, I tried to come off it for a while after Mark died, and again, when Billy went. I did a month each time on methadone, but it didn't work, I just couldn't take it. Now I'm doing a hundred quid a day."

The bitterness in the girl's voice had an instant effect on Ryder. He felt sorry for her. "Why don't you try it again?"

At once he knew he had said the wrong thing. Now there were lines of pain and anguish on her face.

"I couldn't face that, not again. This is better. I can handle this, but not the other shit. No, not that . . ." Her voice tailed away but came back a second later. "Billy dying, you know, it was almost as big a shock as when Mark went." She reached out to lay a feathery hand on Ryder's forearm. Her touch was like a butterfly landing. "I loved Mark, mister. I want you to know that. He was special. Know what I mean?"

Ryder didn't know. "Forget it," he said coldly. "Mark's dead, that's all there is to it."

"And Billy's dead too," she echoed quietly. "He's dead and he didn't deserve to die, he got himself fucked, royally fucked!"

"What do you mean by that?"

Sheila looked away evasively. Then she said, "Those bastards in Dublin did him in. It wasn't smack. He took over where Mark left off and stole some money from them, and then they came around one night and bust his legs with an iron bar. Out in the street - just like that! They were waiting for him when he came home, they stretched his two legs out over the curb and cracked them." She clicked her fingers and the sound echoed in the close confines of the tunnel. "Just like that. I heard it upstairs. It was a sound like a walnut cracking, you know the way it's shell splinters? That's the way his bones were afterwards. He went into withdrawal in hospital and he never survived it. They might as well have murdered him, it was the same thing in the end."

"Who did it?" Ryder wasn't sure if he really wanted to know.

Sheila shrugged her shoulders. "I don't know for sure. There were two of them and it was dark. I couldn't see them clearly from the window." Bitter hatred flashed in her eyes. "Flicker Hennessy, probably. He's responsible for most of that shite. He's the reason I'm here. The debt transferred to me and he sent his lads looking for it, so I had to do a runner."

Ryder sighed. "Won't they follow you over?"

"I don't think so. It's a big enough city. There's no way for them to know where I've gone."

Ryder thought for a moment. "You didn't go to the police?"

Sheila smiled. "Are you jokin'! The cops in Dublin all have their heads up their arses! They're only interested in soft touches, like busting people that they catch driving over the drink limit, stuff like that."

It was Ryder's turn to smile. "Maybe you're doing them an injustice."

"I don't think so. People like me are unimportant. We're the floating shit that everyone wants to see going down the drain."

She glanced over Ryder's shoulder with eyes that were suddenly appraising. He half turned. A man had entered the tunnel and was walking towards them. He looked like an Arab, Ryder noticed, although not a particularly wealthy one. Wearing an oversize grey suit he clutched a battered suitcase and averted his gaze as he saw them looking at him.

Sheila's hand automatically went to her hair, fluffing its wispy strands. "There's a punter coming, so why don't you go now. Just fuck off and leave me alone!" Anger was again creeping back into her voice.

"Fine, if that's what you want, I'll go."

Instantly her eyes changed and he fancied he saw tenderness in them. "I didn't mean it like that," she said hurriedly. "It's just that...well, you know how it is, damn it!"

She was already moving out into the path of the approaching Arab, pouting her lips suggestively again, and making sure that her bomber jacket stayed open so that her ridiculously small breasts could be presented to their best advantage. Her fingers busily trying to peak a nipple into prominence. But the Arab was having none of it. He was already hugging the far wall, hurrying to get by, his eyes nervous and fearful.

Sheila's eyes flashed as she saluted the scurrying Arab with a disdainful two fingers. Then she called out to Ryder who had begun to stride away. "Are you going to do anything? About the stuff Mark was talking about on the tapes?"

Ryder turned and faced her again. "What was that?"

Sheila glared at him. "You heard me!" She snarled. "Are you thick or what? I said you could do something - you should do something. Jesus Christ!" Her tone became incredulous at his blank look. "You didn't even listen to them, did you? Mark was your son. He didn't deserve to die! You never did diddly-shit for him, and you can't even do that?"

"Forget it," Ryder growled. He turned away and quickened his steps.

"That's right," she screamed, "Walk away from him like you did before, you bloody bastard! Some tough soldier you are! Mark looked on you as some sort of a god, you rotten shit! Play those tapes I gave you soldier boy, he talked to you on them, you bloody bastard!"

Ryder kept going. When he looked around again, she was still dancing a jig in the middle of the tunnel, screaming obscenities at him. Then he turned a corner and he couldn't see her any more, but her words remained in his mind. He knew they would never go away.

Later, Ryder sat at a bar in a pub called the Green
Rooster, not far from the Hammersmith fly-over, savagely
drinking a pint of beer. The pub was only a short walk from
where he lived and it was almost ten o'clock at night. The
events of that day were still fresh in his mind and he was
drinking fast, trying to erase them. Nearby, a babble of voices
carrying Irish accents served to keep Sheila's last words
whirling in circles through his brain. What the hell had she
meant about Mark talking to him on those tapes? He couldn't
listen to them even if he wanted to. He didn't even own a
tape player. Who did anyway? He thought. Everything was
MP3s or bloody iPads these days.

He drained his glass and called for another pint. It was like
playing a cracked record with the stylus stuck on the same
repetitive words, he thought. On and on it went, hammering
messages into his mind. You could do something, she had said.
Like what? Shit! He couldn't even hold down a fucking job!
Mark was history, he told himself. But the nightmares had not
stopped, dreams of failure that originated long before Somalia,
dreams that had kept him awake in the jungles of Guyana and
continued to raise feelings that he could not understand.

A television set sat on a shelf at the far end of the bar.
Until now, the sound had been muted, but as the picture of
Big Ben announced the start of *News at Ten*, the barman
turned up the volume. Ryder watched the screen without any
interest and ordered another pint of beer, his sixth that
evening. In a corner of the room a woman had started arguing with her husband and her voice became a plaintive
shriek. "Bert! You drink too much! I'm getting sick of it. I wish
I'd never married you! Leave it behind you, will you, and
come home!" She saw Ryder turn to stare at her and her face
reddened with embarrassment, but she lowered her voice a
trifle, fighting to regain her composure. Ryder swivelled his
stool and turned his attention to the television.

Ryder gulped at his fresh drink, wiping the froth from his
lips with the back of his hand. London had become tiresome.

He longed for a sense of purpose. Already he was beginning to think that leaving the Legion had been a mistake. Maybe Klein was right, he thought. He wasn't cut out for civilian life. He was nothing but a mercenary, no different from the others.

He snapped back to attention at the end of the news bulletin, when the announcer, his tone precise and matter-of-fact, reported that a person, now known to be a Sheila McGuire of Irish origin, had fallen to her death beneath a train at Piccadilly Circus station that evening. Although she was known to be a drug addict, the police were eager to hear from anyone who may have witnessed the accident. Ryder waited for more details, but none came and the picture changed to show highlights of an evening football match between Arsenal and Manchester United. Immediately, those seated around the bar showed more interest and asked for the volume to be turned up.

He ordered another pint. It sickened him to think that a junkie called Sheila McGuire, now dead, was of less importance than a football match. It occurred to him that maybe she had not fallen in front of the train. What if she had been pushed? She had hinted that people were looking for her. Dublin had caught up with her, Ryder thought sadly.

The faces nearest to him were a blur. He drained his glass and asked for another. It was none of his damn business, he thought. But beneath the alcohol's numbness, Ryder realized that nothing would be quite the same again. There were even more ghosts to taunt him now, and they were gathering in strength.

FOURTEEN

Peter Webster stood on a quayside that fringed the oily waters of Southampton docks and stared up in disbelief at the looming black bulk of the container ship as it gently nudged the dockside. The ship flew the flag of Panama and her Filipino crew scurried about making fast the mooring lines that now secured her to the quay wall.

He had never been so close to such a ship before, and the sheer size of the monster that now towered over him left him speechless. The faint tinkling of a bell high up on the navigation bridge reached him, signaling an end to the maneuver as the ship's mighty engine slowed its tempo to an imperceptible throb. As it did, his thoughts were interrupted by the arrival of Sid Phillips who was accompanied by a man that Webster recognized as Commander Gareth Hawkins, the General Manager of Melford's boatyard on the banks of the River Hamble. Webster had met him just that morning and already disliked him intensely. Hawkins, a recently retired naval officer with a distinctive bearing that carried the hallmark of the Royal Navy, wore a navy-blue blazer with a white shirt, lending emphasis to his tanned complexion. He looked relaxed and at ease, nodding his head in casual conversation with Sid and smiling now and then as they came closer.

Phillips looked pleased with himself, Webster noticed. Lately, he had been like that all the time and for days now, he had displayed the demeanor of a man whose plans were coming to fruition. Phillips looked over and nodded at Webster.

"Right, Peter, lets go up and take a look at our new purchase shall we? Commander Hawkins here has promised us a magnum of champagne as soon as she goes in the water."

Phillips followed Hawkins to an accommodation ladder that had been lowered down the ship's side, and beckoned for Webster to follow. A young ship's officer met them on deck and directed them to another level from where they could look down over the tops of a vast number of rectangular steel containers that crammed the forepart of the ship all the way up to her distant bow.

Webster was taken aback as he looked down the length of the monster. He wondered how such a ship could have negotiated its way into Southampton, not to mention squeezing its way through the Suez canal on its voyage from the Far East. Even Sid stopped chattering and gazed over the great ship's decks in silence.

Hawkins, on the other hand, looked very much at ease with his surroundings, his manner indicating that he knew his way about such ships. He spoke with the perfect diction that so annoyed Webster. "Gentlemen," he said, "We will find our boats down there amongst the containers. If you would kindly follow me I will show you. Just watch your feet and you will come to no harm."

Phillips smiled expansively and a gold tooth flashed as sunshine broke through clouds that were clearing away to the East. "Lead the way Commander. We're right behind you!" Sid winked at Webster and signaled for him to follow.

They reached a vantage point that allowed them to see down into a cavernous gap. Webster felt disorientated. His only consolation was that Phillips was breathing a lot harder than he, and visibly sweating in his neat grey city suit.

Hawkins remained unruffled. "Now, gentlemen." His polished accent spoke of a grounding in one of the better British public schools. "Are they not a bevy of the most beautiful ladies that you have ever seen! I told you, Mr. Phillips, that you would not be disappointed. Our sales brochure hardly does these yachts justice. When you see your dream lady afloat..." He broke off and chuckled. "I really think that you should wait and allow her to speak for herself. I promise that you will be enthralled."

Webster peered down at three yacht hulls nestling in wooden cradles that were shrouded in opaque plastic covers. He could not understand what Hawkins was so excited about. The outlines of the hulls didn't look all that impressive to him. To make matters worse, all three appeared to be identical. He glanced quickly at Phillips. "Which one is it, Sid? They all look the bloody same to me!"

Phillips looked equally puzzled for an instant, and Hawkins answered for him. "Yours is the one on the far right gentlemen, the only ketch. The other two are almost identical, but they are sloops. They also do not have the additional strengthening and the larger engine that you specified."

Webster was mystified. "What's a ketch?"

The question elicited a flash of disdain on Hawkins' face and for a brief instant he appeared to be lost for words as though he could not believe his hearing.

Phillips re-lit a cigar that had gone out earlier. "A ketch, Peter my lad," he said with great patience, "has two masts. A sloop has only one!"

Webster felt a wave of annoyance sweep over him. Feeling suddenly foolish, his face reddened slightly. "None of them have fucking masts, Sid!"

Hawkins recovered his composure. Laughing easily, he dispelled the awkward exchange. "Don't worry, Mr. Webster, tomorrow your yacht will have her two masts. The masts and sails are waiting to be fitted at our yard." He turned to Phillips. "I might point out that you were wise to select British made masts and sails, sir. The Taiwanese products are much inferior, even though their boat building standards rank with the best in the world. Now gentlemen, if you have seen enough, I suggest I drive you back to your hotel. It would be my pleasure to entertain you to dinner this evening in Hamble. One of the best restaurants in the South of England is within walking distance of our yard."

Hawkins was about to lead them away when he stopped short. "I almost forgot," he said, smiling now. "What are you going to call her? I need to know so that I can arrange for painters to take care of it tomorrow."

"Call it?" Webster retorted. "Who cares? What does it matter?"

"Don't show your bloody ignorance, Peter!" snapped Phillips. "All proper boats have names."

Phillips gave Hawkins a knowing nudge and placed his arm around the sales-manager's shoulders. Although the action did not appear to please Hawkins greatly, he made no attempt to shake off the arm. "Peter is new to boats, Commander," Phillips said. "You will have to forgive him. I'd like to call her *Wind Song*."

"How very romantic, Mr. Phillips," replied Hawkins dryly. "A very appropriate name for such a fine yacht. I must say. Gentlemen, I wish you luck and safe sailing on *Wind Song*."

Three days later, Sid Phillips led Peter Webster onto a series of pontoons that jutted out into the muddy waters of the River Hamble. It was a day that held all the omens of further fine weather to come, with fluffy white clouds drifting slowly, high overhead and only a warm southerly wind to dapple the waters of the river.

Phillips took hold of Webster's arm and stopped for a moment to admire their yacht, now floating proudly alongside her two sister ships. Although neither of them knew enough to tell one boat from another, they could see that *Wind Song* was special. Her teak decks were pristine and the sunshine glinted on superbly varnished woodwork. Even to Webster, there was something purposeful about the boat. Phillips looked equally impressed.

Hawkins was already on board, waiting for them in the cockpit. Beside him was a bottle of Krug in a stainless steel ice bucket. He stood up as they approached and held out his hand to assist Phillips in negotiating the lifelines as he stepped onto the freshly scrubbed teak decks. Pointedly, Hawkins ignored Webster. "Welcome aboard, gentlemen," he said.

As Webster clumsily climbed on board without assistance, he noticed that Hawkins was dressed casually in jeans, a blue denim shirt, and leather sailing shoes without socks. Hawkins managed to wear the clothes with an elegance that suggested they had been tailored for him on Saville Row. Webster's dislike for Hawkins heightened in that instant, and although Hawkins continued to cloak his thoughts in the professional veneer of a salesman, Webster could sense that his own feelings were reciprocated. From the occasional flash in Hawkins eyes and the use of a phrase or a word that was designed to discomfort him, he knew instinctively that Hawkins saw him as an inferior. It wasn't just because he knew little or nothing about yachts, he thought. It went deeper than that. He knew that it came from the educated, upper class Hawkins having to rub shoulders with the great unwashed, those who originated in the back streets of London, but who now had the power and the money to force him into contact with them. For the moment at least, he gained some consolation from that thought.

Webster found the other two men in the cockpit laughing and joking together. Hawkins picked up the champagne. "Let's go below shall we?"

The pop of the champagne cork sounded excessively loud in the confines of the sumptuous, but relatively small main saloon. Hawkins filled their glasses, raising his own in a toast. "To your everlasting pleasure, gentlemen! *Wind Song* is now yours to carry you where you will. May she do so in comfort and in safety."

Phillips touched glasses briefly. "Thank you, Commander. It has been a pleasure doing business with you!"

To Webster, Sid sounded unusually animated. Phillips had already shed his business suit in favor of a more appropriate yachting rig that he had bought the previous day in one of the Marina boutiques. Webster felt that the yachting cap that Sid now sported was certainly overdoing it. He knew enough to hide his feelings. In response to the toast he nodded politely and sipped his drink.

Hawkins drained his glass and rose to his feet. Although he was over six feet tall, his head did not touch the deck-head in the saloon. Refusing the offer of a refill from Sid, he placed a set of keys on the polished oval saloon table. Then he handed Phillips a bulky plastic folder. "Here are all the necessary papers, Mr. Phillips. Guarantees, customs clearance paperwork, and of course, registration papers. The ship is yours, sir, but do not hesitate to call on me if you need further advice or assistance." Hawkins nodded politely to Webster, and then climbed the short ladder that led through the open hatch into the cockpit. Seconds later, they heard his footsteps fading away on the wooden planking of the pontoon.

Webster got to his feet and poured himself another drink, his impatience breaking through. "Right Sid! Where's the stuff?"

Phillips smiled dreamily, gazing around the cabin. Then he looked at Webster as his smile broadened into a triumphant grin. "You're standing on it, mate! A million quid's worth of eighty per cent pure Thai heroin! Think of it, Peter. Think about all that money. Then you can say, thank you, Sid, for putting bread on the table!"

Webster allowed himself to be swept up by Sid's good humor. He grinned. "Thank you, Sid, for putting bread on my table!"

Phillips responded with a great gut-wrenching laugh and clinked glasses. "To *Wind Song*," he toasted.

"To *Wind Song*," Webster echoed.

FIFTEEN

For almost five minutes, Richard Critchley admired the vessel floating alongside the pontoon. In a daze he double-checked the gold-lettered name on her stern to make sure he had found the right yacht. The yacht looked magnificent and he could only hazard a guess at what she had cost. What two men such as Phillips and Webster were doing with a craft such as this was beyond his comprehension.

Critchley had not been completely truthful with Webster for he had done some formidable sailing in his time and recognized a good boat when he saw one. He had even crewed an Admiral's Cup race and a number of Fastnet races. Thanks to influential friends, he was no stranger to floating luxury. That is, he remembered, until a few of his checks had bounced. And when Air Commodore Howard's wife, Vera, had returned home half pissed one night and shot her mouth off about their affair...his friends in high places had deserted him quickly after that and he became an untouchable.

Now, however, he could be reaching a turning point, he realized. He had already successfully ripped off Sid Phillips for several grand on the purchase of the house. Most of the repairs were almost completed, and here they were, handing him a pristine forty-footer direct from the builder's yard! Life could hardly be better, he thought.

Critchley climbed on board and dumped his bag into the cockpit. "Permission to come on board!" he called. He did not wait for a response, but vaulted down into the cockpit and ducked is head under the spray-hood.

"We're down below, come on down!" The reply issued from the open companionway. Critchley recognized the deep boom of Phillips' voice. He swung through the open hatch and negotiated the short ladder leading down into the accommodation. Webster and Phillips were sitting on either side of the saloon table, flanking an upturned magnum of champagne. Critchley instantly saw that both men were slightly drunk. The saloon was comparatively gloomy after the brightness outside; he stood for a moment, allowing his eyes to become accustomed to the semi-darkness. Gradually he noticed an overhead skylight and a pair of brass-rimmed portholes on either side of the cabin. He noted that the settees and bunks were upholstered in a gold colored material that looked like fine soft leather, and that the interior was fitted out in burnished, golden brown teak. The galley contained lockers with Formica tops, and a double sink with a cooker mounted on gimbals, all of which were in stainless steel. On the opposite side, was a full-size chart table mounted below a console in which was set a number of instruments. Critchley became aware that Phillips was watching him intently. Eventually Phillips smiled. "Like what you see?"

Critchley gave a low whistle of approval. "She is simply a superb yacht," he replied. He ran his fingers delicately across the surface of the inlaid saloon table. "I didn't know they still built them like this." He wondered again what two street thugs like Phillips and Webster were doing with such a boat. It didn't make sense. Gradually the unease that he usually felt in their company returned and he felt a tic of apprehension in the muscles of his jaw.

Webster had learned to detect when Critchley was worried and noticed it now. He smiled. "How's the house coming along?" he asked.

Although the question was put innocently enough, it was unexpected. Critchley experienced a vague sense of alarm at its directness, but he covered his surprise well and neither man seemed to notice his instant of hesitancy. "Fine," he replied lightly, seating himself opposite to the two men. "It's almost finished and they start decorating tomorrow. I'll move in next week as soon as the furniture arrives."

"Good," said Phillips. "I'm glad to hear that. How soon can you take the boat over there?"

"The boat! You mean you want me to sail her over?"

"Of course, what else?" Phillips looked slightly annoyed.

Webster frowned. "You did say, Richard, that you could handle a boat? I hope you're not telling us now that you can't do it! That would be just too bad. For you, I mean."

"Of course not," Critchley replied evenly. "I can certainly do it, even on my own if necessary. I assume that she has some sort of auto helm?"

"What's that?" Webster shot a look at Phillips.

Sid Phillips snickered. He seemed to derive pleasure from Webster's ignorance of boats. "He means an automatic pilot gadget, Peter." He turned to Critchley. "The boat's got one somewhere, but you'll have to find it. Neither of us would know what one looks like." The look of amusement faded from his face and he stared coolly at Critchley. "Just supposing, Richard, that you wanted to return to the same spot in the ocean every day. The exact same spot, mind you. How would you do it?"

Critchley concealed his surprise at this question "Well," he began, "you could do it by using traditional methods of navigation, but there would be a high risk of error at times, depending upon the weather. Personally I would use GPS. Then you could be sure of getting there in all conditions, by day or night, time and time again. It's certainly not rocket science."

Webster glanced at Phillips, who looked impressed. Phillips lit a cigar and opened a locker beside his seat. Rummaging inside it, he produced a bottle of Scotch and three glasses. Placing them on the table, he poured three generous measures. "You seem to know what you're talking about, Richard," he said softly.

Critchley picked up his glass and studied the amber liquid for a moment. He sniffed it and took a sip. "Good Scotch," he said. He looked about the cabin and tried to relax, but found it difficult. He felt like a student sitting a final important examination, and the thought worried him. Phillips appeared to be lost in thought behind a cloud of cigar smoke; Critchley picked up his drink and wandered over to the chart table. There were no charts stored beneath the hinged lid of the chart table when he opened it. He glanced at the bookshelf. It contained nothing more than a maintenance manual for the 80-hp. Volvo diesel engine. "We need charts and a couple of Pilot books," he said.

"Order what you want," Phillips replied without hesitation. His voice sounded distant and uninterested. Critchley noticed that he had chewed the end of his cigar so that it had become wet and pulpy.

Critchley studied the instrument panel for a minute or so. He could see that it contained a number of engine gauges besides an echo sounder and a speed log, but there was nothing else. "She's not very well equipped for navigational instruments," he ventured. "It's common in most new boats. They don't throw in much in the price."

Phillips sighed and stubbed out his cigar. "Get whatever you think is necessary," he repeated.

"Including a GPS plotter with charts?"

"Yes. If you say we haven't got one, then get one. It's a prerequisite from what you've told us. Go see Hawkins, in the boatyard."

"What about radar?"

At that Webster lost his patience. "Critchley! Will you for Christ's sake listen to Sid? Get whatever the fuck you want!"

Critchley stiffened and went quiet. He moved away from the chart table and opened a door that was set in a small alcove beneath the companionway steps. The door gave access to a small but comfortably furnished aft cabin that contained a double bunk, a vanity unit, a wardrobe and another door that opened into a toilet and shower area. Built as a capable ocean cruiser, the yacht was certainly exquisite. The more Critchley thought of that, the more confused he felt. The two hoodlums sitting outside in the saloon just did not fit the picture.

When he returned, he saw that Phillips had spread a large drawing on the table and was discussing it in lowered tones with Peter Webster. Critchley could see from where he stood that it was a detailed engineering drawing of the boat. He could also see that some of the hull frames and what looked like a tank of some sort had been marked in red ink.

Phillips looked at Critchley as he closed the door to the aft cabin and waved him over. "Sit down Richard. I want to show you something." Phillips paused for a moment, studying him intently. "I'm going to level with you. I want you to understand that I am giving you an opportunity to share in a considerable amount of money."

Critchley nodded. His mouth felt dry, and he poured himself another stiff shot of whiskey, gulping it down to steady his nerves. He suspected that by the way Webster was looking at him that he might be better off not knowing what was going on. Whatever it was, he knew that he was not facing any choices in the matter.

Phillips cleared his throat. "You owe me a lot of money, Richard. I mention it just so you know that I haven't forgotten. Luckily for you, Peter came up with a way for you to repay the debt, that's why you are living comfortably in Ireland and not feeding the worms right now. Obviously I didn't buy Clonbar House for the good of my health either. It's a business investment, nothing more. We want to ship some very valuable merchandise through Ireland, that's why you are there, and that's why we are giving you the tools to do the job. Our partners in this venture are a Chinese outfit called South East Asia Enterprises. These people are highly experienced merchants," he finished.

Critchley was acutely aware that not once did Phillips refer to drugs, he only spoke of merchandise or shipments but he had no illusions about what all of this was about. The enormity of it terrified him.

Phillips paused for a moment to allow what he had said to sink in. Then he glanced across at Webster, and with a reassuring smile, he continued. "Less than fourteen days from now, a ship en-route from Panama to Rotterdam will deliver an initial consignment off the Irish coast quite close to where you live. Later there will be other regular deliveries, from North Africa, the Far East, and South America."

Inwardly, Critchley felt paralyzed by fear, but he struggled to remain calm and detached as though everything he had heard was an every day occurrence. The risks were obvious. Anyone caught with an involvement in this operation could be assured of a lengthy imprisonment. For a brief moment he considered the implications of telling the police but rejected the idea instantly. That was a sure route to an early grave. He became aware that they were waiting for him to say something. "Hence, *Wind Song*," he managed.

Philips nodded. "Exactly. The yacht will be used to collect our merchandise, as and when we require it. We will have the safest warehouse in the world, without need of guards. The beauty of our operation is that it allows us to control the supply. Because of that, we also control market prices. It's like turning on a tap that pours money instead of water."

Critchley felt sick, but he forced himself to grin. He had to look pleased, he told himself. Otherwise he was finished. They had divulged too much.

"We'll organize a courier service to pick up the merchandise from the house in Kinsale. There need never be product on the premises for longer than a few hours to minimize the risks. Do you understand that, Richard?" Phillips waited for Critchley's nod of comprehension and then he continued. "The plan is meticulous and fool proof. You can be assured that we have thought of virtually everything."

Critchley considered it for a moment. "You expect me to bring the stuff up from the bottom of the sea? I'm not a diver, let's get that straight."

It was Webster's turn. "No," he said. "We don't expect you to do that. You are simply there to drive the boat. We will provide an experienced diver, one of our lads from the North East. You have the easy part of the job. You can continue in your lifestyle as a wealthy squire and play with your yacht. I should think that it would suit you." The sarcasm in Webster's tone was all too obvious.

Critchley coughed. "I take it that I have a choice?"

"Of course you do, Richard." Sid's voice sounded reassuring. He picked up a briefcase from the seat beside him, placed it on the table, and thumbed the combination locks. Opening it, he turned it towards Critchley. "You can choose the top compartment or the bottom, Richard, whichever you like." His eyes had the hard brilliance of a surgeon's scalpel.

In the bottom of the case Critchley saw a half bottle of Hennessy brandy and several neat bundles of crisp dollar bills, each of which was neatly labeled. He raised his eyes slightly. Held by clips in the lid, was a small automatic pistol. He didn't know what type or caliber it was but he read the name Walther engraved on the butt.

He reached out and took the bottle of cognac and broke the seal. "I'll take the street level if you don't mind. I never did like heights!"

Phillips withdrew the briefcase, placing it on the seat beside him. "A wise choice, Richard, I had a feeling that we could rely on you." His voice was barely audible as his eyes dropped to the drawing that still lay on the table.

Phillips cleared his throat and twisted the drawing so that they all would be able to view it together. "May I draw your attention to the details' of the boat, Richard?" He jabbed a fleshy forefinger at the areas on the drawing outlined in red. "As you know," he said. "This yacht was built in Taiwan, but before she left there, certain modifications were made to enable us to receive our first shipment." Phillips paused for a second and sipped from his glass. "My partners suggested that it would be a wasted opportunity to ship her over here empty." He used a pencil to circle a square object on the drawing that resembled the tank that Critchley had noticed earlier. "This stainless steel tank contains a false bottom.

Inside it are six kilos of number four-grade heroin, best quality stuff from Thailand, virtually pure and uncut. The sort that is easily soluble and best liked by European syringe users." He moved his finger to the frames that had also been outlined in red. "These are extra glass fiber frames indistinguishable to the real ones beneath the cabin floor. We specified extra strengthening during construction. You'll need to cut them out to get at the contents, making ten kilos in all."

Critchley allowed a low whistle to escape from his lips. "How much is all this lot worth?" he breathed.

Phillips grinned. "Far more than the boat. We've quadrupled a very small investment indeed." He sat back and studied Critchley for a moment. "As soon as you reach Ireland, retrieve this merchandise and it will be collected from you. Other than that, there is nothing else for you to do except to enjoy yourself, keep your mouth shut, and await further instructions."

Critchley pursed his lips and lapsed into thought for a moment. "Why Ireland? Why not do it all here, somewhere on the South coast? Wouldn't the dangers be lessened by being closer to the market?"

Phillips sighed before he replied, as though he was tired of this particular question. He choose to ignore the smirk that had appeared on Webster's face. "I have spent considerable time and effort studying all the equations before committing ourselves to Ireland. I'm not alone in this you know. Others are equally convinced that Ireland is ideal for our purposes. Look around you, Richard; police patrols are up and down this river day and night. The coasts are crowded with boats. Damn it! The entire British coastline is littered with coast guard stations all of which have modern communications and radar systems. There are none of those things on the south west coast of Ireland. The Irish authorities are uninformed and under-resourced. Jesus! We even have a politician over there who is about to buy his first Mercedes because of our generosity!"

Webster seemed visibly startled. Critchley saw Webster draw in his breath as though he was about to say something, but Phillips continued as though he had divulged nothing of importance.

"One thing that you need to remember, Richard, is that I came up the hard way. I've made a bundle of money in my time without ever spending a single day in the nick. That's not going to change now."

Critchley didn't quite know what to say for a moment. The enormity of what he was about to embark on was overwhelming. On the other hand, if all went well he could become independently wealthy. He'd surely find an opportunity to extricate himself before it got too late, he decided. "I like it, Sid," he said finally. "It sounds as if you've done your homework well."

Phillips opened the briefcase beside him and extracted a single stack of money which he tossed to Critchley. "Good," he said. "Get everything you need and take *Wind Song* to Ireland as soon as you can."

Sixteen

Ryder awoke after a short but restless nap when the pilot of the Boeing jumbo-jet made a progress announcement. Coupled with an unfamiliar Thai accent, the voice that came over the intercom had a hollow metallic ring to it, "Ladies and gentlemen," the voice said, "This is the captain speaking. I hope that you have enjoyed your meal. We are now eighty miles south of Moscow, flying at a height of thirty-five thousand feet and heading east towards Afghanistan. Our ground speed is five hundred and twenty miles per hour. Please direct your needs to the cabin staff and enjoy the remainder of your flight."

The intercom clicked into silence. On the seat back in front of him the entertainment screen was still showing *Casino Royale*, the movie he had been watching earlier. Ryder raised the back of his seat and sat upright. His hand went to his pocket searching for a packet of cigarettes, and then he noticed that the no smoking signs were all illuminated and remembered where he was. It was going to be a long night, he thought morosely. Not being allowed to smoke added to the sense of unreality of waking to find himself on the flight. His searching fingers found a crumpled packet of chewing gum instead, stuffing the wrapper into the seat pocket in front of him, he glanced around the vast cabin of the aircraft. Only the reassuring roar of the four big Pratt & Whitney engines reminded him that he was in an aircraft thrusting itself through the night. It was very different from the functional realism of a military Transall filled with sweating Legionnaires weighed down by the trappings of war.

That thought brought back memories of Mogadishu. He had gone there to save lives; instead, in a split second he had blasted an innocent child into eternity. That was one death that left him feeling unclean, and the thought was sobering enough to provide the excuse for another drink, raising his hand, he attracted the attention of a passing stewardess.

The lights were already dimmed, but in the beams of numerous overhead reading lamps the rich purples and mauves of the seat upholstery lent an air of tranquility and here and there he could see the shadowy figures of the cabin crew moving with effortless grace amongst the passengers. Their multi-colored silk sarongs and sashes were shot with gold, so different from the stark uniformity of the clothes worn by the staff of European airlines, he thought.

A Thai hostess who wore her jet-black hair in a curled coiffure brought his drink. Ryder could only imagine what length her hair would be if it was uncoiled and in the dim cabin lights her white teeth gleamed as she raised her hands together in a traditional *wai*, bowing her head slightly as she did so. Ryder murmured his thanks. He continued to stare after her retreating figure for some time until he eventually picked up his whiskey and soda and sipped it thoughtfully, trying to put his thoughts into some sort of order so that he could relax.

What was he doing on an aircraft that thundered over Asia towards Bangkok? He asked himself. Only yesterday he had stood in the station tunnel at Piccadilly Circus talking to Sheila McGuire who was now dead, and laying no doubt, on a mortuary slab somewhere in London. He remembered that it was only this morning that he had gone out simply to buy a newspaper in the hope that it might help him in his search for work. It had been a typically grey morning with a soft drizzle that brought an unseasonable chill to the air. At that moment, the streets of Hammersmith had never seemed so dreary, but passing a travel agency, he had stopped to stare at a poster displayed in the window, standing as a child would, with its nose pressed to the window of a candy shop. The poster showed the golden domes of Thailand's Royal Palace and he had been mesmerized by it. That, and the woman pictured in the foreground. She was quite the most beautiful woman that he had ever seen, and she had lured him inside like a siren with all thoughts of his search for a job in disarray.

Several hours later, after a visit to the Thai embassy to secure a visa for an extended stay, he had drawn money from his bank and returned home to pack and settle up the rent that he owed on his room. Then he had left for Heathrow with more than ample time to join Thai Airways flight 917 to Bangkok. Thinking about it now, it all had the semblance of a spur of the moment decision that he might yet regret, he thought. Certainly it was unnecessary.

Slowly, alcohol had its desired effect and soon afterwards drowsiness overcame him. Ryder relaxed his seat and fell into a deep sleep.

It must have been several hours later when he awoke again with a growing feeling that something was wrong. He looked about him, but everything seemed normal as the jet rushed on through the night. The gentle swishing sound of the air-conditioning brought a sense of quiet and calmness to the cabin, and few passengers were moving about, but something had woken him.

Then he heard it again. A soft sobbing sound, that came from the window seat right beside him. A woman, who had only moved once from her seat since leaving London, was quietly crying. Huddled in her seat, as though seeking the anonymity of its shadows, her shoulders shook silently. With the fingers of one hand, she worried and twisted at a thin gold wedding ring as though she was trying to remove something that offended her.

Except for noting that she was European, Ryder had taken little notice of her when he boarded the plane and beyond a muttered "Good evening," he had not spoken to her since,

although he had noticed that she had only picked at a delicious meal of curried prawns. He twisted in his seat to glance
at her, and she met his gaze with a startled look. She sat up
straight in her seat and blew her nose loudly into a paper tissue, which she afterwards quickly stuffed back into an open
handbag that lay on the table in front of her. "I'm sorry," she
said in a low voice as she tried to compose herself. "I must
have woken you. Please forgive me."

Even in the darkness of her seat, he could see that her eyes
were red-rimmed and still full of held back tears, and he felt
suddenly unsure of himself. Unused to any display of emotion, he felt more like a bashful schoolboy than a man of
forty-one who had seen enough anguish to last a lifetime. "Is
there anything I can do for you?" He found himself saying the
words although he felt he had little hope of comforting her.
Soldiers were not trained to deal with women who had tears
in their eyes, he told himself.

"No," she replied quietly. "There is nothing you can do,
but thank you for asking."

Her voice was almost inaudible and filled with the timidity
of a small bird. It was almost as if the sound of her own voice
frightened her, for she became tense again, her fingers again
working at the ring on her wedding finger.

"You're English?" The tone of his voice was more in the
form of a statement than a question.

"No. I'm from Ireland. And you?"

He glanced at her quickly before replying. He should have
recognized the accent before this. "I was born in England, but
I'm a French citizen now. I think my mother came from the
Limerick area, but she died a few years back."

"Oh!" She fell silent as though she expected that to be the
end of the conversation. Ryder looked at her again. She
seemed to have recovered slightly and her eyes were now dry
but filled with incomprehension, as though she did not understand what she was doing here. He judged her to be middle-
aged. The lines on her face and her dark hair, liberally
flecked with grey, suggested over fifty. He had already

noticed that the skin of her hands was red and that she had broad fingers thickening at the knuckles, suggesting that life for her had never been easy. He couldn't help thinking that she looked out of place. She was certainly not a tourist, he decided. "My son lived in Dublin once," he said eventually.

"Not anymore?"

"No. He died there last March."

The woman suddenly dissolved into tears, sobbing so violently that the back of her seat shook causing the passenger seated behind her to stir uneasily. Ryder handed her a folded pocket-handkerchief, which she accepted gratefully, dabbing at her eyes with shaking hands. "I'm sorry," he said, "I didn't mean to upset you."

"Please don't apologize." She placed her hand on his arm reassuringly. "I'm sorry about your son. He must have been very young?"

Ryder's face hardened. "He was twenty, but I hadn't seen him for many years." For a moment he hesitated, then he said bitterly, "I was not a very good father to him, I'm afraid." The admission shocked him. He had never admitted it before, not even to himself. He fell silent as he realized that he was confessing it to a complete stranger, and when he sensed that she had turned to look at him, he couldn't raise his eyes to meet hers.

"How did he die?"

Ryder released his breath and his voice took on a sudden harshness. "He died from an overdose of drugs. He was a heroin addict. A junkie," he added fiercely. The word filled him with bitterness and hatred.

At that, the woman seated next to him drew in her breath and went rigid. She started to shake violently. Then she went quite still, her face drained of all color and her eyes stared at him as though he had suddenly shown her the gates to hell.

It was some time before either of them spoke again. Ryder was the first to do so. "Are you all right? Can I get you something? A drink perhaps?"

"No, there is nothing you can do." She spoke in a voice that was dead and listless and barely above a whisper, as though the effort of doing so drained her of all energy. "I'll be all right in a moment. What you said was as a shock to me that's all. I didn't expect it, you see." She hesitated for a second as though she was gathering her thoughts, trying to put them in some sort of order. "I'm sorry, but I don't even know your name."

"Ryder," he answered. "Robert Ryder."

She held out her hand and he took it in his own squeezing it gently, trying to reassure her. Her hand felt unnaturally cold. "My name is Josephine Lynch, everyone calls me Josie at home."

Ryder inclined his head and smiled, waiting for her to continue. She withdrew her hand and took a deep breath. When the words finally came, they came in a torrent, as though she couldn't wait any longer to unburden herself.

"I'm not going to Thailand on a holiday, Mr. Ryder."

"Robert - or Rob if you prefer," he corrected her gently.

"As I was saying, Robert, I'm not going to Bangkok for pleasure. I don't even know where the place is, although I looked it up on a map once before I left Dublin." She paused to again blow her nose into a tissue.

When she continued, her eyes seemed clear of tears and her voice sounded stronger. Ryder no longer had to strain to hear her. "We're working class people who have never been anywhere. Never wanted to, really. Traveling was something we never thought about much. We never had a holiday even, because we couldn't afford one. When the kids were young, we took them to Bray for the day now and then in the summer, but that was all. We were able to get a bus, you see."

Ryder waited, aware that a wistful look had come into her eyes. Whatever she was thinking seemed to calm her, strengthening her resolve to go on.

"Bray is at the seaside, near Dublin," she said. Then she stopped as though she expected him to say something, but he just nodded, encouraging her to continue.

"My husband has always worked. He spent all his life in the Guinness brewery, but now he has a bad chest - he's always been a bit chesty - so he couldn't come with me. Not that we could have afforded for both of us to come. You see, the lads where he worked, they had a whip-around and gave me the money for the ticket." She choked back more tears. "I wish he was here with me now. I've never been away from him before, not even for a single day in the thirty-five years we've been married."

She stayed silent for a considerable time as Ryder waited patiently, fighting off a desperate urge to smoke. "Mr. Ryder...I'm sorry, Robert. Our second youngest is only nineteen. His name is Steven. He's always been the wildest one out of the five, but at heart he's a decent lad. He wouldn't harm anybody, not for the world would he do that. But he never got himself a job, not a proper one at least but he was always helping people. He'd run errands for neighbors, or do a bit of gardening for them, things like that. Sometimes, they'd give him a few bob so that he'd have the price of a pint."

She stopped and stared at him intently for a second and when she spoke again, hardness had entered her voice. It was as though bitterness was mixed with hatred, forming a cocktail of emotions, bringing her renewed vigor.

"That was until last year. Then he suddenly seemed to have money all the time. He even started paying towards his keep, until one day I found some tablets in his room. Afterwards I found out that they were called Ecstasy pills. He was selling them, you see, around the streets of Dublin."

Her words jolted Ryder, and for a moment he wondered if Mark had been involved. "We found out that Steven had got in with a really bad lot who were doing drugs all over the city," she continued. "He said he didn't use them himself, but I didn't believe him and I told him that if he didn't stop, he could move out. So he did. We're respectable people, Robert. We might not have much, but I brought up the kids to go to Mass and not to rob. Or to hurt other people."

Ryder inclined his head. He felt suddenly trapped. "We didn't see Steven for a while after that. My husband tried to find out where he lived, but before he could, Steven disappeared altogether. We heard he'd gone to England. I didn't worry because I thought that maybe he had gone there to get work. I knew that eventually he would get in touch." She stopped suddenly and rummaged in her handbag. "I'm sorry, may I have a cigarette?"

"We're not allowed. I'm a smoker myself and I'd die for one right now." Ryder grinned. "Anyway, I'm trying to give them up." He fished in his shirt pocket for the packet of chewing gum. "Try this," he said. He noticed that her hands were shaking again.

"It's just as well, I only smoke when I'm upset about something," she said. She took a sliver of gum and started to unwrap it. She seemed totally lost in thought.

Ryder glanced at her and broke the silence. "What happened to your son?"

"Six month's ago the police came and told us that he had been arrested in Thailand and that he was in prison in a place called Chiang Mai." Her voice faltered. "They said that he was charged with smuggling drugs and that it was a very serious charge. For a while, we didn't know what to believe. I couldn't accept that Stephen would do anything like that. Then we got a letter from the government, the Foreign Affairs Department, saying that they were doing all they could to have him released." She sat quietly twisting the empty gum wrapper into a tight spiral until it slipped from her fingers.

Ryder waited, seeing that she was summoning her strength to go on. "Two weeks ago, they wrote and told us that Steven had been found guilty and that he was being moved to Bangkok. They sentenced him to death. They are going to execute him..." She choked on the words, fighting to get them out. "The day after tomorrow." She slumped in her seat, drained by all she had told him. It was as though a well had suddenly dried up.

Ryder had heard of the severity of Far Eastern courts in such cases, and was saddened that this innocuous woman should have to endure what lay ahead and take the memory of it to her grave but he knew there was nothing he could do to prevent it. He had neither the power nor the influence to change anything for this woman. Only force could change anything he thought angrily. He thought of his comrades, Klein had one leg, and Chen was dead, as was Perez, but they had died or suffered their wounds in the dice roll of the fortunes of war, with honor, unlike this woman's son, who would die in ignominy at dawn, tied to a stake, with his head hooded.

Suddenly, Ryder dived into the pit of his own loneliness. The silence that existed between himself and the woman became unbearable. "Is there anything I can do to help you when we reach Bangkok?" he asked. "I mean, have you got somewhere to stay until it's - until you go back?"

She turned to him and smiled. "It's kind of you to offer, but I'll be fine. Arrangements have been made with the British Embassy to look after me."

"Have you thought about appealing the sentence?"

"Of course, but Steven was apparently caught with a kilo of high-grade heroin, or so they said. I don't know what to believe, but the quantity was seen to be very serious and he was sentenced with no right to appeal."

Ryder gave a low whistle of amazement. "I don't know how much a kilo of heroin would cost, but I suspect that it would be worth a very large sum of money if he got it back to Europe. Where did he come up with the money to finance the trip?"

"Someone gave him the money. He was definitely being paid to do it. There is no way he would have had the money himself."

Josephine sounded emphatic, but Ryder had doubts. If the boy had been peddling drugs, it was conceivable that he could come up with the money himself and had decided to take the risk for the sake of instant wealth.

"How can you be so sure," he asked quietly.

"I just know it, that's all. Call it a mother's intuition if you will, but Steven would never have thought of the idea himself.

He was always easily led. All his life he allowed his mates to tell him what to do. Anyway, all of Dublin knows who put him up to it. There is one man that controls the drugs racket in Dublin, for all of Ireland as far as I know. Steven was seen with him a lot before he disappeared."

"Do you know this man?"

"I don't know him personally, but every dog in the street knows who he is. His name is Hennessy. The cops know him as well, but they don't seem able to do anything. He just thumbs his nose at them. He's a right bastard!" Josephine Lynch spat out the word as though she was ridding her mouth of some poisonous venom.

Ryder went rigid. Hennessy! He remembered choking the same name out of Mark's friend, Billy. Sheila McGuire had known it too. Now Billy and Sheila were both dead.

Ryder slowly became aware that Josephine Lynch was leaning towards him. He opened his eyes and looked at her in bewilderment.

"Did I say something to upset you, Mr. Ryder?"

Ryder tensed his shoulders, staring at the plane's ceiling for a moment. "My son knew Hennessy too, and he died because of it."

"Mother of God! What a terrible coincidence." Josie Lynch reached out and touched his hand where it lay in his lap. "Both of us losing our boys because of an animal like that."

They fell into silence. Ryder could think of nothing else to say. Minutes later, she closed her eyes in exhaustion and her face relaxed in sleep. He felt drained, but a chain had been forged that bound him to another dead son. Slowly, Ryder also closed his eyes and sleep overcame him as the jet thundered across the sub-continent of India, heading for the Bay of Bengal.

Shortly before six o'clock in the morning the undercarriage of the jumbo jet rumbled into place and the Fasten Seat

Belt signs in the cabin flickered a warning. A tired hostess silently removed Ryder's untouched breakfast tray as he clipped his seat belt in preparation for the landing.

He glanced across at Josephine Lynch. She sat hunched up, staring out of the window as the plane descended over the sprawling environs of Bangkok, her face a white mask pressed tight against the Perspex. Ryder could only imagine what she must be thinking. Seconds later the great plane thudded down on a myriad of blackened skid marks and its brakes locked, slowing its forward progress, before it made a sweeping turn onto a taxi-way that faced the terminal building.

As the plane rumbled across the concrete, the woman beside him gripped his forearm fiercely and looked into his eyes with intensity. "I want to thank you for listening to me," she said. "I needed that last night. I wish I could help you with your troubles. You're not responsible for the death of your son. Neither of us are responsible for the paths our children chose to take." Her eyes traced the scar that ran down his face as though she was following a road on a map. "Whatever you were, Robert Ryder, you were not a bad father to your boy. Maybe you just couldn't be there."

He wanted to lean across and kiss this dumpy woman on the cheek, to hold her gently in his arms and tell her he would take care of everything, that she need worry no longer. Instead he mumbled, "Good-bye, Josie," before he lost her in the scramble to vacate the plane.

Above the emigration desks inside the airport, a banner carried the words, "Welcome to Thailand - Land of Smiles." The letters, emblazoned in three-foot-high characters, glared at Ryder as he walked beneath it. He glanced over his shoulder and caught a final glimpse of Josephine Lynch, Dublin housewife and mother, dragging herself away with no smile on her face and only abject sadness in her eyes.

SEVENTEEN

Rain swept across Kinsale, turning its narrow streets into cataracts that shed themselves into the harbor with uncanny eagerness. Seated in his brother-in-law's cluttered kitchen, Matthew Brennan clumsily picked up his mug from the table and slopped tea down the front, of what was for him, a relatively clean white shirt. "Damn it!" He muttered in irritation. He stood up and dabbed at his front with a tea cloth, ignoring the multitude of stains already on his tie.

Harry Meadows looked up at him and smirked. "Serves you right, Mattie," he commented with a wicked glint in his eyes. "Snappy suits are best left in the wardrobe and kept for Sundays."

Brennan scowled. Usually his sister was there to protect him from Harry's remarks for she shared the Brennan family's ability to put on airs and graces and was obsessively protective of the Brennan side of the family. She could never understand why her husband, a builder, could not also go to work in a suit just as her brother did.

Brennan threw the dishcloth in the sink. "I heard that you finished the house?"

"Clonbar?"

"Yes." Brennan slurped tea from his mug. "Did you get paid yet?"

Harry grinned. "I finished it last week and he paid me the very next day, in cash. You can't do better than that, Mattie.

He handed me the money just before he left for the airport on Saturday."

"The airport, you say. Has he gone away, then?"

Meadows nodded. "He was flying to London. Said he'd bought a yacht and was sailing her over."

"A yacht!" Brennan's eyebrows shot up.

Meadows selected another fig roll from an open packet on the table. "That's not the end of it; he's looking for a horse now too. "He has Billy-the-Jock keeping an eye out for a good hunter. He's joining the hunt this winter and he wants me to sort out the stables at the back of the house before then."

Brennan nearly choked on a mouthful of tea before he recovered his composure. "You don't say." He poured himself another mug of tea. "I'd like to know where all his money comes from. He's a strange one all right, our Mr. Critchley!"

"You must have done all right out of him." Harry chuckled. "You had that dump on your books for long enough. Although, even if I say it myself, it's turned out well."

Brennan gave a noncommittal shrug. "I got my commission if that's what you mean."

Meadows looked at him in disbelief. "No more than that?" He sniggered. "That's not like you, Mattie, not like you at all. What did he pay for the place, anyway?"

"That's confidential." Brennan's voice was stiff. "He's a client."

Harry laughed. "Would you like to know something else?"

Brennan glared. It was not often he did not know everything that was going on in Kinsale and its environs, and it troubled him that Harry seemed to know more than he did. "What else?"

"When I called out there the other day to check the roof of the old stables, there was a security firm from Dublin working in the house."

"Doing what?" Brennan tried to sound disinterested and failed.

"They were installing an alarm system."

"So what! Most houses are putting them in nowadays.

Christ! Mary Kelly was burgled only a couple of weeks ago, and she lives in the middle of town." Brennan sighed. "The trouble is, Harry, half the gurriers up in Cork city have cars now, and if they don't own one, they steal one. It wouldn't surprise me if they went as far as Galway to rob these days."

"Oh, I know that, Mattie, but how many places have surveillance cameras at their front gates? Tell me that! The gates are automatic, too. Now you have to speak into a wee box to get into the place."

Brennan straightened up. "You don't say!"

Harry chortled, enjoying the effect of his words. "I do say. And after I've finished doing up the stables, I have to renovate the estate walls. He wants them two feet higher all round. He's going to pay for that, I can tell you, what with the price of cut stone these days."

Brennan's hauled himself out of his chair in a huff. "I don't have time to listen to all this foolishness right now, why don't you fuck off back to work!" He brushed ineffectually at his tie and stomped out of the kitchen.

Brennan drove slowly. He was in no rush to get back to his office; he had too much on his mind to even realize that the rain had stopped but he couldn't get one thought out of his mind; Clonbar House was miles from its nearest neighbor. Why was Critchley turning it into a fortress? The man hardly needed more privacy but then again, Ireland had always attracted odd individuals, he knew that. Foreigners of all sorts had long gravitated to its shores, the Brits were no exception and much as he disliked the whole lot of them, he had to admit that they were his bread and butter. Without them, he admitted to himself, times would be hard, perhaps very hard indeed.

When he parked his car, he was still thinking of Critchley. He would have to keep a closer eye on his client, he told himself. Maybe this particular goose hadn't finished laying its golden eggs just yet.

Critchley finished securing *Wind Song* to the pontoon and returned below to shed his oilskins. Although rain still gusted fitfully across the marina, a break in the cloud layer was showing out to the West of the harbor. He didn't need a forecast to know that the front had almost passed through.

He poured himself a stiff whiskey, changing his clothes whilst he sipped thoughtfully at the drink. Although he felt tired, he also felt satisfied and almost euphoric. The trip had taken only four days; a little less than what he'd planned. After ducking along the South coast of England he had used the Helford River as a final departure point well before dawn on the previous day. Anchoring overnight in the lower reaches of the river had suited him perfectly; he had been able to come and go as he pleased without raising attention. Thirty-eight hours from there to Kinsale was good going for the final leg, even though the weather had become boisterous enough as he neared the Irish coast. *Wind Song* had proved herself, sailing like the thoroughbred that she was. The voyage had also given him valuable time to ponder on his circumstances. It was only now, back in Kinsale, that worry seeped back into his mind. Faced with clearing the boat through customs, the knowledge of his hidden cargo weighed heavily. He lay down on his bunk and pulled a sleeping bag over himself. He would face that when he had to.

Critchley need not have worried. In the late afternoon, as the rain faded to sunshine, two customs officers appeared and carried out a cursory inspection of the boat before stamping the importation documents.

Now as he sat in the cockpit and watched them trudge up the ramp that led to the road above the marina, his spirits rose. Exultantly, he realized that he was about to become a wealthy man. His reverie was short lived.

"Richard!"

Critchley swiveled to find Matthew Brennan standing alongside him on the pontoon. He hadn't seen him approach. The auctioneer's presence was about as welcome as a flea on

a dog's back, he thought, but he hid his displeasure and nodded courteously. "Hello, Brennan." It was difficult to sound
enthusiastic, but he tried.

"I heard you had arrived in." Brennan's eyes swept over
the decks. "She's a beautiful boat. Might I come on board?"

Critchley hesitated for an instant. There was no point in
making enemies he thought. As much as he'd prefer to keep
his distance from the auctioneer now that his main business
with him was over, there was nothing to be gained from
antagonizing him. "Of course," he replied. "You're welcome
to a drink, if you'd like."

"I would indeed." Brennan clambered aboard and seated
himself in the cockpit. He peered through the hatch as Critchley poured a generous measure into a plastic beaker. "How
long did it take you to come over?"

"Thirty-eight hours."

"On your own?"

"Yes."

Brennan fell silent. "She's a fine yacht," he said, as Critchley re-joined him and handed him his drink. "Good luck!" He
raised his glass in salute.

"Your health, Brennan." Critchley took a sip of his drink.
"How did you know that I was here?"

"It's a small town, Richard."

Critchley choked back his resentment at the use of his first
name.

"Harry told me this morning, and I checked with the
marina to find out if you had arrived."

"Your brother-in-law?"

"Yes indeed. He also told me that you're joining the hunt.
Fair play to you."

Critchley scowled. "You should tell your brother-in-law,"
he said coldly, "that I don't appreciate having my business
discussed. That is of course, if he still wishes to get work from
me."

"Of course, of course." The words tumbled from Brennan
in a hurry. "No offence meant. I'm sure he just thought that I

might be able to help." He quickly changed the subject. "Have you settled into the house comfortably?"

"Yes indeed, although I've had little time to enjoy it. But now that I have more time, I'm looking forward to having guests over soon. You can tell Meadows that I am pleased with the way it turned out."

"I'll be glad to pass that on." Brennan swallowed the remainder of his drink. "I won't delay you any longer, Richard, I'm sure you have much to do. If you need anything, just call. I'm here to help at any time."

"Thank you, I appreciate your offer."

Critchley remained in the cockpit, sipping his drink as he watched the auctioneer making his way towards the ramp. He wondered what had inspired Brennan's visit. It was a timely warning, he decided. Talk in small towns like Kinsale could crucify him if he wasn't careful. The idea of that was enough to drown out his earlier feelings of well-being, but he tried to console himself with the thought that by tomorrow he would be rid of the merchandise. Later he would call Webster to announce his return. Then, tomorrow morning, he would sail around to the mooring in the bay below Clonbar and extract the cargo. Everything was fine he reassured himself. There was no need to worry.

EIGHTEEN

Webster exhaled an audible breath of relief as he hung up the phone. All along he had worried that Critchley would somehow blow the whole thing before reaching Ireland in the yacht and he had half expected the drugs squad to come hammering on the door at any moment. As he replaced the receiver, he stole a glance at his watch. Ten o'clock. Sid should still be at home, he thought, as he dialed the number.

Phillips answered on the second ring. His voice sounded muffled, and Webster could hear a dog yapping madly somewhere in the background. Webster hesitated for a second. As far as he knew Phillips didn't have a dog, and he wondered if he had rung a wrong number.

"Hello?" The voice was Sid's, suddenly stronger, as though he had turned and was speaking directly into the mouthpiece.

Webster relaxed. "He's back, Sid! The bastard did it!"

"I thought he would." Phillips did not sound surprised. "Maybe you underestimated him, mate." There was a pause "Peter, why don't you come over? There's someone here I would like you to meet."

"Right now?"

"Yes, right now." The line went dead.

The weather front that had brought rain to Ireland earlier, had now reached England, but it was rapidly moving northeast. As Webster drove past the gates of St George's

College in Weybridge, only a light drizzle remained, forming a fog that turned the road to West Byfleet into a slick black ribbon as street lamps flickered on, earlier than usual. Reaching Byfleet railway station, he turned onto the old Woking Road, slowing as he searched a line of beech trees for Phillips' house. He was humming an old Carpenter's tune in time with the car stereo when he swung off the road and entered a tree-lined drive where gravel crunched thickly beneath the wheels of his car. Lights showed in most of the downstairs windows of the double-fronted house, and a brass coach lantern emitted a welcoming twinkle from a tiled porch at the entrance.

Phillips' silver-grey Rolls Royce stood in the drive near the front door, and Webster parked behind it. He got out, not bothering to lock the driver's door, and walked slowly past the Rolls, trailing his fingers along the bonnet until they touched the silver lady mascot. He stepped up to the door and pressed the bell push. Chimes echoed from behind the weathered oak doors, in which twin mullion windows glowed like the eyes of an owl, then the door swung open. Beyond the woman framed in the opening, he could see a wide reception hall; at its end a staircase swept in a graceful spiral to the upper floor.

"Peter! Darling!" Sid's wife, Zoe, swept her arms around him and planted a wetly effusive kiss on his cheek.

"Hi, Zoe." The air held a trace of expensive but cloying perfume and he caught a flash of ample cleavage above a low-cut black cocktail dress. Her streaked hair was cut short in a bob, and her false eyelashes fluttered in welcome. He had always thought that Zoe shared Imelda's propensity for flashiness, but not at this moment. Tonight she looked surprisingly elegant, if he excused the plethora of gold bracelets that jangled on her wrists.

Webster realized that he had never had an opportunity to get to know her. All he knew about her were a few superficial details that Sid had divulged over the years, but he knew that she had been married to Sid ever since he lived in Beirut, years ago, long before Webster had met him. Not once had she appeared in the club, nor did she seem to accompany Phillips anywhere. Yet, to his knowledge, Phillips had never had an affair, even though the nature of his business offered him every opportunity. On the face of it he seemed to be devoted to his wife.

"Do come in," Zoe gushed, "It's so lovely to see you again, Peter. You really do not call out often enough, Sweetie! Sid's waiting for you in the drawing room. How's Imelda? Fine, I hope?" Not waiting for a reply, she clutched his arm and ushered him across the hall. From somewhere in the back of the house he could hear a dog clamoring and scratching at a door.

"We have the sweetest Pomeranian now, darling," Zoe announced gaily. "I can't wait for you to meet him. We call him Bubbles, it reminds me of Michael Bublé. I love Michael Bublé, did you know that? I go all squishy when I play his songs!" Her laughter and endless patter swept him through double doors that showed scratch marks low on their otherwise pristine white paint.

"Sid! Peter's here!" Zoe's voice echoed in the room. Phillips rose from an armchair on one side of a red brick fireplace that dwarfed the end wall. Another man, whom Webster did not know, also got to his feet.

Phillips beamed and moved towards him. He saw that Sid was wearing a new light grey suit rather than his usual navyblue. Phillips noticed Webster's glance and his fingers went to the lapel of his jacket. "Giorgio Armani. Like it?" He grinned, placing his arm protectively around Webster's shoulders. "We're on the pig's back, mate! What do you think?"

Webster nodded numbly. The warmth of his welcome, coupled with Sid's exuberance, was disconcerting. It all seemed contrived and overdone, as though Sid was out to impress someone who was important.

Just then Zoe sidled up again, her face beaming. "I'll leave you boys alone for a while. You'll want to talk business and Bubbles needs his walkies! She swept from the room, closing the doors behind her.

Phillips released him from what had ended up as a bear hug. "Drag up a chair Peter! I want you to meet Frank Sullivan."

Sullivan smiled and shook hands. "Pleased to meet you, Peter," he said. His voice was soft and well modulated. "Sid's been telling me all about you. I understand you're his right-hand man."

Webster's smile wavered for a moment at the sound of Sullivan's Irish brogue, but he quickly recovered and conjured up an uncomfortable smile.

"Sid and I go back a long way, Frank," he replied. He noted that the Irishman was unusually short in stature, his thin frame casually dressed in a Donegal tweed jacket and open necked shirt. His grey trousers looked creased, as though he had just got off a plane. He was a dapper man, perhaps in his fifties, with thin strands of yellowish hair combed flat over his forehead. Heavy spectacles framed a narrow face that spoke of a lack of sunshine. Sullivan looked oddly bookish, he thought. Nondescript enough to be an off-duty teacher or a banker even. The man's voice suggested that he was well educated and at his ease.

Phillips lit a cigar and flopped into an armchair. "Peter, get yourself a drink. Sit yourself down, Frank. Now that Zoe is out of the way, we can talk business."

Webster crossed the room to a well-stocked drinks cabinet. Selecting a fine malt whisky, he splashed a generous measure into a cut-glass tumbler as he appraised the room. A tapestry covered the nearest wall, and tailored curtains were drawn on both windows. Beautifully arranged flowers and strategically placed bowls of potpourri battled against Sid's cigar fumes. Phillips certainly lived well, Webster thought. Admittedly, his house in Hampstead could hardly be described as a slum, but it paled in comparison to this. Not for the first time, he wondered why Phillips was running such a risk. He heard the mumble of Sid's voice, conscious of thick carpeting, soft under his feet as he returned to the others.

"Did you hear what I said, Peter?" Phillips sounded vaguely irritated.

"Sorry, Sid, I was miles away just then."

"I said that Frank is taking over the responsibility for distribution in Ireland. He recognizes the benefits of our organization, although until now he has worked purely on his own behalf."

Sullivan nodded his confirmation and his spectacles slipped on the ridge of his bony nose.

"I'm glad to hear that." Webster wondered if his voice betrayed his disinterest. He smiled at Sullivan, raising his glass perfunctorily in salute.

Sullivan leaned forwards in his chair, one finger poking his glasses back into place. "I'm already handling most of the business in Ireland, but we've been troubled by erratic supplies," he began.

"Not anymore," Phillips interjected.

Sullivan smiled, showing tiny teeth, like those of a rabbit. He re-adjusted his spectacles. "Demand is building every day," he went on confidently. Ireland is not the place it was, you know, - it's opening up all the time and the need has never been greater. Why, it's not that long ago that you couldn't even buy a bloody condom openly. Now all the pubs have them in machines! He chuckled hoarsely.

"What sort of stuff do you want?" Webster wasn't sure why he asked, but he felt that they were waiting for him to say something.

Sullivan sucked in his cheeks so that his already thin face became instantly emaciated. "Heroin is always difficult to get in sufficient quantities and the demand for E and hash has become frantic recently. I'll take all I can get."

Phillips interrupted. "You will have all you need in a few days, Frank," he said. "We've got plenty of hash on the way right now."

Webster's eyes widened in surprise. He had known about a cargo in transit from South America but had thought that it was cocaine. There had been no mention of anything else.

Phillips glanced at him, becoming aware of his raised eyebrows. "Sorry, Peter," he said. "I only heard today that a shipment is about to leave Rotterdam. I didn't have time to tell you."

Sullivan looked pleased. Rubbing his hands together he said, "That's the best piece of news I've had in weeks. I have a man in Dublin who manages that side of the business, but he's been threatening to go elsewhere if I can't deliver." Then, noticing a flash of disapproval on Phillips' face, he sat upright and pushed his glasses back into place. "Don't worry about him," he said. An icy tone crept into his voice. "He's going nowhere. We've marked his card. He now knows what's good for him."

Sullivan's choice of words and the way in which they were delivered brought a slight chill to the room. Webster felt it immediately and studied the Irishman more closely as the word "we" stuck in his mind. It was hard for him to fathom how such a mild mannered man could induce a feeling of dread with a few innocuous words.

"What about coke? He asked.

Sullivan's glasses slipped again and he pushed them back into place. "The demand is growing." He smiled. "Coke used to be for yuppies, like designer jeans, but it's seen to be the respectable drug of choice now, even the Irish Country-women's Association are snorting the bloody stuff." Sullivan gave a short bubbly laugh.

Phillips chimed in. "You know your market, Frank," he commented softly.

Sullivan nodded emphatically. "I do, Sid. You can bet your life on it." He glanced at his watch. "I need a shot, would you excuse me for a moment?"

"Sure, Frank, there's a bathroom attached to your room. Upstairs, first door on your left."

The door clicked shut behind Sullivan. Webster could hear the staccato clack of the Irishman's heels on the hardwood floor of the hall as he made his way to the stairs, then silence as his footsteps were absorbed by carpet. He turned and looked at Phillips, an unspoken question on his face.

Phillips grinned, his eyes dancing. "No, Peter, he's not a junkie. He's a diabetic. Sullivan told me earlier what a pain in the arse it is. He needs to take an injection before dinner."

"You seem sure of him, Sid. I mean, you seem to like him."

Phillips frowned. "I don't know what gives you that idea, mate." He looked thoughtful for a moment. "It's business, that's all, but Sullivan knows his stuff, I do know that. The Chinese respect him too and it says a lot that they accept him and are prepared to overlook the established Triads in Ireland. Besides, he's got connections over there that go all the way to the top, right into the government. Some buddy of his is a junior minister in the Irish Ministry of Defence and that's gold dust, Peter. We get to know everything that's going on before it happens. For instance, the Irish Government is jittery at the moment. They don't like the Europeans pointing the finger and accusing them of having an open coastline, even if it is true. Sullivan told me that they have been holding secret talks recently with the British and the French. The Irish are coming under pressure to agree to a joint coast guard service because the others know that the Irish navy can't hack it. Not enough ships they say, and what they have are too busy trying to keep the Spaniards out of their fishing grounds. That coastline, Peter, is still wide open. Sullivan told me that there are only four revenue officers assigned to it."

Phillips looked at Webster to see if his words were sinking in, reading the doubt still evident on his face. "Whatever they may eventually agree to, it's a long way off. The Irish don't like being pressured, especially by our lot. You and I will be long out of it before they sort it out, I promise you that. Christ! We're not talking about a job for life are we? It's cash, Peter! Quick and easy, then out long before they organize themselves. Take my word for it, Sullivan is useful. He has the means to move our stuff without us having to touch it."

Webster fought off a sense of unease. "He doesn't look the type, Sid," he protested. "You know what I mean? Jesus! He looks like a bloody school teacher!"

"He was. Before he got chucked out." Phillips got up and went over to refresh his drink. "Sullivan was a primary school teacher until he started meddling with the IRA, ask him yourself. Then he lost his job and went full time into the organization. Now the violence is all over, or so they say, but they still need money. The IRA, or Sinn Fein - whatever they like to call themselves - need nine million a year to stay in business.

For a moment, Webster felt that he might explode. The tremble in his hands forced him to put down his glass on a nearby coffee table before he dropped it. Had he not warned Sid right at the beginning that Ireland was home to terrorists, political thugs who accepted brutality as their birth right? Now, not content with linking up with The Big Circle gang in Europe, which was against Webster's better judgment too, Phillips had progressed to a new alliance without even a word about it. Christ! "Sid," he hissed. "You have just made the greatest mistake of your life. Don't even think for one moment that Sullivan is like us. If he's political, how can you be sure he's not trying to do us? We're English, and he's IRA, peace initiative or not. This is fucking crazy!" His eyes were pleading. "Don't you understand that, Sid? Jesus! I've mortgaged myself up to the hilt to row in with you, and I don't want to see it all blown away by some bloody Paddy!"

Phillips glared back at him. "Peter," he said, his voice menacing and barely above a whisper. "Your bigotry is becoming too much, even for me. There is no choice over Sullivan, he was given to us and whether you like it or not, you'll have to live with him, otherwise . . ." He shrugged and looked away. "It's out of my hands."

"Given to us by Kung?"

"Yes."

The sound of heels was clicking again in the hall, and Webster fought to control his anger before Sullivan returned.

Phillips leaned forward, pointing the red tip of his cigar at Webster, stabbing the air with it. "Drop it now," he said firmly. "For your own good, Peter. Drop it. There are no choices."

Webster swallowed hard as the door opened. Sullivan crossed the room, smiling and looking relaxed. "Sorry about the interruption, but it couldn't be helped." He sat down and plucked at the knees of his trousers. "You have a beautiful home, Sid."

"Thank you, Frank. I'm told you live quite well yourself."

"In Galway?" Sullivan looked wistful. "Only on those rare occasions when I see it, Sid." There was a hint of regret in his voice but he brightened again immediately. "Perhaps this investment will allow me to become a home bird, God knows, its time for that. I'm getting old, Sid, its time for me to consider my position in life." He swiveled in his chair to look more directly at Webster. "And you, Peter, what do you dream of?"

Webster gave an involuntary jump, nearly spilling some of his drink. Without looking up, he was conscious of their eyes boring into him. "What you have already," he replied evenly. He returned Sullivan's gaze and forced a smile. "It's not a lot to ask," he added.

Phillips chuckled, regaining his confidence. "And so you shall, Peter," he said quietly. "And so you shall."

Sullivan seemed lost in thought for a moment, as though he was weighing some imaginary odds. "Last week," he said in a low voice. "I was getting sixty quid a gram for smack. Today, I can get one hundred and forty. So, Peter, I believe you've gambled wisely."

Sid released a low whistle of approval. "I'll drink to that," he said.

Webster calculated what it meant. They had ten kilos on the boat, pure and uncut. It represented at least one and a half million at those prices. Slowly, he realized that a quarter of a million of that was his, less expenses, of course. And he had hardly raised a finger to earn it. "How much are you getting for E?" he asked hoarsely.

Sullivan adjusted his spectacles and peered at him appraisingly. There was amusement in his eyes. "Twenty quid a shot."

"That's almost twice the going rate over here," said Phillips cautiously.

"The secret is," replied Sullivan, "Keep the punters guessing, never swamp the market. Always have a shortage."

Phillips grunted his approval and crossed the room to freshen his drink. A small cloud of cigar smoke accompanied him as he filled his glass with ice cubes. Except for the clink of ice a momentary silence descended over them. Webster returned to his mental calculations. He was so engrossed that he was unaware of Sid returning to his chair. When Phillips spoke, his voice startled him.

"How do you propose to move our shipments, Frank?"

"That's the least of your problems, Sid," replied Sullivan without hesitation. "Most of it will go through the North of Ireland, but there are other routes too. You need not concern yourself with the details." He laughed softly. "You will get an express delivery service. I guarantee it."

Webster shuddered inwardly. Semtex explosives came to mind instantly, and he remembered the Birmingham bombings with a clarity that surprised him. Phillips seemed satisfied, however. "Enough said," he replied. "We'll turn over the first shipment to you in the next couple of days." He turned and looked directly at Webster. "You need to arrange that with Critchley, Peter. Okay?"

"Okay, Sid."

"Good. Now lets get down to the main reason why I wanted you two to meet."

Webster waited while Phillips selected a fresh cigar. Impatiently, he watched him run it lightly under his nose before he clipped off the end and lit it.

"There is one small snag." Phillips exhaled blue smoke, forming a screen that failed to hide the worried expression on his pockmarked face. "The Balkan countries are still in a hell of a mess."

Webster glanced at Sullivan and he could see that he was perturbed too. He felt gratified that the Irishman shared his inability to understand. "What has The Balkans got to do with us, Sid?" His stomach rumbled and he belched loudly.

"Until now, Kung's regular supplies of heroin have originated in Turkey and have been routed across the Black Sea, then overland through the Ukraine and Georgia. Bringing it through Serbia and Bosnia is as unpredictable as it ever was, and to make matters even worse, if that's possible, Russian couriers are capitalizing on the problem and making it impossible to move stuff without their say so."

Webster seethed inwardly. First the Chinese, then the IRA, and now the Russian Mafia had entered the equation. Where was Sid going to stop? His eyes blazed but he held back his temper knowing that Phillips could sense it anyway.

"It's only a glitch," went on Phillips, "But we need to demonstrate our ability to survive without the Russian link. Mo Kung has made an agreement to buy the next shipment elsewhere, and that's where the two of you come in."

Webster glanced at Sullivan. The Irishman's face was impassive.

"Frank has invested a substantial sum of money in our operation and I want the two of you to deliver it and secure our next purchase. These new dealers are looking for cash up front."

Webster's mouth dropped open as though he had been stricken by the palsy. He stared wordlessly at Phillips, horror and disbelief in his eyes.

"No problem, Sid," Sullivan said, as though he was responding to a request to go out and buy a take-away meal.

"Potor?"

Webster was aware of a sardonic glint in the Irishman's eyes. He swallowed hard, fumbling in his pocket for a packet of cigarettes. "Whatever you say, Sid."

"Excellent!" Phillips rubbed his hands together as though he was ridding himself of some distasteful contamination. "That's settled then. We can firm up the details after supper. I have a fine wine I would like you to taste, Frank, I understand

you are something of a connoisseur?" Sullivan smiled and
nodded.

As if a signal had been given, the door opened and Zoe
Phillips released a flying bundle of fur into the room. "Oh,
Bubbles! Isn't he sweet, Peter?"

Webster froze in disbelief as the dog raced across the floor
and landed in his lap. What next, he thought. All I need now
is for the bastard to piss on me.

NINETEEN

A startled plover burst from the grass, taking flight with a short sad cry as Critchley trudged across the field separating Clonbar House from the beach. The bird's sudden eruption shattered the stillness of a dew-laden morning, startling him with the suddenness of its departure. In vain, he cast around for the bird's hidden nest but he could not find it.

He walked on, following an ill-defined path that led to the shore. Over his shoulder he carried a holdall loaded with tools that clinked with each step he took through the wet grass. His jeans, already drenched to the knees, clung wetly to his legs, making the morning seem colder than it really was. Although dawn had broken long before he had left the house, it was still too early for people to be about and nothing moved in the nearby fields but in the distance a thin curl of smoke rose over the nearest farm. Matthew Brennan had told him a man named Driscoll owned it.

Ahead of him, a beach of rounded stones shelved steeply below a low cliff formed at the broken edge of the land. As he drew nearer, he could see that the cliff was little more than a steep bank and nowhere was it more than six feet high. The path ended in an incline, where years before, someone had dug a path that led down to a line of sea wrack piled high above the high tide mark. Beyond it, small waves from a full tide licked greedily at the stones where out in the bay *Wind*

Song rode high in the water, giving the illusion of being much larger than she was.

Watched only by a grey seal that surfaced a few yards offshore, Critchley dragged the dinghy to the water's edge from where he had left it at the top of the strand the night before. He loaded the bag of tools and pushed off with an oar until the water was deep enough to start the outboard engine. With a quick pull on the starter cord, the engine sprang to life, propelling him quickly away from the shallows until the water lost its clarity.

He cut the engine as he steered the dinghy alongside the accommodation ladder and stood to secure the painter to a deck cleat on the yacht, then he collected the bag of tools and climbed on board, allowing the dinghy to drift astern on it's painter so that it could not continue to bump alongside.

Down below in the cabin, he removed a panel from the side of the engine compartment before starting up a small diesel generator that provided 240v to the yacht's electrical system. The generator would not only recharge the boat's main batteries but would also provide him with the necessary power to operate an angle grinder that he had bought the day before on a shopping trip to Cork city.

He switched on the angle grinder and listened to the cabin filling with the shrill whine of the machine. In the confines of such a small space, it sounded louder than when he had tried it in the shop. Concerned, he hurried back on deck to listen to the noise level. Out on deck the whine of the machine was less obvious but still worrying. Even the noise of the generator did little to drown it, producing only a muffled throbbing sound that was interspersed with the occasional splash of cooling water discharging through an outlet in the yacht's hull. Warily, he looked about, searching the shore and the nearer fields for movement, but he saw none. His breathing relaxed as he considered that it was Sunday and still too early for early morning ramblers, and the nearby beach remained deserted except for a heron that waded on stiff legs in the shallows. As he had hoped, most of the local populace was probably busy preparing for Mass.

He returned below and switched off the grinder. Spreading out the engineering drawings on the chart table, he studied them while he puffed nervously at a cigarette. It was immediately obvious that the simplest approach was through the water tank. If he drained off its contents, a bolted inspection hatch at the top would give him access to the inside, where, according to Phillips, a second circular hatch in the false bottom would reveal itself. Once he had retrieved the contents, he could dispense with the second cover, and then it would be a simple task to flood the entire compartment so that the tank took on its true purpose. He could refill it at the Marina tomorrow, he decided.

He went to work. First, he switched on all the fresh water taps in the galley sink and in the two toilet compartments so that the water would discharge overboard. Once that was done, he removed an upholstered mattress from the navigators berth, then lifted a wooden hatch cover out of the way to show the top of the stainless steel tank with its first inspection cover secured in place by a dozen steel screws. Using a small ratchet screwdriver he removed the cover without difficulty and placed it, together with its sealing gasket, to one side. Pointing a flashlight inside the hole, he could see the water level dropping rapidly as the domestic pumps extracted it. He found himself sweating profusely and the flashlight almost slipped from his fingers. He pulled a handkerchief from his pocket to mop his face and realizing his hands were shaking uncontrollably he lit another cigarette to calm himself.

He smoked quietly while he waited for the rest of the water to drain away and as he finished the cigarette he felt confident enough to go up on deck to take another look around. All was quiet. There was no movement along the shoreline. Turning towards the sea he picked out the shape of a fishing trawler moving with infinite slowness across the horizon. It was no more than a speck, about fifteen miles away, and presented no threat. Closer inshore he could see a cloud of white sails as a yacht crabbed southwards making the most of a dying breeze. Perhaps she was heading down from the Blasket Islands and making for Kinsale, he thought idly.

His fear subsided as he heard the gurgle of pumps sucking air with the splash of water from the open taps down below becoming a coughing splutter. Quickly, he returned below and turned them off.

The flashlight revealed a second hatch cover deep inside the recesses of the main tank. He stretched himself out along the bunk and undid the twelve screws that secured the hatch purely by touch. Fortunately, they were still new and came away easily. His breathing was ragged from the nervous tension he felt as he collected the screws and placed them on the bunk beside him. Then he retrieved the cover and straightened up.

The beam from his torch wavered for a moment before settling on the narrow opening in the false floor of the tank. The space looked empty. Only bare steel at the very bottom glinted in the light. He panicked. If there was nothing there...if they had been double crossed...Phillips would never believe him, he knew that. His heart hammered loudly in his ears. Phillips would think that he was the rat. Already he could see Webster grinning in satisfaction.

Feverishly his fingers scrabbled deep inside the tank, but he could only feel cold, silken steel. His mouth went dry as he ran his fingers around the rim of the bottom opening. Finally he touched something that felt like a strip of tape on the underside. He picked at it with a fingernail, and then pulled the edge gently. The adhesive came away suddenly and he heard the hollow thump of soft objects falling to the bottom of the tank.

Sweat dripped from the end of his nose as his hand settled on a parcel that felt soft and pliable. He pulled it from the tank, and then retrieved another. Minutes later, six carefully wrapped plastic packages lay on the cabin floor. He stared at them for some time until his breathing settled down to normal.

At his feet, he realized, lay a fortune in any currency. Those innocuous bundles represented a life of ease and for an instant he contemplated what he could do with such a sum of money. Go somewhere warm? He thought. Somewhere he was not known. Yes, Spain maybe. It was possible. He knew he could do it if he wanted to; he had the boat and the skill to sail anywhere. Brazil, even; they would never find him there, he thought. The dream vanished as quickly as it had come. They would surely track him down wherever he chose to hide, he knew. The Chinese would see to that. There was nothing for it, he realized, but to carry out his side of the bargain. At least he would share in it then, and live to enjoy the proceeds.

He glanced at his watch. Time was passing too quickly. It was time to finish. He left the packages lying where they were and moved into the centre of the cabin where he removed two sections of the cabin floor. Stacking them to one side he went back to studying the drawings while he smoked another cigarette.

He peered into the bilge. The two false frames were easy to identify. Below them at the very bottom of the sump, he could see a few inches of bilge water sloshing about as the boat swung to her mooring. A film of oil glazed its surface, forming patterns of color when the boat dipped now and then to an occasional wave.

He restarted the grinder and concentrated on two rectangular sections of fiberglass straddling the narrowest part of the well, directly above the bilge pumps that lay at the bottom, and above where a line of bolt heads marked the join of the keel. He braced himself and knelt closer until the odor of oil assailed his nostrils, making his stomach churn. Carefully, he applied the cutting wheel and the machine shrieked in protest, kicking up a fine cloud of fiberglass dust that settled on the surface of the water like small snowflakes. It was easier than he had anticipated. In seconds he finished the first cut and started on the opposite side. Switching off the machine, he gently extracted the first cross section, up-ending it until the contents slid out onto the floor by his knees.

He failed to hear the engine approaching. Nor did he feel a slight bump as a boat came alongside. It was only the shout that immediately brought him to his feet in terror.

"Hello! Anyone on board?"

Christ! The cabin floor was littered with the stuff! With no time to do anything else, Critchley dived for the accommodation ladder, skinning his shins in his haste to reach the cockpit before the caller came on board. In his imagination, uniformed figures were already scaling the yacht's sides and he imagined the cold grip of handcuffs encircling his wrists.

He erupted through the open hatch in an agony of fear that was so intense he felt an involuntary trickle of urine escape him. Right alongside bobbed a black currach, its tarred gunwales scraping along the yacht's side as the occupant stood up in the boat ready to pull himself on board.

"What the hell do you want?" Critchley moved to cut him off.

The man standing in the currach swiveled until his eyes were almost level with Critchley's. "Sorry, Mr. Critchley, I didn't mean to startle you." The currach bumped heavily against the hull, leaving a scar of tar on the white topsides of the yacht.

"Jesus, man! Fend off, will you!"

The occupant of the boat looked startled, but he put out a gnarled hand to hold the boat off.

"Who are you? How do you know my name?" Critchley fought to regain his composure.

"Seamus Collins." The man extended his hand but drew it back immediately as the currach surged alongside and another smear of tar etched the topsides. "Sorry," he said, grinning through a line of teeth that reminded Critchley of an unclean fire grate. "I'm Billy's brother, I live over yonder." He waived a ragged sleeve in the general direction of Driscoll's farm. "I thought you might like a couple of lobsters, a sort of welcome to the neighborhood." He scrabbled in the mess of nets and pots that lay in the bottom of the boat and, one at a time, pitched a pair of snapping green lobsters into the cockpit where they clattered at Critchley's feet.

"Billy who?" Critchley continued to glare at the man with undisguised suspicion, unable to summon up any gratitude.

"Billy Collins, my brother. You asked him to look for a horse for you," Collins replied, his grubby features taking on a sour look.

"Oh! Yes, Billy the Jock. I'm sorry, now I've got you." Critchley tried to put some semblance of pleasantness into his tone. "Look," he said, "I'm busy right now, I can't stop at the moment." He suddenly remembered the shriek of the angle grinder. The man must have heard it long before he came alongside. "I've got a few repairs to do. Got a bit of damage a few days ago."

"Anything I can help you with?" Collins made as if he was going to climb on board again.

"No, its nothing." Critchley answered hastily. He was aware that his voice had risen an octave and he quickly released the painter holding the currach to the yacht. He threw the greasy rope into the boat. "I'll buy you a pint sometime, Seamus. Thanks for the lobsters."

With one last smear of tar, the currach drifted astern with Collins hunched over his outboard engine. The engine jumped into life without fuss. Critchley noticed that it looked new, a powerful Mercury that made little noise. Ideal for illegal drift netting, he thought. No wonder he had not heard it approaching. He shivered. Supposing Collins had got on board? What lay on the cabin floor was self-explanatory, even to a bone-thick fisherman.

The currach sidled up again a few feet away. Collins smiled and raised a grimy hand in what was meant to be a friendly wave, then he opened the throttle and the boat sped quickly away towards the gap in the rocks that led to the open sea. *Wind Song* was left rolling in the wash with Critchley staring after the fast disappearing boat. He wondered then how soon he'd be able to free himself of Webster, Phillips, and the whole plan before everything blew up in his face. With renewed determination he returned to the cabin and picked up the grinder. Tonight, he promised himself, under cover of darkness he would move the heroin ashore to the house and by tomorrow morning it would be off his hands. Then he would talk to them again and see if he could extricate himself before it became too late.

TWENTY

Ryder feigned sleep, keeping his eyes tightly closed while he tried to remember when he had last woken to a kiss. He real ized that it had to have been Imelda all those years ago, at a time when their marriage was still fresh and full of hope. There had been other women since her, of course, but none had been the type to show much tenderness other than what he had paid them for. Now they were nothing more than dis- tant memories and long forgotten faces.

At the first touch of lips on his, he had thought that he might be dreaming and had attempted to roll away, but instead the kiss became insistent as soft arms held him and he became aware of legs entwined with his own, another body pressing close and moving gently against his. It was an ethe- real moment that he didn't want to lose by opening his eyes, and he lay for a while longer overwhelmed by the unusual feeling of being wanted.

He opened his eyes and raised a hand to brush away long strands of hair that caressed his face, hair that was jet black and sleek, with a weight and texture that fascinated him, it's glossiness picking up early morning light that penetrated the dimness of the room. He became aware then of the sound of rain pattering gently on the roof overhead, even as small shafts of sunlight worked with tiny fingers at the woven blind covering a window at the far end of the room. Gently, his arms folded around the body of the woman who lay as a covering over his nakedness. Closing his eyes again, he let his dream return, not wanting the functional hotel room to intrude on his thoughts and spoil what was a moment of rare tenderness.

Softly, feather-light lips touched each of his eyelids in turn, moistening them one by one. He felt her fingers tracing the route of the scar on his cheek, following its course tenderly as though she was striving to understand what it meant. He opened his eyes again as her lips caressed his mouth, drawing her closer, responding without lust.

The woman pulled away from him reluctantly. She kissed him lightly on the cheek and moved to sit up in the bed. "I must go now, Lobbie," she whispered.

"Robby," he corrected her.

"Yes - Lobbie," she replied.

He laughed quietly. A deep warm chuckle, knowing that she would never get it right. It had been the same with Chen and his mate, Jody. The two Vietnamese Legionnaires could never pronounce his name correctly either, finally settling for Boss, even in those off duty moments when it was not necessary. He realized that it was the first time he had thought of the Legion since leaving Bangkok airport five days ago and he knew that if he dwelt on it for long Mark would return too. His body stiffened as he moved away from her.

"What's the matter, Lobbie?" There was concern in her eyes.

"Nothing. Nothing's the matter, why do you ask?"

"Because your face changed."

"My face . . .?"

"Yes. You have trouble inside you sometimes. I know that."

He tried to sit up but she pushed him back gently studying him with those great brown eyes that had first attracted him to her.

She touched the scar on his cheek. "What was this?"

"A wound," he replied softly.

"A wound?" The word seemed alien to her, as though she

was thinking where she might have heard it before. "From war?"

"Yes," he said, smiling.

"Vietnam?"

"No. I was injured in Somalia." He could tell from her expression that she didn't know where that was. "It's in Africa," he explained.

Her fingers touched the fresher scar that marked a puckered indentation in his neck. "And this?"

"That is from Africa too – in Somalia also, but not so long ago." He shivered, remembering the bloodied body of a small child hurtling across the room, the smell of gunpowder pungent in his nostrils.

"Somaya!" She struggled with the word and they both started to laugh. Her eyes danced, drawing him to her. She toyed with the sliver of shrapnel on the cord around his neck, turning it this way and that in her tiny brown fingers. He waited for her to ask him, but she didn't. Perhaps she sensed his growing unease and knew instinctively that he didn't want to talk about it. As her eyes roamed over his body where there were older scars still visible, he wanted to shed his past as a snake would shed its skin. His skin was a diary of war, he mused, or at least of conflict. It mapped all the flash points of the Middle East and of Chad, and other places where the Legion had asked that he fulfill his promise to it. How could he tell her about a child that was dust because of him, he wondered? How could she ever understand that? Strangely, the death of the priest didn't disturb him. That was a horror of war that he could live with, but the child was a constant reminder of Mark and always served to bring him back.

She kissed him and moved away before he could embrace her and draw her closer to him. He saw her only as a dusky shadow moving across the room until he heard the bathroom door click shut, and then came the sound of the shower cascading inside. His cigarettes were like a magnet on the bedside table but he resisted the urge to pick them up. Instead, he lay staring at the rafters in the arched roof where a spider worked at an overnight web. All he knew of her was that her name was Wan, and that she worked in the bar of the Princess Village hotel. He had met her there on his first night in Koh Samui, and on the second night she had slept with him, as though she too, realized that there was little time. She had yet to tell him why.

The patter of rain on the thatched roof reached a crescendo blotting out the swish of the shower in the next room. Then the rain suddenly stopped and the blind covering the window brightened in the sudden fire of the sun. Instantly the room became warmer and he switched on the overhead fan. He lay back on the bed quietly watching the blades flick at the warm air, cooling it as the fan picked up speed.

Wan returned to the room, smiling as she toweled her hair. Her nakedness was softened by the semi-darkness, only the glow from the shaded window enhancing the gleam of her skin. Her skin was golden without a wrinkle or a single blemish to deform it. She would never grow old, he thought. She was too perfect for that. He realized that he wanted her but the thought confused him. It was not a sexual need, rather it was a deep longing not to lose her. She had asked for nothing, giving herself with a simplicity that had surprised him. "How old are you, Wan?" he asked.

She moved to the mirror on the wall and shook out her sleek black hair so that it fell in long strands, almost touching her waist as she bent to brush it. He could see her face in the mirror, concentrating as she sought for the English words. "Twenty-five," she said eventually. "Why do you ask?" She smiled into the mirror, her eyes on him as he sat up in bed. "Am I too old for you, Lobbie?" She flashed an impish smile. "You like younger girl, yes?"

Picking up her discarded towel he snapped it playfully at her rounded buttocks so that it cracked in unison with her shriek. "No," he said. "I don't want a younger woman. You're all the woman that I need."

He reached for her as she dodged away and watched her as she slipped on her dress, the material of the sarong-like skirt encasing her and pinching in her waist to make her look slimmer and more girlish than she really was. Silently she pinned up her hair in an elaborate coil before donning a tightly fitted silk bodice. With a trace of lipstick she was ready. "I go now, Lobbie, Wan must work today," she said.

"But you'll come back?"

"Yes," she replied softly. "Tonight, when I finish in the hotel."

Ryder slid from the bed and stepped towards her. "I'm glad," he whispered. He kissed her lightly, feeling the warmth of her body as his arms enclosed her.

She leaned away from him for a second, her eyes appraising him, searching his face, reading what was there. "I not bargirl, Lobbie, you understand? I don't go with every farang on Koh Samui."

"I know that," he replied. "That's why I love you." He didn't mean to say it but it just came out, and for an instant he felt like an embarrassed schoolboy on his first date.

She smiled sadly as she turned away from him and reached for her handbag that lay on top of the dresser. He grabbed her arm roughly, pulling her back so that the handbag slipped from her grasp and tumbled to the floor where a small cassette player spilled out of it. "Wan! I meant what I just said." He released her, instantly aware that he had bruised her with a grip that was too fierce. "I'm sorry," he soothed. "I didn't mean to hurt you."

Without looking at him, she bent to retrieve her things from the floor. "It doesn't matter, Lobbie. Wan understands." She straightened up, moving towards the door.

"We'll talk later," he said earnestly.

"Yes." Her voice sounded as if it didn't matter. Ryder noticed the cassette player was still in her hand.

"Is that a Walkman?"

"Yes. It's a Sony." There was a touch of pride in her voice.

Ryder felt a twinge of jealously, wondering who had given it to her. "I didn't know they were still around. Can I borrow it?"

"Of course." She handed it to him and extracted the ear-phones from her bag. "I go now." She opened the door and the warmth of the morning stole into the room. Then she was gone.

With the tape player in his hand, Ryder watched from the doorway as she crossed the veranda and descended wooden steps leading to a pathway that wound between a series of similar bungalows that made up the Chaba hotel. She didn't look back but he could tell from the tenseness of her shoul-ders that what he had said had disturbed her. For a moment he wondered if she would come back again. Then the blue flash of the Gulf of Thailand through the palms beckoned. It was time for a swim.

Darkness came with a swiftness that was of no surprise to Ryder. He sat slumped in a chair on the veranda of his bunga-low, oblivious to the lights flickering on to illuminate the pathways leading to the beach, even the sudden croaking of bull-frogs in a nearby stream and the ticking of crickets greet-ing the coolness of night failed to make any impression on him. On a low table before him, a half empty bottle of Thai whiskey sat beside the Sony Walkman, the earphones of which now dangled uselessly around his neck.

His mind was numb. Both from drink, and from the tape that he had listened to countless times. Wan had not yet returned. He wondered if she would, and tried to force her from his thoughts. Mark was with him though. He felt his son's presence in a way that he had never felt it before, but his vision was formless this time. Perhaps his ghost was con-tent now that it had delivered its message.

Ryder poured another drink with hands that trembled and he slopped the amber liquid carelessly beyond the rim of the glass. He stubbed a cigarette into an overflowing ashtray with all his good intentions long since flown. Lighting another, he set the headphones back in place over his ears and switched the tape to play.

Most of the tapes that Sheila McGuire had given him in Rathmines were strewn around his feet on the wooden boards of the veranda. He had listened to them all, but they were useless recordings of mind-sapping heavy rock music that had assaulted his ears, almost driving him insane. However the last tape that he had listened to was different. It was an amateur recording, a copy of some songs by Aaron Neville, and Ryder could understand most of the words.

The beat of the music was heavy with drums, and the singer's voice was deeply resonant above muted guitar strings. At the end of the passage the tape hissed for a moment, then faint background sounds from a hollow room crept in and he heard the sound of someone breathing heavily into a microphone. Finally the breathing turned to sobs that were choked off. Mark's voice became clear, although his words sounded slurred and sometimes indistinct.

"Dad - you fucking shit! Listen to the words and you'll know what it was like without you. You did all the running, and for what, you selfish bastard? All my life I loved you and missed you, and what do I have to show for it? A few postcards, and two letters from Chad or some such fuckin' place."

There came the sounds of coughing and the tape hissed. "Oh yeah! And a fucking needle in my arm. The only thing you gave me was a stepfather that I didn't want. Do you know what he was good at? I'll tell you. Giving me tranquillizers to stop me pissing in the bed, that's what he was good at. I'll sum it up for you. My mother was an unadulterated bitch, my father was a runner, and my ever lovin' stepfather fed me junk! How do you like that, soldier? Is it any wonder I'm stoned out of my mind and living in hell. Have you ever been to hell, Dad? Because I love you, I don't ever want you to see it. There's nothin' there anyway - only scabs and pus and broken needles, that's all there is in hell, the fuckin' place is full of 'em. You can't see the grass for fucking needles."

Ryder groaned. There came the sound of choking sobs and the crash of furniture overturning. Then a tinkling of breaking glass and a door crashing somewhere in the background before the voice returned, now weaker and less distinct. "I got some bad stuff tonight, Dad. That fucker, Hennessy..."

Mark's voice faded and Ryder listened to him retching as he vomited whatever was inside him. Somewhere in the background, a woman screamed, then there was a rumbling noise on the tape as though the microphone had been kicked suddenly across the floor. The tape degenerated into an indecipherable mess of noise and voices, then reached its end.

Ryder knew that he had again listened to his son dying. His tears returned in racking sobs that consumed him so that he felt devoid of strength for perhaps the first and only time in his life.

Wan came then. She appeared beside him, and he felt the warmth of her as he drained himself in her arms. In return, the nadir of his life reached out and clasped him with hands that were cold and uncaring.

Three days passed in a morass of emptied bottles. Ryder didn't even remember being thrown out of the hotel, but through it all he had vague visions of Wan, who came whenever she could to administer to his needs without question. Although she was unable to fully understand his crumbling world, she slowly steered him away from his own self-destruction.

Ryder felt that he was in a tomb. He was conscious, but for some reason he was unable to open his eyes. He knew he was lying on something that felt hard, but even though he was aware of his limbs, he could hear no sound. He was surrounded in darkness that was blacker than pitch. Was this what death was like? The thought terrified him. He could feel himself trembling as he struggled to open his eyes. From far away, he heard a scream that sounded as though it would never end. Suddenly his eyes opened and he found himself sitting upright with perspiration pouring from every pore of his skin. He realized that the scream had been his own.

He re-joined the world in a small unfamiliar room that held little furniture except for a small table and a couple of cane chairs. The bed on which he lay was hard and unyielding rattan on a rough wooden frame. The floor was bare concrete. Walls and roof heavy with the rustle of dried palm leaves, and in the rafters, an un-lit electric light bulb dangled on its flex. Through an open door he could see chickens scratching in a dusty yard. One, more inquisitive than the others rested on one leg in the doorway with its head cocked expectantly to one side.

Nobody seemed to be about and the air was hot and still. Stiffly, he got off the bed and tottered uncertainly towards a tarnished mirror that hung precariously on the far wall. He barely recognized his own features. Several days' growth of beard shadowed the waxy yellow of his skin. His eyes were bloodshot and had sunk deep into his skull, which throbbed as though a miniature pile driver thudded in his brain. He stuck out his tongue and studied its grey furriness. He had never felt so bad since the take-off to Somalia and looking down, he saw that he was wearing denim shorts that he did not recognize as his own.

He ventured outside, and in the yard, he found a water tap with a metal bucket beside it near the doorway. He filled the bucket and tipped it in a cascade over his head. Although the water was tepid it revived him enough to take stock of his surroundings and he saw that he was in a tiny compound, beyond which, he could see the roofs of other palm thatched huts amongst the trees. Somewhere, a pig squealed, and he could see dust rising where the noise of motorbikes told him there must be a road.

At that moment, Wan appeared in the path leading from the road. She was smiling and started to run towards him. Ryder grinned awkwardly and spread his arms wide in welcome as she rushed into them, her face flushed and delighted. He held her tightly, sniffing at her hair, drawing in the scent of her, not able to speak. Drawing back she kissed him before taking his hand to lead him inside.

She sat beside him on the bed holding both his hands in hers and studied his face earnestly. "Lobbie," she began, "When you were sick you told me many things."

"I wasn't sick," he interrupted her. "I was as drunk as a skunk, and for that I'm sorry. I suppose the hotel kicked me out?"

"Yes, but that doesn't matter. What matters, is that you are better now."

"I'm sorry, Wan." He glanced around the room. "This is your home? You brought me here?"

Massaging his fingers gently, she nodded. Her touch was cool. He felt a wave of embarrassment.

"What did I tell you?" He looked deeply into her eyes.

"Many things - about your life mostly, and about your son, and what happened to him - how he died. You blame yourself for that, Lobbie, and you shouldn't. It was not your fault, there was nothing you could do to prevent it."

"He ended up hating me." Ryder murmured the words sadly, wishing they were not true.

Wan gripped his hands holding them tighter still. "He didn't hate you; he loved you just as a son should love his father. I listened to that tape, trying to understand it. It was difficult for me. My English is not always good - some of the words I did not know."

"Where is that bloody tape now?"

Wan released his hands and pointed at a battered trunk resting on the floor in one corner of the room. "There, with your clothes. You must learn to forget it, to put it in the past. You must build a new life and remember only the good from the old one. I am Buddhist, Lobbie. The Lord Buddha teaches that sorrow is the universal experience of all men. It is not wrong to have sorrow, but you must live through it. You can live through it," she added fiercely.

"What else did I tell you?"

"You told me about your life, about the army - the things that soldiers have to do - things that you did because you had no other choice. It is not different here in Thailand. We have soldiers too, and sometimes they must do things that they might not wish to do." She paused and looked into his face with eyes that were soft and translucent. "You told me that you love Wan, and that you want to stay here."

Ryder swallowed hard. "Did you believe everything that I told you?"

"Yes - everything, but . . ."

"But what?"

Wan hesitated, her face was serious as she gathered her thoughts. "In Thailand," she stopped, then she began again. "Many people come to Thailand now - many men. You know the word we use for a foreigner, it is farang. I told you before that Wan is not a bargirl. Sometimes other farangs think so. They make many promises that are not true. Soon you will go home and forget Wan, and then I too must live with much sorrow and begin a new life, just as you must do." A small tear escaped and trickled with infinite slowness down her cheek.

Ryder placed his arms around her and held her close nuzzling her hair, aware of her slender shoulders that his arms could crush, they were so fragile. He held her gently while silence descended about them. "Do you want me to stay?" He murmured the words into her ear.

"Yes," she said in a voice that was barely audible.

TWENTY-ONE

It was cooler in the North than it had been in Koh Samui. Chiang Mai, Wan's home, was located in a shallow fold in the hills that was sometimes clothed during early morning in a thin mist that dissipated as the sun invaded its dusty streets. It was home to a quarter of a million people, most of whom toiled in a myriad of handicraft industries that supplied an insatiable tourist demand in the rest of Thailand, and was noticeably free of the hedonists that flocked to the southern fleshpots that insidiously eroded an ancient culture.

Wan had made herself Ryder's personal guide, acquainting him with the city even as she brought him to the green fields of her childhood. Ryder suspected with some amusement that besides wanting to help him, she had another purpose in bringing him here; to show him off. The visit with her extended family of mother, grandparents, one sister, and four brothers proved to be less daunting than he had anticipated. Instead it became a joyous event in which he felt welcomed, even by her eldest brother Sompong, who wore the saffron cloak of a monk and spoke English with disconcerting preciseness. At first, Sompong had been suspicious and unsmiling, plying Ryder with questions about where he came from and what his plans were, but later he relented, smiling occasionally now and then.

They stayed for two days in a small guesthouse off Singharat Road, near the Chiang Mai jail. It was a time for lovemaking in their meager room when the night was cool, but also it offered an opportunity to discuss and plan how they would earn a living once they returned to Koh Samui. They agreed that Wan would keep her job even though it paid little. Ryder was already developing an idea for a diving school somewhere along the Chaweng beach, perhaps near the rocky outcrops at the southern end where the water was deep and crystal clear. The plan excited him, and Wan encouraged it with gentle prodding, as though she was nurturing a tiny garden plant that had just sprouted its first flower.

He loved her, Ryder realized, and at that moment he felt sure of it with an intensity that surprised him. For a long time now he had questioned his ability to love. The permanence of their relationship was still an open question, though, and he had not thought of marriage. There was time enough for that, he believed, though he was aware that without a Thai partner he would be unable to remain in Thailand permanently. In the meantime he would have to return to England to obtain money and apply for a resident visa and even though he had a return ticket to London, he did not know how long it would take to obtain the necessary papers.

His mood changed when he and Wan, while exploring the older walled part of the town, stopped before the prison's main gates. Within minutes he withdrew into himself, becoming morose and uncommunicative. Wan became aware of the depression descending on him like a poisonous cloud as he stood pensively outside the steel doors and studied the fortress-like walls. She stood beside him as his eyes roamed over the barbed wire that hung loosely from the top of a watchtower, where the black snout of a machine gun fingered the sky. Once again, she saw the same icy bleakness in his eyes that she had seen in Koh Samui. She reached for his hand, but he pushed her away.

It was there, he remembered, that Josie Lynch's son had been imprisoned before his transfer to Bangkok. He could see that the walls of the prison were old; how many secrets were locked away inside them, he wondered. Guiltily, he realized that he had not thought of the execution since parting from Josie Lynch at the airport. That pitiful woman would be back in Dublin by now, without any of the joy that Thailand had given him and immediately he wanted to leave, to return to the anonymity of Koh Samui. He was looking for a sanctuary, he realized angrily. Briefly, it occurred to him that the Legion had been a sanctuary too. Then Mark's words on the tape re-entered his mind and his face became a mask of despair.

Sensing his discomfort, Wan tugged at his arm pulling him away. "It is only the prison, Lobbie," she said hurriedly. "There is nothing to see here."

He reacted with fury. "I know what it is, damn it! It doesn't matter a toss."

Unused to anger, Wan sadly withdrew her hand. "Let's go further north," she suggested. "If we hurry we can get the last bus to Fang, and tomorrow, I will take you to Chiang Rai. There is so much to see there."

Ryder shrugged. "Okay," he said. "If that's what you want."

For the next two days they traveled slowly in rickety buses through the hidden valleys of the highlands, where there was a beautiful innocence to the northern hills, inhabited by a variety of tribes, each of whom spoke their own strange language. But in spite of the tranquility Ryder sensed a hidden menace that was more palpable the further north they went. Sometimes he glimpsed it in the eyes of the people who lived here; he wondered if it came from the knowledge that clandestine poppy crops flourished in these remote places, far from the roads. Whatever it was, it was all-encompassing.

Ryder became less and less talkative, until they reached Mae Sai, with its single well-guarded bridge that led across the Sai river into Burma. Here, Ryder sensed an aura of secretiveness permeating the potholed streets that was close to being evil. Maybe it was their proximity to Burma, now called Myanmar by its military regime, evidenced by the sullen Burmese traders thronging the streets. But Wan felt it too, and it affected them both.

Ryder guided her to the entrance of a large hotel not far from the bridge. "We'll stay here," he said, "if we can get a room."

"We can't afford a place like this," she protested.

He ignored her and crossed to the reception desk. Within minutes a porter carried their bags to their room and they unpacked in silence.

Wan sat down on the edge of the bed. Unused to air-conditioning, she felt suddenly cold and started to shiver uncontrollably. She crossed the room and switched off the machine, opening a balcony door so that warm air could enter the room.

"Switch that bloody thing back on," Ryder snapped.

"No. I'm cold, and I'm hungry."

He stomped into the bathroom, slamming the door after him. She lay down on the bed and buried her face in the pillow so that he would not hear her sobbing when the tears came. Eventually, she slept, awaking to a soft touch on her shoulder and the sound of his voice. It was soft and caring, apologetic.

"I'm sorry," he said. "Go take a shower, you'll feel better after it. Then we'll go and eat."

The restaurant was off the hotel's lobby, where huge golden dragons glowered down on the desk. It had windows overlooking a street where hawkers were already setting up their stalls for business that would come with nightfall. Ryder led Wan to a secluded table away from the other diners where they could enjoy the privacy provided by a wall of tall, leafy tropical plants and bamboo that grew out of massive tubs. Once seated, he ordered drinks, a beer for himself and iced water for Wan. She was silent and he felt contrite. Small lines of tiredness were etched on her face, and when her drink came, she only sipped at it, waiting for him to say something.

"Wan," he began, "I'm really sorry. You mustn't take too much notice of me. Too much has happened in such a small space of time, and I'm trying to get used to a world that is far different to the one I came from." He smiled self-consciously. "I'm not used to having a traveling companion, either."

Her eyes flashed a warning. "Is that all I am to you? A traveling companion?"

He flushed. "Of course not. I'm sorry; it was a bad choice of words." He reached for her hand across the table and clasped it in his own. "You mean far more than that to me." He fumbled for the words. "Things will be different when we get back to Koh Samui. I promise, Wan, I won't let you down."

She looked away and made no reply.

A waitress came and lit a candle in the centre of the table where its flame flickered in Wan's eyes, bringing shadows to her face. Her white silk blouse brushed the pointed tips of her breasts. For some reason it reminded Ryder of a shroud, and he shivered involuntarily. Something was desperately wrong here, he thought, and once again he remembered Mark's grave back in Dublin, an empty hole that drew him to it. He gripped her hand tightly, as if he would lose her. God! How he wished that she did not look at him like that. Those eyes! He was sure that beneath their doe-like tenderness they could read his innermost thoughts.

Suddenly she spoke, jerking him back from his turmoil. "Lobbie, I didn't bring you to Chiang Mai just to meet my family, although I wanted that too. I wanted to show you some of the more beautiful places in my country, places that the farang have not spoilt. Most of all, I wanted to help you see a future so that you would forget what troubles you. Sometimes I am frightened. Only time can take away that fear, and only time can take away what you see in your mind. You must learn to understand that."

He nodded gloomily, unable at first to respond. She had an expectant look on her face. It was some time before he answered.

"Wan, we can do it together, I know that." he said softly. "Maybe it's this place. I don't really know what it is. All I know is that the further north we came, the more I felt that we should not be here. This place - Mae Sai - it doesn't feel right, I can't explain it, but I know that it is not for us."

She smiled as she caressed his hand. "Then tomorrow, we will leave and go home to Koh Samui."

Ryder sighed. "It's not that easy," he said. "First, we must stop in Bangkok so that I can find out if I can stay. I might have to go back to England. I have money there that we will need."

Her smile faded. "But you'll come back?"

Ryder withdrew his hand from hers and took a long swallow from a beer that was going flat. "Yes," he replied firmly. "I'll come back, if I have to go. I love you too much not to." His smile became warm and reassuring.

The restaurant was filling with the scent of spices and hot food, and Ryder heard people moving to the nearest table just beyond the barrier of greenery near his shoulder. "I'm hungry," he said. "You must be starving too. We haven't eaten since this morning."

Wan stood up. "I go to toilet, Lobbie, and then we eat." She wagged her finger playfully. "Thai food, not Western food!" She gave a short tinkling laugh. "You must get used to that, too. I am a good cook!"

He laughed softly and watched her walking away, her slim brown legs flickering beneath the hem of a short denim skirt. Get a grip on yourself, Ryder, he told himself. Or you'll lose her, too.

His thoughts were interrupted by the sound of a nearby English voice filtering through from behind the potted bamboo. Ryder heard glasses clinking as he turned to peer through a gap in the green barrier that separated him from the table behind the plant and found himself looking directly into the eyes of Peter Webster. It was a split-second of mutual confusion and shock, but recognition was instant. Webster's eyes widened as though he had just been struck across the face. The color drained from his features and a look of fear replaced it. Ryder stared back in disbelief.

He felt himself grow cold and his muscles tensed as hatred bubbled through him. For the second time in less than a year, he realized, he was face to face with the man who had altered the course of his life, and who he believed, had shortened his son's existence. An image flashed through his mind of Mark dancing a jig of delight in time to Aaron Neville's song. In that brief moment he wondered if he might be going mad. What was Webster of all people doing here in a remote corner of Thailand? He wondered wildly. Was Imelda with him too? He looked about, but she was nowhere to be seen.

A mousy-looking individual bent towards Webster, who had stiffened in his seat. Ryder could not hear what passed between them, but he noticed the glasses slip from the bridge of the man's nose, forcing him to stare implacably over their black rims. There was no fear in his eyes, only a cold calculating look of appraisal. Ryder recognized the look; the eyes were those of a killer.

The whole exchange took place in a few seconds but there was a drawn out quality to it that made it feel like an eternity. Ryder moved first, only split seconds before the others got to their feet. He caught a glimpse of three other men at the same table with Webster. All three were short and stocky in build, with broad moon-like faces that lacked the fine features of a Thai. They must be Burmese, Ryder thought. And angry. He was aware of a movement towards what he knew would be a gun, and he froze, realizing he had stumbled into something that had now become extremely dangerous. Alarms rang in his brain and he acted instinctively, wheeling to escape.

Then he remembered Wan. Jesus, where was she? He almost upended the table in his rush to find her. As she emerged from the toilet he crossed the distance between them in a leap, grabbed her arm, and rushed her towards a fire exit. He hit the crash bar so violently that they spilled out into what seemed like a furnace after the coolness of the air-conditioning inside.

It was pitch dark in the lane where the air carried the nauseous smell of an uncovered drain. At one end there was nothing but darkness, but to the right less than a hundred yards away, the lights from the street at the front of the hotel beckoned. There, they would find safety in the crowds of shoppers that milled about the market where a collection of samlor rickshaws waited. He clutched Wan's hand more tightly and sped towards the street just as the lights of a tuk-tuk swung into the lane, blinding them and blocking their escape.

Ryder knew weapons well enough to recognize a Micro-Uzi sub-machine gun when he saw one, even in the dark. Capable of firing twelve hundred rounds a minute, it was lethal at close quarters such as this. Bathed in the headlights, he stopped and pulled Wan close to him. There was no way out. To run for the dark unknown behind them would be suicide. His training said wait, pull back and regroup for an opportunity that would surely come. What the hell did these men want with them anyway? They hadn't done anything. It was all a mistake.

Three men quickly surrounded them but it was difficult to see their faces in the glare from the headlights. Then the lights went out and the tuk-tuk started to move slowly towards them. There was no sign of Webster or the other European who had been at the table with him.

"Who are you, what do you want with us?" Ryder knew that it was a pointless question. The nearest man jabbed him painfully in the ribs with the muzzle of his Uzi. "No talk! No talk!" His voice was dangerously high pitched, as though he wanted a chance to use his gun. They were bundled quickly into the back of the canvas topped vehicle and their three aggressors climbed in after them. The driver rammed his foot down on the accelerator and the vehicle shot into motion, leaving behind it a cloud of dust. The tuk-tuk, an ornate pick-up truck with wooden benches in the back, rocketed through a series of back lanes, bumping over pot-holes that threatened to rip the suspension out of it, until suddenly it swerved left onto a paved road on the outskirts of the town.

The road was now lined with brooding jungle above high-sided banks that threw back the scream of the underpowered engine. Once or twice Ryder glanced over the drivers head to where the headlights picked up the winding ribbon of road, but each time he was rewarded with a blow from the butt of a gun and a shouted "No look! No talk!"

He felt Wan shivering beside him and placed his arm round her shoulders drawing her close so that he could whisper in her ear. "Who are these men, Wan, do you know?

"Not Thai, Lobbie. Maybe Burmese, but not Thai."

"No Talk!" The guard sitting opposite to them drew back his arm and lashed out with his fist. Wan's head slammed backwards against a metal strut supporting the canvas roof of the truck, then she sagged forwards so that Ryder had to catch her in his arms to prevent her from falling to the floor. He lashed out with a futile kick that only glanced off the man's shin and his reward was an inevitable flurry of blows as all three waded in with their gun butts. Then everything went black.

Ryder regained consciousness as he was being dragged out of the back of the tuk-tuk by his legs. He could taste blood in his mouth and a tooth loosened as his probing tongue found it. Then the road came up as his torso fell from the tailgate. His breath exploded from him and vomit filled his mouth. Rough hands grasped his ankles and dragged him across the road into a dusty lay-by. He was totally disorientated, but his eyes picked out dim lights far below him. He thought he saw what looked like a glimmer of moonlight on water just before he was dragged piecemeal down an interminable flight of concrete steps. Desperately he covered his face with his hands, trying to protect it.

At the bottom, he heard voices as though from a great distance and his sense of smell picked up the muddy odor of a riverbank as he felt himself lifted and swung like a bag of rice into the bottom of a boat. There was something warm laying next to him and when he was pushed over on his face he saw that it was Wan, but he couldn't tell if she was breathing. His wrists were forced back and he felt rope burning as they were tightly tied. His wristwatch was torn off. Then he heard the roar of a powerful engine as the boat accelerated away from the pier. The boat gathered speed rapidly and headed out into choppy water that slapped against the flat section of the hull underneath him as the bow rose under the driving force of the engine.

Ryder managed to angle his head to one side and squinted back to where three men crouched in the darkness. A fourth man, with the slimmer physique of a Thai, nursed the huge engine mounted on the stern of the boat where it coughed flame from its exhausts into a wake that lay behind them like a serpent in the moonlight. The first splash of spray as the boat reached its maximum speed was intoxicating. It tasted fresh and cool as he extended his tongue to catch the drops. His mouth felt full of pain as his tongue searched his swollen lips. When he moved, pain stabbed through his chest. He wondered if his ribs were broken. Then he heard a groan as Wan moved beside him. She was alive! The thought of that took away his fear.

Perhaps an hour passed. It might have been less. Ryder couldn't be sure, but his instincts were returning and he sensed by the noise of the water slapping under the upraised prow that they were powering up river against a strong current. He turned his head and glanced up towards the sky. The moon confirmed his suspicion that they were going north, but up what river? There were so many of them in this region. Then it dawned on him. The Mekong river. Jesus! The Golden Triangle; Mae Sai sat on the edge of it. Realization exploded in his brain. Poppies. Opium. Heroin! Webster was dealing, and he had walked right into it. The fucker was indirectly responsible for Mark's death, and now, if he wasn't careful, he and Wan would be next. He should have listened to his own premonitions and never have come north, but there were many things he should not have done in his life and it was too late now to be thinking of it. He rapidly considered his options for escape. If they were traveling northwards up the Mekong there were only two places the boat could be heading for, Burma or Laos. China was too far, and at least ninety miles further up river.

Just then, the engine throttled back to a low growl and their speed dropped so that the water was only a whisper against the skin of the boat. He felt the hull take on a slight angle as it turned towards the shore. They were making a left hand turn, he realized. It was Burma. Not the most hospitable place in this corner of the world, but Laos would be little better. The boat lurched onto a shelving bank and someone grabbed his hair, yanking his head back. Ryder steeled himself for the slash of a knife blade across his throat. Instead, he felt a blindfold being knotted tightly, and blackness became infinite.

The prow of the boat grounded softly, not in sand but in mud. He could smell the pungent odor of it. His mind was concentrated now. Every sound, every step might be a clue to getting out of this. Now everything that the Legion had taught him mattered. He had to gather information not just with his ears, but with his feet and his nose. Already he could sense the dampness of heavy foliage that surrounded them, while an incessant whine in his ears told him that the air was thick with mosquitoes.

He felt a rope noose being slipped over his head, and then it was pulled tight around his neck, almost choking him. He was dragged roughly to his feet and forced overboard into water that lapped at his knees. He heard Wan whimper as she was dragged out after him. Then a steep bank met him as he stumbled on a slope that felt hard and well trodden. There were more voices around them now. Soft mutters of sound that communicated nothing. He became aware of the rustle of animals, restless movements as though they were waiting impatiently. He felt the warm flanks of one on his cheek as he brushed past it. Short stiff hair and the smell of dung. Mules...of course. Pack mules for the fruit of the poppy that came across the river from Laos. They were on a smugglers' trail. He remembered Wan telling him when they were exploring the hill country that most of the opium nowadays was brought in from Laos, across borders where no roads existed.

A vicious tug on the rope circling his neck jerked him forwards and he stumbled on blindly, counting his steps. Every now and then he heard spurts of sobbing from Wan, confirming that she was not far behind. When the cavalcade eventually halted he calculated that they had covered 3 miles over a path that was hard packed and broad enough to allow a fast march by what he judged to be at least ten men and several mules.

Ryder felt himself forced to his knees. A bullet in the head? Instantly he pictured the killing fields of Cambodia. Then a violent blow from a rifle butt between his shoulder blades pitched him forward through an entrance that he guessed was some sort of cage. He heard shouts of welcome from others further away, and then the sounds of blows being delivered nearby followed by a low scream of pain that subsided into a low moaning sound. Face down, he listened to the shuffle of receding footsteps and the thump of unshod hooves as the mules were led further off. He lay sprawled on his stomach for some time before he sensed it was safe to move. What voices he could hear, came from a long way off. There were no other sounds, although he could smell cooking on the air, feeling the first pangs of hunger as he remembered he had not eaten since breakfast.

With his face close to the ground, he seesawed feverishly at his blindfold. His nose touched something soft and immediately filled with the smell of human excrement, but he worked on, until with the first trickle of blood on his forehead, he forced the bandage up over his eyes and he was able to roll over into a sitting position with his hands still tied behind him. Ryder saw that he was sitting in a low bamboo cage to one side of a wide clearing that was surrounded by thick jungle. On the far side, lay a squashed series of huts supported on short legs to keep them clear of the ground. There were lights there and he could see occasional movement, as well as hear the clatter of pans and low voices. There didn't appear to be any guards posted. Their captors obviously felt safe here, and unworried about the chances of an escape.

He noted that his cage was expertly constructed of woven bamboo, allowing just enough space to sit upright or lie full length on the soiled ground. Nearby, was the dark outline of a similar contraption that contained a prone, unmoving body. "Wan!" He whispered her name as loud as he dare and was rewarded with a slight movement as she rolled onto her side.

"Lobbie!"

He felt his heart soar. "Are you okay?"

"Yes, but Wan very frightened, Lobbie." Her voice choked and she started to cry.

He listened to her sobbing with anger growing inside him like a cancer while he tested the rope that bound his wrists. It was the work of an expert. Without a knife, it was near to impossible to free himself. He looked about him in the darkness but there was nothing inside his cage except bare earth and shit. Even so, he struggled to one side and began a hopeless sawing motion of the rope against the bamboo frame. He knew it would take days for the friction to have any effect, but he didn't care. No matter how hard the road, the Legion would take it. He concentrated his mind on that, knowing that he had to think again as a Legionnaire. Nothing else would do.

Ryder worked at his bonds steadily until he noticed lights approaching from the other side of the clearing. Something was up, and it was unlikely that it meant dinner. He glanced toward the other cage. Wan was sitting up but he couldn't see if she had managed to shed her blindfold. She had her head cocked to one side as though she was listening to him.

"Wan," he hissed. "Lie down. Someone is coming."

Obediently she lay back on the floor of her cage. He rolled onto his stomach and worked the blindfold down as far over his eyes as he could. The skin on his cheeks and nose was burning and he could taste blood.

Ryder heard the sound of a chain being released from the door of his cage before his blindfold was ripped off. He rolled onto his back and blinked into the powerful beam of a torch.

"Welcome to Myanmar, Ryder! Just what the fuck were you doing in Mae Sai, besides poking your nose into my business?"

Webster's Cockney accent was unmistakable. Ryder sat up and glared into the beam from the torch. Webster was only a shadow behind it and he couldn't see his face.

"Get fucked, Webster!" He snarled. "I should have broken your goddamned neck years ago. The world would be a better place for it."

Webster sniggered in the darkness. "He's a soldier, Frank, did you know that? A fucking mercenary. Does he look tough to you? He only looks like a piece of shit to me. I suppose the next thing we'll hear out of him is name, rank, and serial number."

Ryder became aware of another shadow close to Webster. "Don't waste your time on him, Peter. It's the girl that we need to talk to. She'll tell us what the bastard is up to." Ryder recognized the Irish accent of the second man.

"She's just his fucking whore," Webster sneered. "He probably picked her up on Patpong Road."

"Just get the bitch. She'll talk quicker than this bastard. If she doesn't know anything we'll soon find out. Then we can come back to this cunt."

Ryder felt Webster's breath on his face as he leaned close to the bars. "Frank's right, Ryder, we'll try the easy route first. If that doesn't work, I'll personally see to you. And take it from me, mate, I'm going to enjoy that."

Ryder spat straight into Webster's eyes, feeling a tooth leave his jaw as the glob of saliva and blood flew from his mouth. His aim was precise. Webster jerked back and the torch fell from his hand. No longer blinded by the light, Ryder could see his enemy's contorted face more clearly. He laughed coldly. "It's lucky for you, Webster, that I don't have AIDS!"

"You fucking bastard, Ryder! You're going to die anyway and by the time I'm finished with you, you'll wish it were from AIDS. It would be far less painful." Webster wiped the blood and spittle from his face and threw away a pocket-handkerchief. He picked up his fallen torch and turned to his companion. "We'll come back for him later after we loosen up that bitch of his."

They secured the door to the cage and turned their attention to Wan. Ryder held his breath. They had not replaced his blindfold. He watched in silence as they dragged Wan spitting and squealing from her cage and frog-marched her towards the huts on the far side of the clearing. Then he moved back to the bamboo frame, working on his bonds with a renewed vigor.

TWENTY-TWO

Ryder had lost track of time and he was angry with himself for that. The night was hot and he was sweating profusely, which drove the mosquitoes into delirium and they were having a field day feasting on his arms and head, thoughts of possible dengue fever or malaria were never far away. He couldn't feel his hands any longer, and the rope binding his wrists seemed as strong as ever. Earlier, some of the lights on the other side of the clearing had gone out, but sometimes he could still see movement on the veranda of the most central building, from which, the sound of breaking glass was once followed by a scream that seemed to go on forever. Thoughts of what was happening to Wan only served as a spur to free himself.

Clouds moved gently across the face of a new moon and he wished it would rain, so that he could assuage his thirst and clear his mouth of the small clots of blood that filled it. He became aware of a sudden flurry of movement and the sounds of voices raised in anger and the lights came on again on the balcony. Then he saw three shadowy figures dragging something towards him across the compound.

He stopped working on his bonds and lay down on his side. Three men came to the nearby cage and there was a thud as they threw a sack-like body inside and closed the door. A torch flickered as they secured the door and two of them went away. Then he recognized the tall figure of

Webster coming towards him and he sat up. Webster was alone and there was no sign of the Irishman.

Webster went down on his haunches and swung the beam of his torch inside the cage, dazzling Ryder with its intensity. "I've just fucked another of your women, Ryder." Webster's voice sounded high-pitched and dreamlike. "She was a juicy piece. I'll give you that."

Ryder went rigid. Every muscle in his body screamed as he tensed his shoulders in an effort to free himself. His hatred for this man was unlike any he had experienced before. "I'm going to kill you, Webster, do you know that? The one thing you can be sure of, is that you will never live to see old age!"

Webster reached through the bars and hit him a savage blow across the bridge of his nose with the torch, bringing stinging tears of pain to his eyes. "Look at it this way, mate," Webster said. "Your luck finally ran out. You were in the wrong place at the wrong time. You've seen too much for your own good, so you're not going to kill anyone, Ryder. Your killing days are over, mate. Tomorrow, if you're lucky, you'll get a bullet in the head and that will be the end of you, but they might keep your little bitch a bit longer on my recommendation."

"Who are they?"

Webster gave a dry laugh. He jerked his head towards the black fringe of jungle undergrowth. "Not far from here lives a very interesting gentleman named General Khun Sa. Ever heard of him?" He chuckled. "I don't think you'd like him, Ryder."

"Why's that? Is he as big a shit as you?" Ryder could taste the blood dripping from his nose, but his eyes were focusing again.

Webster grinned. "He hates foreigners even more than I do, particularly nosy ones who can't mind their own business. Of course, he's quite an old man now, a bit doddery, if you like. But once, when he was young, he fought the Commies all over this part of the world. The Yanks and their bloody CIA loved him then. Now they're not so sure. They probably wished they'd killed the bastard when they had the chance."

Webster shrugged. "I've met him and I quite like him. She'll be a nice present for him, but don't worry, he won't screw her. He can't get it up any more, he's too old. Instead, he gets his kicks from being plain nasty, if you know what I mean."

"You know, Webster, I always knew you would hit bottom one day, but I never thought you'd go so far down. When did you get involved in drugs? Mark died from the shit. I suppose that doesn't mean anything to a greedy bastard like you?"

Webster sneered. "That little scumbag. Fruit of your loins, was he, Ryder? I never gave a toss about him. I'd have stuck the needle in him years ago, if I'd had my way. Just like fucking your women." Webster got to his feet. "So long, soldier boy! I'm off home soon, but I'll remember you to Imelda, I'm sure she'll be delighted to know that you're dead."

Ryder watched him until he disappeared inside the hut. He struggled to get nearer to the bars of his cage. "Wan! Wan! Can you hear me? Are you all right?" He heard a slight whimper and her body moved, but she made no reply.

Ryder returned to sawing the rope that bound his wrists on the bamboo bars with renewed energy. Minutes later he sensed that he was being watched and he stopped. He heard a slithering movement from behind him. Warily, he turned his head, not knowing what to expect.

The figure of a man lay prone in the dust just outside the cage. The man hunkered up and beckoned him to come closer. In his outstretched hand he held a tin cup of water that dripped enticingly as he passed it through the bars. Ryder felt the water splash over his chest as he slurped insatiably. Overhead, the clouds rolled back, revealing thin strips of moonlight that relieved the darkness. He raised his eyes and stared at his benefactor. The man gave him a toothless smile, and encouraged him to drink more. His face was that of a Mandarin, with cheeks fringed by wisps of grey beard that was like a cobweb on his mouth. The arm that held the pannikin to his lips was old and withered like a dried stick, the forearm showing a faded tattoo. Ryder couldn't see the tattoo clearly, but it triggered something in his brain.

Without thinking, he muttered his thanks in French. "Merci!" he said.

The man nodded. Ryder fancied he saw sudden recognition in the rheumy eyes. "Parlez vous Francais?" he asked.

"Oui."

Ryder felt a surge of excitement. A French speaking ancient in the middle of the Burmese jungle? He felt his heart rate increase as he thought of all the dead of Cambodia. 1954, the battle for Dien Bien Phu. For fifty-seven days the Legion had held it at a cost of 10,483 dead. This man, his savior maybe, was old enough to have been there. "Honneur et Fidélité," he whispered.

The old man nodded, his eyes dropping to his tattooed forearm. "Troisieme Régiment Étranger d'Infanterie," he lisped. "Parachutiste. Veteran de Indo-Chine," he added proudly.

Ryder's heart sang. "Et moi," he said. "Deuxieme Régiment Étranger de Parachutistes."

The old man's eyes widened, but he became instantly nervous, turning his head about to check for threats. All was quiet. He withdrew the pannikin and took a mouthful before emptying the remainder in the dust at his feet. Whoever he was, whatever thoughts were running through the man's mind Ryder couldn't tell. He knew that Cambodians and Vietnamese had fought for the Legion in Indo-China. Probably Burmese too, he thought, if that was what the man was. "Burmese?" he asked gently.

The man scowled, shaking his head. "Non, Cambodia," he replied firmly, as though Ryder had asked him something distasteful. He smiled uneasily and made as though he was about to crawl back to wherever he had come from.

Ryder sensed that he was losing him. He felt a rising sense of disappointment tinged with desperation. "A moi la Legion!" His words echoed like the final rounds in a magazine. The old rallying call that drew the family together, that bound them as brothers and made them one. All were subject to it; the Legion prided itself on never abandoning their dead or wounded. It would not have been different in this man's time.

The man hesitated. His eyes shone wetly and he straightened his shoulders, then he drew a machete from a scabbard at his waist and thrust it inside the cage. He nodded slightly. "Vive la Legion." Instantly he became a slithering shape heading for the edge of the clearing.

Ryder didn't dwell on his good fortune. He forced himself into a kneeling position and managed to clamp the machete between his ankles. Although the blade was not sharp, it was far better than the bamboo. In minutes he was free with a sudden surge of blood rushing into his hands that brought agonizing pain.

He glanced up at the sky, studying the moon to judge how much darkness was left before dawn came. There was not long to go. He cut away the bindings that held the bamboo framework of his cage, squeezed through the opening, and crawled over to Wan. She lay face down in a fetal huddle. The door to her cage was only secured by twine but even when he opened the door and reached for her, she did not move.

Gently, he pulled her out through the opening and turned her over. He brushed away strands of hair that had stuck to the dried blood on her skin. Even in the darkness he could see that her face was puffed and swollen, but whether it was from the earlier beating in the truck he could not tell. The buttons of her silk blouse had all been ripped off and her small breasts showed tiny black specks that looked like cigarette burns. Her skirt was just a torn rag that barely covered her. Her breathing was shallow, and he could feel shivers rippling through her body. Slowly her eyes opened to show a flicker of recognition. It was then that he noticed blood on her hands and discovered that three fingernails were missing from her left hand. Ryder cradled her in his arms, crying softly now, tears that he didn't know he had, remembering what it must have been like for Jody when Chen died in the ruins of Mogadishu airport. With malice in his eyes, he looked back at the huts that protected Webster, and then he hoisted her across his broad shoulders and padded off down a trail that he knew must lead back to the river.

Dawn came with the same characteristic swiftness that also brought nightfall to the tropics, and with its coming, the jungle came alive with a cacophony of sound erupting in the trees. Although he sensed that the river was not far away, Ryder knew that daylight would betray their escape. Already, trackers could not be far behind. His chest pounded and a burning sensation in his ribs worried him. Wan's weight, although slight, added to his discomfort. The dangers of having to hide during daylight seemed little when weighed against the opportunity to rest and sleep, if that was possible. Thoughts of food surged through his mind but he drove them away, destroying them with memories of hardships that had gone before, thanking the Legion for making him what he was. Endurance was now his obsession.

All at once he found himself sliding down the muddy end of the trail with the broad expanse of the Mekong stretched before him, to where pink tendrils of mist caressed the far shores of Laos. He could hear the sound of distant engines but he couldn't distinguish the long-tailed boats that plied the waterway. Fishermen, he thought, but he couldn't be sure. He cast about for a place to hide but there was none. It was getting brighter with every second and he could see no other paths through the undergrowth that strangled the riverbanks. Instinct told him he needed to lose this place. He imagined he heard the sound of a shot in the trees from back the way he had come and it served to drive him on. Settling Wan more comfortably on his shoulders he waded out into the swirling brown water until it was deep enough to let it carry them.

He let the current embrace him, paddling now and then to stay as close to the riverbank as possible. If he were swept too far out he would be an easy target in the full light of day. Wan was conscious now, clinging to him. He placed his hand

gently over her mouth until her eyes told him that she understood she was not to make a sound.

The roar of engines further downstream warned him of
approaching danger. Then he saw the curving bow waves of
three long-tailed boats traveling at speed in line abreast and
approaching rapidly. From the way the occupants were sitting
rigidly upright he knew that they were not fishermen. They
were scanning the water, looking for something. They hadn't
wasted time. Radio, he thought. The word was out and there
was little time to find a hiding place.

Wan pushed him away then indicating that she was strong
enough to swim. A few strokes brought them under the overhanging foliage at the riverbank and Ryder knew that he was
in luck. A fallen tree lay with its branches hiding a deep cleft
in the earth where its roots had been torn free and they were
able to wade into a cave formed by a tangled growth of its
creepers. Underneath the tree roots it was dark and cool
enough to protect them from the sun and nearby, a flat rock
that had dislodged itself from the bank, enabled them to pull
themselves clear of the water. Ryder scooped great handfuls
of dark brown mud over his clothes and limbs until his head
resembled a black blob in which only the whites of his eyes
showed. Gone were all traces of his blond hair; he became
brown earth, part of their surroundings.

Wan smiled for the first time and copied him. Then she
curled herself into his arms and closed her eyes. Ryder lay for
a long time just content to feel the warmth of her body close
to his own. The river outside their refuge was indistinct
through the tree branches, but the sound of engines was constant and many times during the morning they came close
enough for him to hear voices above their roar, although
never close enough for him to see the occupants.

He tried to relax so that he could plan the next move.
The reason for their capture eluded him. How could they
have been any threat to Webster's plans? The bastard must
have panicked. Just like him, Ryder thought. Webster had
admitted as much, but why Webster had not killed him last

night when he had the chance, he could not imagine. He could only conclude that Webster either did not have the authority to do it, or else he was too scared. It was like him to leave the dirty work to others, he thought. Whatever the reason, it would be his undoing. Anyway, none of that mattered now, he told himself. What mattered was that they were alive, thanks to an old Legionnaire who had honored his vow. They were in relatively good shape and free to move in what had to be considered as enemy territory. It was purely a military exercise of escape and evasion now and for that, he had trained with the best.

Time passed slowly. Once, a snake came slithering down the bank close beside him and with hunger searing his stomach, he bared his machete to kill it but at that moment a boat came very close, its engine idling. Angrily, he watched the reptile slip into the water without a ripple to mark its passage.

Late in the afternoon he slept, becoming aware on wakening that the light overhead had dimmed without him noticing it. Boats were still speeding out on the river, although they seemed farther away now and less threatening. A water rat came then, scuttling out of the water onto their stone ledge only to stop suspiciously and sit on its haunches, testing the limp air with its whiskers. Moving quickly, Ryder dispatched it with one blow of his machete. He quartered it neatly and hungrily sucked at the bloody meat with no sense of revulsion but when he offered a section to Wan, she simply shook her head and turned her eyes away.

Darkness was not far off and Ryder felt better now. Soon they could move although his chest was still full of pain, and he could feel that his nose was twice its normal size, but thankfully the swelling around his mouth was fading, leaving only a steady throb of pain where his tongue found an empty socket in his upper gum.

A brittle clap of thunder echoed overhead just before the rain came, crashing overhead in the branches, and drowning out the gurgle of the river. Ryder smiled. Rain would serve them well and conceal their escape. He felt Wan jerk in his arms and he soothed her, cradling her. "Hush," he said softly. "Everything is all right. We're safe and we'll be able to go soon."

"Where, Lobbie? Where will we go?" Her voice was like that of a small child afraid of the dark.

"Into the river," he said. "The river will take us home. It will be difficult but we will do it. You must do everything I tell you, okay?"

"Yes," she whispered.

Ryder wondered at her faith in him. She had been tortured and raped and yet she could respond without thought of herself. Her resilience matched his own, he realized, loving her even more. "When we leave you must stay close to me," he said softly. "And when you are tired, you must rest and hold onto me. Do you understand, Wan?"

"I understand, Lobbie." Her voice was barely audible and a small shiver ran through her.

"We will swim in the strongest current and if we are lucky we will find something to help us. There are trees floating in the river. I saw them this morning."

She moved in his arms and he knew she was ready.

Silently they slipped into the water and swam out from beneath the covering that had protected them. It was black outside. Thankfully the moon was hidden by cloud. Ryder swam close to Wan, appraising her strength and waiting for the pull of the current as rain lashed the belly of the mighty Mekong bleeding to its delta in far-off Vietnam.

TWENTY-THREE

Wan was a fatalist. Her culture had taught her not to fear death for she held a deep seated conviction in reincarnation, but when she felt herself slipping away from the tree trunk as it rolled in an eddy that swirled with the strength of a python, she experienced momentary terror as the tree turned upside down. She had no strength left to hold on, and the slippery bark eluded her. The pain in the fingertips that had lost their nails was intense and the water had begun to feel cold. She sank beneath the surface with her fear turning to a feeling of peaceful contentment. There was a strange sense of pleasure in drowning, she thought. It took away the need to struggle. Perhaps The Lord Buddha would allow her to return in some form that would be free to enjoy the pleasures of life. Then she felt a hand tugging at her ripped clothing and found herself gulping air as consciousness returned. Nothing was easy, she thought sadly.

"Wan! Don't ever do that to me again!" Gripping her with an iron-like fist, Ryder choked on the water that had entered his lungs. He trod water until he regained his breath.

Wan clung to him, love surging out of her for this big oaf of a farang who had shown her an unwanted glimpse of a world that she could never have imagined in her worst nightmare. Then she smothered his face in kisses and wept for sheer joy, glad that she had not died.

The tree trunk that had carried them for many miles had deserted them now, and had lost itself in the darkness. Briefly she thought of where it might have come from, and where its journey would take it. Fate had brought it to them, and fate had taken it away. The Lord Buddha was good, she decided. He protected the weak.

"I see some lights, Wan! Over there! Look!" Ryder clutched her tightly and turned her so that she could see the faint glow of lights through the rain that still sheeted down. He rolled onto his back, holding her in his strong arms as his legs churned the water with renewed energy.

They reached the sodden banks of the river where rainwater cascaded from somewhere high overhead that she could not see and her legs went from under her, devoid of feeling. She felt him pulling her with one big hand as he staggered higher in glutinous mud.

The next thing she remembered was hearing the rustle of leaves stirred by a warm and comforting breeze. Opening her eyes, she saw stars far above in an inky sky that held no cloud. The rain had stopped. Frightened, she sat upright and looked around her. She felt a desolate sense of loneliness. "Lobbie!" She whispered his name, afraid to call out, but he was nowhere to be seen. Then she saw the river shining placidly in the moonlight below where she sat, and apprehension that he had not survived consumed her.

Not far away she could see the white dust of a deserted road, chalk-like as moonlight found it. Nothing moved there, and she could see no houses or lights anywhere along its length. She realized that she could be anywhere. Burma, Laos, Thailand. She started to cry softly.

Ryder re-joined her so silently that she didn't hear him until his hand touched her shoulder. "It's time to eat," he said, as she stifled a small cry of fear. He set a small bundle on the ground near her feet. It held a colored sarong, flip-flops, a plastic bag that contained a variety of scraps mixed with fried rice, and lastly, a couple of overripe mangoes.

They ate in wordless savagery, devouring everything that lay before them. Afterwards Ryder said, "A cigarette would be great now. It would finish off a perfect evening. I hope the clothes fit, but you had better rinse off some of that mud before you try them on; I want you to look your best! There's a stream just over there, near the road."

Her eyes widened in wonderment. "Where did you get these things, Lobbie?"

He laughed. "Don't even ask. Get changed first."

She shed her tattered clothes and tottered over to the stream. The water was clear and un-polluted, a product of the recent rain. Later, when the sun came up it would revert to a drain that carried the spores of dysentery. But tonight it was as fresh as the sky. Happily, she washed away the blood and mud that clogged her hair, combing it with her fingers.

When she returned he was still sitting where she had left him. His broad shoulders hunched forward, studying the moonlight on the river.

"Where are we, Lobbie?"

"I don't know exactly, but I think we are somewhere in miles south-east of Mae Sai, I'm not really sure."

"Where did you get the food?"

A slow smile spread across his battered features. "Are you sure you want to know?"

"Yes," she laughed. "It was good."

"It came out of a bin." He started to chuckle, "It's amazing what people throw away." He leaned towards her and kissed her on the lips. It was a kiss that lingered, sweet and memorable. "You look beautiful again," he said. "I'm glad the sarong fits."

She twiddled her toes. "The sandals are too big. Maybe you should take them back." She smiled.

"Too risky," he said. "The owners might wake up."

Wan put her arms about Ryder and laughed into his chest, stroking his shoulders, feeling the lump from yet another forgotten wound. She looked into his face, searching it, wanting to know how he felt. What were his recollections of the past days?

Were they like hers? Were there memories that he would carry to his grave, too? Would they add to all the other things that troubled him? Slowly she watched his smile fade as his face became serious.

He sat back from her, gripping her hands tenderly so that he wouldn't touch her fingertips. "Who raped you, Wan? I need to know. Was it just Webster, or was it both of them?"

She shuddered. "It doesn't matter, Lobbie," she said in a small voice. "You must forget it. What matters is that we are safe."

"I want to know," he replied fiercely.

She tried to fight back tears. "It was the tall farang."

"Webster!" The coldness in his eyes frightened her.

"Yes."

He sat facing her for some time, not speaking. Only the bleakness of his eyes spoke of what he was thinking. He looked at the blackened scabs forming at the tips of her fingers. "And these? And the burns on your chest?"

"Not him," she responded hollowly. "The other farang, before Webster . . ."

"What did you tell them?"

"I told them what they wanted to know."

His eyes were insistent, and she stroked his arm. "I told them we were on holiday," she continued. "They asked where I was from, where we had met, why we were in Mae Sai."

"What did you say?"

"I said that I was from Chiang Mai and that we had visited my family there."

"You told them nothing about Koh Samui?"

"No. They thought I was a bar-girl that you met in Bangkok."

Ryder looked relieved. "Good," he said quietly.

Wan felt an instant thread of fear. "We must go to the police and tell them about these men," she said.

He shook his head. "Not here," he said. "We cannot trust anyone here. Do you know of a man called Khun Sa?"

"Everyone in Thailand knows of him. He is a Shan

warlord who fought against the Burmese communists. Before, his name was Chang Chi-Fu. He is half Chinese, half Shan. He started the opium wars in 1967 before I was born, but he is very old now. Why do you ask me that, Lobbie?"

"Because he is why we can't go to the police, especially here."

"But, Lobbie, he's an opium smuggler and the police are searching for him. That is why he stays in Burma."

"And that is why Webster was here," Ryder replied. "He came to buy drugs and when he saw me, he panicked."

"Why was he afraid of you?"

"Because he knows me. He's married to my wife - ex-wife - Mark's mother."

The bitterness in Ryder's voice was not lost on her. Wan fell silent. "You are going back to England, aren't you?"

"Yes," he said sadly. "I have to now, but it will only be for a short time. Then I'll come back."

Wan knew that nothing she could say would change his mind. She fell into a gloomy silence.

"It's going to get light soon, Wan, and when daylight comes it will not be safe for us to stay together. You understand that, don't you?" She nodded numbly. "I want you to listen carefully and do everything I ask, will you do that?"

"Yes."

Ryder pointed down the nearby road. "There is a small village about a mile away. Mae Sai must be in that direction also. I want you to go to the hotel. When you get there, take the money and my passport with the airline tickets from the safe. Pay the hotel, but do not go to our room . . ."

"What about our clothes?"

"Forget them," he replied firmly. "It's too dangerous. Someone might be waiting in the room. When you're done, take a bus or a train to Bangkok. Leave my passport and half the money at the French Embassy. I think it is on Charoen Krung road. You can check. Afterwards go back to Koh Samui and wait for me there. Do you understand, Wan?"

"Yes, I understand, but why can't we go together?"

"If they are still searching for us, they will pick me out too easily. It's too dangerous for you. But whatever you do, don't go to your home in Chiang Mai. They know you come from there and they may trace your family."

Wan suddenly felt alone as though he had already left her. "I don't want you to go, Lobbie."

"I have to," he said. "Trust me; it will not be for long."

"You have no money," she said. "How will you get to Bangkok?"

Ryder smiled. "Let me take care of that. Just do as I ask. But be careful when you get to Mac Sai, especially in the hotel. You'll have to look casual, but be very alert. Only go to the desk if no one is hanging around watching it. Then get out as quickly as you can."

"I'll wait for you in Bangkok," she offered.

"No," he replied firmly. "I don't know how long it will take me to get there. I'll telephone you at the Princess Village before I leave."

She could see that he was eager to be gone. She heard the sound of a motorbike coughing into life far down the road. Soon the road would be busy.

Ryder kissed her and held her tightly to him. "Go now," he whispered, releasing her. "When the rains end I will come back."

Wan broke away from him with a heart that felt like lead. Meekly, she walked towards the road without stopping. Once she stole a backward glance towards where she had left him and she fancied he was still there, watching her. Then her tears came in a cascade and she started to run.

Ryder remained standing until he lost sight of her at the first bend in the road. He glanced at the sky and noticed the stars were already fading. Then he set off following a trail that led through trees in a southerly direction. There were many miles to cover. He would forage as he went, just as the Legion had taught him.

Twenty-Four

Ryder did not expect to find what he was looking for quite so quickly. At mid-day he reached a tarred road that scarred the hillside far above a valley that sheltered a number of remote mountain hamlets. The road appeared to lead in the direction he wished to take, but he realized there was more risk of traffic and if he used it, his chances of being spotted would be dangerously high. So for a while he held back and rested amongst the trees.

He guessed that a tarred surface meant that the road was a main highway. Two bus loads of tourists had passed him earlier; and judging by the villages in the valley below, he was probably now on a main tourist route to the hill tribes. These were the insular Akha, Yao, Lisu, and others who, Wan had told him, had emigrated from the borders of China many years ago. He had heard they were reclusive people who lived a frugal life, spurning the Thai culture and he knew it was unlikely that he could expect any help from that quarter.

Ryder calculated that he had covered about twelve miles, mostly uphill, since he had left Wan. At times, his chest ached abominably but his head remained clear. If it were not for his light canvas shoes he would be good for 30 miles a day, providing he had food and water; but hunger was now sapping his energy and he knew that he couldn't go on without eating. Thankfully, water had not been a problem; the recent rains had left the mountain streams full and uncontaminated.

He estimated that he was still roughly 450 or 500 miles north of Bangkok. Some form of transport was imperative. Perhaps not yet, he thought. That could come later when he had distanced himself sufficiently from Mae Sai.

Climbing high into the hills, he had met nobody on the dusty track even though once or twice he had come across isolated communities, but he had circled around them, keeping to the bush to make sure that he remained unseen.

Wan was constantly in his thoughts. Her safety concerned him greatly, and he knew that everything depended upon her success in retrieving his money and passport from the hotel. If she failed, Bangkok would present him with a multitude of problems.

He moved stealthily to another vantage point to get a better view into the valley. His hiding place was on the edge of the road close to where a track led steeply down to the nearest village. He could see no telephone or electricity cables, but he could make out the villagers far below. They seemed to be setting up stalls where the track entered the village proper. Minutes later he knew why.

Two honks of a horn further down the road resulted in increased activity in the village. A mini bus ground slowly up the hill towards him and pulled into a lay-by opposite to his hiding place. Ryder crouched low and counted six tourists emerging from the bus. They all looked hot and flustered, and two of them seemed bad tempered. It was obvious that they had driven for some considerable distance. Bickering voices reached him, the nasal tones telling him that they were Americans. The last passenger out of the bus confirmed it. He was a large ruddy-faced man wearing a Stetson and high heeled cowboy boots. His manner was disinterested, as though he had seen it all before, but even so, he raised a video camera and began to slowly pan the valley, talking all the while into the machine's microphone.

Ryder watched as a harassed tour guide rounded them up and led them off down the dirt track towards the village. So far so good, he thought. At their pace, he could forget them for at least an hour, perhaps more. The driver of the bus was another matter. He remained sitting in the driver's seat smoking a cheroot.

Carefully, Ryder weighed his options. There weren't many. He was miles from Bangkok and still too close to the river. People might be spreading a search even now, he thought. He could see several bags piled inside the rear door windows of the bus. He needed clothes badly, his own were in rags. He also needed money; but most importantly he needed a map. There had to be one inside the vehicle.

He considered his approach for a few minutes longer, reminding himself that it was not a military problem. There was no danger in this. All he had to do was to act normally and walk up to the driver and ask for directions. Then it would be simple to reach in and incapacitate him.

The driver simplified it even further. Just as Ryder was about to emerge from his hiding place, the driver opened his door and stepped out into the road, stretching. Ryder saw him walk to the edge of the lay-by and go behind some bushes. One minute he was standing upright, his head and shoulders in full view, the next he was squatting out of sight. Ryder nearly choked; the guy was taking a crap. He felt like laughing, but he wasted no time. He sprinted silently across the road and circled behind the bushes.

Squatting near a thicket of bamboo, the driver had his back to him. His trousers were around his knees and he held some tissue paper in his hand. The man heard nothing. Ryder moved swiftly across the intervening space and slid one hand over his mouth, stifling any sound, and then probed his neck with the other, seeking the pressure point. It was over in a second. The man slid away from him and crumpled to the ground. Ryder checked the pulse in his throat. He was still alive. Quickly he returned to the bus.

The keys dangled temptingly in the ignition. He might as well take the damn thing, he decided immediately. He reckoned he would have at least an hour before the alarm would be raised, maybe more if there were no telephone lines to the village. An hour was better than nothing. It was 50 or 60 kilometres less walking, if he drove fast.

For over an hour he drove as recklessly as he dared, content to be putting as much distance as possible between himself and Mae Sai. He saw little traffic except for a few trucks, and he passed those quickly. His progress was so good that he pushed on for another half hour, only pulling off the road when he met a Jeep containing two uniformed occupants in steel helmets traveling in the opposite direction. Police, he thought. Although they seemed to have paid no attention to him, it was time to abandon the bus. The alarms might be ringing.

He swung off the road at the first opportunity. The rutted track that he turned onto led into jungle where considerable logging had taken place. It ended in a large clearing in the forest where the red earth lay churned up by logging machinery. He stopped the engine and climbed out. There was no sound of engines, just the hum of insects busy among the trees. He concluded that it was long since abandoned and ideal for his purpose.

In the back of the bus he found a useful rucksack that contained a woman's clothing. Discarding the contents, he ripped off the baggage tags and identification label and buried them in a shallow hole. Another small holdall revealed a purse containing a small quantity of Thai money, enough to buy food for a day or so. In a zippered section he discovered $500 in crisp twenties. There was also a driver's license with a photograph of a woman's face and an address in Chicago. He pocketed the cash quickly and rummaged through other bags until he had outfitted himself with a couple of shirts, jeans that were a tight fit, and a pair of Reeboks that looked new and far better than the canvas shoes disintegrating on his feet. A search of the glove compartment provided him with a map and a packet of Marlboro cigarettes. Not his brand, but they'd do.

He didn't delay. Shouldering his newly acquired rucksack he set off back to the road, disposing of his old clothes on the way. By nightfall he was hammering up the miles, forcing a pace that even Sinbad would have crumbled under.

Twenty-Five

"I've decided to throw a house-warming party, Sid. It's expected of me really. I'll be seen as unfriendly if I don't." Critchley waited for disagreement. "Keep your distance; don't get too pally with the locals over there. Be friendly and don't upset anyone, but don't get too close," Phillips had already said. Now he just sighed into the phone.

"It sounds risky," he began.

"Look, a small luncheon party would be no harm, surely? Things are going fine. You've had three deliveries without a single hitch." Critchley paused for a moment and thought about Matthew Brennan. "One or two over here that are getting a bit nosy," he said. "I don't want to attract any more attention by not acting normally."

There was silence on the line while Phillips thought for a moment. "Okay." he said reluctantly. "Keep it low key though, that's my advice. Tell you what," he added. "Peter is away for a few days, if you put it off for a week, we'll both come over. It's time I had a look at the set-up over there."

Critchley stifled a groan. The last thing he wanted was a visit from Webster and Phillips, he thought. "All right" he said eventually, trying to sound agreeable. "I'll set it up and call you tomorrow." He hung up the phone and stared out of the window and across the fields. Out in the bay, the yacht snubbed quietly at her mooring. He was a fool to have even discussed it with Phillips, he decided. He should just have gone ahead and done it, and not said anything.

With three deliveries safely accomplished, the nature of his task no longer frightened him the way it had at the beginning. The pick up of the drugs had by now become routine, and only once had he suffered a delay when the weather was so bad that it precluded diving for two days. Diving took place mostly at night when the moon was full, or else on a day when the visibility was poor and mist shrouded the coast. He had even formed a close relationship with Nicholls, the diver who flew over from the North of England each time he was needed. Sometimes, the two of them sailed on to Crookhaven afterwards and remained there for a day or so with the cargo still on board. *Wind Song* had become a familiar sight on the coast and excited no undue attention and he knew that the locals saw him as just another eccentric English yachtsman with money to burn.

Who to invite? That was the question. He decided he would limit it to half a dozen people. Definitely he would exclude Brennan and Meadows, he thought firmly, there was no knowing what either of those two might say to Phillips about the house or what he had paid for it. He jotted the name of the Acton Hotel receptionist at the top of the list. He had met Helen Cullen several times on his trips into town. As often as not he had come across her in The Spaniard public house, where once, he had treated her to lunch and as yet they were only on speaking terms, but he planned to change that. His need for female companionship was becoming compelling and she had not hidden her interest, and he felt sure too, that she was not quite the angelic Irish colleen that he had taken her for on the first day of his arrival in Kinsale. He'd start with her, he thought, as he returned to the telephone and started to dial.

"Good to see you again, Richard!" Sid Phillips pumped Critchley's hand and thumped him heartily on the shoulder before following him into the house. Phillips and Webster had taken an early morning flight from London and were the first guests to arrive. To Critchley's surprise, Webster had also brought his wife with him. He greeted Imelda warmly when Webster introduced him, making a mental note to set an extra place in the dining room before lunch.

He took them straight to the drawing room where he had lit a fire in the grate. Imelda clapped her hands in delight. "How lovely and cozy," she said. "And the views! My oh my, Richard! How did you find such a lovely material for the curtains? They're such a delicate pink." She wagged a finger at him. "You've had help, I can tell that. There's the hand of a woman in all of this."

Critchley smiled and made no reply

Phillips looked around the room. "You've done us proud, lad," he agreed. "Peter told me it was a dump when he came over to see it first. You'll have to show me around, if we have time."

Critchley beamed. He could see that even Webster looked happy and it surprised him how well his enemy looked. Gone were the pale gaunt features and even Webster's eyes no longer looked as deep set as he remembered them. The face of the man now standing at the window looking out across the fields was deeply tanned and fresh looking, as though he had just returned from an overseas holiday. "You're looking well. Peter." he offered.

Phillips turned to him. "Peter has just returned from Thailand," he explained. "He's a lucky bugger don't you think, Richard? He gets to do the all expenses paid trips, while you and I keep the home fires burning!"

"Some people have all the luck," Critchley replied smoothly. "Now, what about drinks? Who's having what?"

"Gin and tonic for me," piped up Imelda. She admired herself in a mirror over the fireplace, fluffing up her hair.

"Sid?"

"White wine, if it's chilled."

"I'll take a Scotch, please," Webster responded.

Critchley crossed the room to the drinks cabinet. "Why don't you try Irish, Peter? I've switched to it myself. It's very good you know. It grows on one."

"If you insist."

As Critchley busied himself with the drinks, Phillips settled into a chair. "Is there somewhere in the house where Peter and I can discuss business, Richard? He only arrived back late yesterday, and we haven't had time to discuss his trip."

"Certainly." Critchley served the drinks. "Cheers everybody!" He turned to Phillips and clinked glasses. "I've made one of the upstairs bedrooms into a study; you can go up there if you want privacy. The others won't be here for ages yet."

"Let's do that." Phillips sipped his drink and walked over to the window. "That's a fine wine," he said, smacking his lips. "I must be paying you too much."

Critchley colored. He laughed off a stab of discomfiture. "I was thinking of asking you for a raise," he joked.

Phillips chuckled. "I might surprise you yet, mate!"

"Will you be all right down here, Imelda?"

Critchley shot a glance at Webster. He sounded anxious. Critchley wondered why.

"Of course, darling! I've got my book, and if I need another drink I'll help myself." She blew her husband a kiss.

"Perhaps you'll join us, Richard?" Phillips raised an eyebrow. "You're part of the team now, you know."

Critchley nodded. "Of course. Follow me."

Critchley led the way upstairs to his study. Though it was the smallest room on the top floor, it was big enough to contain a large leather-topped desk with a matching chair and two other armchairs. One wall was lined with the books that he had shipped over from London. A single window overlooked the walled orchard and the stable buildings at the back of the house. He waived his guests to the armchairs and seated himself at the desk.

Phillips closed the door and pulled his chair closer to the desk. "Well, Peter," he opened, looking intently at Webster. "How did you get on in the Far East?"

Critchley fancied he detected a flicker of fear in Webster's eyes, but it was momentary.

"Everything went as planned, Sid," Webster replied. His voice held no hint of unease. "We handed over the money and the stuff was immediately shipped to Bangkok. It's on its way already. They will advise us as soon as the ship leaves the Mediterranean."

"Do you trust them?"

"Yes I do. They are clearly interested in doing a lot of future business with us. Kung's contacts were very reassuring on that point."

Phillips relaxed in his chair and took a cigar from a silver case. "Good," he said. "There is a pile of money at risk." He twirled the cigar deftly in his fingers and sniffed it appreciatively, then he clipped the end with a tiny cigar cutter that he had taken from his pocket.

Critchley came from behind the desk and handed Phillips a cigarette lighter. "It sounds as though this is something special, Sid." He waited while Phillips lit up.

"Thank you." Phillips handed him back the lighter, blew out a cloud of smoke and contemplated the tip of his cigar. "This is the big one," he said eventually. "This is where we really clean up. Over two tons of pure heroin, just like the stuff that came over in the boat, and we made a bundle on that. After this shipment is cut, we could damn near retire!"

Webster smiled at Critchley knowingly, but he said nothing.

"Do you mean that, Sid? About retiring, I mean." Critchley hoped that he didn't sound as anxious as he felt. The though of getting out of this mess while he was still ahead was almost too much to bear.

"Not really. Figure of speech. I reckon we can go on a good bit longer. It's too easy to give up now. You've done a good job over here, Richard. Why rush out of it now? I don't mind telling you, that when we first started, Peter here wasn't too sure about you. I'm glad you proved him wrong."

Phillips peered at Webster through the cigar's haze. "So that's it, eh? Well done, mate. I'll have to call Frank Sullivan and congratulate him, too."

Webster stirred uneasily and took a long swallow from his glass. Critchley watched him as he waited. The signs were minuscule, but unmistakable to him. Webster was frightened about something. He was sure of it now. He wondered who this Frank Sullivan was.

"There was one small problem," Webster said in a low voice. Critchley noticed Sid's eyes narrowing as Webster swallowed hard. "We ran into Imelda's first husband in a place called Mae Sai up in the Golden Triangle. We were in a restaurant." He hesitated, wiping the palms of his hands on his trouser legs.

"Spit it out, Peter!" Phillips' voice rang in the room. There was a harshness to it that startled Critchley.

"We thought he was on to us...me and Frank, that is."

"You fucking panicked, is that it?" Phillips looked flushed and angry. His voice rose to a shout. "Why the fuck would he be on to you? Tell me that!"

"You don't understand," Webster protested. "We'd just met up with the Burmese and I got a shock at seeing him there. Jesus! He was sitting right next to me; I didn't know what he might have overheard. The whole thing got out of hand. When he started to run for it, the Burmese over-reacted. They snatched him and his girlfriend."

"You said nothing about a girl," Phillips snapped.

"Forget her, Sid, she was a whore. Anyway, stop flying off the handle. The fucker is dead."

"You killed him?" Critchley couldn't stop himself from joining in. He felt rising panic.

"As good as."

"What the fuck does that mean?" Phillips rose, his pock marked face looking oddly bloated.

Webster spilled some of his drink as he lifted his glass. He dabbed fussily at his trouser leg with a handkerchief. "The Burmese took him over the border to where we were to make the deal and hand over the money."

"And...?"

"And he escaped!"

"You are shitting me, Peter!" Phillips left a measured space between each word. In his rage he bit right through his cigar and was forced to spit a mouthful of tobacco onto the carpet. "I thought you just said that the bastard was dead?"

"Don't have a seizure, Sid. He drowned in the river. We didn't have to kill him."

"What fucking river, for Christ's sake!"

"The Mekong," Webster snapped back.

"Did you see the body?"

"No."

"Then how do you know he's dead?"

"Sid, there is no way he could have escaped. It was the rainy season and the river was in full flood. Frank will tell you the same thing. Sullivan was as satisfied as I am that the bastard drowned. Christ! We were miles from anywhere. The Burmese told us they'd often seen the river alive with crocodiles when it's in full flood, not to mind the bloody snakes they have out there. There wouldn't have been a body after a few hours. I saw a croc myself. Forget the gators you saw on your trip to Florida last year. Those were midgets by comparison."

Critchley had a hysterical urge to laugh, but he restrained himself. The thought that this could all too easily have been his fate took the humor out of it.

Phillips sat down heavily. "Okay, Okay. Calm down. Let's just recap on this. What does Frank Sullivan think?"

"He's not even worried, Sid. Sullivan saw the place too, don't forget. The Burmese searched every inch of that river and they were satisfied that he couldn't have survived. That was good enough for both of us." Webster fell silent. He looked calmer.

"There's nothing else? Nothing that you're holding back?"

Webster returned an even gaze to Phillips. "No, Sid," he said. "On my mother's grave, that's the truth of it. It was all a big mistake. Ryder happened to be in the wrong place at the wrong time. It shook us, that's all."

Critchley released his breath. He had been holding it for so long that his chest ached. "What did you say his name was? Ryder, was that it?"

Webster glared at him contemptuously. "Yeah. Ryder."

"And you said that he was Imelda's first husband?"

"Yeah."

"Does she know about this?"

Phillips showed renewed interest. He sat forward in his chair waiting for Webster to answer.

"No." Webster responded firmly. "I was going to tell her, but I decided not to. Too many questions. Although I'm sure she would be delighted to know that he was dead. She hated the bastard."

Phillips sighed. "At least you got that right," he commented. "What about the girl? What happened to her?"

"She's dead, too," Webster replied. "She was with Ryder; the two of them escaped together. They both drowned, Sid. There's no doubt in my mind about that."

The sound of a car horn out at the front of the house reached the room. Phillips got to his feet. "That must be your guests arriving, Richard," he said. "We'll have to leave it there but I think I've heard enough. It sounds like there's nothing much to worry about after all. There's no point in getting our knickers in a twist if it's unnecessary."

Helen Cullen was standing on the top step with her hand poised to ring the bell when the front door opened. She wore a black silk cocktail dress that buttoned down the front. It looked transparent in the sunshine so that her legs were outlined as long dark shadows. She smiled shyly when she saw Critchley. "I hope I'm not too early."

"Helen! I'm so pleased that you could come!" Critchley kissed her lightly on the cheek and she blushed as he took her arm to lead her inside. "I want you to meet some friends from London. Business acquaintances really," he said in an aside as they entered the drawing room.

"I'd like you all to meet Helen," Critchley announced. "We've become good friends since I came over."

Imelda wagged her finger at Critchley. "I knew," she said triumphantly. "I knew there was a woman's hand here somewhere!"

Critchley was saved by the sound of his other guests arriving in two cars. Martin Sheils arrived first. He was a shy slightly bohemian poet who was dressed all in black. Critchley had met him on a number of occasions, mostly in the Kinsale yacht club. He liked Martin, even though everyone else in the Club thought him a little odd, but there was something about him that reminded Critchley of his own better times in London. Sheils sailed a small wooden yacht mostly on his own, another reason that Critchley liked him.

Close on his heels was Colonel Dunlop and his sparrow-like wife, Kitty. Dunlop was Master of the Hunt and Critchley secretly hoped that Dunlop's presence might bring Webster some discomfort. The Colonel was a big beefy man who towered over his wife like some gigantic beast of prey, although he was surprisingly gentle in her presence. He was known for his love of gin, preferably Bombay Sapphire when he could get it. Critchley had ensured that he had a bottle especially for the occasion. He held up the bottle so that the sunlight from the window picked up its deep blue haze. "A drop of your favorite, Colonel?"

"Good Lord! Richard! How did you guess?" A great rumbling laugh erupted from Dunlop's belly. He pumped Sid's hand as though it was a lever, and then turned his attention to Imelda. "Charmed, m'dear," he said, kissing the back of her hand and holding it for a little longer than was necessary.

Helen Cullen stuck close to Critchley, as though doing so made her more comfortable. She was drinking brandy rather quickly, he noticed. Critchley refilled her glass and smiled benevolently. He was conscious of her nearness and the tantalizing scent of her perfume. "Enjoying yourself, Helen?"

"I think so. I didn't know you had such a lovely place, although everyone has been saying what a great job Harry Meadows did on it. The views are wonderful. I expect that you are pleased?"

Her breast brushed his arm and he shivered. "I'm delighted with it, but you need not tell Harry that. I hope," he said softly, "That this will not be your last visit."

Her face dimpled as she raised her glass to her lips. Colonel Dunlop had Imelda cornered near the fireplace. She looked flushed; whether it was her nearness to the fire or the effect of the drinks, Critchley couldn't be sure. He overheard her telling Dunlop that they were returning to London on an early evening flight. He smiled. Perfect. He couldn't wait to get rid of all three of them.

Critchley coughed politely. "If you would like to go to the dining room, there is a catered buffet waiting for us. I'm afraid you must help yourselves. Unfortunately, my resources do not run to having help."

Colonel Dunlop looked meaningfully at Helen. "Perhaps you should get married, Richard. Nothing like having a good woman about the house to take care of details, what!" Everyone laughed while Helen blushed attractively.

"If you'll excuse me for a moment, I need to set another place at the table. Don't rush your drinks. There's ample time." Critchley left the room.

In the kitchen, he took a small tin labeled "baking powder" from one of the cupboards and carefully poured two thin lines of white powder onto the worktop. With a straw he sniffed a line into each nostril and threw the straw into the waste bin. It was his new friend. He had made its acquaintance in the first shipment from South America. He extended his fingers and studied them for a second. Not even a shake.

He felt renewed strength flooding through him, bringing such a feeling of confidence that it surprised him. Even Webster was no longer a threat, he thought.

He left the kitchen and quickly reorganized the dining room table. Then he returned and led the others in to lunch.

With Philips and Webster finally off his hands and safely on their way back to Cork airport, Critchley finally felt able to relax. The lunch had gone well and even Webster seemed to have enjoyed himself. He closed the front door and went back into the sitting room where dark shadows were forming in the corners of the room. Outside, the sun sent shards of crimson into a far off wad of clouds. Only Helen Cullen now remained. She stood by the window silhouetted in the red glow from outside. Critchley placed his arm around her shoulders and drew her close as a low crackle came from the fire and its flames danced on the walls. She leaned into him, not resisting.

"It really is beautiful here," she murmured. Her words sounded slurred and she giggled. "I think I've had too much to drink."

Critchley took her glass from her. Pouring her another brandy, he said, "Dunlop was quite pissed when he left. He nearly fell down the front steps. Did you see him? I think his wife was angry."

Helen giggled again and began to weave her way to a settee. She flopped into it so that the hem of her dress rose in disarray. Her legs scissored in the firelight and the rustle of nylon reached him. He felt a surge of desire.

"What about Imelda? Peter had to virtually carry her to the car." Helen hiccupped and her giggle turned to laughter. "Pardon me," she said.

Critchley placed her brandy on a low coffee table and took a seat beside her. Gently he pulled her towards him and kissed her. Her mouth was slightly open in surprise and he tasted the brandy on her lips. For an instant she stiffened against him as though she was unsure of what was happening.

Then she seemed to melt into him, before pulling away and reaching for her brandy.

"Cheers," he said raising his glass.

"I don't mean to pry," Helen said, "But what do you do, Richard? You and Sid and the others?"

Critchley's face clouded for an instant. The question was inevitable and had to be faced, he knew. "Oh, this and that. Property investment, import export, that sort of thing. I'm lucky. I can work from home on the telephone or the internet. Sometimes I have to go over for a meeting with them or to sign something, but that's all."

She seemed satisfied and sipped at her drink. "Are you from Kinsale," he asked.

"No. Not originally, that is. My parents had a farm in Kildare but I don't go there much. My father drinks a lot. It's not a place I feel comfortable in any more. It's too depressing. I have a flat in town not far from the hotel." She looked at her watch and put down her glass, "It's getting late, and I should be going."

Critchley embraced her. "What's the hurry," he whispered into her hair. "Why don't you stay? You shouldn't drive anyway."

"I thought you'd never ask." She kissed him, a wet openmouthed kiss, as her dress rode higher and his fingers plucked at its buttons.

TWENTY-SIX

Matthew Brennan heard of the party at Clonbar House from Seamus Collins, the fisherman, the day after it took place. Delicately, he picked up the plastic bag of prawns that Collins had thrown on his desk and placed it on the floor.

"They're fresh, Mattie, don't you know? I only caught them this morning." Collins sucked on a rotten tooth and smiled apologetically.

Brennan gave a noncommittal grunt. "Getting back to what you were telling me," he said. "Who was there?"

"Well I didn't actually see them, now. I explained that already, so I did. It was the chef up in Acton's that told me about it. I delivered fish there this morning and he said that Helen Cullen had been bragging to the other girls about it. Apparently there were a couple of blokes over from London. One of 'em had his wife with him; the other was on his own. Then there was old Colonel Dunlop and his wife. Martin Shiels was there, too. From what I heard, it was quite a do. They had wine and all that sort of thing. Burke's delicatessen did the catering." Collins stared at Brennan for a moment, his eyes questioning. "You told me to tell you anything I heard," he said hopefully. "They even had caviar."

"Caviar!"

"Yes. Fish eggs, from the sturgeon. I wish we had a few of them fish around here. They're worth a fortune, so they are."

"I know what caviar is, you bloody fool!" Brennan struggled to regain his composure. The auctioneer frowned so that
his bushy eyebrows met like old friends in the centre of his
forehead. "These guys from London," he said. "What did they
look like, Seamus?"

Collins returned a vacant stare. "How should I know? I
told you I didn't see any of 'em. What does it matter what
they looked like?"

"Well, I don't suppose it matters in the least. I just wondered what sort they were, that's all." Brennan smiled disarmingly. "Thanks Seamus." He fumbled in his pocket, extracted
a twenty Euro note and handed it to the fisherman. "That's
for the prawns," he said.

"I'd have thought he would have invited you, Mattie,"
Collins commented as he pocketed the money. "After all you
sold him the place, and your brother-in-law did it up. He
should have been there too, if you ask me. Where would
Critchley be now? Without the both of you?"

Brennan reddened a bit and looked away. "Well he didn't,
that's all there is to it. These Brits can be ungrateful bastards,
Seamus. You know that as well as I do."

Collins stood up, leaving a damp patch on the chair from
his oilskin trousers. Brennan's nose crinkled, detecting the
smell of rotten fish as the fisherman moved towards the door.
"Thanks for the twenty," Collins said.

"For nothing," Brennan replied. "There's more where that
came from. Keep an eye on Critchley for me, Seamus, if you
would. It's important."

Collins paused for a moment with the door to the street
half open. A damp breeze rustled the papers strewn on Brennan's desk. Collins pulled a knitted hat down on his head so
that it covered his wispy hair. Brennan noticed that the cap
had fish scales and spots of dried blood on it. "Why are you
so interested in Critchley, anyway?" Collins asked.

"Business, my man. Just good business. It's good to keep
tabs on what is going on around the town, especially when it
comes to strangers like Critchley. You never know what leads

it might land you in this game. Not that it's any of your business." Brennan glared at Collins. "Close the door after you."

The fisherman showed his blackened teeth. "Keep your pants on, Mattie! I was only asking." He slammed the door hard enough to rattle the glass panes in the frame.

"Nosy fucker!" Brennan muttered. He returned to scanning the morning newspaper but he couldn't concentrate on it. No matter how hard he tried, he couldn't take his mind off Critchley. He felt frustrated and angry with himself for revealing so much interest to Collins. Mother of God! He'd accommodated Critchley in every way he could. Made money for the bastard, too! And then not to be invited to the party...did Critchley think he wasn't good enough company for all his society friends? As if that little piece, Helen was...eventually he could stand his feeling of outrage no longer and he left the office for an early lunch.

Halfway down the street, Brennan almost collided with Helen Cullen as she came out of a shoe shop. She was clutching a shopping bag and appeared to be in a hurry. He drew in a sharp breath and stopped. "Morning, Helen!" Brennan smiled, using his bulk to block her path.

"Oh! Hi! I'm in a rush, Mattie. I was supposed to be at work ten minutes ago." She tried to side step.

"New shoes I see," Brennan commented, holding his ground. "I hear you have a new boyfriend now as well." Brennan tried to make a joke of it, but knew from her face that he had failed

"Helen's eyes flashed angrily. "That's none of your business, Matthew Brennan!" she snapped. "That's the trouble with this damned town. Everybody wants to know everyone else's business."

"Well, I did hear you were invited to a party out at Clonbar House yesterday." he persisted.

At that, she looked startled. "It was not a party. I was invited to lunch, if you must know. Now please, I have to get to work." She pushed past him and hurried up the street.

Brennan turned and watched her for a minute until she

disappeared down a side street leading to the harbor. A snappy little bitch, that one, he thought. If she gets her nails into him, Critchley might yet regret it.

The thought pleased him, but he made a note to himself to be careful. If Helen was blabbing to the staff in the hotel, she might yet be the key to finding out what he really wanted to know about Richard Critchley and the source of his money.

TWENTY-SEVEN

A minor heat wave had settled over London as Ryder's plane from Thailand nudged its way into its disembarkation point at Terminal four. Although it was early morning, Ryder could feel the heat penetrating the fuselage and the air-conditioning seemed suddenly unable to cope with it. Perspiring passengers were already clogging the aisle and he found himself trapped in his seat. He felt groggy after the flight even though he had slept through most of it. He ran his hand over his jaw and wished he had taken the time to shave earlier before the toilets became blocked. He noticed that none of his fellow passengers looked fit enough to face a full day of activity either, but that was of little consolation. He found space and left his seat to join the crush forming to leave the aircraft.

As he pushed his way towards the door he reminded himself that he was lucky to be here at all. The frustration of Bangkok yesterday was still fresh in his mind and it was only assuaged by his relief in finding that Wan had done all he asked of her and had left his passport and tickets together with money at the French Embassy. His one abiding comfort was that although he had not been able to get through to her on the phone before he left, he felt sure that she was safe and would already be back in Koh Samui. The thought of that freed him to do what he had come back for, and that was to kill Peter Webster. Every hard earned mile of the road to Bangkok from Mae Sai had branded hatred on his brain.

Two names, Webster and that of an Irishman named Frank. Even at the town of Fang, where he had been able to hide and find rest in a truckload of teak logs traveling south, his hatred had not diminished. Webster had become a monkey on his back that he was determined to get rid of.

Carrying only a light bag containing a change of clothes that he had bought in Bangkok he cleared customs and emigration without difficulty. Then he collected his kit bag that he had left in a storage facility before the flight out and followed the signs to the Underground.

The train was crowded and he was forced to stand, but it was only a short ride before he emerged into brilliant sunshine in Hammersmith. He looked about him, squinting in the sun. Nothing had changed except for the weather. It was hard to believe that he had been gone for only a few weeks and he realized how much he still disliked the place. He had forgotten how early it was; the banks had still not opened. He crossed the street and found a cafe opposite to a branch of Barclays'.

Taking a seat near the window, he sipped his coffee and tried to formulate some sort of plan of action. He didn't even know where Webster lived, he realized. All he knew was that Mark had told him a long time ago that Webster and Imelda were still living somewhere in London. It occurred to him then that he hadn't thought of Mark in days. Had his ghost finally left him?

London was a big place. Ryder sipped his coffee and contemplated how many Peter Webster's he would find listed in the telephone directory. Probably hundreds he realized numbly. He felt defeated by the size of the task facing him. He wasn't a detective, he thought. He was a soldier. Suddenly he needed a drink so badly that it frightened him. He searched for his watch. Jesus! He didn't have one, he realized. Those bastards out in Burma...

Gloomily, Ryder collected another cup of coffee and stared through the window at work-bound faces hurrying by, faces of uninteresting people that he had never seen before and would never see again. Finally he saw movement over at the bank as the doors opened. He drained his fourth cup of coffee and hurried from the cafe.

A cashier slid a piece of paper across the counter. "That is your current balance, Mr. Ryder," he said, stifling a yawn. The teller's expression said it all; the amount was trifling, not worth worrying about. Ryder glanced at the slip of paper. Seven thousand. He realized gloomily that he had gone through three thousand in a few weeks. "I'll take it in cash," he said. "Close the account, I'm moving on." He watched the teller riffling through a pile of bank notes, knowing that if he still wanted to open that dive school on Chaweng beach he was going to have to watch his expenditure, otherwise he could forget that idea for good.

The Hammersmith library was an even greater disappointment. Ryder dumped a pile of telephone directories on a vacant reading desk and settled down to what he knew would be a time consuming task. An hour later he was still adding to a scribbled list of Webster's in a notebook, all of which were annotated with the letter P or the first name, Peter. His stomach rumbled telling him it was time to eat, but the futility of his task dulled his appetite. He realized that he was searching for the proverbial needle in a haystack. There had to be a better way, he thought. This was not going to work unless he had the luck of the devil. Suppose the bastard had an unlisted number? It would be just like Webster, especially if he was now living on the fringe of the law. Even the internet was unlikely to throw anything up on the bastard, he realized.

Angrily he slammed the last book shut so that the noise resounded around the room and a discreet cough from someone nearby reminded him where he was. Mark came then, flickering into his mind like some comic demon. He was laughing and dancing that infernal jig of his that had driven Ryder to desperation so many times before. Mark always chose such a time as this, he thought. It was as if he knew that he was beyond caring and was at his most vulnerable.

Ryder glared at the scribbled pages of names and addresses from all over London; he could hear himself on the phone already. "Hello, is that Peter Webster? The one married to Imelda? The one that raped a girl in Thailand!" It was so ridiculous that he almost wanted to laugh himself and join Mark in his insane scream of derision.

What else did he know? He tried to think clearly. He knew a man named Frank something or other - an Irishman. A lot of good that was, he thought. The Irishman could be anywhere, and anyone. If he couldn't even locate Webster, what chance had he of finding a man simply known to him as Frank. The thought was too ridiculous to even contemplate. Then he remembered Hennessy. Flicker Hennessy, who lived in Dublin, and could be found in a club called the Mandarin. Suddenly he was aware that Mark was no longer laughing hysterically. His son was smiling now, and fading from his mind. Ryder fished in his pockets and lit a cigarette.

"No smoking, mate, not here in the library."

He looked up to see a man at the next table staring at him. Further away, a plump female librarian was already leaving her counter and making her way towards him. "Sorry," he said, grinding out the cigarette on the floor. "I wasn't thinking."

The man grunted something and returned to his book. Ryder folded his sheets of notes and stuffed them into his shirt pocket. He looked about him. Shafts of sunlight filtered through grimy windows set high up in the walls of the room, and dust particles hung suspended in the beams of light. Dublin was the key, he decided. At least there, he had an address - a starting point, even though there might be little chance of finding a connection between Hennessy, Frank, and Webster. He was going to have to tackle this whole affair differently, he realized. There was no quick and easy answer. The growing complications made him feel exposed and vulnerable. He might even need a weapon, he decided. Then he remembered Corporal Klein in Hamburg. He still had Klein's address somewhere in his kit bag. Hans would help him get started. He was family.

TWENTY-EIGHT

If anything, it was hotter in Hamburg than it had been in London. Ryder vaguely remembered someone on the plane telling him that the whole of Europe would experience a drought before the summer ended, and even though he was wearing light clothing and a silk shirt that he had bought in Bangkok, the air was humid and his clothes clung to him. The smell of his own perspiration told him he needed a shower too, but there was no time. It would have to wait.

Evening shadows shaded the narrow streets off the Reeperbahn in St. Pauli as Ryder left the cab that had brought him from the airport. The taxi driver pointed to a narrow opening beside a run down theatre where lurid signs promoted a live sex show. Ryder thanked the driver and paid his fare.

He entered a lane that was just wide enough to allow a car to pass. On either side there were closed doorways topped by emergency exit signs, but at the far end he picked out a battered garage sign hanging precariously over the entrance to a workshop. The doors to the garage were rolled up and he could hear the sound of a compressor coming from somewhere inside. He reached the entrance and paused. Inside, a bulky man wearing greasy overalls was paint-spraying the wing of a Mercedes. He didn't look up when Ryder walked past him.

At the rear of the workshop he found a lighted, glass-fronted office. Through the window he could see a faded pin-up poster on a wall and a steel filing cabinet in one corner. He hammered on the door and pushed it open. There was no one in the office, although an open program illuminated a computer terminal. He heard the sound of a toilet flushing, then a second door opened and Klein limped into the room.

Klein stopped in surprise, his face widening in a grin of recognition. "Ryder!" he shouted. The German grabbed his hand, pumping it up and down furiously as he slapped him on the back. "Come in, come in! What are you doing here!"

Ryder's sense of pleasure at seeing his old comrade surprised him. Klein dumped a pile of greasy service manuals from a chair and pushed it towards him. "Sit down," he said. "This calls for a drink."

"It's good to see you, Hans. I'm glad I found you." Ryder slumped onto the chair feeling oddly light-headed. The Legion suddenly leapt into focus, bringing a pang of regret that he had ever left it behind him.

Klein rummaged excitedly in a desk drawer and pulled out a bottle of schnapps. He sloshed the spirit into two china mugs with oily fingerprints around the rims and handed one of them to Ryder. "A toast to old times," he said. "Prost, my friend!"

"Prost, Hans!"

Ryder took a long swig from his mug and felt fire hit his belly. "So, you've settled down, Hans. How's the leg?"

"Good. I can walk well now. Soon I won't even need a stick." Klein's eyes twinkled over the rim of his cup. "What about you? You didn't get that tan of yours in Europe. The summer has only started here."

"I went out to Thailand for a holiday."

"A sex holiday, eh!" Klein roared with laughter. "You should read the papers, Ryder. Even a bishop was caught sneaking back from there recently. Ever heard of a place called Pattaya? He said he went there for a third world charity seminar."

Ryder laughed. "Yeah, I know all about Pattaya, but I never went there. From what I heard, I doubt if there is any charity work going on in a place like that."

"I'd say he was fucking his brains out!" Klein snorted. He took a long swallow from his mug and eyed Ryder expectantly. "How long will you stay? Hamburg has more than Thailand to show you, I can tell you that."

Ryder's face clouded for an instant. "Not long, Hans," he replied. "I've got business to attend to. That's why I'm here. I need your help."

"Anything. If I can do it, I will."

"I need a car, Hans."

Klein laughed. "Is that all! No problem, just tell me what you want. Cars are what we Germans are good at."

"Something reliable but cheap, enough to take me a few thousand miles before I dump it."

Klein waved his mug towards the office window. "That Mercedes out there, I can let you have it for eight hundred. It was crashed but we've put a new gearbox in it and patched it up. The engine is good."

Ryder glanced into the workshop. The mechanic had just finished spraying. He heard the sound of the compressor splutter to a halt. "That'll do me fine," he replied. "Is that your brother out there?"

Klein poured more schnapps into their mugs. "No. That's Klaus, our mechanic. What he doesn't know about autos is not worth knowing. My brother has given the garage to me to run. He's off doing something else now."

"Things are going well for you then? I'm glad."

"I can't complain," replied Klein. "Sometimes now, I don't even miss the Legion."

"Have you heard from any of the others?"

"No."

"Nor have I." Ryder hesitated for a moment, aware that Klein was watching him. "I need something else as well, Hans."

The look of welcome on Klein's face faded a bit. "I thought you might." he said. "You didn't come all the way to Hamburg to see me, or just to buy a car."

"No. I need papers; a passport, driver's license, that sort of thing."

Klein pursed his lips and thought for a moment. "I know a man," he said eventually. "He can do that, but it will cost you more than the car."

"I realize that," Ryder replied.

"You want them quickly and in a different name, right? Not your own, I mean?"

"Yes, that would be best."

There was a moment's silence during which Ryder studied Klein. There was no change to his narrow battered features, the moustache, or those arrogant brown eyes. "You've put on a bit of weight I think, Hans," he commented.

"Unfortunately." Klein patted his stomach and smiled loosely. "I don't get the same exercise anymore. But you," he said. "You look as if you might be just back from a war zone." His eyes were quizzical. "Someone did a job on your face too, by the looks of it."

Ryder avoided his gaze for a moment as he wondered how much he should tell him. "I got into a bit of a scrape out in the Far East," he said slowly.

Klein nodded. "Woman trouble, I'll bet?" His eyes twinkled.

"Something like that." Ryder extended his mug. "I think I need another one." As Klein poured the drink, Ryder took a deep breath. "There's something else, Hans." Ryder saw renewed suspicion leap into Klein's eyes. "I need a weapon."

"A pistol?"

"Yes."

"That's not too difficult," Klein replied eventually. "We can get one from the same man."

Ryder looked up and fixed the German in a steady gaze. "With a silencer."

Klein shook his head uneasily. "A silencer is a different matter, Ryder. That costs money."

"Forget it, then," Ryder responded flatly.

A tap on the door interrupted them and the mechanic poked his head inside. "Auf wiedersehen, Hans!"

Klein smiled at the mechanic. "Ja, auf wiedersehen, Klaus." He turned to Ryder. "The mechanic is going home," he explained.

Ryder watched the mechanic switching off the lights in the workshop. He noticed it was dark outside, the only light coming from the hissing neon sign over the door. "What about the gun? Can you do it, Hans?"

Klein didn't reply. Instead he picked up the phone, dialed a number and spoke rapidly in German. He placed his hand over the mouthpiece and looked at Ryder. "How soon?" he asked.

"Quick as you can. I'm running out of money."

Klein said something into the phone and replaced the receiver. "Tonight for the pistol, tomorrow for the papers. You will need photographs. We'll get them later."

Ryder felt exhausted. He tried to think how long it was since he had slept in a proper bed and he couldn't remember. But he would sleep tonight without worry. "I owe you, Hans. I won't forget it." he said.

Klein shrugged. "You owe me nothing, my friend, but you will need five thousand euros for what you want, in cash."

"That's steep."

"That's because you are in a hurry. If you can wait a week or so...."

Ryder shook his head. "No, it's not a problem. I can't wait around."

"It must be very important to you."

"It is. Did I ever tell you about my son, Mark?"

"No. I didn't even know you had one. You only told me that you were married once." Klein seemed disinterested.

Ryder reached for the bottle. "I cut him out of my life after the marriage ended, and I regret that now. Maybe if I hadn't done that he would still be alive. After we got back from Somalia the first time, I spent six weeks in hospital, you remember that?"

Klein nodded and picked up his mug.

"I was convalescing in Marseilles, I had a bit of leave coming when I got a message telling me he was dead so I went over to Ireland to bury him. I found out he had been doing heroin. It was supposed to have been an overdose, but there was more to it than that. He crossed up some dealer over there." Ryder paused and lit a cigarette. "Anyway," he said. "I came back and tried to forget it, but I couldn't. It fucked up my head and after the Mogadishu raid things got a lot worse. That's why I quit." Ryder stopped.

Klein rocked back in his chair and stretched out his artificial leg. "I wondered about that," he said. "Some of the lads thought you had gone soft."

Ryder smiled coldly. "Maybe I did. I didn't know what to think anymore. After I saw you in the hospital I went to London and it didn't work out, but while I was there I met up with Mark's old girlfriend, another junkie. She ended up under a fucking train. I think she was thrown under it. Anyway, I went to Thailand after that. On the way out there I heard about some other kid who was in the shit with the same dealer in Dublin, some guy called Hennessy. About ten days ago, up in the North I ran foul of a guy called Peter Webster - he was Mark's stepfather - that son of a bitch was out there setting up a heroin deal and he thought I had rumbled him, so he tried to pull down my curtains." Ryder stubbed out his cigarette viciously. "So now I've got a score to settle. I'm going to put the bastard in his box."

Ryder stared into space for a moment. He'd said enough, he thought. There was no point in mentioning Wan or what had happened to her. Nor did he want to divulge his plans to return to Koh Samui. He glanced at his watch but realized he still did not have one. All he knew was that it was late, and the bottle of schnapps was almost exhausted.

Klein massaged the joint of his artificial leg absentmindedly. "You are embarking on a very dangerous mission, my friend," he said slowly. "If these people are in the drug business they are not to be messed with. You do realize that?"

Ryder nodded. He thought of Wan, and wondered what she was doing right at this minute. "There's more to it, Hans, but I don't want to go into it right now. It's something very personal, but that bastard Webster has been a thorn in my side for a long time now. Its time to pluck him out."

"Even with an army it would be difficult. I know these people, Ryder." Klein waved his arm expansively. "Right here in the Reeperbahn, it's full of them. How else could I get you the things that you need so easily?"

Ryder felt a twinge of anger. "Don't try and talk me out of it, Hans."

"I'm not. I'm just trying to warn you about what you might be getting into."

Ryder lit another cigarette. It was not getting any easier to do without, he thought. There was the sound of music filtering in from the nearby streets. The night was coming to life and he felt suddenly hungry.

"I need to find a hotel, Hans. Not too expensive though. I think I've spent enough for one night."

Klein reached for his walking stick and stood up. "There's one right around the corner from here. I can get you company, if you like."

"Sleep is what I need, Hans, not company."

Klein laughed and then he belched. He picked up the bottle and studied it. "First," he said, "We'll finish this, and then we will eat. Afterwards I'll take you to see someone who will have your pistol ready."

Ryder could feel the schnapps taking its effect. He squinted at Klein. They had never been friends. On the contrary, he had disliked Klein as much as anyone else in the squad. Now he felt a deep sense of gratitude.

He put down his drink. "You are a good friend, Hans, thank you."

"For nothing. Wir sind kamaraden." Klein raised his mug. "Prost!"

"Kamaraden!" Ryder mouthed the word, hearing again that strange song of the Legion. He swallowed the remainder of his drink not wanting to reveal the emotion that suddenly welled up inside him.

A small raised balcony area overlooking the main hall provided the only space for dining at the beer hall where Klein brought him, and the smoke and noise from the main area below offered a constant challenge at their table. There was only one advantage, Ryder realized immediately. The noise level masked any sounds of nearby conversation.

Ryder pushed away his empty plate as Klein ordered more beer. The food rested uneasily in his stomach but his strength was returning and he felt less light-headed.

Klein grabbed his arm, pointing downstairs. "See that table right at the back, Ryder, the one with six guys sitting at it?"

Ryder sought it out with difficulty. The noise coming up to them was clamorous. "Yeah," he said.

"Ex-Legionnaires," Klein shouted in his ear.

"Para's?"

"No." Klein's voice was disdainful. "Infantry. I know a few of them. They meet here every Friday night. They like to act the hard men. You know - singing the songs and all that shit when they have enough drink in them." His voice changed. "Your man has just come in." Klein waved to someone far below near the entrance amongst the crush of bodies pouring into the beer hall.

The man who came to their table could not have been more startling. He was a hunchback who walked with a sideways shuffle as though his hips were disjointed and out of line. His hair was more green than yellow, and tied in a pony tail at the back so tightly, that it stretched the skin of an ash white face. His eyes were mere slits. It was impossible to determine their color. Klein introduced him as Gustav. The hunchback refused to sit down and made no attempt to shake hands.

Klein leaned across the table. "Gustav is Danish," he shouted. "He doesn't speak English, but he is probably the best gunsmith in Europe. Follow him to his car."

Ryder nodded and got to his feet. He realized that he was a full two feet taller than the Dane. Obediently he followed the strange creature that pushed and shoved a passage through the crowds on the ground floor until they reached the door.

Outside, the street was thronged with people, mostly men, all making their way past the more garish nightspots. It was a melting pot for all the nationalities of the world. Many were seamen. Jews rubbed shoulders with Arabs, Turks with Koreans. Some were just nervous voyeurs, but all had that air of expectancy common to men seeking sexual relief.

He followed the hunchback inside an amusement arcade where a myriad of machines whirred and clicked under blinding white neon lights. At the rear was an instant photo booth, Gustav pointed at it and smiled. Minutes later the Dane took the strip of photos that Ryder handed him and beckoned for him to follow. He moved so quickly in his odd sideways shuffle, that Ryder found it difficult to keep up with him against the tide of humanity that funneled down the street. Gustav's gait reminded him of the bloodless crabs that appeared in darkness to scuttle about the deserted beaches in Koh Samui.

Gustav climbed into the back of a large BMW saloon that was parked in a side street under a street lamp, leaving the rear door open. Ryder got into the back of the car, feeling soft plush leather seating under him. The engine was running inaudibly and the dark outline of another man filled the driver's seat. The nearby streetlight provided light and it was refreshingly cool inside as the air conditioning whirred softly.

Without speaking, Gustav handed him a small zippered holdall with the word "Nike" emblazoned in white on the outside. Ryder unzipped it. Inside was a pistol and two clips of ammunition. He removed the gun and looked it over carefully. It was a 9 mm semi-automatic having an eagle engraved on its slide, and the name "VIS" etched within an inverted triangle on the butt. It felt heavier than other automatics that he had handled, but it was well finished and had obviously seen little use.

Gustav slid closer on the rear seat and grinned slyly. "Sehr gut, eh! Polish pistolen."

Ryder checked both magazines. The clips held eight cartridges, both were full. "How much?" he asked.

"Zwei thousand," Gustav replied swiftly.

Ryder eyed him warily. It was expensive, but the eyes staring back at him were uncompromising. It was a seller's market.

"Okay," he said. He pulled a bundle of notes from his
pocket and counted them out on the seat. "What about the
passport?"

"Tomorrow morgen," replied the Dane. He jerked his
head over his misshapen shoulder. "Garage, mit Hans," he
said as he pocketed the money.

Ryder nodded and left the car. He stood for a moment on
the pavement as the car moved away. Then he returned the
way they had come.

Klein was still sitting at the same table where he had left
him. A Bavarian band had taken to the stage, adding to the
deafening clamor downstairs where the crowd was roaring its
drunken approval. He looked at Ryder with an unspoken
question in his eyes.

Ryder placed the holdall on the floor by his feet. "Everything's okay."

"Good. More beer?"

Ryder nodded. "Why not."

Dawn was not far away when Ryder returned to the hotel
that Klein had taken him to earlier. Only a few drunken stragglers were making their way homewards in the streets. The
concierge handed him a key and his kit bag as he carefully
counted the money Ryder gave him and pointed towards a
coal-black stairway.

Ryder found his room on the top floor, after twice taking
the wrong corridor. The bed was unmade and still warm from
an earlier occupant. There were sticky semen stains on the
pillow and he threw it into a corner of the room in disgust.
Without bothering to switch off the light, he fell onto the bed
fully clothed and fell asleep instantly.

He woke as sunlight searched the window, feeling disorientated and unsure of where he was. His head was pounding and when he moved, the pain in his chest became so unbearable that he thought he would vomit. He collapsed back on the bed and stared at the ceiling while he waited for the pain to subside. The sound of someone coughing penetrated through the thin walls separating him from the next room and the naked light bulb suspended from the ceiling swam before his eyes. Instead of one, he could see two bulbs.

Slowly, his eyes focused and he was able to sit upright and risk getting out of bed. To his surprise, the shower located in a squashed recess in the room worked well. After his shower, dressed in clean clothes, he felt as close to normal as a surfeit of German beer would allow. He put the bag containing his pistol inside his kit bag and left the room.

Klein was waiting for him when he arrived at the garage. The German's reddened pupils reflected his own misery and it satisfied him to know that Klein felt as bad as he did himself. "That was one hell of a night, Klein," he said.

Klein gave a sheepish grin. "Like old times. Will you take some coffee?"

"Please. Make it strong and black, no sugar." Ryder noticed that the workshop outside was empty. "Where's the car?" he asked.

Klein poured boiling water into a grease-spattered coffee maker. "Klaus has taken it for a test drive. I told him to make sure it was in good order. I wouldn't want to sell a friend a heap of shit."

The coffee was scalding but it steadied his nerves. Ryder belched, tasting the sauerkraut that he had eaten the night before. "I feel like dog shit," he said.

"You look like it too," Klein replied.

"Speak for yourself." Ryder began to laugh, but he stopped quickly as his head started to pound. "Gustav told me he would have the papers here this morning. Can I rely on him?"

"He'll be here," replied Klein. "Where there's money to be made, that fucker is more reliable than a Volkswagen."

The mechanic returned with the Mercedes and got out to open the hood. Ryder watched him fiddling with a screwdriver inside the bonnet as he revved up the powerful engine. Then he slammed down the hood and switched off the motor. He glanced at the window and gave the thumbs up sign.

"You want to try it out, Ryder?" Klein poured more coffee.

"No, I'll take your word for it." Ryder counted money out on the desk and Klein stuffed it into a drawer.

There was a light tap on the door. Gustav sidled into the office, "Guten morgen." He handed Ryder a German passport and a driving license. Ryder flicked through the pages. He didn't know what to look for in forged documents, but these looked excellent. The name on both documents was Helmut Heinecke. "These look good," he said, putting them in his pocket.

Klein spoke for Gustav. "He's the best," he said. "I doubt if anyone will pick you up with those."

Ryder handed over another three thousand euro, wondering just how much was left of his dwindling funds.

Gustav nodded at him, getting up to leave. He paused and said something to Klein "You need a phone?" the German asked. "He has a very good Samsung."

"No thanks. I don't need one where I'm going. They're too easy to trace."

Gustav smiled knowingly. "Danke," he said and shuffled outside to where his car and driver waited at the entrance.

"He's a strange bastard," Ryder commented as he left.

"I wouldn't like to cross him," Klein replied.

Ryder got to his feet and stretched. There was no point in delaying longer. He extended his hand. "Thanks for all you've done, Hans," he said. "I won't forget it."

Klein shook hands and picked up his walking stick. "If you've got any sense, Ryder, you should forget all about this man Webster and get on with your life." As he walked with him to the door, Ryder noticed that his artificial leg seemed to be dragging more than it had the night before.

Ryder threw his bag into the back seat of the Mercedes

and got into the front. He wound down the window and looked at Klein standing in the doorway. "One other favor, Hans?"

"Sure."

"Keep everything I told you to yourself."

Klein's face tightened momentarily. "Of course," he said. "Good luck!"

Ryder started the engine and drove off. When he reached the corner of the street he glanced in his rear-view mirror. Klein was still standing in the open door of the garage as though he was lost with nowhere to go. He lost sight of him as he turned right into heavy traffic.

Klein remained in the doorway for some time before he went back inside. His face was troubled. He returned to the office and stared blankly at the computer screen. Eventually he laid his stick against the side of his desk and picked up the telephone. Then he thumbed through a grubby address book and dialed his brother's mobile number.

"Gunter?"

"Ja."

"It's Hans. Where are you?"

"On the autobahn, just outside Rostock. I'm on my way home."

"Does the name Peter Webster, from London, mean anything to you?"

"No, why should it?"

Klein felt a wave of relief. "It's nothing. It's just that he's in the same line of business. Someone is looking for him. I thought he might be one of your contacts."

"I never heard of him. The name means nothing, but I'll check."

The phone hissed in Klein's ear as though the signal had just faded out for a second. "Are you still there, Gunter?"

"Yes, I just went under a bridge." The voice was weaker now. "I'll talk to you this afternoon when I get back."

Klein put down the telephone and wandered out into the

workshop where Klaus was backing an Audi into the service bay. He felt edgy and almost unclean. Ryder had saved his life back in Guyana, of that he was sure. The others would have left him there. Forget it, he thought. He had given Ryder what he wanted. The slate was clean.

Twenty-Nine

Peter Webster knew there was trouble the minute Sid Phillips entered his office. Sid's familiar self-important strut was gone, and the man looked more like a deflated football than the rotund and jaunty Phillips that he had seen only that morning. Phillips threw a folded newspaper on his desk. "Read that," he snapped.

Webster unfolded a creased copy of the *Irish Times*. His fingers twitched as he spread the newspaper on top of his desk to read the headline in extra large bold type. "Second Journalist Brutally Slain in Broad Daylight."

With rising panic gnawing at his stomach he read of the murder of a journalist, Monica Flaherty, in Dublin the day before. The words swam before his eyes. Shot three times in the head at close range, he read. Thought to be a gangland hit by contract killers. Irish Government in an emergency session promises a crackdown on organized crime.

He finished the article and looked at Phillips helplessly. Sid was fidgeting with the ring on a finger of his left hand as he always did when something worried him. "Does this mean what I think it means, Sid?" His voice faltered in the stillness of the room.

Phillips coughed. "Probably... no... oh, shit! I don't know, Peter. Why do you always expect me to have a fucking answer for everything?"

"It's Sullivan, isn't it? She was on to him."

Phillips shrugged. He seemed to be regaining his composure. "I don't know, Peter. I haven't spoken to him and I'm afraid to call him in case they have his telephone bugged. It's in all the English papers too. The media are going mad. Even our PM has taken enough interest in it to speak to the Irish prime minister."

"I warned you about him, Sid. I told you we couldn't trust his kind."

"I know, but there is nothing we can do about it now. If Sullivan is behind this, as they seem to think he is, he must have been forced to do it. He's not a fool. Remember, we don't have all the facts yet."

"Have you spoken to the Chinese about it?"

"Yeah. They're checking on it right now. They're going to call me back."

Phillips stood up and started to pace the office restlessly. Webster watched him. He had never seen Phillips so agitated. It worried him even more than what he had just learned. "The paper said that they expect early arrests. If . . ."

"I know what the fucking paper said, Peter," Phillips shouted. "For Christ's sake, leave it off, will you! Like I said, we don't know what went down yet. Even if the cops do pick up Sullivan, he won't crack. You can be sure of that. That's not what worries me."

"What then?"

"The next shipment, that's what. It's due next week and it's the biggest yet. We might not be able to move it if Sullivan is under threat."

"And Critchley?"

"That little shit is your problem!"

"My problem?"

"Yes, yours."

Webster gave Phillips a cold look. "Well, I suggest we waste the bastard now and replace him with someone more to my liking."

"You would, wouldn't you?" Phillips sneered. "Where would that get us? I ask you? Critchley is the least of our problems."

Webster eased himself from his chair and went over to the drinks cabinet where he poured himself a large brandy. He swallowed it quickly. The drink steadied him and he poured another before returning to his desk.

Phillips studied the gaming floor, his hands clasped behind his back, deep in thought. At that moment Webster hated him. He could see all his plans evaporating before his eyes, all because of a goddamn Paddy terrorist that Phillips had forced on him. Restlessly, Webster joined Phillips at the window. "Shit!" he exclaimed. "How did he get in?"

"Who?" Phillips appeared startled.

"That bastard in the pinstriped suit over at the blackjack table. I barred him two weeks ago. Excuse me, Sid. I'll have to go and take care of him." Webster hurried from the room closing the door behind him.

Phillips watched as Webster made his way through the crowds down below. He knew that whatever else he might think of him, Webster ran a tight ship where the Club was concerned. As for the rest of it...he knew all about Webster's little scams, he thought. Even Webster's earlier dealings in small amounts of dope were no secret to him, and they had largely died out since he had moved to more lucrative pastures. Phillips saw Webster collect a bouncer from the door before cutting the punter from the herd and firmly guiding him towards the entrance. He smiled. It was all done discretely. None of the other gamblers had noticed a thing.

No doubt it might be a different matter at the door. If there were no witnesses, Webster would personally reinforce the barring order. No, Phillips told himself, when it came down to it, Peter rarely shirked what was required of him.

The telephone on the desk rang. Phillips walked over and picked it up. "Speaking," he said quietly. He listened intently to the voice at the other end of the line. "Good," he said. "I'm delighted to hear that. Is there anything you want me to do from here?"

Phillips gazed at the wall, his face a blank. "Okay," he said after a pause. "We can do that. No, it's not a problem, leave it to me. Is there anything else?" There was a long pause while Phillips listened and fumbled in his pocket for his cigar case. "That's a different matter," he said eventually. "No, I don't think it's serious. We can handle it. I'll be in touch. Leave it with me."

Webster returned to his office to find Sid sitting in a trance behind his desk, smoking a cigar. Instant irritation flooded through him.

"Did you get rid of him?" Phillips expelled a cloud of smoke so that his features were hidden for an instant.

"Yeah." Webster poured himself another drink and sucked on the knuckles of his right hand. "He won't be back," he said.

"What did he do, anyway?"

Webster turned to face him. "He tried to work a card scam. There were two of them at it, him and a woman."

Phillips sighed. "Sit down, Peter," he said softly. "I want to talk to you. I've just spoken to Mo Kung. Sullivan is okay for the moment, but he's gone to ground. That reporter was about to dish the dirt on him and he had to take her out. But now there's another problem, and it's potentially more explosive."

Webster felt a cold thread of fear penetrate his brain. "Now what?" he groaned.

"You told me he was dead," Phillips spoke evenly, without emotion, as he watched Webster's face for a reaction.

"Who?" Webster fought for time and his hand trembled as he raised the glass to his lips.

"Ryder."

Webster jumped. He stared across the desk at Phillips. Sid's eyes were cold. "He's dead, I'm sure of it," he whispered.

"No, Peter. He's alive, and he's looking for you."

Webster felt a thin film of perspiration breaking out on his forehead. He dabbed at it with his pocket-handkerchief. "How do you know?"

"Mo Kung told me that a guy in the German organization was tipped off by his brother. Apparently, this guy's brother and Ryder were in the Foreign Legion together, and Ryder went to see him yesterday in Hamburg. Ryder told him he was going to do you. I don't really know what stunt you pulled on this guy out in Thailand, but whatever it was, you are in deep shit, mate!"

Webster pulled himself together. "I can take care of Ryder," he muttered.

"He sounds dangerous. He's a wild card in this other mess," Phillips replied. "I don't want him sniffing around here."

"I'll take care of him if he turns up, Sid. What else can I do?"

"I think you should get out of London for a while. I've been thinking it over and so has Kung. With Sullivan having to lie low, we can't rely on Critchley to handle the size of the next shipment on his own. I want you to go over there and take charge of it. It will kill a few birds. Sullivan was to have brought over money in the last few days, but he's afraid to move while the heat is on. You can pick it up and bring it back with you. Besides, it will get you out of here for a while."

Webster could not disguise his dismay. "Sid," he said. "I hate Ireland, I don't see the point."

Phillips' face flushed with anger. "Just do it, Peter!" he snapped. He leaned back in his chair and exhaled a thin curtain of smoke. The corners of his mouth were set as he spoke. "It's for your own good."

THIRTY

Late evening shadows were already hiding some of the unsightly tenement buildings when Ryder drove slowly along Gardiner Street in Dublin, but the pavement was still full of small knots of youngsters enjoying the warm evening air. He pulled into the curb outside a dilapidated terrace house where a sign advertised B&B. Switching off the engine, he studied the building for several minutes, realizing that the average passer-by would not give it a second glance. He was getting good at this, he told himself.

He climbed out of the car and pulled his bag out of the boot. His muscles felt cramped, like compressed springs. It had been a long drive, and apart from occasional pit stops for food and fuel, he had driven virtually non-stop from Hamburg. He had rested in Paris only briefly, after buying a sleeping bag and a few other essentials in an army surplus store. On the ferry from Le Havre, he had slept.

Shouldering his kit bag, he glanced up and down the street. Each house had an identical steep flight of steps leading up to the front door but the building next to the one he had selected looked derelict and empty. A group of teenagers lolled on its steps, appraising him steadfastly with pinched street-wise expressions. Ryder walked over to them and dumped his kit bag on the pavement. He pulled a twenty-euro note from his pocket. "The car's not worth much," he said. "It's left hand drive and it doesn't go very fast anymore. If it's still here tomorrow morning, complete with wheels, you get another tenner. Savvy?"

The oldest youth, not much more than fourteen, gave him a sly look. He reached for the money. "You've got it, mister."

Ryder studied them sternly. "Fuck it up and I'll break your legs, okay?" He smiled, picked up his bag, and mounted the steps of the doss-house. He pressed the bell push and entered a gloomy hall that held a rancid smell like lingering bad breath. An overfed black cat scurried past him and disappeared down the steps into the street. Then a door at the end opened, allowing light to spill through from the kitchen. An obese woman in a filthy pink dressing gown switched on a light and looked him up and down, a cigarette dangling from her bulbous lips. Behind her he could see bedclothes spread on an airing frame around a coal-fired range that might have dated back to the last century and he heard the sound of a television or a radio. He flashed her a smile that was meant to be pleasant. "Do you have a room?" He asked.

She nodded and the ash spilled from her cigarette, but she didn't remove it from her mouth.

"How much?"

"Thirty-five a night, in advance." Her voice was husky. "Breakfast is between eight and nine," she added.

"I'll take it," Ryder said, handing her the money.

The woman selected a key from a rack on the wall near a coin-operated telephone. "Room five," she said as she handed him the key. "Second floor. The second key is for the front door. House rules are no females in your room." With that she disappeared back into the kitchen, closing the door firmly behind her.

Room five was little different from room twenty-five in Hamburg. The same threadbare carpet that could have been bought from the same store and it had a narrow window with glass that was opaque with filth. A bed with springs that squeaked under test, and a midget's bathroom containing a shower that reeked of disinfectant, hair clogging its drain. The only difference was a fly-specked picture of the Sacred Heart over the head of the bed.

Ryder went to the window and looked down on the street. The teenagers were still where he had left them, proprietary eyes on his battered Mercedes. Good, he thought. He flopped on the bed fully clothed and fell asleep instantly.

It was dark when he awoke. A faint breeze stirred unfamiliar curtains at the open window. He walked over and looked down, good, the car was still where he had left it.

He shaved and showered, feeling better immediately. Dressed in clean clothes, he sat on the edge of the bed and clicked a clip of ammunition into his pistol before slipping it into the waistband at the back of his trousers. He put on a loose fitting jacket and checked himself in the bathroom mirror. The bulge was not too obvious, but he would be happier with a gun of a smaller caliber; it felt too heavy. He returned to the room and fumbled in his kit bag for a small coil of stainless steel wire and a roll of duct tape, which he stuffed into his jacket pocket.

Downstairs, the hall was still in darkness. He found a light switch at the bottom of the stairs, made a note of the telephone number and stepped into warm air. A figure detached itself from the shadows. "Your car's still here, mister, we're looking after it."

"Good lad," Ryder said quietly. "What's your name?"

"Jimmy," the boy replied.

"Well, Jimmy, how do I get to Rathmines from here?"

The boy gave him directions. "Are you coming back?" he asked.

"Yes, but I might be late."

"Okay," Jimmy said. "We'll be here. Don't worry, we'll watch out for you."

Ryder patted the boy on his shoulder, unlocked the door, and climbed into the car. The traffic was light and Jimmy's directions were faultless. He glanced at the dashboard clock as he entered Rathmines; eleven o'clock.

He felt hungry. The lights of Rathmines were familiar, surprisingly so. He slowed as he passed the house on Grove Road where Mark had lived and glanced up at the lighted windows trying to remember which one had been his. He saw that the bicycle was still there, chained to the railings. A year from now it would still be there, he thought sadly. Then the house was gone, but he still felt its nearness, and a small shudder of bitterness ran through him.

He pulled in and parked outside a steak house that was squashed between a church and a dry cleaner's. His stomach rumbled as he went inside. Later, over coffee, he sat at a table near the window and watched the crowds passing by. Hopeful faces in the streetlights, and girls wearing light summer dresses or tee shirts that showed their breasts. Across the street he could see a pale moon rising over the rooftops and he thought of palm trees swaying in a warm breeze, and of Wan, somewhere far away waiting for him. At that moment he felt like the loneliest man in the world.

He finished his coffee and glanced at the watch that he had bought on the ferry. It was nearly midnight. He paid his bill and got directions from the waitress.

The Mandarin Club was no different to thousands of others. Ryder thought he might have been there before, but knew he had not. A long bar sold watered-down spirits and beer from taps, all at prices that reflected the lateness of the hour and there was a jammed dance floor heavy with the scent of perspiration and cheap perfume. In defiance of any ban, smoke hung in swirling clouds over a litter of sodden tables, techno music throbbing, the constant beat of sex moving the bodies of those jamming the room.

Ryder ordered a pint of beer and settled himself on a high stool at the bar, further down he could see four bar tenders working feverishly to supply the insatiable demand for drink. One looked older than the others and seemed to be in charge because he was the only one not wearing a nametag. He was a heavyset man with a stretched waistband and a Pancho Villa moustache that glistened with sweat. Thin reeds of black hair covered his balding scalp. Ryder caught his eye and beckoned him closer.

"What can I get you, pal?" The man shouted to make himself heard, his voice nasal and true Dublin.

"Whiskey chaser."

The barman slid a glass of amber towards him. "Eight euros," he snapped.

Ryder counted out the coins. "I'm looking for someone," he said.

"Isn't everyone!?" The barman smiled.

"A man called Flicker Hennessy."

The barman's eyes narrowed for an instant, just long enough for Ryder to recognize the warning sign. "He's not here right now. Come back later." The man moved away quickly and stationed himself further up the counter, but Ryder knew he was being watched. A little later he saw the barman pick up a telephone at the end of the bar. So far so good, he thought.

Ryder ordered another beer from a passing waitress whose nametag read "Deirdre." He sipped it slowly. He knew he should pace himself. It might be a long night.

An hour later, as the place was filling up, he felt someone pushing closer to the bar beside him. "Are you the guy looking for Flicker?" The voice in his ear carried a trace of a lisp.

Ryder glanced over his shoulder. The man standing close to him was short, perhaps only just over five feet tall. His face was round and nondescript, his smile genial, but the brown eyes were wary as though he was summing him up. "Yes," he replied.

"He won't be here tonight." The man grinned, his face friendly.

"That's a pity."

"Why?"

"I was told I could get some stuff from him."

The short man's face hardened for an instant. "I don't know you," he said. "Who told you that?"

"A guy in a pub. I'm new in town." Ryder flashed a casual smile.

The man sipped from a pint of Guinness, leaving a thick stripe of creamy foam across his mouth. He put the glass down and passed a hand across his lips. "What kind of stuff?" he asked.

"Coke."

The eyes studying him flashed a warning. "That's heavy," he said. "We only deliver."

Ryder scribbled the address of the B&B and his room number on the back of an empty cigarette packet and handed it to him.

"Be there in an hour," the man said quietly. "I'll see what I can do. Have a hundred in cash, understand?" Ryder nodded and the man faded away into the crowd.

Ryder took his time and drove slowly back to Gardiner Street. He pulled nearer to the curb and drove more slowly as he entered the street. Nothing seemed out of place and few people were out so late, but a new looking BMW was parked half way up the street, looking out of place in the drab surroundings. No one was in it as he passed.

He stopped outside the B&B. No sign of Jimmy or the other kids. For an instant he was worried. He didn't want to come out tomorrow morning and find he didn't have a car.

Ryder inserted his key in the front door and stepped into the hall. The lights were on, just as when he had left but there was no sound coming from the kitchen and briefly, he wondered if he was the only person in the house.

He climbed the stairs and fumbled with the lock on his door. The light bulb in the corridor was no longer working, he noticed. Had he left the light on in his room? He couldn't remember, but it was in darkness now. He pushed the door open. Without warning, a powerful torch flashed in his eyes and he felt a fist bunched in his jacket hurling him into darkness.

The lights came on instantly and he felt a boot thudding into the side of his head as he sprawled on the floor. He tried to get up and another boot took him in the ribs, filling his chest with agony as he rolled into a fetal ball to protect his face. Jesus! Did the Legion teach you nothing, he thought desperately. In the corner of his eye he saw a pair of black Doc Martin's close to his face as their owner bent to frisk him. Ryder moved with all the pent-up fury that he could summon. He rolled and grabbed the two feet, heaving upwards with all his might, lifting the man clean off his feet and hurling him across the room, hearing the glass in the window shatter as the man's head penetrated it. He was on his feet now. Vaguely, he saw a second blurred figure coming at him. He whirled then, delivering a lightening-fast muy thai kick that landed with such force that he felt the man's ribs crack as his chest collapsed.

It was all over quickly, but the room was in a shambles. One leg on the bed had broken and the mattress leaned at a drunken angle towards the floor. The contents of his kit bag were strewn around the carpet, and the empty dresser drawers gaped open like mouths without teeth.

The man with the broken ribs sat up clutching his chest. He let out a weak moan. Ryder booted him in the face and saw his nose explode in a bloody mess as though he had just kicked an over-ripe tomato. The second man sagged near the window, blood filling his eyes from a multitude of facial cuts. Ryder gripped him by his hair and hurled him against the wall, letting him slide into a sitting position on the floor.

Breathlessly, Ryder sat down on the lopsided bed. "Now," he said softly. "Which one of you two is Hennessy?"

Neither answered, they just stared back at him blankly. "Me ribs," one of them moaned.

Ryder picked up his pistol that had skidded into a corner of the room. He flicked off the safety catch, and there was an audible click as he cocked it. Carefully he inserted it into the man's open mouth. "It's not your ribs, pal, it's your brains this time. I asked you a fucking question!"

The eyes staring along the barrel of the gun were like saucers. Whoever had sent these two goons didn't know what he was doing, Ryder realized. He withdrew the gun and stood up. "Hands behind your backs!" he shouted. "Just stay sitting, and extend your legs with your feet together!"

They did as he ordered. Swiftly he wound strips of duct tape around their wrists and ankles, then he dragged them back to the wall and propped them against it. He went to the door, opened it, and listened. No sound came. The house remained as silent as a tomb in spite of the noise they must have made.

He wondered how they had got in. It was irrelevant, he told himself; he should have known they would be there. Get sharp, he reminded himself viciously, remember your breeding. Remember what you've learned, or you are dead.

Ryder closed the door soundlessly and returned to squat on the edge of the bed. He studied the men for a full minute, sizing up their strengths. The eyes of the man with the smashed chest seemed to be wavering. It made his decision easy. Ryder stood up and brutally clubbed the other man on the head with his pistol and watched him slump onto the floor.

"Wotcha do that for? He didn't do nuthin'." The man with the crushed ribs started coughing. Pain etched his features as blood dripped steadily from his nose.

Ryder sat down on the bed again. He smiled "So that you can tell me what I want to know," he replied. "Unfortunately for you, you're the weak link in the chain, mate." He placed his pistol on the bed beside him and lit a cigarette. "Let's start again," he said. "What's your name?"

"Paddy."

"Okay, Paddy. So neither of you is Hennessy? Is that a good guess?"

The man made no reply. Ryder sighed wearily. "It doesn't have to be like this, Paddy, but you're making it difficult."

He stretched out his foot and prodded the man's chest. He increased the pressure tentatively and was rewarded with a scream of agony. "Now, Paddy," he said slowly. "You're getting the message. Your pal over there is out of it and will never know you snitched. I've got all the time in the world to make you understand, savvy?"

The man nodded glumly.

"Good, I'm glad we understand one another." Ryder smiled. "Now, I want to know what Hennessy looks like, where he lives, and where I can find him. All that kind of stuff. You're going to tell me, and if you don't, you're going to die. It's your choice. I don't really give a shit either way, because I'll find him anyway."

Paddy's mouth sagged open. His eyes showed that he understood perfectly.

Ryder looked at his watch; it was just after two o'clock in the morning. "You've done the right thing, Paddy." he said. "Don't feel bad about it. No one will know, and you've saved your mate's life as well as your own." He wound duct tape around the man's head, gagging his mouth, and then severed the end with his combat knife. He did the same for the other man who was still unconscious. Then he re-packed his kit bag and left the room.

He reached the hall where the floor squeaked under his weight but there was no other sound, then he noticed that someone had switched off the downstairs lights. So much for not being heard, he thought. That bitch in the back knew all about it. He had been set up and the thought of that annoyed him intensely. He should have been better prepared. Angrily, he yanked the telephone cable out of the wall as he made his way to the front door.

The street was deserted and there was again no sign of Jimmy or the other kids. He started the car and drove down to where the BMW was still parked. He stopped in front of it and got out. Then he slashed all four tires with his knife before driving off into the night.

To Ryder's surprise, Rathmines was still alive with small clumps of people making their way home. Many of them were drunk and because the night was warm, they lingered in the streets as though they had no homes to go to. Through the open window, he heard the sound of voices singing on the night air. It drew him back instantly into the bosom of the family and he remembered campfires, long distant memories, that lingered still.

He found the block of flats without difficulty and drove past it. At the next corner, he turned left into a street where trees lined the road side and the black faces of sleeping houses were set well back from the road. He parked there and walked back.

A short flight of marble-like steps led to glass doors that showed a vestibule where he could see a collection of potted plants and a pair of elevator doors, one of which was open. There was a plush look about it that surprised him. Hennessy was obviously living well. The doors refused to open when he pushed against them. Then he noticed a keypad set in the wall next to a panel of bell pushes and a small communication speaker. Damn! He thought. He retreated to the bottom of the steps and looked up at the balconies above him. A few windows showed lights but no one moved overhead. Without climbing gear, there was no way up, he realized. A lawn surrounded the building with thick shrubbery huddled close up to the walls. Ryder withdrew into the shadows and waited, he was rewarded almost instantly.

A taxi slowed to a halt at the pavement, and the sound of giggling and stifled laughter rang on the night air. A young man and a woman got out and the cab drew away. The couple climbed the steps close to where Ryder remained hidden. The man had his hand on the girl's bottom, kneading it gently. She snuggled closer to him as he keyed in a code. The scent of whiskey was heavy in the air as she dropped her handbag and her giggle became laughter. The door clicked open and they staggered inside.

Ryder leapt silently up the steps and inserted a cigarette packet in the door before it closed. He stepped back from the entrance and watched them cross to the lift. Oblivious to his surroundings, the man had the girl's dress up now as his fingers searched her panties. The door of the lift closed and in spite of lingering pain in his chest, Ryder took the emergency stairs two at a time. He came out on the top floor onto an L-shaped landing. Four apartment doors faced the elevators. He crossed quickly to number fifteen and pressed the bell. There was no response. He pressed it again and held his ear to the door. He could hear nothing from within. Either Hennessy was sound asleep or else he was not back yet.

Probably the latter, Ryder decided. It was not yet three o'clock. The nature of Hennessy's business obviously involved working unsociable hours, he thought dryly.

To his left, he saw a small area containing some indoor plants with heavy foliage, a coffee table, and a small settee. Ryder removed a light bulb from a wall fitting in the recess and settled down on the settee to wait.

Ryder was at the point of dozing off when he heard the click of electric doors followed by the whine of an ascending elevator. The doors swished open and a man walked confidently towards number fifteen with a key in his hand. Hennessy was alone. Ryder recognized him instantly from the description he had dragged out of Paddy earlier. He was on his feet in a flash.

As Hennessy stepped into the open door of his apartment Ryder hit him with a powerful chop to the back of his neck, sending him flying into a softly lit living room. Then he stepped inside and closed the door.

Hennessy lay prone on the floor. Ryder quickly searched the single bedroom, the bathroom and the kitchen. He relaxed; there were no other occupants. They had the place to themselves.

He dragged Hennessy across the carpet and propped him up in a soft, grey leather armchair. Swiftly, he wrapped duct tape round Hennessy's upper arms and the chair, leaving his hands free and he sat down on a matching leather settee facing his captive. Pulling a glass topped coffee table closer, he placed his gun and knife on the table and took stock of his surroundings.

A cheap form of affluence stifled the room, but it looked unlived in, as though Hennessy had been unable to establish his presence here. He let his gaze wander back to the slumped figure in the armchair, to the man he held responsible for the death of his son. Hennessy's clothes were casual but expensive looking, he noted. They covered a scrawny body that had sticks for arms and legs. His hair was unfashionably long, falling in thick strands over his face, momentarily hidden on his chest.

Hennessy stirred. His head snapped back and his eyes opened, then widened in surprise. "You!" The word was indistinct and slurred; it hung in the air like a cloud.

The word hit Ryder like a punch in the stomach. He jerked upright. "Do you know me? Who told you?"

Hennessy snorted derisively. "You think you are smart, don't you? Go fuck yourself, Ryder!"

Lost for words, Ryder stared at him. Disbelief flooded through him. Hennessy even knew his name! How? Ryder shook his head, knowing he had to regain control. "You set me up tonight, Flicker. It wasn't a friendly sort of thing to do. I'd like to know why."

Hennessy turned sullen. His face was good looking in a petulant sort of way, Ryder thought. "I know all about you, we've been expecting you. Your name is Ryder, or are you using your German passport now?" he sneered.

Ryder felt a cold shock of surprise. "I'd like to know how you know that," he replied coldly. But even as he spoke, he remembered Klein. A member of the family had betrayed him and the thought was evil. The reason didn't seem to matter.

"Fuck you!" Hennessy struggled, unable to release himself.

Ryder sighed wearily and stretched out his legs. "I've been through this once tonight already with a couple of your friends, and I'm getting tired of it. I'm going to kill you,

Hennessy, I want you to know that, but whether it is easy or
hard is up to you. It makes no difference to me."

Hennessy remained silent as Ryder searched his face. "I'm
a good judge of character, Hennessy, you need to believe
that. When I look into a man's eyes I know whether he can
stand pain or not, and administering pain has been my calling. I'm good at it, you understand?"

Hennessy jerked in his chair and spat at him. The small
globule of saliva landed harmlessly at Ryder's feet, white on
the maroon carpet. Ryder moved swiftly then. Snatching up
his combat knife he got to his feet and reaching over, he
jerked Hennessy's head back by the hair and severed his right
ear. Then he returned to his seat and threw the bloody ear
and knife carelessly on the glass topped table. "Let's start
again," he said softly.

A tiny whisper of sound issued from Hennessy's mouth.
The swiftness of the action horrified him, he was beyond
screaming. Numbly he watched his blood trickling down the
shoulders of his jacket, and then he became aware of searing
pain. His eyes returned to the ear that leaked a sticky pool on
the table.

Ryder lit a cigarette. He exhaled a cloud of blue smoke
nonchalantly, and then he turned to Hennessy. His voice was
sharper than the knife. "I'll cut you up piece by piece if I have
to, you had better understand that, and only you can prevent
it. I wonder why people call you Flicker? Is it because you
like to use a knife too? You killed my son, Flicker. He's dead
because of you."

Hennessy's eyes widened in astonishment. "It's occurred
to me that maybe his death was not accidental." Ryder continued. "What did you cut his fix with? Was it rat poison or
something even worse?"

Hennessy's face paled. He opened his mouth but no words
came. Beads of perspiration popped on his forehead.

"You're a dealer, Flicker. You peddle in death. I'm looking
for a man called Peter Webster. Do you know him? He's in
the same business."

Hennessy shook his head. Drops of blood fell in small blobs, staining the arm of his chair. "Never heard of him," he muttered.

Ryder picked up his knife again. "Are you sure of that?"

"Yes! For Christ's sake!"

"I believe you, Flicker." Ryder smiled reassuringly. "We're getting places now," he added. "What about a guy called Frank something or other? An Irishman like yourself."

"Don't know him."

Ryder took one long step, inserted the tip of his knife in Hennessy's nostril, and jerked it upwards, slitting the nose neatly. Hennessy issued a low moan as Ryder returned to his seat.

Hennessy felt blood flowing down into his mouth, he gagged on the taste of it. His eyes rolled frantically. "I'm going to bleed to death!" he howled.

"Yes, you are, unless you get honest with me. Answer the fucking question!"

"His name is Sullivan." Hennessy's voice sounded choked, as though he was drowning. "He warned me to look out for you."

"Excellent." Ryder stubbed out his cigarette and put the butt in his pocket. "I wonder how he knew? Where does he live?"

Hennessy hesitated. Ryder picked up the knife and the words flowed from him in a torrent. "He lives somewhere near Galway, near a village called Moycullen. I don't know exactly where, I've never been there. He's IRA, Ryder; he'll fuck you, as sure as shit!"

"Maybe, but I doubt it. Describe him."

"I've never met him. I don't know what he looks like. He's the main man." Ryder made a small movement as though to get up. "I swear to God, Ryder, it's the honest truth. Sullivan operates from a distance. I only get to meet his go-betweens."

"Who are...?"

"You met them already."

"Ah! Paddy and his pal!"

"Yeah." Hennessy's voice was a croak of despair.

Ryder lapsed into thought for a moment. If Sullivan was the same man he had met out in Burma, he would recognize him. How could he forget? The burns on Wan's breasts and her mutilated fingers were indelibly seared on his mind. Find Sullivan and he'd find Webster. He stood up and slipped the pistol into his waistband. He slid the knife into a scabbard and put that in his inside pocket. Then he moved behind Hennessy, who jerked in terror, too frightened to cry out. Ryder's voice came from behind him now, sounding more menacing than before. "What about Sheila McGuire, Hennessy? Did you throw her under a train in London?

"No," he choked.

"But you ordered it, right?" Hennessy made no reply and started to sob uncontrollably.

Ryder thought of Josephine Lynch, and he could almost taste the tears that he had seen in her eyes. She was in Dublin, too, he remembered. Briefly he wondered if she was nearby. "There was a guy called Steven Lynch. He was only nineteen when he got himself topped in Bangkok for smuggling heroin. You didn't kill him, but you were responsible for his death. You financed him, didn't you?"

"Yes." Hennessy's voice was barely above a whisper.

"I don't think I heard that."

"Yes!" Hennessy screamed.

"Confession is good for the soul, Flicker, I can see that now." Ryder fumbled in his jacket pocket and took out a small coil of wire. "Now, I want you to do something else for me," he said softly.

"Anything," the man sobbed.

"I want you to remember my son, Mark. You can do that, can't you?"

Hennessy nodded vigorously.

"He was a good kid that didn't get enough chances, perhaps I should have done more for him, but I didn't. It doesn't matter what he did to you. All that matters is that you gave him the stuff that killed him. You're sure you're thinking of him right now, Flicker?"

"Yes," he screamed. "I'm thinking of the fucker!"

"That's good."

Ryder coiled the wire in his powerful hands and slipped it swiftly around Hennessy's neck. In an instant, he garrotted him, only releasing the wire when Hennessy's feet stopped drumming on the floor.

THIRTY-ONE

"Well! Well! So Flicker finally got his comeuppance!" Inspector William Brophy came through the door surveying the room with a smile of satisfaction on his face. He looked almost angelic in his white scene-of crime cover-all and his mood was buoyant, like that of a man who had picked the right horse in the Grand National. He noted the expensive stereo equipment, television, and video units, and a display of flowers in a bowl. That's strange, he thought. He would never have believed that Hennessy of all people would have flowers in his room.

Flashes of light came from the police photographer's camera, swallowing any shadows in the room and through an open door to the kitchen he could see a plain-clothes man methodically searching the cabinets. Across the room, John Smith, the State pathologist, hunched over the body, his gloved hands turning the head slightly to gain a closer look. "Evening, Bill," he said without looking up.

Brophy moved nearer and studied the blood-soaked body slumped in the chair. "Who found him?"

"I believe it was a cleaning woman. About an hour ago. She comes in around six every evening." Smith stood up and removed his white plastic gloves, dropping them into his open bag. "Isn't that a bit odd?" he mused.

"What?" Brophy studied the angle of the body slumped in the chair.

"That she does the cleaning at night."

Brophy straightened up. "Why?" he asked.

"I would have thought that cleaners work days."

Brophy smiled wickedly. "No," he replied. "Our friend here is like Dracula, John. Vampires sleep during the day and rise at night. You should watch the movies more often."

"Ah! I see. You know him, then?"

"Oh, yes. Hennessy is well known to us. He has been in and out of the nick since he was sixteen, small stuff mostly. He's a petty crook that's gone up in the world lately. Self-promotion, I suppose you would call it. We've been interested in him for a while." Brophy angled himself so that he could study the side of Hennessy's head. "Jesus!" He exclaimed. "He's missing an ear!"

"It's on the coffee table." Smith replied. A slight smile crinkled the edges of his mouth and his eyes twinkled beneath his shaggy eyebrows.

Brophy drew in his breath sharply. "How long is he dead, John?"

Smith pursed his lips. "At least twelve hours, possibly a bit more. Difficult to say yet."

"Cause of death?"

"Strangulation certainly. A wire garrotte, I should think. The killer is certainly male, a very powerful man by the looks of this mess. There are severe lacerations to the neck."

Brophy stared at Smith with renewed interest. "Garrotting!" he exclaimed. "I've never come across that before, not in all my days. It sounds professional. Continental, if you know what I mean. The lump hammer or a baseball bat would find more favor with our lads here."

"The garrotte originated in Spain, I believe." Smith gave Brophy a tired smile. "I've never really been in favor of joining the European Union. It's brought us many things that we could do without, don't you agree?"

Brophy chuckled. "Yes indeed," he said. "It's increased our workload, too, that's for sure."

Smith put a large thermometer into his brief case and

closed it. "One more thing, Bill," he said as he moved towards the door.

"What's that?"

"I think he was tied to the chair before he was murdered. There are bloodstained fibres clinging to his jacket. Some sort of tape I would suspect."

"And the killer removed it before he left?"

"Yes. I'll have more for you later after I get him on the slab." Smith gave him a slight wave and left the room.

Other detectives from forensics were filtering into the room. Brophy issued his orders quickly. "You know what to do in here," he said. "Be thorough, but I've got a feeling you won't find much. By the way, who got here first?"

"I did sir."

Brophy looked up. Detective Sergeant Colm O'Dwyer from the Rathmines station had just re-entered the lounge from the bedroom. Brophy liked O'Dwyer. "Glad you are on the case, Colm. Find anything interesting?"

"A couple of thousand quid's worth of dope, in a suitcase in the wardrobe."

"Careless bastard, wasn't he?" Brophy scowled. "Anything else?"

"Well, there's no money in the place. None that I can find, anyway, and there doesn't seem to be anything taken."

"No money!"

"No."

"Not even in his pockets?"

"Zilch! Not even a wallet."

"He must have had money on him. Christ! The guy was dealing!" Brophy frowned. Robbery as a motive? Possible, but he didn't think so. There was something more. Hennessy had suffered before he died. They were still looking for Monica Flaherty's killer but whoever had killed Hennessy had done it for some other reason. Maybe they were witnessing the start of a drug war, he thought. "What was in the suitcase?" he asked.

"Hash mostly. A few packs of heroin and a small amount of cocaine by the looks of it." Colm walked over and looked down on the glass coffee table where the ear lay in a small blot of congealed blood. It resembled the sort of white fungus that might grow on a rotted tree stump. "They slit his nose as well," he said.

"They?"

"Figure of speech, boss, sorry."

Brophy gave a noncommittal grunt. What about the other apartments on this floor? There are four in total, right?"

O'Dwyer consulted his notebook. "That's correct. The two adjoining this one are empty. A Mary and Francis Hickey in number fourteen are away on holiday in the Canaries. They've been gone for over a week. Number sixteen is also empty and up for sale. A man called Donald Swift occupies number twelve. He was in all night and heard nothing. He sounded pleased about it. From what he told me nobody liked the victim too much."

"That doesn't surprise me. Who told him?"

"The cleaner. She phoned us from there; she was sensible enough not to touch anything."

"Good." Brophy pondered on what O'Dwyer had told him. "What happened to number thirteen, Colm?"

"There isn't one boss." O'Dwyer smiled. "Swift said something about it being an unlucky number. The builders left it out."

Brophy laughed gently and moved towards the window. "Maybe Hennessy was a naughty boy and fell foul of his suppliers. Perhaps he stole something that wasn't his. That might account for him having no money."

Colm coughed politely. "Would they have left the stuff in the suitcase?"

Brophy shrugged. "I guess not," he replied. He parted the curtains and looked down on the street. Several police cars were scattered by the curb where a small group of onlookers were gathering behind the yellow tapes marked

"Crime Scene. No Entry." An ambulance with its doors open was parked directly in front of the steps. On the other side of the street a metal waste skip sat outside a building site. "Tape off that skip across the road and have someone check it," Brophy ordered.

"What are we looking for?"

"Murder weapon. Probably bloodstained wire or rope. Plastic tape that sort of thing. Anything else that shouldn't be in a builders' skip."

Brophy turned away from the window and studied the coffee table. A small quantity of ash lay in an ashtray. Tiny flecks of it were also resting on the congealed blood from the ear. "He was a smoker," he said. "We know that much. I doubt if Flicker was in the mood for a fag before he died."

He stuffed his spectacles into his inside jacket pocket. "Okay, Colm. Enough chat. Let's go and have a few words with the cleaner woman and Mr. Swift. We'll leave forensics to get on with what they do best."

THIRTY-TWO

Ryder parked his car at the end of a dirt road that had led him into thick pine forest. It was already dark but that did not matter; he had reconnoitered the area on foot in daylight and already knew the terrain intimately. He was now only a mile from the house.

Like menacing soldiers, the trees encircled him, taking on threatening shapes in the darkness. He got out and opened the car boot. Everything he needed was there. He slipped on an army camouflage smock and trousers, and then picked up a bundle of additional items, including a sleeping bag, and stuffed them into a rucksack. The smell of pine was heavy on the night air, but he felt at home here, far more than in the city streets of Dublin that were now many miles behind him. The Legion had prepared him for surroundings such as this.

He moved off down a rutted track that had been used by foresters, following it for perhaps half a mile until he reached a tree that he had marked with a nick in its bark, seeing nothing other than a fox that hastened through the gloom just before he turned off into the brush. There was time for one last cigarette, he thought. It might be some time before he could risk smoking again. He went to ground in a gully floored with loose rocks. Edged by nodding ferns, it would be a stream in rain, but now it was dried up like a withered crone. He lit his cigarette, cupping it in the hollow of his hand, and contemplated what he had accomplished so far.

It had felt good to avenge Mark's death. Hennessy shouldn't have messed with his family, Ryder thought, then realized with some surprise, that he was thinking of Mark differently now. While he had always known that Mark was his son, it had never occurred to him that he was family. It was a category that Ryder had always reserved for his brothers in the Legion. Until this, Mark had been a specter who encumbered him; now he was a son who he remembered with fondness. Wan was family too, he mused. Harm the family, and you brought down swift and merciless retribution. The code of the Legion had demanded that, and he would honor it.

Hennessy's bulging wallet had provided him with three thousand pounds. The spoils of war, he thought. He had dumped the empty wallet and the blood stained tape in a trash can in a Dun Laoghaire car park at the ferry terminal where he had slept until dawn, awakening in the car as the first rays of light crept over the harbor.

Now he was in Galway. An online telephone directory enquiry had made Sullivan surprisingly easy to find, if Sullivan was indeed the man he sought. He would know that soon enough. If he was, Sullivan held the key to the next locked door that led to Webster. After that it was over. He could withdraw just as he had done in Mogadishu, with his honor intact. Honor, he thought sadly. A dead child surfaced in his mind. He shook his head. There would be no more killing after Webster.

He ground out his cigarette and followed the gully until it emerged from the trees near a walled field where cows grazed, moving as blacker humps in the darkness. The house was just visible as a pale white square through other trees across the meadow, its roof flat, and black, like an aircraft carrier's deck. A single light showed as a tiny speck in a downstairs window. Ryder circled the field, keeping close to the wall, losing sight of the lamp as he moved to lower ground.

He reached the end of the wall and eased himself over without dislodging any stones. He could see the light clearly again now. It seemed to be coming from what looked like

French windows that opened onto a wide lawn at the rear of the house. He studied the gardens for several minutes. Just inside the boundary wall, dark banks of shrubbery gave thick cover right up to the lawn. Off to his right, an orchard of fruit trees stretched almost to the building itself. He judged that the grounds extended over several acres. He couldn't see what was at the front, but earlier that day he had driven past a long gravel drive that led from the main Moycullen road. The gates at the entrance had been open. Sullivan obviously lived without fear and in considerable affluence.

He climbed over the boundary wall and slid silently into the shrubbery. If he needed to, he knew that he could remain here for days. Even in daylight, no one would see him, not unless they stepped directly on him and even then there would be doubt if he exercised his skills. He took a small pair of field glasses from his rucksack and scanned the building, wondering if there was a dog. He could see nothing that resembled a burglar alarm clinging to the walls of the house, unless there was one at the front or off to one side. The binoculars magnified the lighted window. Someone was there, but he couldn't see movement in the room. He had to get closer.

Before he left the shrubbery, he prepared a hide so that he could return there instantly if he had to. He left his rucksack and headed towards the orchard, moving quickly from tree to tree until only a narrow concrete path separated him from the house. Three short paces had him nuzzling the wall of the house. He sidled left and took a quick glance through the patio doors.

The room was a comfortably furnished study. A television flickered in a corner showing what appeared to be a news broadcast. Faintly he could hear the voice that issued from it. Bolder now, he craned his neck. He caught a glimpse of a man sitting at a desk with his back to him. The man was alone in the room.

Ryder ducked back and hugged the wall. Without seeing his face he couldn't be sure. He considered his options. The man he was looking for was IRA as well as being involved in the drugs trade. Surely a man like that would guard himself? He had a choice, he could go to ground and wait until he was sure, or brazen it out. Silently, Ryder retreated to the orchard to consider his next move.

Frank Sullivan stared blankly at the television screen, oblivious to it. He had missed the main news broadcast at nine o'clock, and the late summary that he had just watched was condensed and lacking in information. But it still depressed him. The media was over reacting to the death of that bitch Monica Flaherty, he thought morosely. The whole country was now clamoring for a Garda crack down on organized crime, baying like hounds that had picked up a scent but it was too late now to have regrets; she had driven him into a corner and given him no other choice.

His telephone had never stopped all day, even though he had issued warnings that it was no longer safe. Calls from different parts of the country brought threats that he could no longer ignore. Even from The Organization, he thought savagely. After all that he had done in his time to drag this country toward a better future. Now, even they seemed to think that he was rabid and out of control.

To top it all, he mused; there had been no word from Paddy or Michael since he had responded to Hennessy's call last night. It was unlike them, and he wondered what was going on. No word from Hennessy since, either.

Things had become suddenly complicated. The arrival of that fucking English bastard, Ryder, was but another complication, and one that he could have done without. Thankfully, Ryder should be at the bottom of the Liffey by now. Webster owed him plenty for that, he thought. He should have insisted on doing the job himself out in Burma, and not left it to Webster.

Then there was Phillips, who wanted the money that was in the safe on his study wall. He had to rid himself of it. Not just to satisfy Phillips, but in case the authorities responded to the clamor and closed in on him.

Momentarily, he thought of calling Martin Dennihy at Leinster House, but rejected it immediately. Dennihy would be in touch if the Government really planned a crack down. He'd need to save his own skin, if nothing else.

The mobile phone lying on his desk jangled. Sullivan picked it up. "Yes."

"Frank, it's Paddy. I'm going to keep this short. It was him right enough, but he gave us the slip."

Sullivan cursed into the mouthpiece. "Where is he?" he snarled. "You had better find him."

"We're looking, Frank and believe me he's dead meat when we find him. The fucker stove in my ribs and Mossy has a busted nose."

"Have you spoken to Hennessy?" Sullivan heard a sharp intake of breath. "Hennessy's dead, Frank, I don't know any more than that. Call me in the morning."

Sullivan threw down the phone. "Shit!" he shouted.

He stood up and strode to the patio doors, then wrenched them open, and stood on the step sucking in the cool night air. He looked up at the sky where a shadow passed across the moon as a cloud crept across its face. The fine weather was over. He could sense it. He stood for a minute longer, breathing deeply, calming himself.

He fancied he saw a movement somewhere in the trees but heard no sound. Often, he had looked out to see a fox crossing the lawn on its nightly prowl. He shivered. Worry was not an ally. He stepped back into the room as a gloved hand that was scented by the forest engulfed his face, another circling his neck before blackness descended on him.

Ryder closed and locked the double doors to the patio. Sullivan lay crumpled on the carpet where he had allowed him to fall. He switched off the television and went out into a darkened hall and listened. There was no movement anywhere. It was as if no one lived here. He returned to the study and picked up a table light that lay on the floor, adjusting the shade before placing it back on the desk from where it had fallen.

He wrapped tape around Sullivan's arms and legs and turned him over, then dragged him to a nearby chair and propped him in it. Sullivan breathed rhythmically, his chest moving in and out in small movements. His mouth was slack, his lips slightly parted, and his spectacles dangled incongruously from one ear. The face held remnants of a tan that disguised what otherwise would be skin that was like moldy white bread.

Ryder reached across and adjusted the glasses on Sullivan's face. He thought of Wan and what she had suffered at the hands of this man, wishing he could hate him for what he had done to her. But no rage invaded his mind; nothing came to remind him that he was here to kill.

Sullivan opened his eyes. The room was blurred. Slowly, he focused his gaze on the man watching him. Recognition flashed across his mind as the scarred face registered on his brain. His mouth went suddenly dry but he felt no fear. He sensed his spectacles slipping on his nose and moved to adjust them, realizing instantly that his hands were bound behind him.

"I told Webster he was a fool," he said quietly.

"Oh?" Ryder stared back at him.

"He should have killed you when he had the chance."

Ryder smiled. "I agree," he said. "That's why I'm here. I want him. I need his address in London. We have a score to settle."

"Is that all?"

"Yes."

"You're lying, Ryder. I can tell."

Ryder shrugged. "Think what you like."

"How did you find me? It was Hennessy, wasn't it?"

"Yes."

"And you killed him. Why?" Ryder made no reply. Sullivan found himself staring at the scar on Ryder's face. There were fresh bruises too, he noticed. Webster had told him

Ryder was a Legionnaire; a mercenary. Such a man could be useful if handled correctly, he thought.

"How did you get out of Burma, Ryder?"

"I swam."

"You swam, just like that! Down that river? They told us it was impossible."

Ryder looked bored. "Nothing is impossible. I was never allowed to think of impossibility."

Yes, Sullivan decided. A useful man indeed. "And the girl?" he asked.

"She survived too. I haven't forgotten what you did to her."

A hardness had crept into Ryder's voice. It was time to change the subject. "I have money," Sullivan said calmly. "Five thousand, ten maybe. Just leave now while you can, otherwise you'll never get off this island alive."

"You think that I can be bought?"

"Everyone has a price."

Ryder's eyes seemed to turn to steel. They drilled into him remorselessly. Ryder intended to kill him, Sullivan knew instantly. Bleakly, he contemplated what that meant. There were enemies waiting for him on the other side too. Scores to be settled. He shivered. Stall for time, he thought. He would live only as long as he could hold back the information that this man needed. "Maybe I can give you what you want," he said softly.

"Don't try to sidetrack me, Sullivan. Who else is in the house?"

"Nobody."

"You live alone?"

"No, but my wife is away visiting relatives. She could come back at any minute."

"Don't screw with me, Frank. You're a fucking drug dealer. What I don't understand is that anyone could walk in here."

"I've got friends in high places, Ryder. I don't need guards." Sullivan thought of Paddy and Michael up in Dublin.

He should have ordered them to come down once he knew
Ryder had given them the slip.

Ryder stood up. "I'm going to take a look around," he
said. "When I come back you'd better have the answers I
want to hear."

Ryder checked every room in the house. Sullivan had told
him the truth; no one else was in the house. He went outside
and raised the door of a double garage. A BMW was parked
to one side but there was room for a second car and there was
an oil stain on the concrete floor where it had stood. Perhaps
Sullivan's wife really was on her way back. Killing her was
not part of his plan. He was wasting time.

He returned to the study and sat down in front of Sullivan.
"Tell me where I can find Webster," he said.

"Get fucked!" Sullivan grinned.

Ryder studied his adversary for some time. A clock
chimed somewhere in the house. Sullivan was not like the
others, he concluded. He showed no fear. Physical pain for
this man was no stranger. It would work in the end...it always
did...but it would take time, and time was not on his side.
What then? Everyone held secret fears of something, he
thought. For some, it was snakes. For others, rats. Perhaps dis-
ease or death itself. What was Sullivan's fear? His eyes
dropped to a small pouch on the desk and he opened it.
Inside was a small set of syringes.

"Are you on drugs?"

"No. I'm a diabetic. That's insulin."

A diabetic. Ryder wracked his mind. Something about an
excess of sugar crossed his mind. He picked up a syringe and
looked at it, holding it up to the light. Sullivan stirred. Ryder
glanced at him. Something had been in those eyes just then
but now it was gone. He had missed it. "What happens if I
stick one of these into you Sullivan?"

Sullivan tensed. His eyes flickered. This time Ryder saw it.
"You don't seem to like that idea much. Why not?"

"Do what you want." Ryder heard the instant of hesitation before Sullivan spoke, and the hint of flatness that betrayed his false bravado. He squatted in front of Sullivan, the syringe in his hand. "Okay, you know what I'm going to do, Frank?"

Sullivan shook his head. There was a trace of perspiration on his upper lip.

"I'm going to take a chance and dump this into you. It can't kill you, can it? I mean, you take it all the time, right?" He didn't wait for an answer, but stabbed the needle into Sullivan's thigh. Then he sat back in his chair, lit a cigarette, and waited.

It was not long. Sullivan's head swayed as though he could no longer control it. His eyes rolled in reddened sockets. His face looked like a mound of grey putty and his mouth moved sloppily as though he had difficulty controlling it. Ryder felt a rush of panic. He slipped to his knees in front of Sullivan and slapped his face hard. The skin felt unnaturally hot, and dry, like ancient parchment. Sullivan's head rolled to the blow like that of a rag doll. "Sullivan!" he shouted. "Where's Webster?" He slapped him again, a resounding crack that echoed around the room. "Don't pass out on me, you bastard!"

"Sugar," Sullivan whispered, as though all the strength had gone out of him. "In the kitchen." His voice sounded slurred, like that of a drunk.

Ryder wrenched open doors in the hall, switching on lights everywhere. His mind was racing now. If he lost Sullivan, he lost Webster too. The third door revealed a glaring white-tiled kitchen. He flung open cabinet doors scattering their contents in a shower of shattered bottles and jars until he found the box of cubed sugar. He grabbed it and sprinted back to the study.

Sullivan seemed almost comatose. Ryder held up the sugar. "This what you want, Frank?" Sullivan went rigid at the sight of it, his eyes blazing. Ryder searched his eyes looking for a sign. To give it to him or not, that was the question. Supposing he didn't? He rattled the box. "Where do I find Webster, Frank?"

There was desperation in Sullivan's face. His eyes were those of an addict craving a drug. Strange, Ryder thought. The same drug that he needed in order to live could also kill him. Then he thought of Mark dying in that squalid squat in Rathmines and his momentary pity evaporated.

A small stain spread on the crotch of Sullivan's trousers. Ryder caught the warm scent of urine. He slapped Sullivan hard across the face. His head flopped lazily. "Where, Frank!" he shouted. "Tell me where, Goddamn it!"

Sullivan seemed to shrink away from him. Ryder returned to the desk and selected a second syringe. Then he went back and fell to one knee.

"Supposing I give you another splash of this stuff, will that speed things up?"

Ryder didn't inject the full amount this time. There was no need to. Sullivan's eyes were wild now; they were like that of a man drowning in his own vomit. Ryder bent closer. He could smell the sweat of fear. "Webster, Frank. Then you get sugar."

"He's here." Sullivan's voice was barely audible, his words slurred and indistinct.

Ryder jumped. "Here in the house? In Galway?"

"No. Kinsale. With Critchley."

"Where in Kinsale?"

"Clonbar."

Ryder thought for a moment. Suppose Webster was no longer there?

"London, Frank. What's his address there?"

"Don't know. Ask Phillips. Marbella club."

What the hell was he talking about? Ryder wondered. Who was Phillips? Critchley? The Marbella club? Ryder stared into the distance, no longer seeing Sullivan. Did it matter? Webster was in Ireland. He was that close.

There was no time to waste. He emptied the box of sugar cubes onto the floor. "The money, Frank. Where is it?"

Sullivan's mumbled something that was incoherent and Ryder shook him. "Combination safe," he slurred. "On the wall."

Ryder could barely hear him. "What's the combination?"

"Five...eight...nine..." Sullivan stopped for a long pause, almost unable to complete the thought. "One...two. Sugar. Need sugar."

Ryder swept his eyes around the room. There was nothing that resembled a safe, but there was a framed picture on the wall near the fireplace. He wrenched it off the wall and the glass shattered as he threw the picture aside. He punched in the numbers on the keypad and the door clicked open. Inside it were thick stacks of money, and an old fashioned Webley revolver. He left the safe gaping open and returned to Sullivan.

Sullivan was dying; that much was clear. Ryder remembered Wan, the mutilation of her fingers, the burns, her scars. He remembered her telling him that they must make peace with the past and move on, as instant hatred for this pathetic creature flooded through him. Coldly, he picked up the syringe and plunged the remaining insulin into Sullivan's leg.

THIRTY-THREE

An incessant hammering on the front door filled the house, echoing hollowly from room to room. Critchley stirred in his sleep, wishing the noise would stop. Psychedelic flashes seared his brain as he finally opened his eyes, trying to make sense of what he was hearing. In a daze, he switched on the bedside lamp. What time was it? He glanced at his watch; it was only midnight. When had he gone to bed? His thoughts felt like they were moving through treacle as he tried to shrug off a feeling of disorientation.

He sat up and looked at Helen Cullen sprawled beside him. She lay on her back, naked, with her mouth open. He could see the fillings in her teeth. At that moment she no longer looked attractive, he thought. She moved restlessly in her sleep as if, she too, was conscious of a clamor in her ears.

The hammering on the doorknocker continued unabated. The gates were locked for the night, he thought. How had anyone reached the house? He got out of bed, and pulled on a silk dressing gown before making his way down stairs. "I'm coming," he shouted from halfway down. "Jesus Christ! Whoever you are, I'm coming!"

Critchley opened the door and Peter Webster stepped quickly inside, dropping a small suitcase unceremoniously on the hall floor. "What the hell kept you, Critchley," he bawled. "I've been hammering on that damned door for at least fifteen minutes."

Critchley gaped in surprise. "I was in bed," he replied eventually.

"I can see that." Webster glared at him. "You look like shit. Where's the fucking bar? I need a drink."

Critchley guided Webster into the sitting room, still trying to clear his head. At the moment he wasn't even sure what day it was. "Brandy?" he offered.

"Fine, and make it a bloody large one."

"I wasn't aware that you were coming over," Critchley remarked as he poured the drink. "How did you get through the gates?"

"You gave me the code for the gates the last time I was here, you cretin, or have you forgotten?" Webster accepted a glass gratefully and flopped into an armchair.

Critchley sat down opposite to him. Something was wrong here; he knew it instinctively. "I forgot I gave you the code," he said. "What's going on, Peter? You're not here just because you like my company."

"You're right about that," Webster replied. "But we'd best get used to each other. A large pile of shit has hit the fan in the past few days. That stupid bastard Frank Sullivan put a contract out on a journalist in Dublin recently, and now they want to gut him for it."

"Monica Flaherty?"

"That's right. It was bad enough when the first one was killed a few months ago, but now a second . . ." Webster crashed his fist on the coffee table. "That's just plain bloody stupidity," he muttered into his glass.

"I read about it," Critchley said. "The papers here have been full of it ever since. One of them all but named him. But what does that have to do with you?"

"Sid reckons we've got to cover for Sullivan until it blows over. Or until they arrest him," Webster added ominously. "Work doesn't just stop, you know."

Critchley felt a wave of nausea sweep over him and he wanted to puke. He realized that Webster was staring at him and he didn't like it.

"Excuse me for a moment," he said. He stood up and rushed headlong from the room.

In the bathroom, Critchley splashed cold water on his face and glanced into the mirror over the washbasin. He fought to regain his composure. The face staring back at him did not seem to be his. He restrained an impulse to smash the mirror and blot out the image. He opened the medicine cabinet, his hands scrabbling at the contents. Nothing resembled what he was looking for. He wanted to scream, but dashed to the bedroom instead. Helen was still asleep, but was now curled up in a tight ball, her hands between her naked legs as though she was protecting herself from a recent nightmare. Critchley fought off an urge to drag her out of the bed and kick her senseless.

He rummaged in the dresser drawers, feverishly scattering clothing onto the floor. Nothing! Jesus! What had that stupid bitch done with it? He moved to the bed, checking her hands, feeling the mattress around and under her body. He slipped a hand under her pillow; thank God, he thought. She was going cracked on the stuff, he realized with horror. He did two quick lines of the cocaine, rubbing the residue into his gums.

The tremors stopped. He took a deep breath as renewed confidence surged through him like an incoming tide.

Webster had refilled his glass by the time he returned to the lounge. He was sitting with his eyes tightly closed, massaging his forehead with the fingers of one hand.

"I'm sorry, Peter." Critchley sat down and smiled. "Where were we?"

"We were talking about covering for Sullivan. There's two tons of stuff coming in and you and I may have to handle it."

"I usually handle it, don't I? Or are we going to have to do the delivery as well?"

"Only if we have to," Webster replied. "Sullivan might be lying low, but he'll still make the arrangements."

"That's okay then," Critchley replied. "If we have to, Sullivan tells us where to take it and we deliver. That's simple enough."

Webster looked at him as though he couldn't understand what he was hearing, then put down his brandy and leaned forwards suddenly. "You stupid fucking bastard!"

Critchley stiffened and half rose from his chair. "What do you mean?"

"You know what I fucking mean. You're using, aren't you?" Webster sighed wearily and picked up his glass. "I might have known it," he said.

Critchley looked away evasively. Was it that evident?

"What are you on?"

"Just some Charlie, but only now and then. Nothing serious. It's no worse than taking an occasional glass of Champagne. Fuck you Webster, I'm on the front line here. There's pressure in that, I can tell you, you'll find out soon enough. It's all very well for you and Phillips and that sod Sullivan. You lot don't have to get your hands dirty."

Webster looked at him in disgust. "I knew there was something different about you the last time we were here," he said, but you're the same bloody fool that you always were, aren't you Critchley? If you screw up..."

A small sound came from overhead and a floorboard creaked. Webster turned on him in panic. "Who's upstairs?"

"A friend."

"A woman?"

Critchley nodded. "Yes. Nothing to worry about. It's Helen Cullen."

"Jesus!" Webster drained his glass and handed it to Critchley. "Pour me another," he snapped. He passed a hand across his face as though he was trying to blot out the memory of something painful.

Critchley listened to the sound of a toilet flushing upstairs. He prayed that Helen would not come down. Whatever state she was in, it would do nothing to lighten the blackness of Webster's mood and he didn't want the situation to worsen. He heard the gratifying squeak of the floorboard directly overhead and he knew she had gone back to bed. "There's something else, isn't there, Peter?" He pushed the decanter of brandy on the coffee table closer to Webster.

Webster scowled. "There's a man looking for me in London, and he's partly the reason I'm here. He'll either get tired of it, or one of the boy's will take care of him. Sid just didn't want any more complications while this thing with Sullivan is going on. That reminds me; I had better call him and let him know that I've arrived."

Critchley pointed to the telephone. "Help yourself," he said. He half listened to Webster mumbling into the phone, but his thoughts were on Helen Cullen upstairs in the bedroom. He still wanted to fuck her, rut with her like an animal, but right now he needed to get her out of the house, he realized. She was a liability now, and one he could do without. He had found out early on that she was over-fond of drink, but now she was heavily into drugs as well. Early in their relationship she had told him that Ecstasy made her more loving, and because of that, he had plied her with it. Now it was mostly cocaine, but he knew that she would take anything on offer.

He had given it all to her, as much as she wanted, and her addiction had progressed rapidly. The sex, too, was addictive, he thought. She was no longer the same person he had met when he first arrived in Kinsale.

He glanced at Webster, who was listening intently on the telephone. Webster's face was pale in the light emanating from a small table lamp. As he let the receiver drop into the cradle, he remained standing near the phone as though he was afraid to move from the spot. "He's here."

"Who?"

"Ryder, the guy who's looking for me."

Critchley almost upset his drink. "I thought you said that he died out in Thailand?"

"I believed it myself." Webster shook his head in disbelief. "How he got out of there is beyond me, but he ended up in Germany a few days ago and our contacts there tipped us off that he was heading for London to find me."

Critchley thought for a moment. "How does he know you're here?"

"He doesn't. Only Sid, Frank, and you know that."

Critchley laughed hollowly. "There's only you, me, and Helen here. If you're seeing anyone else, you're seeing a ghost, Peter."

Webster wheeled, as if to lash out at Critchley, then stopped himself as Critchley took a threatening step towards him. "Get a grip, you fucker! I said he's here in Ireland, that's what I meant, not here in the fucking house! He was spotted in Dublin yesterday evening. A dealer named Hennessy was murdered there last night. Sid just told me about it. By the sounds of it, Sullivan sent a couple of his men to head Ryder off from Hennessy and they failed. We had warned Sullivan about the information we got from Germany, but how the hell Ryder got on to this guy Hennessy is beyond me." Webster returned to his chair. His face was a mask.

Critchley seemed unconcerned. "Could Ryder get to Sullivan through Hennessy?"

"Maybe, but Phillips doesn't think so. Frank stays out of the limelight. Even the cops can't get near him."

"But you don't agree?"

"No," Webster looked ravaged.

Critchley felt a slight thrill. It was good to see the tables turned on Webster, he thought. Let the bastard sweat for a change. His own job had become so easy that he had been lulled into a feeling of security. He went to the window and stared into the night. Supposing this man Ryder was already out there, watching the house right now? It might be nice to deliver up his prey, he thought. "Do you think he will come here?" he asked eventually.

Webster shook his head. "How can he? Hennessy knew nothing about this place. Only Sullivan knows. I've told you how Frank operates. Only his most trusted people know any details, and Hennessy was not one of those."

Critchley sat down and faced Webster. "We should expect the worst," he said.

Webster swallowed his brandy and refilled the glass. "Sid has taken care of it. Two of Sullivan's men are coming down tomorrow, and Nicholls, the diver, will be here later. They'll bring weapons."

Weapons! Critchley's heart raced. He'd love to turn a weapon on Webster, he thought. Too bad he hadn't had the opportunity before this. But gang warfare in a place like Kinsale? What a mess. He had an urge to escape now, make a run for it before it was too late.

Webster seemed to read his thoughts. "And you're staying in this with us, Critchley," he said harshly. "If he comes here; we'll be ready for him."

"What does he look like?" Critchley found himself asking without really caring.

"You'll know him," Webster said. "He's big, about six-two with a scar on his face and half an ear missing. He's no shrinking violet, I can tell you. He's the sort that stands out in a crowd."

At that moment there was the sound of a heavy thud from upstairs, followed by a tinkling sound like a bottle rolling across the floor in the room above them. Shit! What was that bitch doing now? Critchley made for the door and took the stairs two at a time. He didn't realize that Webster had followed him until he got to the bedroom.

Helen Cullen had half-fallen from the bed onto the floor. She was no longer naked but was half dressed in a denim shirt and a pair of panties. Her jeans were grasped in her hand.

Critchley felt a stab of momentary panic. There was something unnatural about the way she lay. For a moment, he wondered if she was dead. There was a thump as her left leg, still on the bed, fell to the floor. He crossed the room and turned her over. A small trickle of blood escaped from a cut on her forehead. "She must have knocked her head when she fell. Stupid bitch. Give me a hand with her, Peter, lets get her back on the bed."

Together, they lifted her gently onto the bed. She didn't move. Her eyes remained closed, her body corpse-like. Webster took her hand, her skin felt cold to the touch. "She's in a bad way," he said gruffly. "What sort of shit is she on, anyway?"

"Anything she can get," Critchley replied. "Probably a cocktail." He picked up an empty jar that lay on the floor. The cover was missing. Two brown tablets still remained inside. "Ecstasy this time."

"How many were in that jar?"

"I don't know," Critchley replied. "I didn't know she had them."

"I want her out of here, right now!" Webster snapped angrily. "We need to clean this place up, get rid of everything."

Critchley's eyes widened. "You think she's overdosed?"

"I don't just think it, I know it, mate!" Webster glared at him. "You've opened up a Pandora's box that we've got to lock shut. Where does she live?"

"In town."

"Right. Help me get her dressed, she's going home right now."

"We're taking her to a hospital," Critchley growled.

"Forget it! I'm calling the shots on this one." Webster grabbed her shoulders and started to haul her from the bed.

Once a week Matthew Brennan played poker with a group of Kinsale businessmen. It was a meeting that he usually enjoyed because he played well and rarely lost. What was more important, the arrangement allowed those who saw themselves as town policy makers to exchange ideas and discuss developments that might have a bearing on their individual businesses. Sometimes the parish Priest, Father Concannon, attended, too. He was the epitome of the Kinsale schemers; his brother, Ignatius, owned the pub.

By the time he left the back room in Concannon's pub, Brennan was drunk, had lost fifty euros, and was now committed to Father Concannon for five hundred euros towards his youth club fund. Not exactly one of his better nights, he thought, as Ignatius let him out through the side door.

He made his way unsteadily homewards. The back streets were deserted at two thirty in the morning, so when a car rocketed the wrong way down a one-way street that crossed ahead of him, even his befuddled mind registered the fact.

Brennan turned the corner, but ducked back into a doorway when he saw that the car was parked only yards away with its engine still running. He focused his eyes with difficulty and recognised Critchley's BMW, the only large BMW in town with British plates. He saw two men get out. Both went round to the nearside rear door and opened it. Brennan recognized one of them as Critchley. He narrowly resisted calling out a greeting, but instead, withdrew further into the shadows.

Critchley reached inside the back of the car, seeming to struggle with something heavy. Muffled voices reached Brennan in his hiding place. He saw them pull a woman from the back seat of the car. The two men supported her between them and dragged her into a doorway.

Brennan heard a muttered curse then a door slammed loudly. He looked up and down the street; nobody was around. He scuttled down the street on tiptoe and looked at the number over the door. Just as he had suspected, it was Helen Cullen's apartment.

Quietly, Brennan retreated and continued his way home. Pissed out of her mind, she was, he thought. He almost laughed. Maybe he should have offered to help Critchley out. Not that he'd get any thanks for that, he thought bitterly. Anyway, it was none of his business. Everyone knew she was seeing a lot of Critchley. It was common knowledge now that they were an item. For a moment, he wondered who the second man was. Some friend of Critchley's, no doubt. Maybe one of his hunting or yachting pals, but no one local, he was sure of that. Maybe another Brit, but he had more important things to worry about right now, he decided. Five hundred euros, he thought mournfully. He recalled Father Concannon waffling on about needing to raise money for a youth club. A place to keep the kids off the streets, he had said. A Catholic place, and strictly run. No nonsense, Concannon had said.

A place of protection from the drug culture now sweeping the cities of holy Ireland.

Drugs, Brennan thought. As if a place like Kinsale needed protection from that! He did laugh this time, just before he missed his footing on the curbside and sprawled full length on his face. Then everything went black.

Thirty-Four

Ryder did not take all the money. He replaced a large bundle of euros in the safe and stuffed only sterling and dollars into the pockets of his combat jacket. Without counting it, he could tell that it was more money than he had ever possessed in his life. He left the revolver untouched and closed the safe door. Carefully, he wiped off the door with his handkerchief but when he tried to replace the painting that hid it from view he realized the hook was missing on the wall, unable to find it, he left the painting on the floor as though it had fallen from its place. Then he dusted off the lamp and anything else that he might have touched.

He crossed the room and felt for a pulse in Sullivan's neck, finding none. Quickly he stripped off the duct tape that he had used to tie Sullivan up and allowed the body to slump naturally in the chair. Picking up the syringe, he cleaned everything thoroughly and replaced it in its container, returning it to the desk where he had found it. He glanced at his watch. It was just after midnight.

Retracing his steps to the kitchen, he carefully tidied up the scattering of jars, wiping off all traces of his fingerprints as he did so. After one last careful look around he locked the patio doors on the inside and quietly left the house by the main entrance at the front.

The moon flirted with a dark cloud as he ducked across the back lawn to retrieve his rucksack from the shrubbery, and he felt a soft sprinkling of rain on his face before climbing over the wall and heading for the fringe of trees high on the hill where he had left the car. Half an hour later, he turned onto the road to Limerick and relaxed. The roads were virtually empty, but he resisted their temptation and drove slowly, not wanting to run into problems with a possible speed trap. Everything now depended on his ability to protect his anonymity and complete what he had come to do without delay. If he were lucky, Sullivan's body would not be found until the morning at the earliest. After that he could expect the shit to hit the fan. If the police were not already looking for him for the job in Dublin, it would only be a matter of time before they did. He regretted again the impulse that had kept him from killing Sullivan's goons.

The next three hours were a blur. He was tired, so tired that he missed the turning to Kinsale soon after passing through the deserted streets of Carrigaline and found himself entering the unfamiliar village of Crosshaven just before dawn. On his left lay the river with the dark silhouettes of moored yachts lining the waterway as the first tentative light showed over the wooded slopes on the far side. He pulled into a deserted car park near the entrance to a yacht Club to consult his map. Good, he thought. He was not too far off track. Kinsale was not far away and he had the whole day to rest up if he could find a suitable hiding place. Reversing back onto the road, he drove slowly along a village street that circled mud flats left behind by the tide. He caught a glimpse of a boatyard and a marina on a far point where the river obviously opened into Cork harbor, but there was no one about and the village slept on.

Soon he found himself on high ground overlooking a great expanse of water where in the distance he could see a town with a prominent cathedral in its midst. Looking at the map, it had to be Cobh, he decided. Far below him, navigation buoys still blinked their warning lights even though daylight was approaching rapidly and directly before him lay a fortress that looked abandoned. Closer inspection revealed a drawbridge leading over a defensive ravine to its massive locked gates. "Fort Meagher. Department of Defence. Keep Out," a notice read. "Trespassers will be prosecuted." The place looked deserted and had fallen into decay and as far as he could see there were no nearby houses.

Ryder parked the car in a lay-by that overlooked the water far below. Shouldering his rucksack, he walked quickly towards the drawbridge. As he drew nearer, he could see broken windows in the small embrasures that perforated the granite walls along one side of the road. His footsteps echoed back at him as he walked onto the bridge.

Perhaps eighty feet below he could see a deep ravine choked with brambles that fell away to a steep cliff right above a small pier that seemed to be still in a good state of repair. Seagulls wheeled above the water as tiny white dots far below but nothing else moved. He peered through the iron gates into an entrance courtyard where a raised walkway led to a guardhouse on one side. Slits for long departed weapons gashed the walls. Judging from the rusted state of the gates, the fort had not been used for some time, although the locks on the gates were well oiled. Once, it would have been the pride of the British army, but not now. Now it was a decaying tomb for the ghosts of soldiers long dead.

He thought of similar Legion forts, long since abandoned to desert storms, ghostly places lost in the vastness of the Sahara. It brought a shiver to his spine. But if he could get inside, he could hole up here for days if necessary. There was only one problem. There was no way over the gates; and without climbing equipment, scaling the granite walls was not feasible.

He looked over the railings of the bridge and studied the walls closely. From below in the tangled undergrowth, he could hear an invisible stream of water trickling slowly towards the cliff edge above a tiny harbor. Then he made out the dark cavern of an old gun embrasure in the stone wall about twenty feet below where he stood. Even if it did not give access to the inside of the fort it would be a secure place to hide the money.

He returned to the car and lit a cigarette as he sat and mulled over his options. On the far side of the harbor he could see a ship moving away from what looked like an oil refinery. He wondered if anyone worked in or around the fort during the day but by the look of the place it seemed unlikely. Switching on the radio he was in time to catch the first news bulletin of the day. The bright voice of the announcer spoke of another fine summer day in all parts of the country, again confounding meteorological predictions of a break in the weather. He went on to announce another increase in the price of petroleum and issued a warning that the government was considering the introduction of a household tax.

Ryder became alert when the broadcaster reported that a known drug dealer had been murdered in Dublin. It was suspected, he said, that the killing resulted from a feud in the drugs underworld. He went on to say that the police were following a definite lead in their enquiries and expected an early arrest.

Ryder reached over and switched off the radio. What did a definite lead in enquiries really mean, he wondered. An early arrest of whom? Were they on to him already? This could become just like that torturous road from Mae Sai all over again, he thought wearily. Night would be his ally, daylight his enemy. He needed a place like the deserted fort.

To add to his worries, he could now see the roofs of bungalows not far from where he sat. They were set lower than the road on the slopes of the cliffs. Soon people would be moving about, and all it might take was some nosy-parker walking a dog to spot him. The car was safe in an official parking place and hopefully would not excite attention if he left it there. He quickly retrieved a length of rope from his supplies in the boot, and tried to gauge if it would be long enough. Instantly he made up his mind. He shouldered his rucksack and returned to the bridge. Swinging over the railings, he clambered underneath onto the steel girders that supported the bridge. One slip, and all his plans would end in a bone-shattering plunge into the ravine but he put the thought of that from his mind.

Precious moments were lost when his backpack snagged on one of the supports as he wormed his way towards the stonework below the gates. For a moment he thought he might have to release the pack but he managed to wrench it free. As soon as he was close enough he attached one end of his rope to one of the transverse struts and let it drop down. The rope was perhaps three feet shorter than he would have wished, but it would enable him to swing inside the emplacement. He could see that his difficulty would come when he wanted to climb back up.

Breathlessly he slid down the rope and swung himself into what resembled a concrete cave that narrowed at the far end. He couldn't believe his luck. There, he found gaping steel shutters that reluctantly gave way as he applied his shoulder to them. He dropped into semi-darkness and found himself standing in an old gun emplacement where rusted steel mountings were still bolted to the floor.

Ryder resisted the idea of a cigarette. Dumping his Bergen on the floor, he looked around him. An oblong concrete gallery extended away to his right from where he stood and thin shafts of daylight invaded the embrasures in the walls to relieve the darkness. Particles of dust lay suspended in the beams of light, reminding him of the night skies over Koh Samui where the stars of the universe seemed to stretch to infinity.

The floor was thick with dust and littered with rubbish, and a dank airless smell pervaded the place. He wished he could throw open the steel shutters in the gun slits to allow fresh sea-borne air to cleanse the atmosphere and as his eyes became accustomed to the gloom he could make out slicks of wetness streaking the walls where deposits of a green-white crystalline substance formed long ridges that extended to the floor. He knew immediately that he was safe here; it was a catacomb that had lain undisturbed for many years. A man could die here, he realized, and perhaps never be found. He took a torch from a pocket of his pack and set off in search of an entrance.

The only door that he could find was at the top of a flight of granite steps at the end of the gallery. It was constructed of steel and securely locked. The hinges were welded by rust that powdered when he touched it. It had not opened in years. Satisfied, he retraced his steps and stood for a moment in one of the firing positions where he could look directly down into a sloping ravine that was choked with furze and wild blackberry briar. From far below the supports of the bridge came the sound of the sea making sucking noises in the kelp fringing the rocks. It was a lonely sound that echoed like muttering voices from the granite facing of the defile.

He returned to where he had left his rucksack and rolled out his sleeping bag. Sitting on it, he lit a cigarette while he nursed a small chemical fuelled stove into life and heated a can of minestrone soup. The soup warmed him, and he followed it with great chunks of bread and cheese. Then he zipped the sleeping bag around him and closed his eyes.

Inspector William Brophy collected a plastic cup of lukewarm coffee from a machine and took it inside his cluttered office. He sat down at his desk and surveyed the disorder of the room with an acute feeling of despair. At his feet, the contents of his waste paper bin had long since overflowed and a collection of plastic coffee cups littered the floor like pulled teeth. Thumb-stained brown manila folders rested in drunken piles everywhere. How much longer could he go on, he wondered. Ten years ago Ireland thought it had a crime wave when the murder rate climbed to one or two in a year. Now it was one or two a day and most of those were drug related and it was not just in the cities either, it seemed to him that every hidden village was touched by brutality of some sort. As a result the prisons were choked with the living scum of the streets, drug ridden and odious, like blocked sewers that

spewed filth back into circulation with the regularity of a lavatory being flushed.

He fished a crumpled packet of cigarettes from his pocket.
Selecting one that wasn't broken, he lit it and sipped at the
tasteless coffee. He didn't give a fig for Flicker Hennessy's
demise. The world was better off without that little bastard, he
thought. It was the reason for his murder that concerned him.
That, and the method used to kill him. It was the work of a
professional, that much he was sure of. He drained his coffee
and picked up the phone to call O'Dwyer. "Any news,
Colm?"

"Well, as a matter of fact yes. One of Hennessey's favorite
haunts was the Mandarin down in Rathmines. I had a chat
with the guy who runs the place and he let it out that someone was in there last night looking for our friend Flicker
before he got himself topped."

Brophy felt a surge of excitement. "That's good work,
Colm', he said. "Did you get a description?"

"Not great. Six feet tall or thereabouts, scar on his face.
Hard looking, not the sort you'd want to pick a row with.
Thinks he was English but he wasn't sure about that."

"Well that's something to go on at least." Brophy murmured.

O'Dwyer was silent for a moment. "There's another
thing," he said. "The supply of drugs has taken a big hike
recently. Anything you want is out there at the moment. The
city is awash in the stuff. Someone has been very busy
recently, that's for sure. What about you?"

"Confirmation on Hennessy's cause of death, that's all. He
was strangled. The coroner says it was definitely done with a
wire, which worries the hell out of me."

"How so?"

Brophy fumbled for another cigarette. "The killer used a
garrote, that makes it foreign, doesn't it? Forensics say the flat
was as clean as a whistle except for the cigarette ash. They say
it was from a Gauloise. That's French. How many of our hard
men smoke French fags? I'd guess not many. An internal drug

war is one thing, but if it's gone international...brace yourself for a load of bodies and I'm afraid we've just witnessed the start of it."

There was a moment's silence before O'Dwyer replied. "I don't think so," he said. "Hennessy was small fry. Anyway, maybe he smoked Gauloise cigarettes himself."

"There was a packet of Rothmans in his pocket," Brophy retorted. He looked up as his office door opened. A uniformed sergeant stepped to his desk and handed him a flimsy sheet of paper. "Hold on a minute, Colm," he said.

Brophy drew in a sharp breath and let the sheet of paper drop to join the other debris on his desk. "It's started, Colm." he said.

"What's that?"

"Frank Sullivan was found dead this morning in Galway. We've just received a fax from Millstreet." Brophy heard O'Dwyer's whistle of surprise at the other end of the line.

"You don't say! How did he die?"

"Natural causes, they think. Apparently his wife found him this morning when she arrived home from a trip to see her mother."

Brophy listened to the pause as O'Dwyer considered what he had told him. "I don't understand." O'Dwyer said eventually. "What could that have to do with Hennessy? It sounds like a coincidence. Sullivan was no youngster, you know. Was it a heart attack?"

Brophy scorned the suggestion. "You are admirably forgiving, Colm. I'll give you that much. I don't know what he died of yet, but there is not a gram of junk coming in here that Sullivan doesn't have something to do with. You know that as well as I do. If supply is on the upsurge as you say it is then you can bet that Sullivan is behind it. On top of that, every dog in the street knows that Sullivan was behind the killing of that journalist, Monica Flaherty, too. She was on to something, you can be sure of that. Christ! She virtually named him for the Brink's robbery last year and we know that she wheedled information out of Hennessy on more than one occasion." He glanced at the files littering his desk. "I've got dossiers on that fucker that would fill a bloody museum; it's evidence that I don't have. Take my word for it, boyo. Hennessy was the start of it and Sullivan is linked to it in some way, even if they tell me he died of chicken pox."

"You think someone is settling a score?"

"Maybe. There's three main families that have an interest in this, it could be any of them. It just takes one to get greedy and want a bigger slice of the cake." Brophy glared at the institutional walls of the room. "I'm going down to Galway to take a closer look. While I'm gone I want you to drag in every little snot-rag that Hennessy had any dealings with. Frighten the shit out of them if you have to, but by the time I get back I expect you to have something for me. Understand?"

"Okay, boss. It'll be a pleasure!"

"Good lad, Colm! Don't forget to ask 'em what they smoke!" Brophy let the telephone slip into its cradle and threw his plastic cup onto the pile of others beside his desk.

THIRTY-FIVE

Matthew Brennan regained consciousness as a light sprinkling of rain fell on his face. He slowly became aware that his clothes felt damp and there was a throbbing pain in his head. He sat up in surprise and looked about him. The street remained deserted, the pavement a damp sheen under the streetlights. He was cold and his forehead felt sticky. He put a hand to his head and felt the soreness of a bruise with a lump the size of a pullet's egg.

Numbly, he studied the blood on his fingertips in the light of a nearby street lamp and wondered how long he had been lying there. He remembered leaving Concannon's pub at two thirty, after the card game and glancing at his watch, he realized that he had been out cold for more than thirty minutes. Then he remembered seeing Helen Cullen being carried into her home by Critchley and another man. He glanced up the street, but Critchley's BMW had gone. He stood up, swaying unsteadily on his feet. Helen Cullen's house was in darkness. Groggily, he made his way home, deciding that later in the day would be a good time to pay a visit to his old client, Richard Critchley.

Critchley slept only fitfully during the night. Helen had never regained consciousness even when he and Webster had undressed her and placed her in her bed. He tried to convince himself that she was still alive, but he worried that she could not survive without expert attention. On the other hand, he was too aware of the risk he would run by bringing her to a hospital. Her drug abuse would be immediately evident and the source would come under scrutiny. He felt chilled and sickened by what had happened.

Webster's attitude to the whole affair was beyond his comprehension but he had been very thorough and had even strewn a number of the tablets she had taken around her bed before they had left the room. Critchley realized he would never have thought of that.

He glanced at his bedside clock. It was nearly ten o'clock. Webster must have fallen asleep for there was no sound in the house now, only the harsh twittering of starlings from outside his open bedroom window. He considered what lay ahead throughout the day. Nicholls would be returning after another of his delivery trips to the border and another dive was scheduled that night. He shivered in spite of the warm bedclothes that covered him.

Webster was sitting in the kitchen, drinking coffee and listening to the radio when Critchley finally came downstairs. He looked relaxed. "Morning," he said, as Critchley came into the room. He was holding a mobile telephone, but he put it down immediately. "There's coffee in the pot, if you're interested."

Critchley muttered his thanks and picked up the coffee pot. "We've got a busy day ahead of us," he said, sitting down. "Nicholls will be here later this afternoon and I have to recharge his air bottles before tonight's dive. The boat needs refueling as well," he added as an afterthought.

Webster nodded. "That's not all we have to worry about," he responded.

Critchley glanced up over the rim of his mug. "What does that mean?"

"Frank Sullivan is dead. I just heard it on the news."

"Dead!"

"Dead as a dodo, mate. Don't look so worried...it was natural causes, but it presents us with one hell of a problem all the same. Not only does he have a pile of our money, but we might have to cap the well for a while until things sort themselves out."

Critchley felt a wave of relief. Maybe this was the end of it for a while. He opened his mouth to say something but Webster interrupted him. "Don't look so pleased, Critchley." he said. "I've spoken to Sid this morning, and he wants us to bring up as much as we can tonight and ship it north. The other thing you need to be thinking about is that bitch of yours. Have you leveled with us on how much she knows?"

"She doesn't know anything," Critchley protested.

"That's what you say. I'm not so sure. She's not a fool."

"Did you tell Phillips about her?"

Webster shook his head. "No," he said. "Sid's got enough on his plate right now. You had better call round there later to check on her."

"What if she dies?" Critchley moaned.

"That's a problem you're going to have to take on board, mate. You should have thought of that before you started pushing stuff into her other than your dick. Think yourself lucky that I was here to clean up after you." Webster's gaze was cold. "Left to your own devices, you'd have fucked it up!"

Critchley bristled. "What about your friend, Ryder? It sounds to me that I'm not the only one to have blotted my copy book."

Webster scowled. "I was coming to him," he said. "The cops are looking for him. He won't get too far. They want to talk to him about Hennessy's murder."

Critchley was startled. "How do you know?"

"Don't get up-tight about it," Webster snapped. "It was on the news...they don't even know his name yet. But the report will frighten him off. We can forget him for a while. I might even give the cops a helping hand."

"What do you mean by that?"

"Never mind. It doesn't matter."

"Did he have anything to do with Sullivan's death?" Critchley asked.

Webster gave a dismissive wave of his hand. "I thought of it, but it doesn't make sense. Sullivan died naturally."

"I hope you're right," Critchley countered, and for the first time he saw real fear in Webster's eyes.

Matthew Brennan opened his office much later than usual. It was nearly midday when he unlocked the door. He had a profound headache and his stomach felt bilious. Foregoing breakfast, he had left the house quickly, before his wife had time to question him about the bruise on his forehead. He had no desire to face an inquiry and there were too many other things occupying his mind.

He boiled water in an electric kettle and made himself a cup of tea. Yesterday's milk was just beginning to curdle but he ignored the scum forming on the surface of the tea and carried his cup to the doorway. Sipping his tea slowly, he contemplated where to begin. How to approach Critchley was paramount in his thoughts. He had to do it in such a way that would ensure his inclusion in Critchley's wealthy lifestyle. The identity of the other man who had carried Helen Cullen from the car last night puzzled him. Step carefully, lad, he told himself.

A passer by stopped to inspect the list of properties displayed in his window. Brennan eyed him sourly for a moment, and then adopted a false smile of encouragement. "Good morning, sir!" He said. "'Tis' a grand day for buying a house, that's for sure."

The man smiled self-consciously. "If you've got the money," he countered. "Kinsale prices have gone to the dogs. Mark my words. The bubble will burst one of these days."

Brennan gave a noncommittal grunt and moved away from the doorway, closing the door behind him. He could do without time wasters like the man still standing outside. He was reaching for the telephone to ring Critchley when Seamus Collins pushed the door open and slid inside. The usual aura of rotten fish preceded him, and Brennan's stomach churned. "What the hell do you want, Seamus? Can't you see that I'm busy?"

"This won't take but a minute, Mattie." Collins was unsmiling, not his usual simpering self. He pulled up a chair and sat down as though he carried the weight of the world on his shoulders. Even the sly sparkle usually in his eyes was missing. "It's terrible news I have for you, Mattie, and that's for sure." His eyes settled on Brennan's cup. "I suppose there's no chance of a cup of spit?"

Brennan reached over and switched on the kettle. "Get on with it, Seamus." he snapped. "I'll have a tea bag for you in a minute. I hope you don't mind sour milk in your tea?"

"Tis all the same to me now. I'm parched with the thirst and that's the God's truth." Collins picked absentmindedly at a layer of fish scales on his hand. "I suppose you've already heard," he said eventually.

"I've heard bugger all this morning, Seamus." Brennan dropped a tea bag into a mug and poured in the hot water. He handed it to Collins and pushed a milk carton towards him. "There's no sugar," he said. "I don't use it. The wife says it's bad for my arteries."

Collins slurped from his mug and eyed Brennan warily. "It's about Helen Cullen," he said in a low voice.

Brennan hid his surprise. "Go on," he said. "What about her?"

"She's dead," Collins replied. He made the sign of the cross and bowed his head. "They found her an hour ago dead in her bed, the poor girl. That's a robbery by God, I say. She was the finest bit of stuff in the town and He's snatched her from underneath our noses. What age would you think she'd be, Mattie?"

Brennan stared blankly at Collins. This was some turn up, he thought. "I'd say she was only about twenty-six or so," he replied eventually, before adding, "She had too many airs and graces for my liking."

"She was never like that to me," replied Collins. "Anytime I took fish to the hotel she'd always have a pint lined up for me at the bar when I finished my delivery. That's the sort of kindness a man with my occupation appreciates. You build up a hell of a thirst hauling pots, I can tell you. I must go to the funeral."

"When is it?"

Collins drained his tea. "I don't know. They say there will have to be an inquest. Because she was so young I suppose."

"Oh! There would have to be at her age, of course." Brennan peered at Collins for a moment. "Is that all you heard, Seamus? I mean, did anyone say how she died?"

"Well, I only saw the coffin being brought out of the house as I passed, but Mrs. Gibbons was standing outside as well. Twas she that found her dead. She told me it might be suicide. She said she found the bedroom covered in pills. They were all over the place, according to Mrs. Gibbons."

Brennan grunted and looked away. Collins had saved the best for last, he thought. Maybe there was more yet. "Have another cup of tea, Seamus." he said.

"I will indeed. Don't stir yourself, Mattie, I'll get it myself." Collins got up and went across to busy himself with the kettle. "She was seeing a lot of your man, Critchley, out at Clonbar House lately." Collins said from behind him.

"Is that so?" Brennan half swiveled his chair and watched Collins dumping his tea bag carelessly beside the kettle. A slow brown stain seeped to the edge of the shelf and dripped slowly down over a pile of newspaper clippings. "You've been keeping an eye on thing's then, Seamus?"

"You told me to, don't you remember?" Collins came back and sat down at the other side of the desk. "He's been very busy with that boat of his lately."

"Oh?" Brennan fished in his pocket and found a crumpled twenty Euro note. He passed it to Collins and it disappeared instantly into a salt stained pocket of his oilskin jacket. "That's generous of you, Mattie. I'll bring you in a couple of lobsters tomorrow."

"Fuck the lobsters! Spit it out!" Brennan growled.

Collins colored slightly and sipped his tea. "There's been a lot of coming and going at night lately," he said. "That mooring of his out at the house is not the easiest place to get in and out of in a big boat like that, especially in the dark. The way in through the rocks is very narrow. Sometimes when the visibility's really bad he lines her up on a pair of lanterns that he leaves on the shore for leading marks. But I could never get close enough to see much else. It seems a bit strange though, when he has a berth in the marina anytime he wants."

"I wouldn't worry yourself about it, Seamus. Critchley is eccentric. The Brits are funny that way." Brennan studied Collins for a moment. On the face of it, he thought, the man was an idiot but Brennan had long since learned that it was impossible to know what went on in someone else's brain. At any rate, he felt sure that he had learned all that he could from him. "I'll have to go now, Seamus," he said. "I've got an appointment with a customer."

Collins stood up to leave. "Thanks for the tea, and the other," he said. "Will I still keep an eye open for you, Mattie?"

"Do, Seamus. I appreciate what you've told me." Brennan showed Collins to the door and watched him thoughtfully as he made his way back down the street towards the harbor. In a few minutes all his plans had changed. Helen Cullen's death was not suicide. He felt sure of that. Briefly he wondered if she was already dead when he had seen her being carried from the car. If she was, then Critchley might be involved in a murder.

Whatever it was, Critchley was wide open to blackmail, but the thought did not excite him the way it should. He was no longer sure that he wanted to get into water as deep as that.

THIRTY-SIX

The tourist season was making itself felt in Galway and strangling the city center as Inspector Brophy followed a serpentine line of cars crawling towards Eyre Square. To add to a sense of chaos, the day was overcast, the air muggy and laden with the fumes of impatient engines. It took nearly forty-five minutes for him to make his way from the outskirts of town through the snarl of traffic that blocked the narrow streets to a parking place outside the police barracks at Mill Street. When he finally climbed out of his car his shirt was sticking to his back.

The station was cool, but its activity matched that in the street. Brophy forced his way through a raucous crowd of itinerants who were arguing noisily with a harassed desk sergeant. As he reached the front of a wedge of sweating bodies he flashed his warrant card. "Brophy," he said sharply. "I'd like a word with Superintendent Forbes."

The desk sergeant glanced at him without interest. "Upstairs," he replied. There was frustration in his voice. "First door on the left."

"Thanks."

Brophy knocked politely on the door, opening it after a moment's hesitation and went inside. Superintendent Forbes was seated behind a desk piled high with files. The air was filled with smoke from a pipe that he clenched firmly in his teeth. Forbes took the pipe out of his mouth and placed it on the desk as he smiled in welcome. "Drag up a chair, Bill," he said. "Forgive the pipe; the bastards haven't managed to break me yet! It's been a long time. How are things up in the smoke?"

Brophy shook hands and sank into a chair opposite to him. "Just as fucking bad as your place downstairs," he said, grinning. He had trained with Forbes when they first joined the Gardai. That was ages ago he realized. Now, Forbes looked as old as he felt.

"Galway is becoming a war zone," replied Forbes sourly. "The tinkers are arriving for the races and we have our hands full." On top of that, we've got pickpockets, pushers, you name it, this year. And the usual shit, not enough man power. Can you believe we even have hookers coming over from Cardiff to set up shop for the easy pickings!" He gave a hoarse laugh. "Galway used to be one of the nicer places, a great posting...but that's beside the point. What can I do for you, Bill?"

"I wanted to pick your brains."

"About what?"

"Frank Sullivan's death."

Forbes frowned. "What's to know? He died at home of natural causes. If you want my personal opinion, the country will be better off without him. He's one less to worry about, and I can do with that at the moment."

"You have no suspicions then, Jerry?"

"No. Why should I? His doctor certified the death. Sullivan wasn't a young man, you know, and he's been in bad health. He was a diabetic and his doctor had been treating him for angina for some time. The cause of death was given as heart failure."

Brophy toyed with his cigarette packet. Thinking better of it he put the pack back in his pocket. A wasted trip, he thought morosely.

Forbes gave him a quizzical look and picked up his pipe. "Why the interest? I'd have thought you would be pleased."

"I'm investigating the murder of a Dublin dealer named
Hennessy. Sullivan was linked to him. It's just that the idea of
both of them doing us a favor at the same time seemed too
convenient." Brophy smiled through a haze of tobacco smoke
as Forbes brought his pipe back to life. "Maybe I got it
wrong."

"I think you have," Forbes responded without hesitation.
"We've been keeping an eye on Sullivan since the murder of
that journalist, you know. We haven't been able to pin him to
anything. I can assure you, there's nothing to suggest foul play
in this, Bill."

"I should have talked it over with you on the phone. I
could have saved myself a trip; the traffic was lousy."

Forbes adopted a conciliatory tone. "Well," he said. "As
you're down here, you can always have a word with Sullivan's wife just to satisfy yourself, although I doubt if you'll
hear anything different from her. How's the investigation
going, anyway?"

Brophy shrugged. "Murky. Not a lot to go on yet. We're
looking for a guy with a scarred face, but other than that we
have little to go on. He could be English or maybe a foreigner
because I think he smokes French cigarettes." He smiled. "I'm
not close to arresting any one on that, am I?"

"You think it was a hit?"

"Possibly." Brophy shifted uneasily in his seat and stubbed
out his cigarette in an ashtray. "There's some kind of war
going on that I can't put my finger on, but I can tell you
there's a lot of stuff on the streets up in Dublin lately and if
I'm right that Hennessy's killing was the work of a professional from outside, I'd say the killer is long gone by now.
From what you say, there's probably no connection with Sullivan." He stood up and prepared to leave. "Thanks for your
time, Jerry. I'll call out to Mrs. Sullivan before I head back to
Dublin."

Superintendent Forbes saw him to the door and shook
hands. "Good luck," he said. "You'll need it. Sullivan's wife is

just as crafty as he was. The desk sergeant will give you directions to the house."

Brophy followed the winding road to Moycullen stuck behind a motor caravan with French registration plates and a truck laden with sand. With each shift in gear, the lorry belched black fumes that had the consistency of treacle, burning Brophy's eyes and throat. It was not his day, he decided.

He found Sullivan's house without difficulty and followed a curving drive, glad to be rid of the lorry that had frustrated him for six miles. A number of cars were parked in front of the house and he came to a halt behind a Mercedes with opulent leather upholstery. The front door bell chimed hollowly when he pressed it, and he waited patiently until a man wearing a blazer and a tie that had some type of nautical insignia emblazoned on it opened the door. The man's eyes were suspicious and he neither spoke nor smiled.

"Good afternoon." Brophy flashed his warrant card. "Detective Inspector Brophy," he announced. "Might I have a word with Mrs. Sullivan?"

The man blocking the entrance scowled. "She's not up to speaking to anyone." he replied coldly.

"This will only take a minute." Brophy insisted. "It's important that I speak with her."

"Her husband has just died, don't you people understand that?"

"I know that. That's why I am here. I have one or two questions I'd like to put to her."

The man's jaw tightened. "I'll ask her if she wants to talk to you."

The man led Brophy through a wide hallway with a floor of gleaming pine and showed him into what appeared to be a comfortably furnished study with French doors opening onto a wide sweep of well-kept lawns fringed by fruit trees. "Wait here," he said as he closed the door behind him.

Brophy glanced around the room. It was well furnished but uncluttered. There were a number of paintings on the walls, one of which had a cracked glass in its frame. Against one wall was a well-stocked bookcase. Set at an angle to the glass doors leading to the garden, a polished rosewood desk reflected a gleam of sunlight from outside. He walked to the French doors and looked outside. Where the lawns ended, he could make out a low stone wall behind an expanse of shrubbery. Behind that was a series of fields that ended far up on the hillside where a forest of pine trees covered the skyline. The gardens were secluded and not overlooked, but the lack of security surprised him. Anyone could easily gain access from the fields to the rear of the house. He would have expected a man like Sullivan to live in something more like a fortress.

He turned away from the window as the door opened. A diminutive woman hesitated in the doorway. She wore a simple black dress without jewelry except for a plain ring on her wedding finger. Her face was pale without make-up; her eyes red-rimmed from recent tears. "You wished to speak with me?" she said in a low voice.

Brophy advanced towards her. "Mrs. Sullivan?"

"Yes," she replied hesitantly. "What do you want? This is not a good time. My husband has just died."

He noticed that her hair was tightly coiled and held in place by a clip from which a wisp of fair hair had escaped. It made her face look unusually severe, but she must have been beautiful once, he could see. "I understand that. You have my condolences, Mrs. Sullivan."

She ignored his extended hand and stood for a moment appraising him, holding the door open as though she needed a means of escape. "Condolences!" she snorted. "I would have thought you would be celebrating."

"I'm sorry?" Brophy sensed an inner strength to the woman that suggested she was no pushover. Her eyes did not waiver. As though she had reached a decision, she closed the door shutting out the mutter of voices coming from further down the hall.

"The police made my husband's final years a misery," she sniffed. "He didn't deserve that." She extracted a tissue from the sleeve of her black dress and dabbed at her eyes. Then she blew her nose and composed herself. "Let's get it over with," she said sharply. "What do you wish to ask me?"

"I understand that your husband died of a heart attack. Is that correct?"

"Yes. He had suffered from severe angina for some time."

"Where was his body found?"

Mrs. Sullivan's eyes suddenly became watery again. "Sitting right there, in that armchair near to you," she replied, tugging at her sleeve for her tissue.

Brophy glanced at a leather armchair near to where he was standing and tried to visualize the body. "Was he alone in the house?"

"Yes. I was visiting my family in Dublin." She made a snuffling sound and forced her eyes away from the chair. "I always feared it would end like this...that I wouldn't be here when...that I would find him dead one day."

"I know this is difficult for you, Mrs. Sullivan." Brophy paused and dropped his eyes for a moment. "You noticed nothing out of the ordinary?" He raised his eyes and looked at her.

"What do you mean by that?" For an instant she looked startled.

"No sign of a forced entry or any indication of a disturbance of some kind? Nothing missing from the house? Money, for instance?"

He followed her gaze to the painting with a cracked glass. "Why would you suggest such a thing?" she said. "Nothing was taken. There was a small amount of money in my husband's safe and in his wallet. The only thing that was out of the ordinary was that a painting had fallen off the wall. The hook had come out of the plaster and the glass was broken.

Otherwise, everything was intact and all the doors were locked. I've told you that my husband had been ill for some time. He was a diabetic. He died from natural causes. You people were always suggesting things about him that were untrue." Her voice had become brittle and angry.

"I'm not suggesting anything, Mrs. Sullivan. I'm investigating the murder of a man in Dublin that was known to your husband, an associate of his. I wanted to be certain that the two deaths were not connected in any way, if you follow me."

"I'm not sure that I do."

"How much money was in his wallet?"

"About two hundred euros."

"And in the safe?"

Her face grew suddenly pale. "Another seven hundred or so."

"Where is it?"

"In the bank," she replied quickly.

"No. I meant where is the safe?"

"Oh! It's a wall safe behind that painting."

"The one that is broken?"

"Yes." she said softly. "He probably needed something from the safe and dropped the painting, or it fell of its own accord. I don't know, but the safe was locked when I found him."

Brophy studied her face for a moment. Suspicion nagged at him. It was no more than a gut feeling, but he had been around long enough to trust his gut; and right now his gut was telling him that she was not really coming clean on the amount of money in the house. "I have to say that your husband was no angel, Mrs. Sullivan. We know he was involved in the drugs trade. Are you sure there wasn't more money in the house?"

Her face flushed with rising anger. "I am perfectly sure," she retorted. "I suggest you leave right now, Inspector whatever your name is! I have nothing further to say to you." She opened the door to show him out. "You can find your own way out," she said coldly.

Brophy followed her into the hall. "Just one further question, Mrs. Sullivan."

She stopped and wheeled to face him. "I just said . . ."

"What was your husband wearing when he died?"

She eyed him suspiciously for a moment before she answered. "He was dressed in a suit. A better one than that which you are wearing, Inspector."

Brophy ignored the gibe. "Where is it now? Could I see it?"

"No." she replied. "I had it burnt."

"Brophy raised his eyebrows. "And why was that?"

"Because he...because he had soiled himself." she said. "They removed his clothing in the morgue and I instructed them to dispose of them."

"I see. I won't trouble you any further, Mrs. Sullivan."

"Please don't." She turned away.

Brophy let himself out through the front door and climbed wearily into his car. His mood was bleak, but he could not stop thinking of the cracked glass in the painting in Sullivan's study. Nor could he think of a reason why the widow should want to cover anything up.

He drove slowly back down the gravel drive and turned right onto the winding road that led back to Galway. Reaching a straight stretch of road devoid of traffic, he accelerated just as his mobile phone buzzed. It was Sergeant O'Dwyer.

Brophy slowed down. "What have you got for me, Colm?"

"A name, boss. The guy we are looking for is an English man named Robert Ryder. I've got a complete description of him too."

Brophy's spirits lifted in an instant. "Great." he replied. "I'm on my way back and I'll be with you in three hours or so. How did you track him down?"

"I didn't. It was pure luck, boss. An anonymous phone call."

"Any idea who from, or where?"

"Haven't the foggiest."

Brophy sighed. "Well, it's something to go on." he said. "Make sure the ferry terminals and the airports get this information. I've wasted my time down here. Looks like our friend, Sullivan, just upped and died on us after all. I'll discuss it with you when I get back to Dublin."

Brophy pressed the finish button on his phone and stuck a Pavarotti tape into the stereo system. So, he thought. Maybe the day was not entirely wasted after all.

THIRTY-SEVEN

The ravine was filled with evening shadows when Ryder awoke. He was surprised at how soundly he had slept but he felt rested. A shiver of anticipation ran through him as he readied himself for what was to come.

Before leaving his hiding place, he carefully wrapped his false passport and the money he had taken from Sullivan in a stout plastic bag, and then secreted the package in a crevice in the wall. He left behind him a second bag containing a supply of tinned food and unwanted items of clothing. Then he re-packed his Bergen and stuffed it through the firing slit, easing himself after it through the narrow opening. He crouched in the embrasure for several minutes, sniffing the air like an animal. Nothing moved above him on the bridge and the road leading to the car was empty. He glanced at the rope that dangled a couple of feet away. He suddenly realized how short it was and looked down into the blackness of the canyon where jagged rocks lay in the shadows. This was not where he wanted to die, he thought grimly.

Tightening the shoulder straps of his Bergen, he steeled himself, and then drawing in a deep breath he launched himself into space. For a brief instant he thought that he had missed; then he felt the rope burning his hands as he swung in a wild arc beneath the girders of the bridge. He hung for a moment, waiting for the gyrations to slow, and then climbed swiftly upwards until his boots touched the first strut where he quickly coiled the rope and secured it out of sight for his return later.

Although it was a fine evening, Crosshaven was surprisingly quiet as Ryder drove through the village. It was too early yet for the pubs to be doing much business, and the scattering of shops overlooking the harbor looked empty. What few passers-by were about paid him no heed. Reaching the yacht club, he accelerated as the road opened before him.

A mile further on the River Owenabue lay snake-like and silent as he drove past Drake's Pool, where a cluster of yachts swung to their moorings. Here, Ryder pulled in at a lay-by above the riverbank to consult his map. In Carrigaline, a few miles further on, he would reach the main road leading to Kinsale. He got out of the car and walked to some bushes that fringed the road debating whether to take the back roads instead. He relieved himself and lit a cigarette knowing he had plenty of time before true darkness descended. As before in Somalia and in Thailand, darkness would be his ally, he knew. The back roads might be safer, he decided. Twenty feet below him, the water was black in the shadows of the trees, moving sluggishly against the steep banks as the tide flowed in from the sea. Ryder noticed how different it was from the swirling torrent of the Mekong that flexed its muscles in far off Thailand. He thought of Wan waiting for him, and glanced up at the sky where faint stars were beginning to show themselves, feeling her presence, remembering her smile, the touch of her finger tips warm upon his face. Soon he would be with her again, he promised himself.

He studied the boats on their moorings for a moment, recalling the warm waters of the Mediterranean where, in brief respites from the business of war, he had sailed dinghies off the shores of Corsica. In contrast, many of these looked neglected to Ryder, as though they never moved from the anchorage. They lay like forgotten toys, their owners lost somewhere in the jungles of commerce. A few yards away from where he stood lay a small stone pier where several dinghies moved uneasily as the incoming tide attempted to lift them from the muddy bottom. It was a place of peace and solitude, he thought. Another time, he would have lingered there. But he was here to kill. He thought of Mark then but his son's ghost no longer came to taunt him, as though he was content in some distant place. It was a strange thought. Putting it aside, he returned to the car.

He drove on until he picked up a sign for Fountainstown, turning left to follow a winding uphill tree-lined road. Now and then he passed expensive houses that were set back from the road, whose lights showed a briefly passed welcome. Unknown people lived in those homes in a way that Ryder wished he could. Correction, he thought firmly. In that way he would, once this was over. The beaches of Chaweng village beckoned.

He glanced at the clock. It was nearly nine o'clock. Surely there would be news. He switched on the radio. The voice of the announcer sounded friendly and matter of fact as he recounted the issues that concerned the outside world, and only at the very end did he disclose details of the murder investigation into Hennessy's death.

"Detectives involved in the investigation into the murder of drug dealer, Martin Hennessy, known to the underworld as Flicker, carried out a number of raids in Dublin today and several males were taken in for questioning. It is understood, that they have since been released without charge. It was also revealed this evening that the police are now interested in interviewing a Robert Ryder who is believed to be a foreign national, and was last seen in Dublin but is thought to be driving a left hand drive Mercedes car that is believed to be light brown in color. The registration number may be German. The driver is over six feet in height, of powerful build and is believed to have a noticeable scar on his face. Members of the public are advised not to approach this individual as he might be armed and dangerous."

They had his name! The announcement was so unexpected that Ryder took an approaching bend too fast, narrowly avoiding ending up in the ditch.

"Further to this development," the announcer went on. "The death occurred this morning, of Frank Sullivan at his home in Galway of natural causes. Although Sullivan was the source of much speculation in the press recently as being a major figure in the drugs underworld, his death is thought to be unconnected with that of Hennessy. Recently, there have been unproved suspicions that Sullivan was connected with the tragic murder of journalist, Monica Flaherty. His funeral will take place in Galway on Thursday. Now, for news of the days sporting events..."

Ryder switched off the radio and braked hard as he saw an open gateway leading into a field on his left. He reversed back through the opening and brought the car to a halt in a field of recently cut corn stubble. He got out of the car and looked about him. He could see no houses, only the blurred shapes of hedges that led to other similar fields but far away on the other side of Cork harbor, bright lights from an industrial complex sent a glow into the darkening sky.

Calmly, he lit a cigarette and considered his options. The element of surprise was no longer his primary weapon he realized. However they had managed it, the police now had his name. The whole world knew it now. He wondered if the two thugs in Dublin had known. He should have killed them, now it was too late. Webster was no fool, Ryder knew and if he was still in Kinsale he would be prepared. Even if he was to abandon his mission, he thought, getting out of the country was more difficult now, perhaps even impossible. The police would be watching all exit routes and his scarred face exposed him in a way that he had never suspected it would.

He rested his elbow on the roof of the car that was now just another encumbrance that could trap him. He could easily abandon it and steal another, he thought, but what about the risk? Feeling suddenly defeated he climbed back into the car and sat in silence while he wrestled with the problem.

All his instincts told him to withdraw now, to forget Kinsale. Then Colonel Marchand's brooding features entered his mind. What would he have done? Marchand would not hesitate, he decided. Not with the objective un-taken. Give me your body, he would say, and let the Legion take care of your soul. Your blood is the only price we ask of you.

Ryder switched on the interior light to study his map. Cork airport was not far away. The answer lay there.

THIRTY-EIGHT

Matthew Brennan drove out to Seamus Collins' house as shadows grew along the hedgerows fringing the fields. He drove slowly, squinting his eyes into the red blaze of a setting sun that made the road in front of him almost invisible.

He didn't really know what he was going to say to Seamus if he found him at home and all day he had struggled with his thoughts trying to decide what action to take. He knew that the right thing to do was to go to the police and tell them what he had seen the night before outside Helen Cullen's house. But she was dead and he wondered if it mattered anymore. Certainly it would not bring her back.

Kinsale was awash with rumor when he'd left. Everyone now knew that she had died from an overdose, but whether it was by accident or by design, nobody seemed to know. Except himself. Earlier, he had contemplated going out to Clonbar House and facing Critchley, but he had rejected the idea out of fear of the consequences. He needed to know who he was dealing with. Critchley was not alone in whatever he was up to. Of that he was certain. The truth was that Brennan was scared now.

He passed the turning that led to Clonbar House without even glancing to his left and accelerated as the sun became hidden behind distant hills. A few miles further on he turned off the main road onto a rutted boreen with clumps of grass at its centre that swished under the floor of the car as he followed its winding passage towards the sea. Shortly afterwards he entered a farmyard littered with the remains of rusted farm machinery. To one side, stacks of lobster pots were piled against the walls of an open-fronted hay shed. The door of the cottage facing him was open, and someone switched on the lights inside as he drew to a halt.

Seamus Collins appeared in the doorway chewing on a lump of bread, a mug of tea in his hand. His eyes had a faint gleam. "How 'ya, Mattie," he said as Brennan eased himself out of the car.

"Grand, Seamus. Yourself?"

"Not so bad, Mattie. This is a surprise. I can't remember the last time you came out this way. Is there a farm for sale, or what?"

Brennan scowled. "Just being sociable, Seamus. That's all."

"Well, you had better come inside then. There's tea in the pot."

Brennan followed him into the kitchen where the red embers of a fire glowed in a great stone fireplace. A half eaten loaf of bread and a chunk of suspect-looking cheese lay on a table covered with a sheet of farmyard plastic. The concrete floor showed through holes in what was left of its linoleum covering. "It's a warm night for a fire, Seamus," Brennan said as he lowered himself into a rocking chair at one side of the hearth.

"Believe it or not, Mattie. That fire has not gone out for near on a hundred years. No, I tell a lie. It went out the day my mother was buried, God rest her." Seamus wrestled with a blackened iron teapot and poured tea into an enamel mug. "Help yourself to milk and sugar," he said.

Brennan got up and stirred his tea at the table then returned to his chair. He glanced about him. There was nothing much in the room except for a picture of the Pope on one wall and a painted dresser that held a pile of plates and a few cracked cups. A flight of stairs climbed up one corner. "Nice place you have, Seamus." he said, sipping his tea.

Collins nodded and sat down at the table. "It does the job," he replied.

"You were right about Helen Cullen, Seamus. She took an overdose."

"Sleeping pills was it?"

"I don't know. But the whole town is talking of suicide."

Collins made a tut-tutting sound. "The Lord have mercy on her. "I'd say her boyfriend must be upset. It'll be a big shock to him, that's for sure." Collins' eyes were as bright as a stoat's over the rim of his mug.

Brennan ran a hand through his tousled hair. "Yes." he said, swallowing a mouthful of tea. "I suppose he will."

"Something's on your mind, Mattie. I can tell."

Brennan stared at Collins for a moment but the fisherman's face was innocent. "I haven't seen Critchley since," he offered.

"He refueled his yacht today in the marina. That's a sure sign."

"A sure sign of what?"

Collins smiled craftily. "A sure sign that he's going to sea again. He always fills her up before he does a trip."

"When do you think that will be?"

Collins buttered a slice of bread and carved off a slice of cheese from the lump on the table. "Probably tonight. He likes sailing at night. Then he'll probably go up to Crookhaven for the weekend. That's often what he does. He had another man with him. Some pal of his from London, I think."

Brennan walked over to the table and refilled his mug. "We could follow him if you like." Collins said quietly.

Brennan let out a long slow breath. Seamus was way ahead of him, he thought with a sense of surprise. "And why would we do that, Seamus?" he asked.

Collins shrugged. "Because I know that's what you want to do, Mattie. That's why you're here isn't it?"

"I suppose it is, Seamus. I suppose it is."

"If there's money in this..."

Brennan looked at Collins sharply. "If there is, you'll get your share."

The fisherman smiled. "Let's go and get the boat," he said. "We wouldn't want to miss him, would we? There's a set of oilskins there on the chair to keep you dry."

The approach road to Cork airport was surprisingly quiet as Ryder left the main road and he could see the landing lights of a plane making its descent far in the distance. He drove slowly past a line of waiting taxis in front of the terminal. The building was brightly lit, and through the glass entrance doors he could see lines of passengers forming at the check-in desks. Instantly, he thought of Wan, wishing that it was all over and that he was amongst them, queuing for a boarding pass. He wondered what it would be like to touch her again, to lie with her and feel her warmth, hear her laugh, and listen to her whispering in the darkness.

He forced her from his mind and followed the signs to a long-term car park, stopping at the entrance to take a ticket from a machine at the barrier. Then he slowly circled the car park, checking the cars. He hoped to pick one whose owner would be absent for a few days longer. Vaguely, he remembered someone telling him once that Fords, in particular, were more difficult to steal, but he didn't know if that was true or not. He eventually selected a Renault that was unlikely to attract much interest and parked the Mercedes some distance away, nearer to the terminal building. Removing everything of a personal nature from his own car, he walked unhurriedly back to the Renault.

Ten minutes later he had paid his parking charge and was back on the road to Kinsale.

Brophy arrived back in Dublin later than he had planned. He had stopped earlier at a motorway service station where he had eaten an all-day breakfast that now lay as a leaden mass in his stomach. As he followed the motorway at the approaches to the city he picked up his telephone and punched in Sergeant O'Dwyer's number.

O'Dwyer answered almost immediately. "Colm," Brophy said, "Its too late to go to the office. Why don't you meet me in Ryan's pub in Rathmines? I've had a feed of rashers the likes of which you've never seen. I could do with a pint of beer."

O'Dwyer chuckled into the phone. "I'll be there in fifteen minutes."

"I'll be a bit longer than that. Any developments?"

"None." replied O'Dwyer. "We pulled in a number of Hennessy's associates but only one of them was of any help."

"Who was he?"

"A guy called Scratcher Shaughnessy. He was one of Hennessy's runners. He told us that Hennessy had been warned to look out for Ryder, but he doesn't know why. They sent a couple of heavies to head off Ryder but we haven't been able to track them down."

Brophy grunted. "Any names?"

"No, Boss. Scratcher wouldn't give way on that one. He would only say that he warned Hennessy that Ryder was in town and that he wanted to buy a hit. That was all."

"Okay, I'll see you in a while." Brophy wondered if he was reading too much into this. If this Ryder was only trying to buy drugs, maybe the deal had gone wrong and he...Oh to hell with it. Brophy switched off the phone and accelerated into the fast lane.

Rathmines was at its frenetic best, but Brophy found a parking spot easily enough not far from Ryan's pub. All the fast food outlets were doing good trade and the pubs were overflowing. He found Colm O'Dwyer perched on a bar stool at the far end of the bar. He had an untouched pint of Guinness in front of him.

Brophy squeezed in beside him and signaled to the barman for a pint of the same. "It's been a long day, Colm." he said. "I'm bushed, and I feel like shit!"

O'Dwyer smiled. "A pint will settle your stomach. So Sullivan was a lost cause, was he?"

"Yeah, looks like it anyway. They're burying the bastard tomorrow."

"But you're not happy, right?"

Brophy paid for his drink and picked up his pint. "Cheers!" he said. He took a long swallow and wiped the foam from his lip. "I've been looking forward to that all day. No, Colm. I'm not entirely happy. The widow was holding out on something. I think she wanted a nice respectable funeral without any unpleasant autopsies, know what I mean? She said there was no sign of a disturbance but somehow I know there was money taken from that house. Just a feeling, mind you."

"Maybe Sullivan had a payment to make. You know, to someone he knew. Then he just upped and died."

"That might be the way it was. But there was a broken picture in his study that covered a wall safe. She said it had fallen off the wall and the glass broke when it hit the floor. She was adamant that there was money still in his wallet and in the safe and that nothing was missing."

"Well then..."

Brophy shrugged. "I'm probably imagining things."

O'Dwyer's mobile phone buzzed and he extracted it from his inside pocket. With one hand over his ear to blot out the noise around him he listened intently. "Good," he said eventually. "I'll tell him." He put the phone back in his pocket. "They've found Ryder's Mercedes," he said.

Brophy picked up his glass and gulped greedily from it. He put down the glass and belched. "Where?"

"At Cork airport. A security guard spotted it at the end of his shift."

"Shit!" replied Brophy. "He's long gone."

"Maybe not, Boss. The airports have his description and his name. Surely they'd have picked him up?"

"That security man had sharp eyes. That doesn't mean to say the rest of them have." Brophy sounded despondent.

He picked up his pint and drained it. "Finish your drink." he ordered.

"Where to?"

"Cork. You drive and I'll sleep."

THIRTY-NINE

There was a sickening smell of rotten fish in Seamus Collins' tarred currach and several inches of water sloshed about in the bottom of the boat as Collins pushed off from the shore. Brennan struggled to find a comfortable perch amongst a tangle of polypropylene ropes and a number of lobster pots containing herring bait that had lain all day in the sun. Already, his shoes were filling with cold water. "I hope this is not a wasted trip," he said glumly.

Collins grinned at him and pulled the starter cord of the engine. "If it is," he said. "At least the fresh air will do you good, Mattie. You spend too long in that office of yours. I don't know how you stick it." A low mutter came from the powerful outboard motor as he opened the throttle and Brennan watched the shore quickly receding behind them.

Brennan became colder over the next half hour as the dampness from his oilskins slowly penetrated his inner clothing and reached his skin. How any man could stick making a living from the sea in an open currach was beyond his comprehension. "How much longer?" he moaned.

"Not far now, we're nearly opposite Critchley's house." Brennan let his eyes search the black outline of the land but he could recognize nothing. Only a few distant lights showed but they seemed to be a long way off.

The low growl of the engine subsided as Collins throttled back, and then the bow of the boat dropped as their speed decreased, giving respite from the chill wind of their passage. "We're off the entrance now," Collins whispered. "If he's there we should be able to see the yacht." He stood up to get a better view. "There she is now," he whispered. Collins killed the engine and the boat slowed even more until it began a rhythmical rolling motion with just the faint splash of tiny waves against its sides.

The sudden stillness was eerie. With an uneasy feeling, Brennan started to contemplate the pork chops he had consumed for dinner earlier. "I can't see a damn thing," he protested.

"Raise your eyes towards the sky. You'll see her masts above the rocks if you look carefully."

Brennan squinted into the darkness. The outlying rocks were close now. He could smell the seaweed and the sea was making low sucking noises as though it was feeding there. A powerful light swept briefly across a gap in the rocks and instantly went out. "I see something," he said with bated breath.

"Keep down; they're coming out," Collins growled. He tugged at the starter cord and the engine obediently came to life and he nursed the currach closer to the black shadow of the rocks. Stopping the engine again, he quickly threw an anchor overboard, paying out the rope until the anchor bit and the boat swung into a gentle onshore breeze. "Keep still now," Collins ordered. "Keep your head down and say nothing until they get clear."

Brennan became aware of the pulsating sound of a powerful diesel engine above the slap of the waves. The approaching engine sounded alarmingly close. He risked a quick peep over the gunwale as a green navigation light appeared in the entrance. Moments later he saw the outline of the yacht as she lifted her forefoot to the open sea. Brennan ducked lower in the boat. The smell of rotten fish filled his nostrils and his stomach churned both from fear and the stench.

Slowly the throb of the engine faded as the yacht powered past in the darkness. When he next looked up he could only see a white stern light receding into the night.

Collins started the engine and calmly heaved in the anchor until it clanked against the bow, then he lifted it on board. Without a word he steered the currach away from the rocks following the white light out to sea.

A steady bleep-beep sound issued from the GPS repeater mounted in a cluster of cockpit instruments and a tiny green light flashed. Critchley immediately throttled back the engine and the yacht slowed perceptibly. With power and running lights off, the boat lay quietly under the faint light from a waning moon rolling gently on a sea that gave the illusion of a great pool of molasses.

"Okay," Critchley said. "We're here."

He produced a powerful pair of night vision glasses and made a careful sweep of the horizon. "I'll just check the radar, and then we can get on with it."

A few minutes later Nicholls, the diver, appeared in the hatchway dressed in his black diving suit. Nicholls glanced at the GPS readout and pulled on his head cover. There was the clink of metal on metal as he shouldered his air bottles on his powerful frame and strapped them on. "Okay, guys. Here we go!" He slipped on his goggles and inserted his mouthpiece. There was the faint hiss of air as he adjusted valves and tested the tanks before he slipped overboard with his flippers in his hand and sank from sight.

Peter Webster gaped uneasily at a small flurry of bubbles that formed on the inky water, only to instantly disappear. "How the fuck does he do that!" he exclaimed. "I mean, that son of a bitch has guts going down there in the dark."

Critchley smiled inwardly. Rarely did Webster praise anything. "He's good at it," Critchley replied. He lowered a stainless steel boarding ladder over the side and secured it. "Nicholls is the nearest thing to a fucking fish that I've ever met. He actually likes it down there. Did you ever look at his eyes?"

"No."

"Take a close look when he comes up." Critchley laughed softly. "They're the closest thing to fish eyes you've ever seen. Normally divers like to go down in pairs if it's deep, and especially at night. It's safer. But Dave doesn't give a shit! It's probably where he wants to die anyway."

Webster stared over the side. "Did you ever go down yourself?"

"Yes, once or twice just for the hell of it, but I prefer to do it in daylight and in shallower water." Critchley sat down in the cockpit and lit a cigarette. "Now all we have to do is wait," he said. "He'll do the rest."

"How deep is it?"

"About twenty metres."

"How the hell does he see anything down there at night?"

"He's got a powerful underwater light and the stuff is in white containers. As soon as he locates them, he'll send them up with an air bag."

Webster shook his head. "Sooner him than me," he said firmly.

Critchley gave a dry chuckle. "I told you this was the front line, Peter. Now perhaps you'll believe me."

Webster grunted and looked up at the sky. It seemed huge, as though there was no end to it where it met the sea. Except for a sliver of moon, there was nothing to see, just a sprinkling of stars. Far away a light flashed. "What's that?" he asked nervously.

Critchley looked in the direction Webster was pointing. "That's the light on the Old Head of Kinsale," he said. "Group flashing twice, every ten seconds."

Webster stared at the light for some time. He had never been out on the sea at night before. This was more than a sea he realized. This was the edge of an ocean that stretched all the way to America. He wondered what it would be like in a storm, then decided he didn't want to know. "You know, Critchley. You've changed a lot since you came over here."

Critchley glanced up. "What do you mean by that?"

"Well, I was against sending you here in the first place. I didn't think you had enough guts for this. I only agreed because Phillips insisted."

Critchley gave a dry laugh. "It's all down to breeding, old boy!" His tone was mocking.

Webster felt some of his old dislike surfacing. The insufferable little bastard had not changed at all, he decided. He closed his mouth and listened to the tide sucking at the hull of the yacht as it rolled restlessly. Soft groaning noises reached him as the yacht rolled and he began to feel the first twinge of seasickness. "And another thing," he said testily.

"What?"

"I don't know if it's because you are coked up to your eyebrows or what, but out here you are your own man. What I mean is, you don't seem so jumpy. You seem to know what you are doing, and the risks don't seem to freak you out. Ashore it's a different matter. Back there, you're like a headless chicken, and with about just as much bottle."

"Fuck you, Webster! I happen to like the sea. It's clean, and it helps me to forget that I'm mixed up with the scum of this world. Don't get any illusions. I didn't choose you either, and I can't wait to be rid of you. That can't come soon enough." Critchley turned on him angrily. "A woman is dead because of you. I might as well have killed her and it will be on my conscience for a long time."

"You didn't kill her, you asshole! The stupid bitch overdosed."

"I don't see it that way. She might be alive now if we had got her to a hospital. Sooner or later I'm going to have to answer questions about that."

"You just keep your goddamned mouth shut and everything will be alright." Webster snapped.

"Nothing's alright. Things are coming apart, Webster. This operation needs to shut down for a while."

"Right after this lot. I told you that."

"What about Ryder? You seem to have forgotten him."

"He's fucked, Critchley. You can stop worrying about him. I've spiked his guns." Webster laughed coldly. "I wouldn't be surprised if he's already nicked."

Critchley shot Webster a venomous look. His voice had a measured tone when he eventually replied. "What do you mean, you spiked his guns?"

"I told the cops who he was. I gave them a complete description."

"You did what!" Critchley sounded incredulous.

"Don't worry about it. I made an anonymous call, that's all."

"When?"

"After lunch. From a call box, so forget about it."

"I don't believe this! How could you take such a risk!"

"What else could I do, for fuck's sake! Sit and wait for the bastard? Serve him tea and biscuits and say, nice to see you again, Bob? Get real, Critchley! I know how to handle the likes of Ryder!"

Critchley glanced at the GPS repeater. He reached over and pushed a button. Instantly, its screen began to glow with symbols. Webster heard the muted throb of the engine as Critchley opened the throttle. "What are you doing now?"

Critchley put the engine into gear and swung the wheel as the boat moved slowly forward. "The tide has pulled us down," he said. "I'm just getting back into position."

Webster slumped deeper into the cockpit, fighting off increasing nausea and wishing he was back on the familiar streets of London where the sky never looked so immense or so ominous. Earlier, when they had filled up with fuel at the marina in Kinsale, it had all seemed a bit of an adventure, almost fun. They had enjoyed a lobster salad for lunch at The Spaniard and sat in the sun drinking beer. Now he wished he had not eaten. He wished he had waited back at the house with those two goons of Sullivan's who had come down from Dublin.

The GPS instrument bleeped as Critchley slowed the engine and took it out of gear. "Back on station," he announced.

At that moment Webster vomited his dinner onto the side decks as he struggled to reach the guardrail. The effort exhausted him; he lay half in and half out of the cockpit until his dry retching subsided. "How much longer?"

"Not long." Critchley chuckled to himself somewhere in the darkness.

Seconds later a small sound startled Webster as something bumped heavily alongside the hull up forward. Critchley disappeared into the darkness clutching a boat hook, only to reappear dragging on a rope as he brought the first package abreast of the cockpit. He wound a couple of turns of the rope around a winch and passed the end to Webster. "Hold this," he hissed. "And don't let it go!"

Numbly, Webster held onto the rope's end and watched Critchley rigging a purchase to the end of the boom. He gave a fleeting thought to Phillips, deciding he was probably tucked up in bed back in West Byfleet. Critchley hung over the side and attached a snap-shackle to a loop in the rope and swung the boom out board. "You can let it go now," he breathed. "Help me pull on this rope."

Webster was aware of a splashing sound in the darkness and he started to shiver uncontrollably. "It's only Dave," Critchley snapped. "He'll look after himself. Just do as I say and pull on the bloody rope!"

The first bulky package swung overhead dripping seawater into the cockpit where Critchley released it. He attached the tackle to rescue the next. Soon there were six piled up so that they took up all the available space, and Webster forgot his sickness as excitement overcame him. He became aware of the diver clambering up the stern boarding ladder. In the darkness Nicholls resembled some sort of sea monster, his air hose writhing like a serpent about to strike.

Nicholls collapsed onto the helmsman's seat and threw his fins on top of the pile. He shucked off his head covering and sucked in a deep breath of the clear night air.

"Another fine job, Dave," said Critchley.

Nicholls grinned. "Smooth as shit!" he said. "There's four

more still down there. They're not as scattered as the last lot. It was a lot easier this time, not as deep either." Nicholls released his air tanks and wearily eased them from his shoulders.

"Right. Let's get rid of them down below and get out of here. You relax, Dave. Peter and I will do it."

Nicholls took over the helm and headed the yacht slowly towards the distant coastline as Webster struggled to pass their cargo below decks and by the time it was over he had forgotten his earlier sickness and was perspiring lightly from the effort. His clothes felt cold and damp against his skin and he pulled on a heavy jacket that he found on one of the bunks and re-joined the others on deck.

"What happens when there's bad weather out here?" he asked Nicholls.

"Then we don't dive if it's too bad. The risk of not being able to find the container when it comes up in a breaking sea is too high. Calm conditions with rain or fog is best for us. Next best is a dark night like this when we can't be seen from the shore," Nicholls added.

"What I meant was," said Webster, "What happens to the stuff down on the bottom, is there any chance that it could wash ashore in a storm?"

"Possibly, if the load is left out there for too long. The containers are well weighted," interjected Critchley. "Our biggest worry is that a fishing boat might drag one up in a net, but we chose the position carefully. It's an area that has a number of wrecks on the bottom and the fishermen tend to avoid it because of that. Nets cost money. They're too valuable to risk.

"Ever heard of the Lusitania?" asked Nicholls.

Webster looked up. "No."

"She was a big White Star liner that was torpedoed during the First World War. She lies just a few miles away, but in deeper water. I dived out there one day. She's covered with nets that got snagged on her. There's something eerie about it. It's like cobwebs hanging on a corpse. Twelve hundred passengers went down on her."

Nicholls paused and looked at the sky. "I think there's a

blow coming, Peter. It's just as well we got this job over."

Critchley poked his head out from under the spray-hood and sniffed the air suspiciously. The rigging had started to thrum softly. "I think you might be right."

"How do you know?" Webster asked.

"It's written in the sky." Critchley replied. "Look at the cloud building up. There's rain and wind coming. That halo on the moon is a bad omen."

Webster fell silent and watched the flash from the lighthouse on the Old Head of Kinsale. He tried not to dwell on the bodies of those lost at sea right underneath them, or the steadily increasing wind. Instead, he considered that he was sitting just a few feet away from more money than he could ever use. It was then that he remembered Ryder and felt suddenly cold as though the temperature had plummeted. He wondered if Ryder was watching them even now, perhaps from one of those tiny lights that were now showing as they neared the coastline. He should have killed him while he could, he thought, and not left it to the Burmese. They were fools, he told himself. He would not make the same mistake again.

It seemed an age before Collins stopped the engine and allowed the boat to drift. The waves seemed bigger further out and they slapped angrily at the hull of the currach causing it to roll drunkenly. Brennan was freezing. He shivered and hugged his arms about him. "Where the hell are they?" he growled. "I can't see a light anymore."

"Neither can I." Collins whispered. "They must have switched off their lights. But they're somewhere right ahead of us. We should be able to hear the engine. We're down-wind of them." He held up his hand for silence. "I think they've stopped." he said.

"What do you think they're doing?"

Collins stuffed a wad of chewing gum into his mouth. "I don't know," he said. "But if I was to guess, I'd say they were picking something up. Or else meeting someone out here."

Brennan shivered. "You know what that means?"

"Don't tell me. I don't want to know."

"What about radar, Seamus? Could they see us on radar?"

Collins thought for a moment. "No," he replied slowly. "Its unlikely. This is just a currach, there's no metal in her and we're low in the water. I was on trawlers once. We had radar on them and sometimes we couldn't even see big yachts unless they had radar reflectors."

Brennan felt satisfied. "If we can't find 'em," he said eventually. "Is there any point in staying out here, Seamus? I mean, we can't see what they're up to can we?"

"There's truth in that, Mattie."

"Well then..."

"Well then, we can go in if you like and wait for them to come back to the anchorage."

"How do you know they'll come back? I thought you said Critchley might sail to Crookhaven."

"They'll be back." Collins responded firmly. "I don't like the look of the sky, there's a blow coming. I can feel it in me bones and I know the way he operates. He'll be back before first light, just like a fucking vampire. I've seen him do it before."

"Are you suggesting we stay out here all night?" Brennan was appalled by the idea.

Collins gripped his arm fiercely. "You want to know what Critchley is up to, don't you?"

"Of course I do," answered Brennan.

"Then shut the fuck up and do what I say!"

FORTY

In the early hours of the morning, thick cloud built up over the South coast of Ireland. Even the Shannon meteorological station was caught unaware by the vigorous depression out in the Atlantic, which had quickly changed direction to track northeastwards, and the gale struck without warning. Its winds came howling out of the southwest at forty knots. At Shannon airport a light aircraft was picked up and blown across a runway just seconds after an American military plane, en route to its base in England, had made an emergency landing with engine trouble.

Wind Song was just three miles southwest of her anchorage, running downwind under engine in seas that were building by the second. On board, Webster was terrified. "This is madness!" he howled, only to have his words snatched away by the wind screaming through the rigging.

Critchley ignored Webster and clung to the spray hood to steady himself. He peered into the darkness, trying to find some distinguishing mark on the shore that would lead him to the entrance to the bay. This was white-knuckle sailing with a vengeance, he realized. His stomach was in a knot of apprehension but outwardly he was calm. He had no fears for the seaworthiness of the boat, although he knew that the seas would already be breaking right across the mouth of the harbor, such as it was, making their approach an act of lunacy.

Normally he would not have attempted it. The nature of their cargo was the spur. He would risk anything rather than run for the safety of Kinsale, and to stay at sea and battle it out with the stuff on board was equally unthinkable.

Nicholls was on the wheel. With his feet braced, he unerringly controlled the giddy plunge of the yacht as she careered down the face of another sea that broke with the noise of thunder around her. He was laughing, exhilarated by the speed of their passage. His diving suit glistened with phosphorescence, flashing a multitude of fairy lights but to Webster, he looked like some demon that had erupted from the bottom of the sea.

Webster forced his eyes away from the seas advancing behind them. He retched but there was nothing left in his stomach to come up, and only a green slime of bile filled his mouth. Another cresting sea roared out of the darkness from astern, picking up the yacht as though she were a toy. Nicholls wrestled with the wheel as the wave broke over the stern and thundered into the cockpit, filling it to the coamings. "Drive her under!" roared Nicholls, his laughter filling the air, as Webster was slammed back under the spray hood. For a moment Webster was sure that they were doomed, but to his surprise the yacht righted herself and he could hear the surge of water releasing through the cockpit drains.

"Keep her steady, Dave!" Critchley screamed. "I see the entrance!" Ahead of him was a black void where seconds before, a few points off the bow, he had glimpsed an area of white foaming water. He struggled aft to the wheel. "I'll take her now," he shouted. "Clip me on and get Webster down below!"

Nicholls attached Critchley's safety line to a ringbolt, then manhandled Webster through the hatch, almost throwing him down the accommodation ladder. Webster landed in a heap at the bottom of the ladder. The cabin was claustrophobic and the noise and darkness was even more frightening than on deck. The heaped up containers had all fallen to one side and the cabin table had broken away from its supports under their weight. Stunned, he lay looking up at Nicholls' legs filling the entrance. Then the yacht heaved on another approaching wave and he was sent sliding across the cabin sole, ending up with his head jammed between the cooker and a bulkhead. He heard Critchley scream, "Hold on, we're going in!" The noise reached a horrifying crescendo. In moments Webster was up to his armpits in water cascading through the open hatch.

Matthew Brennan and Seamus Collins crouched low in the shelter of a clump of furze bushes near the beach and watched in astonishment as the yacht approached the entrance. It seemed impossible that she could survive the maelstrom of white water that lay to seaward of the rocks that sheltered the bay. They had been lucky; when the wind came they were already just off the entrance and had ducked inside, anchoring in the lee of the rocks to wait for Critchley's return but their position had become untenable as the sea rose to break over the barrier threatening to swamp the currach. Collins had beached the boat further up the bay well away from Critchley's anchorage, and they had made their way back on foot to a vantage point where they could wait in safety.

Brennan switched his horrified gaze to Collins crouching beside him. "Surely they can't get in through that, can they?" he asked.

Collins shrugged. "We'll see in a minute," he replied. "The man's a fool to try, God help him. He should have run for Kinsale or else stayed out at sea until it blows itself out."

"Jesus! Seamus, will you ever look at that!" Brennan clutched Collins' arm tightly in his fist. Collins drew in his breath as he saw the yacht making a ponderous turn to brave the entrance. She was picked up by a huge wave that seemed to have the might of God in its maw, and rolled on her beam-ends right in the gap in the rocks. For a second she seemed to have gone right over and her masts almost touched the surface, but instantly she righted herself. They could just make out a dark figure struggling with the wheel in the cockpit; then she surged through the entrance with her bow clear of the water in one last dizzy spell of acceleration as she reached the calmer waters inside the bay.

"He did that well. I'll give him that." Collins whispered. He shook off Brennan's grip on his arm. "Let go of me arm will you? You're cutting off me circulation."

Still rolling uncomfortably, the yacht swept closer until she turned up into the wind. They saw someone running along the deck to pick up the mooring. He missed it with the boat hook on the first pass, then the yacht surged away for another attempt. This time, whoever was on the foredeck made no mistake, and soon there were two figures on deck hauling in the mooring warp to make it fast.

"Now comes the interesting bit," Collins said softly. "This might be where we find out what they were doing out there in the first place."

With the mooring line secure, Critchley followed Nicholls back to the cockpit and switched off the engine. Webster emerged through the hatch. "What happened?" he spluttered. "I thought we were sinking!" He was clearly shaken.

Nicholls gave a short laugh and braced himself as the yacht rose to snatch at her mooring. "You weren't the only one," he said. "That was as close as it gets, sport. You can thank your lucky stars that we had an engine that was man enough for the job."

Webster's legs folded and he collapsed in the cockpit as though all the strength had gone out of him. "I never want to go through anything like that again," he said quietly as his fingers explored a lump forming on the back of his head.

Critchley glanced inside the darkened cabin at the water sloshing about down below. It was halfway up to the saloon bunks. Sodden charts and books moved sluggishly on the surface.

"I'd better pump her out," he muttered. He slid down the ladder and felt for the switch panel over the chart table. The cabin lights came on followed by the whir of the electric bilge pumps. He sat down heavily on the navigator's seat and fumbled in a locker for a packet of cigarettes. Lighting one, he hungrily dragged in the smoke and contemplated the chaos below decks. Every locker in the boat seemed to have emptied its contents and the starboard settee was littered with canned food, broken bottles and other debris. He took in the piled up containers of drugs and the smashed saloon table beneath them. "Jesus!" he groaned.

Nicholls joined him. "We'd better get this stuff ashore, Richard." His voice was quiet. "We've never brought in such a load. The sooner it's off our hands, the better I'll feel."

Critchley's hands started to shake uncontrollably and his fingers lost their grip on his cigarette. It sizzled for an instant as it hit the water. "Get the dinghy ready, Dave." he said. "We'll drop Webster ashore first and he can go back up to the house." There was a tremor in his voice that he was unable to control. "He'll be bugger all use to us out here. He can send down the other two to carry the stuff up when we get it ashore."

Nicholls made to go back on deck but he paused halfway up the ladder to look down at Critchley. "You know," he said. "I thought we were a goner for a moment back there."

Critchley cracked a weak smile. "So did I, Dave. So did I." He surveyed the packages of drugs piled high all around him. "They didn't help. All that weight down here, when she went over..." He rested his hand tenderly on the teak fiddle of the chart table and caressed it. "She's a lady, this one. She'll live longer than any of us."

Brophy and O'Dwyer arrived at Cork airport long after the last incoming flight for the day and only a few stragglers remained in the concourse, haranguing a distraught official about their lost baggage. They found two of the local plainclothes-men waiting for them near a coffee machine. One of them stood up as they approached. "You must be Brophy," he said, extending his hand. "I'm Sergeant Reynolds."

"Glad to meet you." Brophy replied. "This is Sergeant O'Dwyer."

O'Dwyer smiled and shook hands. "You guys did a good job," he said. "We didn't expect to find the car that easily. Where is it?"

"In the car park. Forensics are waiting to take it away to do a check on it."

They followed Reynolds outside and walked the short distance to where two other men waited beside the Mercedes, which was illuminated by the powerful lights of a police recovery vehicle. A gust of wind howled across the car park, sending a scattering of rubbish scurrying into the air. "Hell of a night," Brophy growled. "There was nothing about this on the forecast earlier."

"There's trees down all over the county," one of the Cork detectives replied. "We heard there's a lot of trouble around the coast and lifeboats are out everywhere."

Brophy peered inside the car and flashed his torch over the seats. "Clean looking," he said with a grim smile. "I doubt if it will tell us much."

O'Dwyer carefully opened the boot and shone his torch inside. In a corner, lay a half-used roll of duct tape. "Take a look, Boss. It's our man all right."

Brophy peered into the boot. "See if your lads can get prints off that," he said. "My guess is that it's the only thing he has forgotten."

He straightened up and looked back at the airport building. "I'd say he's flown out of here back to wherever he came from. The car's got German plates all right, but he could have gone anywhere. We need a list of all the flights and passengers that have gone out of here.

O'Dwyer looked thoughtful for a moment. "Maybe that's what he wants us to think, Boss."

Brophy gave O'Dwyer a searching look. "Why do you say that?"

O'Dwyer shrugged, looking uncomfortable for an instant. "Just look at where he left the car. I mean, would you have done that? Right close to the terminal, where it could easily be seen. That's why it was found so quickly."

"Maybe he was in a hurry to catch a flight," offered Reynolds.

"This guy's a professional," Brophy countered. "I think O'Dwyer might have something. Let's go back inside and see what we can turn up in the airport. Maybe there's a passenger list or some damn thing that can point us in the right direction."

Ryder glanced nervously at the fuel gauge as he negotiated a sweeping bend in the road. A red light flashed intermittently on the dashboard and the wind buffeted the car as he crossed a bridge over a river where the water was choppy. His grip tightened on the steering wheel, willing the car to go an extra few miles.

A few minutes later he topped a hill and saw the lights of a town directly in front of him. He caught a glimpse of a Texaco sign ahead on the right-hand side and coasted slowly towards it. The garage consisted of a large corrugated iron shed with fuel pumps outside. There were lights in a shop off to one side. The engine spluttered, leaving him with no choice. He swung into the forecourt, picking a pump that was furthest from the line of vision of the attendant that he could see sitting inside a pay window. He knew he was running a risk and for a moment he debated whether to fill up and drive on, but where to? He had to ask for directions whether he liked it or not. At least the place was not well lit, he thought as he got out of the car. He picked up the hose oblivious to the wind swirling about the forecourt and hammering on the overhead canopy. Finished refueling, he walked towards the lighted window behind which a youth was reading a newspaper. Ryder slipped sixty euros into the cash tray. "I'll take a couple of bars of chocolate as well," he said. He kept the scarred side of his face averted as the young man looked up and turned down the volume of a portable radio on the counter.

The attendant reached for the chocolate and rang up the sale. "That'll be fifty-eight fifty," he said.

"I'm looking for a man named Critchley, he lives in some place called Clonbar."

The garage attendant peered at him through the window. "That'll be Clonbar House. Are you here for Helen Cullen's funeral?"

"Funeral?" The question took Ryder by surprise. "I don't..."

"She was Critchley's girl friend," the youth interjected. "She died this morning. Suicide." he added mournfully.

"I didn't know about that." Ryder felt taken aback by the turn in the conversation. "I just need to find the house," he said. "I'm supposed to be staying with him, but my flight was delayed."

The youth squinted at him suspiciously. "It's easy enough to find," he replied. "When you get into the town, turn left and go round by the harbor past the Trident hotel, over the bridge and take the R600 to Clonakilty. About two or three miles out you'll come to a pink bungalow on your right, you can't miss it. It's the worst shade of pink you've ever seen. Everyone's been talking about it. Just beyond it there's a turn to the left. Drive all the way down towards the sea and you'll find the entrance to Clonbar house at the end of the road."

"Thanks." Ryder turned away and walked back to the car, trying not to hurry.

Brophy and O'Dwyer had little success with their enquiries inside the airport. The check-in staff had already gone home and it was some time before they were able to track down an official who reluctantly agreed to search the boarding lists for passengers who had flown out that day. "Nobody named Ryder is listed," the man said after an interminable wait.

Brophy scowled. "Are you sure? Just run a check on all the UK flights again."

"Inspector, I'm perfectly sure about it. Nobody of that

name checked in. If he flew out of here he did so under another name. I work in a back office, so I wouldn't be able to help you with the description you gave either. I rarely see the passengers. You'll have to come back in the morning when the check-in staff come back on duty."

O'Dwyer gave a discreet cough. "I think we're at the end of the line here, Boss."

Brophy nodded slowly. "I suppose so." He smiled at the airline official. "Thanks for your trouble. We'll try again in the morning."

The two men walked slowly towards the door, coming out just as the recovery vehicle carrying Ryder's Mercedes passed by. "I still think he flew out tonight," Brophy said as he watched the truck disappearing into the darkness.

O'Dwyer shrugged. "I'm starving," he said. "Do you think we might find a take-away still open?"

Brophy unlocked the car and climbed into the driver's seat. "I'll buy you the biggest burger we can find," he said. "Then we'd better find a B&B for the night."

"Hold it!" O'Dwyer shouted as Brophy started the engine.

"What's up?"

There came the sound of running footsteps and Brophy caught the flash of a car's headlights in his rear view mirror. Reynolds leaned heavily on the car for support as Brophy wound down his window. "We think we might have your man," he said breathlessly. "I was afraid you had already gone. We were on our way home ourselves."

"Where?" Brophy snapped.

"Kinsale," the detective replied. "Fifteen minutes ago someone fitting his description stopped for petrol just outside the town. The attendant thinks he recognized him from a description he heard on the radio at nine o'clock. He's driving a blue Renault. We have the number and we know where he's going. If it's him, the silly bastard asked at the garage for directions."

"Jump in," Brophy said tersely. "Your mate can follow us."

FORTY-ONE

Ryder braked as he rounded a bend in the road. Seconds later his headlights picked out a garish pink bungalow, and he slowed even more to pass the road on his left that he had been told led to Clonbar House. It seemed too risky to drive there, he decided. It would be safer to find a hiding place for the car and reconnoiter the area on foot.

A little further on, he found just what he was looking for. An overgrown track led him into a disused quarry, now used as a dumping ground for the rusted remains of skeletal cars, long since picked clean of anything useful. It was quiet, and sheltered from the wind that drove in from the sea. He removed his pack from the boot, slipped a clip of ammunition into his pistol, and sped back to the main road.

Fifteen minutes of fast walking along the deserted by-road brought him within sight of the gates to Clonbar House. He was aware now of being close to the shore, the roar of the sea combining with the wind drowned out the sound of his own footsteps as he kept close to the perimeter wall. He studied the locked gates from a safe distance, noting a spot lamp that illuminated the electronic keypad that controlled them. Then he froze, hardly daring to breathe, as his eyes picked out a surveillance camera mounted on a pillar above the light. He recalled the lack of security he had found at Sullivan's home in Galway. This wouldn't be quite as easy, he thought.

Across the lane from where he stood was a low stone wall, overgrown with briars. Beyond it lay fields, as far as he could judge in the darkness. He tried to estimate the line of vision of the camera, then retreated back up the lane before crossing quickly and taking to the fields. Soon he was opposite the lighted gateway again, and then he was past it, with the noise of surf louder as he neared the beach. Seconds later he slid down a bank and his boots crunched on a shelving beach of rounded stones near where the lane ended. The wind buffeted him as he moved to his right until he lost sight of the wall that guarded the grounds at the front. He had no idea whether his route was taking him towards the house or not, but he continued to follow the beach for some distance until he judged it safe to make his way back to higher ground.

Ryder found himself in a plateau-like field of long grass where clumps of wild furze rose towards a scattering of trees higher up. In the distance, perhaps half a mile from where he stood, the lights of the house relieved the darkness. Suddenly, he became aware of the sound of voices carried on the wind and he dropped to the ground instantly, not knowing from how far off they had come. He raised his head, straining for any sound above the roar of the surf and wishing the moon would show itself, if even for an instant. He glanced up at the sky but its light was blotted out by cloud.

He moved forwards at a crouch, staying close to the beach, stopping only when he thought he picked up the sound of an engine above the crash of waves. Seconds later he heard the crunch of a boat striking shingle and a muttered curse reached him. He wormed his way slowly towards the lip of the low cliff above the beach and peered over the edge. Further along the beach a boat was leaving the shore with a man standing up in it to pole it out into deeper water. The man squatted down and an outboard motor stuttered into life. Small flashes of white came from the boat as it ploughed into the waves. Minutes later, Ryder saw the light of a torch further out and he caught a quick glimpse of a large yacht rolling heavily to her anchor. Then the light disappeared and he fancied he heard the sound of voices.

He became aware of sudden movement nearby and hugged the ground. A man carrying something heavy on his shoulders appeared as a dark shape perhaps fifty yards from where he lay. The man disappeared into the darkness following a well-trodden path through the grass leading in the direction of the house.

Ryder sensed urgency in what he had just seen. The man had been furtive and careful to make as little sound as possible. Ryder recalled the soft padding noises of unshod mules on the night he had last seen Webster. Nobody in their right minds would be out moving supplies or equipment from a boat at anchor in the height of a storm, and in the dead of night to boot. It had to be drugs. Briefly, he wondered if either of the men he had just seen was Webster, and a cold wave of excitement consumed him. One shot, he thought. That's all it would take. Then he could go. The mission would be over. He got to his feet and took to the path.

As he closed on the house, Ryder circled to avoid a gravel forecourt and sped across the drive to the safety of dense shrubbery on the opposite side. Lights showed in two of the downstairs rooms and he could see steps leading up to the front door. Noises were coming from the rear and he moved off in that direction until he found himself facing a courtyard. What looked like stables or a large garage was directly before him.

A floodlight illuminated the courtyard and through an open doorway in the building he could see a large van backed inside with its rear doors open. Behind the van he spotted a green BMW parked under bright electric lights. He heard the thud of something heavy being dropped onto the floor of the truck, then saw a man jump down from the tailboard and step into the light. Ryder recognized him instantly as one of the men who had waylaid him in Dublin. A second man joined him in the doorway and a match flared as they lit up cigarettes. Their voices reached him clearly.

"My chest is killing me, Mossy! How many more for Christ's sake!"

"There's only two or three left on the boat, I'll do it, you stay here, Paddy. Critchley and Nicholls can bring up the last two."

"About time they did some of the heavy work!"

Ryder went to ground as one of them stomped out his cigarette and started to cross the courtyard. He passed close to Ryder, who held his breath until he heard the man's footsteps receding across the gravel in front of the house. The other man moved back from the doorway and Ryder lost sight of him as he went behind the van.

Ryder shed his pack and crossed swiftly to one side of the door. The lights exposed him with no room for error. Flicking off the safety catch on his pistol, he stepped quickly inside, keeping close to the van as he edged towards the rear. His heart rate increased and his adrenaline flowed as he coiled himself. He moved with barely a sound, and suddenly the two men were face to face.

Paddy was sitting on the edge of the van floor, swinging his legs idly as he finished his cigarette. His eyes widened, first in surprise, then in recognition. As he opened his mouth to scream a warning, Ryder thought of the waspish dwarf back in Hamburg who had sold him the automatic. He remembered thinking then that the pistol was heavy. Now he was glad of the weight of it as he brutally clubbed Paddy in the mouth, shattering his front teeth with a metallic crunch. Ryder caught him by the throat as his head flew back.

Ryder pocketed his pistol and went to work with his roll of duct tape. He dragged the unconscious body into the shadows at the rear of the BMW and left it there. Paddy had more than the pain in his chest to worry about now, he thought. He probably had a broken jaw as well. One down, three to go. Then Webster, wherever he was. Even if it meant going to London again, he would do it. He moved back into the protective shadows inside the van, wishing that he could risk taking out the lights, but that would be a dead give away. Surprise was still on his side.

Twenty minutes later, as Ryder listened to the shriek of the wind reaching its peak rain spattered explosively on the exposed area of the truck, sweeping through the open garage door to slick across the concrete floor. He strained his ears but it was difficult to hear anything outside. No one had returned. He debated whether to leave his hiding place then something bumped heavily against the side of the van and he steeled himself.

A man appeared at the rear and slammed a soaked package onto the floor. In the instant it took for Ryder to spring forward, he knew he had left it a micro second too late. The man threw himself sideways and screamed a warning into the night air as Ryder lost his footing and fell from the rear of the truck, cursing his own clumsiness. Regaining his feet, he brought up his pistol and started to run after the man sprinting across the courtyard. He heard a door slam, then came the chatter of a weapon from somewhere ahead of him and he heard the whine of ricocheting bullets whipping off the concrete. He pumped off two shots and whirled to one side, throwing himself down and rolling back to the relative safety of the garage.

Ryder sprawled inside the doorway as another burst of gunfire slammed into the van, shattering one of the headlights. He instantly recognized the rabid splutter of an Uzi sub machine gun, the sound filling him with dread. How could he have been such a fool? He looked around desperately for some way out, but there was none. No rear door, no window, just lights everywhere that exposed his every move. He rolled onto his back and took careful aim at the floodlight just outside and above the entrance. He felt the buck of the pistol in his hand, closing his eyes protectively as glass rained down on him and the light went out, turning the yard into rain-swept blackness. A light flashed up at the house, and the air filled with bullets. A front tire on the van exploded and it sagged forwards. Whoever was firing the Uzi knew little about it, Ryder thought. It was a close quarters weapon. The distance was too great. Ryder felt grateful that his foe was an amateur.

Near to where he lay, a long handled shovel rested against the wall. Two bare electric bulbs illuminated the garage but he could see no switch on the wall. He heaved himself upright and fired several shots into the night hoping that it would at least cause someone to duck. Picking up the shovel, he sprinted across the floor and smashed out each of the light bulbs, going to ground as another withering burst of gunfire swept the building. There seemed to be two of them at it now. Ryder felt something tug at the heel of his boot as he regained the protection of the truck; a bullet had nearly found him. He stretched out prone on the concrete, waiting to pinpoint the next muzzle flash, ducking his head when it came. He pumped off two more shots then the pistol clicked on empty. His fingers scrabbled in his pockets for his remaining clip of ammunition. Eight shots left, then he was out of it. He had to make a dash for it, he decided, before the gunmen moved in for the kill. If either of them had been Sinbad or any of his comrades, they would have done it already, he thought. He took careful aim and squeezed off four shots in quick succession, hearing glass shattering, as he dived through the doorway.

He was halfway to the trees when the answering burst of gunfire swept the building behind him, there the van exploded into flame, which became an instant inferno as the wind sucked it towards the roof. He crouched low, fired two shots, and flung himself headlong into the shrubbery.

At the first sound of gunfire, Critchley dropped his bale onto the ground and froze. For an instant he wondered if he had imagined it. He was only yards from the house. Maybe something had been torn loose by the wind.

Then it came again and there was no mistaking it this time. He saw the lights go out in the courtyard and he started to run in panic back towards the sea. He collided with Nicholls in the darkness halfway down the path and sprawled full length, his breath knocked out of him.

Nicholls dropped his bale and dragged him to his feet. "What the fuck is going on!"

"Gunfire!"

"Where?"

"Up at the house," Critchley croaked. "I'm not waiting around to find out about it. If you've got any sense, you'll come with me. It could be the cops."

Nicholls hesitated. "Come on!" Critchley shouted, breaking into a run.

Mathew Brennan and Seamus Collins heard the shots too. Like a pair of startled rabbits they poked their heads up as Critchley and another man hurtled past them heading for the beach. Brennan's greed evaporated in an instant as though the heat from the flames he could see shooting over the house had sucked it out of him. Critchley was welcome to whatever he was doing. He wanted no more part of it. "I'm getting out of here," he whispered.

Collins licked his lips nervously. "Me too."

Without another word they set off at a stumbling run across the field towards the distant gates.

Brophy was half asleep in the front seat of the car as O'Dwyer swerved to a halt at the gates. The second car pulled to a stop behind them. Brophy got out of the car and walked closer to the gates. "Locked," he shouted.

O'Dwyer got out and joined him. "Maybe we can get in over the wall."

"Maybe you can, but I'm too fucking old for that shit!" Brophy growled. He raised his hand. "Hear that?"

"Hear what?"

"Shots!" Brophy snarled. He ran for the car and jumped into the driver's seat.

O'Dwyer had hardly closed his door when the car plunged forwards and rammed the gates. The crunch sounded expensive. For an instant he thought of the endless forms they would have to fill in to explain it. Then Brophy was reversing to have another go as the gates sagged inwards.

On the second attempt they burst through as flames leapt skywards just over the hill.

There had been no further gunfire for several minutes. Ryder lay in the bushes debating whether to make a run for it. He watched the flames from the van lick into the roof timbers, then the wind rose again as though it was determined to fan it into a holocaust. It was time to consider what few options he had left. A direct assault on the house was out of the question. He had lost the initiative. Marchand would withdraw, conserve his energy and attack again when the time was right. He thought of the man he had left trussed up inside the blazing building. He would die, Ryder knew, and he rebelled against the thought. It was Webster he wanted, and he would have to wait.

The sudden roar of flame shooting into the sky instantly transported him back into the ruins of Mogadishu airport where the smell of death was more overpowering than the fire that destroyed what was left of it. He saw again the young boy on the roof, his jacket smoldering at the edges of the hole in his chest and he remembered acutely how he had felt after he had placed the muzzle of his MP5 to the boy's forehead and squeezed the trigger.

The anguish of the memory galvanized him into action. Ryder got to his feet and raced across the open space. His heart pumped fear to his brain just as it had done on the mad dash up the runway after landing in Mogadishu. Again he tensed himself for the searing shock of bullets that didn't come. Then he was inside the smoke-filled garage, fighting for air as the flames became intense.

The man had managed to roll clear of the BMW. Still gagged by adhesive tape, he could not cry out. His eyes were wide with terror as Ryder grabbed him by the feet and dragged him to the door. As he did so a thunderous noise silenced the wind as the roof sagged downwards, and a great gout of flame leapt for the sky as it collapsed.

Ryder didn't hear the gunfire when it came, but he felt the tug of bullets striking the man's body as he dragged it away from the flames. In panic, he abandoned it halfway across the courtyard and leapt for the bushes. He lay perfectly still gulping air into his lungs, thankful that he was not hit. The bitter taste of failure was worse than the smoke in his lungs. His fingers probed his right boot where the entire heel was missing and only a shred of the sole remained. He knew he had to find a way out while he was still able. His luck could never last.

FORTY-TWO

Inspector Brophy brought the car to a sudden halt as he crested the hill. Beside him, Colm O'Dwyer was shouting instructions into the radio microphone to a Special Branch team already racing down from Cork to join them. Directly in front of them, flames eerily lighted Clonbar House. "Call in the brigade too," Brophy ordered. "While you're at it, order up an ambulance. God knows what we are going to find down there."

Out of the corner of his eye he spotted two figures running wildly across the field off to one side. "Nab those bastards!" he shouted, jumping from the car.

Reynolds had already seen them and he was out of the back seat in a flash, racing at full pelt to head them off. As the second car slammed to a halt behind them, the second Cork detective spilled out to join the chase. When they reappeared, they were shepherding Matthew Brennan and Seamus Collins between them. They stuffed them into the back seat. "You two are nicked," Brophy shouted as he put the car back into gear and raced down the hill.

Wide eyed, Collins huddled into a corner of the rear seat. "We didn't do anything," Brennan protested. "They've all gone mad down there."

O'Dwyer wheeled on them. "You heard the man! You're nicked! We'll get to you two after we sort out that mess down below."

Nicholls summoned all his strength and struggled willfully with the mooring rope, releasing it as the yacht dipped her bow into a trough. "All gone!" he roared, scuttling back down the side deck to the cockpit.

Critchley rammed the gear lever into ahead and opened the engine throttle. The yacht fell off the wind momentarily before surging forward into the darkness as the rudder brought her under control. She slammed into a wave that broke ferociously over the bow, swamping them in icy water that ate into their bones. "Drive her under!" Nicholls screamed into the wind. He laughed wildly.

Critchley had had enough of Nicholls' lunacy for one night. "Don't start that shit, Nicholls!" he bellowed. "Make yourself useful and harness us up."

The gap in the rocks became clearer, becoming a maelstrom of white water that seethed across the entrance directly ahead of the plunging yacht. It was enough to turn a man grey before his time, Critchley thought. His legs shook. But he knew that if he could nurse her through it, freedom and the open sea lay beyond. Once into deep water, he could go virtually anywhere. He shot a quick glance over his shoulder to where flame lanced into the night sky. Burn, Webster you bastard, he thought vehemently. He tightened his grip on the wheel as the boat felt the first big swell rolling through the entrance, he didn't hesitate. It was all or nothing now. There was nothing back there for him.

He slammed on full throttle as a great bearded sea towered in front of them with its malevolent teeth bared on the crest. With infinite slowness the yacht clawed her way skywards, hesitating at the top as though she were about to fall backwards into the abyss. She shuddered like a dog shaking itself and broke through to skid giddily down the back of the wave as Critchley fought with the wheel to regain control. The wind tore at his clothes and on either side the rocks roared while Nicholls screamed his defiance back at them.

They were almost into clear water, when the next great comber reared its head in the darkness just outside the gap in the rocks. At that moment the hitherto faultless engine lost power. "What the hell . . ." Critchley hammered the throttle with his fist. "Give her power, Critchley!" Nicholls screamed. He was no longer laughing. "Don't let that engine die!"

Critchley shot a terrified glance at the plummeting rev counter. "Fuel," he shouted. "Water in the fuel!" He knew that he was facing his nemesis.

They were powerless as the wave towered over the yacht and roared out of the darkness. It's maw rose above the main mast, gathering strength to strike. As the yacht teetered, the crest broke high overhead gathering them in its grip and hurling them onto the rocks. Neither man felt pain as they shattered on impact.

Ryder was about to leave his hiding place in the shrubbery and make a run for it when two cars skidded to a halt on the graveled forecourt. He ducked back into cover as four men piled out. It was clear that they were police. Seconds later, a fire truck thundered down the approach road with its blue lights flashing and siren blaring. One of the men signaled for the others to take cover and scurried towards the steps leading to the front door. "This is the police!" he thundered. "Lay down your weapons and come out!"

The fool, Ryder thought. He didn't know what he was dealing with. Perhaps he'd figure it out soon enough when he got a taste of that Uzi. But to his utter surprise the door opened and a man appeared in the entrance silhouetted by the light from inside the hall. He had his hands up. Then a second man joined him and they both stepped outside into the light from the headlights of the cars. Webster! Ryder recoiled as a feeling of infinite hatred shot through him. He had been there all the time.

The policeman at the bottom ascended the steps cautiously, and for a moment Ryder lost sight of them as the fire engine passed in front of him. Then an ambulance and another police patrol car arrived and the whole forecourt became filled with running figures. The courtyard became a tangled morass of hoses, firemen, and flashing lights. Clouds of white steam billowed up into the night as water found the searing flames of what remained of the garage block. One of the firemen released a terrified horse from the stables and the animal thundered off into the night.

They were all coming down the steps now. Ryder braced himself. Calmly he got to his feet and walked quickly across the intervening space. No one challenged him. They were concerned only with the three men now halfway down the steps.

Webster recognized Ryder as he reached the bottom step. His eyes widened in fear and he tried to turn back but the policeman restrained him and forced him forward. They were only yards away as Ryder coldly raised his pistol.

The whole scene seemed to unfold in slow motion in Ryder's mind. "Gun! Watch out!" He heard the warning shout from somewhere behind him and ignored it. He gripped the pistol tightly in both hands, took careful aim, and squeezed the trigger as he heard a rush of bodies descending on him. One shot to the chest, a second to the head. A technique called the double tap, calculated to kill instantly. The first shot was for Wan and what this man had done to her. The other was for Mark, that he could rest in his grave and find peace wherever he was. Then he was thrown sprawling on the ground under a surge of bodies, the cold snap of handcuffs circling his wrists.

FORTY-THREE

The room was small and airless, with one tiny window set too high up in the wall to see anything outside. It contained a metal-framed table, three chairs, and a tape recorder on a small shelf. Overhead, a single powerful bulb turned the sickly green walls into the color of puke.

"Please sit down," O'Dwyer said, as Ryder was ushered into the room. O'Dwyer sat as he motioned to the chair opposite to him. Ryder slumped into the chair and placed his hands on the table.

Brophy remained standing, quietly studying the man who had brought his own private war to Ireland. He didn't like what he saw. Ryder's cold blue eyes were unnerving. His scarred face spoke of an ability to withstand pain and hold back anything he wished to. Ryder looked like everything Brophy thought he would be, a hard son of a bitch. He sensed that this would be no easy task as he reached over to switch on the recorder.

O'Dwyer jotted a note into the open notebook that lay on the table before him. "I'm Detective Sergeant O'Dwyer, and this is Detective Inspector Brophy. We're investigating the murder of a man named Martin Hennessy in Dublin on the night of the 26th." He paused to glance at his notes. "He was probably better known to you as Flicker Hennessy. You have already been charged with the murder of a Peter Webster, and I must warn you that you are still under caution."

Ryder made no reply and switched his gaze to a spot on the wall behind O'Dwyer's head.

Brophy groaned inwardly. He had seen it before. It was a tactic adopted by the hard men from the North. Find a spot on the wall, concentrate on it, and then say nothing. He should have expected it. This bastard was a professional, all right. He leant over and placed an ashtray on the table. "You can smoke if you wish," he said, adopting a friendly manner. "We don't abide by every rule in the Government's book." He threw a packet of Gauloise cigarettes carelessly on the table. Ryder's eyes did not even flicker.

"Where were you on the 26th?" O'Dwyer asked softly.

Ryder made no reply. Brophy pulled up a chair and sat down heavily next to O'Dwyer. He took one of the cigarettes and pushed the packet towards Ryder. "I bought these for you especially," he said. "We already know a lot about you, Mr. Ryder. For instance, you have a French passport but you are not French, are you? You're an English mercenary. An ex-Foreign Legionnaire, a trained killer. We checked you out in England. The Parachute Regiment is not exactly popular over here either, by the way and although you have no criminal record in either country, that doesn't mean to say that you're not a criminal. I mean, the Legion is full of bloody criminals, isn't it? After all, that's where it got its reputation. What we would really like to know is why you killed Hennessy and Webster. Who paid you to do it?"

Ryder selected a cigarette and lit it. He spoke for the first time. "I'm not a mercenary," he replied gruffly. "I'm a professional soldier."

Brophy sensed a weakness immediately. He glanced at O'Dwyer, his mind racing. Ryder had pride in what he was. He believed that soldiering - killing and maiming others - was an honorable profession, comparable to the practice of medicine or the law. Maybe it was time to change tack.

"Not anymore, you're not. The French authorities told us you were honorably discharged from the Legion a few months ago. They said you left with the rank of Sergeant and that you had been decorated for valor in the Siege of Sarajevo." Brophy stared at him coldly for a moment. "So you're saying nobody ordered you to do it? You expect us to believe that you're not an everyday scumbag. Instead, you want us to believe that you're some kind of war hero."

Ryder calmly pulled on his cigarette and made no reply. His face remained blank

"We were there when you killed Webster, you know. There are a dozen other witnesses that will testify that it was an assassination, a professional hit. You're going to get life, that can't be avoided but if you come clean with us, it might act in your favor."

Brophy was rewarded with a flicker of understanding in Ryder's eyes. "What does that mean?" Ryder asked.

"It means that a full admission of guilt might help to mitigate your sentence. It will certainly speed things up. It might even help us in other on-going investigations and I'd be prepared to recognize that in court." Brophy smiled cautiously. "It could help your case."

Ryder looked at the two men facing him and stubbed out his cigarette. There was a calculating look in his eyes that hadn't been there before.

O'Dwyer stirred in his chair. "We can prove that you killed Hennessy too," he said softly. "Webster is an open and shut case, as you perfectly well know. We just need a little more time to prepare the charge for Flicker's murder."

"What about Frank Sullivan?" Brophy probed. "He's dead too. What do you know about that?"

"Never heard of him."

Brophy sighed. "Okay," he said. "Forget him for the moment. Tell us about Webster. Why did you blow him away?"

"He was scum!" Ryder snapped. "He was a drug dealer."

"We know that," O'Dwyer said. "That became clear after we tracked you to Kinsale. Two of the men arrested there were closely connected to both Hennessy and Sullivan. If it's any consolation, one of them said that you dragged him out of the fire and saved his life. It doesn't add up. I mean, killing one and saving the life of the other."

"I'm glad he's alive, I thought he was dead," Ryder countered. "I didn't try to kill him; he was hit while I was dragging him out. Whoever was firing the Uzi was using it like a fly spray."

Brophy grunted. "He took a bullet in the leg and another in his shoulder, but he's doing okay. He says you bust his jaw and that if he ever meets you again he'll knock your teeth down your throat, and then he'll thank you for pulling him out of the fire. Why did you do it?"

"Why did I do what?"

Brophy scratched his chin. "Why did you pull him out of the fire? You smashed his teeth out, why not let him burn?"

Ryder took another cigarette and lit it. "Because I had nothing against him."

O'Dwyer leaned forwards. "But you had something against Webster?"

"Yes. He was my son's stepfather and caused him a lot of misery. He turned him onto heroin. The kid is dead now. Webster's dealing would have killed a lot of other people too. Besides, he. . ." Ryder stopped abruptly as though he knew he was saying too much.

"Besides what?"

"Forget it."

"You're not making this any easier on yourself," O'Dwyer snapped.

"I didn't expect it to be easy."

"Look," Brophy said calmly. "Paddy Mullins, the guy with no teeth, he told us about your run in with him in Dublin. We know you were there on the 26th and that you were looking for Hennessy. I thought the Gauloise might jog your memory."

Ryder took a deep breath. "Okay," he said. "I killed Hennessy for the same reason that I killed Webster. My son was a junkie.

He lived in Dublin until he died. He ran foul of Hennessy, who gave him some bad stuff. He might as well have triggered him. I decided to even the score." He hesitated for a second. "There was another thing, too. He set up some kid named Lynch to bring in heroin from the Far East. Lynch got himself topped out in Bangkok for it."

"That was in all the papers here. We didn't know there was a connection."

Brophy glanced at O'Dwyer who was sitting back in his chair, rocking it gently. "That's the first we heard of your son," he said. "So you're telling us this was just a personal vendetta. Revenge for your son's death?"

"Something like that."

O'Dwyer blew his nose into a spotless white handkerchief. "Where did you get the gun, Ryder? Ballistics are testing it but we don't see many like it. They tell me it's a Polish Radom."

"I picked it up from a guy in the Legion. Its okay, but they'll find that it throws off to the right."

Brophy eyed Ryder coldly. "Why did you cut Hennessy up? You used a knife on him before he died."

"I needed to know where to find Webster. He needed to tell me. There was no time to be delicate about it."

"What about Sullivan?"

"Never heard of him."

"You said that before."

"Yes, I did."

Brophy felt momentary anger. "We could dig him up, Ryder. You know that, don't you? We could do all the tests and find out what killed him."

"Dig the bastard up." Ryder shrugged.

Brophy leaned back in his chair and thought for a moment. "Webster had a deal going with Sullivan didn't he?"

Ryder gave him a cynical smile. "I suppose that's possible," he said. "They were in the same line of business according to you." He took another cigarette and puffed it alight.

"But I've already told you, I know nothing about this Sullivan guy. I can give you a name that might be a lot more important, though."

Brophy rested his arms on the table and leaned forwards expectantly. "Is that so? Who might that be?"

"A man called Phillips. I don't know anything about him but Webster worked for him. Try the Marbella Club in London."

Brophy nodded to O'Dwyer and the Sergeant left the room. "We'll take a short break," he said. "Like a cup of tea?"

"That would be nice, Inspector."

"You're a polite son of a bitch, aren't you?"

Ryder smiled. "You learn that in the Legion," he replied. "I can give you another name to check, too."

"Go on."

"Hans Klein. He lives in Hamburg. He's got a garage in the Reeperbahn. I think you'll find that he's mixed up in this as well. Just a hunch, mind you." Ryder's gaze bore into Brophy like a steel drill.

Ryder's words silenced Brophy. He got up and left the room feeling angry.

Ryder tried to relax in their absence and contemplated what he had told them. They had him dead to rights for Webster, and he knew he was going down for it. He should have made them work a bit harder for Hennessy, he decided. But there was nothing to connect him to Sullivan, only Hennessy and Webster could do that, and they were both dead. He sensed that Brophy had nothing to go on and was shooting in the dark.

He stubbed out his cigarette and lit another. Why was Brophy so concerned about Gauloise cigarettes, he wondered. He didn't remember smoking in Sullivan's house. He tried to remember if he had done so at Hennessy's flat. He vaguely recalled that he had, but he had taken the butt with him when he left. Maybe that was it. Perhaps they were able to do something with the ash.

He was surprised that he had given them Klein's name. But Klein had betrayed him, too. He could be dead now because of it. So much for family, he thought.

His thoughts turned to Wan. She was going to have to wait a long time for his return, he realized sadly. He felt suddenly tired. There would be a lot of time for sleep from now on, he thought. Perhaps for the rest of his life. The thought numbed him.

The door opened and Brophy came back into the room. He placed a mug of tea in front of him. "I forgot to ask you if you took sugar. I put it in anyway."

"Thanks. It'll be fine the way it is." Ryder stared at Brophy over the rim of his mug. He was beginning to like the bastard, he realized. "Are you checking up on Phillips?"

"It's being taken care of."

"Good."

"I don't like you, Ryder."

"I don't like you either, Inspector."

Brophy chuckled. "Then we understand one another," he said. "Are you prepared to sign a statement?"

"Yes." Ryder drained the remainder of his tea and put the mug down.

"I'll arrange for legal representation. I don't suppose you have a lawyer?"

"Do that," Ryder replied. "I never needed one before. What happens next?"

"You'll appear in court tomorrow to be formally charged. Afterwards you'll be remanded in custody until your trial. We will not be recommending bail."

"I didn't think you would," Ryder replied dryly. Brophy raised his eyebrows and gave him a quizzical look. "You know that I'd fuck off the first chance I got."

"I'm absolutely certain of it," Brophy replied.

Ryder laughed quietly. There was a moment's silence between them. "What happened to the others?" Ryder finally asked.

"Two of them made a bolt for it in a yacht. Their bodies were fished out this morning."

"What about the two in the car?"

Brophy shrugged. "Just a couple of locals that were out fishing and came in when it got too rough. They're witnesses now."

Sergeant O'Dwyer came back into the room and placed a pen and a sheet of paper in front of him. "Read it first, then sign at the bottom," he ordered.

Ryder glanced at the printed words. He controlled the shake in his hand and picked up the pen.

Brophy turned to O'Dwyer after Ryder had been led away to a holding cell. "What do you think, Colm?"

"Open and shut case, Boss." O'Dwyer sounded pleased.

Brophy squinted up at a shaft of sunlight that had penetrated the small window above his head. "Maybe," he said.

"There's no maybe about it. He signed a confession."

"I wasn't thinking about that. I was thinking about how easy he was to crack, he was holding something back, I'm sure of it."

"Like what? The guy is a moron, Bill. Did you look at his eyes? I've never seen eyes as cold as that. Ryder is a born killer if ever I saw one. I think he gets pleasure just out of smashing people up. Legion my arse! That bloody outfit is full of psychopaths. He killed Webster and Hennessy just because he wanted to. He didn't take his complaint to the police. Instead he planned it and did it, just like that."

Brophy uncrossed his legs. "Perhaps you're right, but I have a feeling he's mixed up in this whole sorry mess a lot more than he says he is. Maybe he's into the drugs scene deeper than he wants us to know about. I can't get it out of my head that he wasted Sullivan, too."

"We'll never prove it."

Brophy sighed. "I don't suppose we will," he replied. "There wasn't a mark on him and the death cert was clean."

"Well then?"

"Well what?"

"Are you going to pursue it?"

"Let me think about it. Let's see what the British turn up when they pull in Phillips. Ryder has opened up a Pandora's box for us. We've got him to thank for that."

"Do I detect a hint of admiration?" O'Dwyer chuckled.

Brophy smiled and walked towards the door.

FORTY-FOUR

Ryder was woken by the sound of an inspection grill being drawn back on the metal door of his cell. The metallic double click reminded him of a weapon being cocked and he sat up, instantly alert. Suddenly he remembered where he was. He was in prison on the first day of the next quarter of a century. It was a sobering thought to realize that it was a noise which would wake him every day for the next twenty-five years. He might as well be looking into infinity.

He got out of bed and padded quietly to a small barred window and looked outside. It had been dark last night when they brought him from the court and he had been too exhausted to do anything other than flop onto the iron-framed cot.

It was grey outside. Even the sky was the color of slate above the granite walls and black roof tiles. Directly below him he could see a rectangular enclosed courtyard that contained pools of water in the hollows and a miserable basketball net that clung resolutely to a wall at the far end. Someone had painted the outline of goal posts with whitewash on the opposite wall. There was a drab reality to the exercise yard that defied his worst expectations and he turned away from it in total despair.

His cell contained two cots, a pair of small lockers and a washbasin. There was also a lavatory bowl that didn't flush too well when he tried it, and a cracked wall mirror over the sink that was blackening at the edges. Linoleum tiles of an indiscriminate color covered the floor and a strong smell of disinfectant clouded the air. As yet there was no other occupant, but he suspected it wouldn't be long before there was.

He sat down on the bed to pull on his socks. The Legion had offered little in the way of home comforts, he thought. Perhaps even less than this in his early days of service, although he couldn't recall it easily. But at least the sun had shone in Calvi, and there was always the risk of a quick death to expunge any regrets. Here there was nothing but time. Each minute of it, measured by the tick of a clock and not by a calendar. If there was a choice, he thought fervently, he would return and jump without a parachute. He dressed himself, shaved in cold water that was a dull brown color, then sat waiting for the door to be unlocked.

Soon afterwards he heard the jangle of approaching keys and found himself standing outside his cell. He was conscious of faces turning towards him, a multitude of suspicious eyes weighing him up and searching for the first sign of weakness. They wouldn't find it. He squared his shoulders and followed a line of men towards a metal staircase and when he passed a uniformed warder at the top of the stairs, the man studied him, too. His manner was that of an animal sniffing the air for potential danger.

The canteen was as Ryder had expected; a noisome barn of a room with a high ceiling that threw back the noise of voices and the clatter of plates and cutlery. He followed the line, collecting a bowl of porridge that was the same color as the morning, a mug, and a serving of bread with a spoonful of marmalade. Then he found himself a seat at a long table. Metal pots of tea banged and slapped while he ate in silence, oblivious to the enquiring glances of those nearest to him.

Afterwards he followed the stream out into the yard where the others gathered in small groups smoking or chatting in a way that he found disturbing. He wondered what they found to talk about. Certainly it was not about the latest exciting thing in their lives. The realization that he was banged up inside a prison for a long time to come flooded over him, bringing a sense of acute despondency. Unless he changed it, he thought suddenly. He started to jog then, round and round the yard like a caged animal with his eyes on the walls, constantly measuring their height. There was always a flaw, he thought. He just had to find it.

Ryder returned to his cell when he was ordered to. That it had gained an occupant while he was away didn't surprise him. From what he had heard while he was on remand, Mountjoy was bursting at the seams and he was lucky not to be sharing with more.

His new cellmate was sitting on his cot busily sticking photographs on the wall with blobs of plastic adhesive. He looked up as the door slammed shut.

"Hi! What's you name?"

"Ryder."

The other man swiveled on his bed and eyed him uneasily. "I've heard about you," he said. Then he smiled slowly. "My name's Dinger. Dinger Bell - get it?" He gave a cackling laugh, but his eyes showed no amusement.

"Glad to know you, Dinger." Ryder sat down on the opposite bed and gazed at him warily. He didn't particularly like what he saw. Dinger was a wasted runt of a man with thinning hair that lay on his domed skull like drying seaweed. His features were pale and pinched so that his cheeks looked as though he was constantly sucking them in. His eyes were weak and edgy, flickering beneath shaggy eyebrows that belonged to a much stronger man.

"Been here before?" Dinger asked without looking up.

"No," Ryder replied.

"I thought not. You don't look like someone who knows the ways of the Joy."

"The Joy?"

"Yeah, it's what we call this fucking place. Mountjoy - the Joy - understand?"

Ryder smiled uneasily. "I get it," he said.

"I know all about it," Dinger said proudly. "It's not bad, once you know your way around. Winter is best though, then its warmer here than outside. Summer is a bummer." He gave a cackling laugh again. "I should have been a poet!" The faint twinkle disappeared from his eyes. "I heard they gave you twenty-five?"

Ryder scowled and stayed silent.

"That's a hell of a sentence. You pulled the wrong fucking judge. Are you going to appeal?"

"I hope to," Ryder answered.

"You should. Anything I read about you in the papers said you did the fucking Guards a favor. Is it true that you were a mercenary?"

"No, that's not true." Ryder's eyes flashed.

Dinger looked at him sharply. "No offense," he said.

Ryder lay down on the bed and stared at the ceiling. "None taken," he replied softly. He listened to Dinger rummaging about with his photographs.

"You want me to put you wise about a few things in this place?"

Ryder rolled onto his side. "Like what?"

Dinger thumbed another snap shot onto the wall and turned to him swinging his legs over the edge of the bed. "Well," he said. "First of all, you can get just about anything you want in here, if you go about it right. Fags, drugs - booze, even. Heroin is easy."

"I just came from there," Ryder interjected angrily. "That's why I'm here."

Dinger's eyes clouded. "Some of the guys in here won't take too kindly to what you did, I wouldn't brag about it if I was you."

"I'm not bragging about it."

"Okay, calm down. Like I was saying, do things right and you won't find it too bad. The Governor is okay. He likes to think he's rehabilitating us, know what I mean? But he's a sound shit behind it. Doesn't take any nonsense, but a sound shit all the same. The Chief Warder - his name is Flynn - watch him because he's from the old school. We call him the Bishop, because he likes nothing better than giving you the belt of his crosier if you give him the chance!" Dinger laughed softly. "The rest of 'em are only doing a job and couldn't really give a shit so long as they get home to the wife every shift without any agro. You're English, right?"

"Not anymore. I'm French."

"That's a pity."

"Why?" Ryder stirred himself.

"Visitors." Dinger replied.

"There won't be any."

"None?"

"None at all."

"Shit!" Dinger gave him a long sad look. "You must have friends," he said.

Ryder smiled coldly. "They're either dead or they're on the other side of the world."

Dinger shook his head. "I couldn't handle that. Not for the sort of time you're doing." He gestured at the photographs. "They mean a lot to me. The wife - the kids - mates, even the fucking dog."

"Don't let it worry you, Dinger. I can handle it. What are you in for?"

"Aggravated assault and burglary. I couldn't get a job the last time I got out and I've got a habit, you know what I mean? They gave me five this time, but I'll probably get out in two." He looked away for an instant. "Two is bad enough for fuck's sake! I'll only be here for a few days though."

"How's that?"

"I've put in for a transfer to Limerick, that's where I come from."

Something triggered in Ryder's brain. He sat up with his feet on the floor and looked closely at Dinger. "What do you mean, you put in for a transfer?"

"Simple." Dinger replied, selecting another photo from the bundle on his lap. "If you're doing a long stretch they try to put you near to your family, if you ask. Mine are in Limerick, so I went and asked the Governor for a move there on compassionate grounds."

Ryder thought about what he had just heard. "My mother had a sister in Limerick once," he murmured. "I think there were cousins too, but I never met them."

"Well, there you are then," Digger said triumphantly. "There's your fucking visitors for you. If those are the only people you've got, you can ask for a transfer. Doesn't mean to say you will get it, but you can try if you want to."

"Ryder grinned. "Dinger," he said softly. "I think you and I are going to be good mates. You've just made my day!"

Dinger's face flushed. "I'm glad."

With three weeks of his time served, Ryder had settled into a monotonous but purposeful routine. He was on good terms with most of the warders and was well on the way to establishing himself as a model prisoner without antagonizing his fellow inmates. Dinger Bell shepherded him constantly, paving the way to ensure that he was accepted as one of their own. He seemed inordinately proud of his newfound friendship with Ryder and had guided him skillfully in his approach to the prison Governor. The only thing that he didn't share was Ryder's passion for the library and pumping iron in the gym. Keeping the body and mind fit consumed Ryder and he made the exercise yard his own private racetrack where he jogged endlessly at every opportunity.

When the time came, neither man was prepared for it. It was after the evening meal, both men were watching television when the Chief warden came in and spoke in whispers to the guard on duty.

The warder nodded his understanding and came over to where they were sitting. "Okay, you two. Get back to your cell and pack your things. There's a vehicle going down to Limerick and you're both on it. You have half an hour, so get moving!" A chorus of mocking cheers broke out among those sitting closest to them.

Ryder packed his few belongings oblivious to Dinger's excited chattering. His mind was too preoccupied with what he would find in Limerick. But his thoughts of getting outside even for a few hours were euphoric. Nothing in life remained the same, he thought. Round every corner lay something new. Bad luck for some, opportunities for others. Behind every change lay something else. The family had prepared him well.

"I told you we'd get it!" Dinger chortled. "Didn't I tell you that, Robby boy! Has Dinger ever left you down, mate!"

"Yes, you told me, Dinger. Now shut the fuck up and stop wasting time. If that truck goes without us, I'll kick your arse from here to eternity!"

"How do you know it's a truck, you shit! It might be a car. If it's a car we'll be able to see out, and it's a grand evening for that!"

Dinger's enthusiasm became infectious. Ryder punched him playfully on his shoulder. "Move it, you bollocks!" he shouted.

The transport waiting for them in the yard turned out to be a dark blue Ford Transit van. A uniformed driver was waiting in the driving seat and a second warder accompanied them into the back. Then the gates opened before them and they were driving along Dublin streets that were almost frightening in their normality.

Ryder glanced at his watch, it was almost nine. The evenings were drawing in. It was still daylight, but a soft glow in the western sky spoke of approaching darkness and as they left the busy city streets for the main road leading to Limerick lights were flickering on in the pubs and late-opening shops.

Dinger nudged Ryder. "What does it feel like, Robbie?"

"Great! Bloody great!" he whispered.

"Pity its getting dark; you'd enjoy the drive. I love the country. One day I'll sort myself out and get a place out in the country. It's better for the kids, you know? The wife would like that too."

Ryder doubted if Dinger would every sort himself out, not unless he gave up the junk that he was on, he thought, but he refrained from saying it. "You'll do it, Dinger." he said instead. "If you want to, you can do that, but you really have to want it. If a man puts his mind to something, he can accomplish the hardest thing in the world. I've done the hardest things in my time, and I know."

Dinger fell into silence for the first time and Ryder turned his attention to the dark shadows of fields speeding past. He squinted out of the window up at the sky. Not a bad night, he thought. A half moon that appeared now and again high in the clouds that held a hint of rain, but only that.

It was growing dark inside the van now and the warder sitting opposite was only a blurred shadow, with his chin nodding on his chest as he fought against tiredness. The driver switched on headlights, dipping them now and then to approaching cars, but the traffic was thinning. His face was visible in the glow from the instrument panel. Ryder noticed that he wasn't wearing a seat belt. He strapped on his own with difficulty because of the handcuffs that were tight on his wrists. Beside him, Dinger was nodding too, lulled by the motion of the van and the soft purr of the diesel engine. Ryder remained awake, noting every sign and bend in the road.

The headlights picked out a sign for Nenagh, and then soon afterwards they were on the open road again. Not far to go now, Ryder realized. He wondered what Limerick prison would be like, Dinger had said that it was a grand place but he doubted that. No prison was a grand place. Koh Samui was a grand place, but only he knew that.

The scream of tires and the ensuing crunch as the van left the road came with a swiftness that even Ryder was unprepared for. He heard the whinny of a horse just before its head suddenly exploded through the windscreen. Then the van became airborne for a second before plunging down a steep bank, turning on its side as it did, so that the roof crumpled inwards like tin foil.

Ryder found himself suspended by his seat belt. The seat next to him where Dinger had been seconds before was empty. He released his belt and slid into a heap on top of the warder who had been sitting in the back. He could feel him breathing under him but the man was unconscious and did not stir. Ryder peered into the front. The engine was still running and the headlights threw their beam into a boggy ditch that had a stream running through it. The horse's eyes were lifeless, two bulging orbs that glowed eerily in the lights from the instrument panel while blood flowed steadily from its nostrils. The driver was crumpled over the steering wheel and was not moving. Ryder struggled closer and felt for the keys. He switched off the engine and the lights went out so that it was suddenly pitch black inside the crumpled remains of the van.

He heard a sound from behind him and crawled back to where Dinger was moaning softly. "Dinger! Dinger, are you all right mate?"

"I think I bust me arm," Dinger moaned. "What the fuck happened?"

"We hit a horse, I think the driver's dead."

"Shit!"

"Stay there. I'll be back in a minute." Ryder crawled back to where he had last seen the warder who had been seated with them. Feverishly, he searched his pockets and found the keys. Seconds later his handcuffs clanked away into the darkness. He went through the man's pockets one by one, taking anything of value. Then he returned to where Dinger was lying. "Hold out your wrists," he ordered.

"What do you mean?"

"Hold out your fucking wrists, I'm going to un-cuff you."

"No!" Dinger shouted.

"What do you mean, no? This is your fucking chance, you clown!"

"There's no chance, Robbie. Not for the likes of us. If you try to fuck off from here you'll get no appeal, and if I go with you I'll have to do the full five. I'm staying."

"Suit yourself, mate. I'm heading for the fucking hills. There will never be another chance like this."

"Fuck you, Ryder! You're fucking nuts!"

"I'm off," Ryder replied. He wrenched open the rear door and slid outside into the darkness. He hesitated and peered back inside. "Are you sure, Dinger? You're okay, right!"

"Yeah, I'm sure. We'll be found pretty soon. If you're determined to go, you had better do it."

"What's your address?"

"Limerick fucking prison!"

"No. You're home address, I'll drop a card to your wife."

Dinger laughed. "You're kidding! You'll be back with me tomorrow."

"Just tell me the address."

"Poulduff Lane, Limerick. That'll find me."

"Okay!" Ryder reached inside and searched in the darkness for Dinger's hand. He gripped it. "Good luck, mate! It was nice knowing you."

"You're a mad bastard, Ryder. But good luck, I hope you make it."

Ryder searched the night sky for a guiding star and seconds later he took to the fields.

Inspector Brophy took the call from O'Dwyer just before dawn. "He's out, Boss!"

Brophy's head was muzzy with sleep; he laid his hand on his wife's shoulder and soothed her as she moved restlessly beside him. "What was that?"

"I said he's out. Ryder has busted out and is on the loose."

Brophy came instantly awake and sat up in his bed. "How in the name of Jesus did he manage that?"

"They were moving him and another prisoner to Limerick last night. The van hit a rider-less horse outside Nenagh."

Brophy felt that he would choke. "Why were they moving him to Limerick? For Christ's sake! Didn't they know what they were dealing with? Ryder, of all people!"

"Apparently he put in for a transfer because he had people there."

"That's the first I heard of it!" Brophy exploded. "He pulled the fucking wool over their eyes, that's what he did! The bastard suckered them."

"Well, he's out." O'Dwyer replied gloomily.

"I heard you the first time, Colm. It doesn't surprise me that much. I just thought it would take him longer. Jesus! A fucking horse! I'll bet it was a tinker's horse. What happened to the rest of them in the van?"

"The driver was killed; he died on the way to hospital. The guard who was in the back is okay but he's suffering from concussion and the other prisoner has a broken arm."

"I'll bet you any money that Ryder hasn't got a scratch. That sod has the luck of the devil!"

"I'm not taking the bet," O'Dwyer responded dryly. "I'm going down to Nenagh."

"Pick me up on the way, I'll come with you." Brophy put down the phone and swung his legs out of the bed. He patted his wife on her shoulder. "Something's come up," he whispered softly. "I have to go out."

Fort Meagher was bathed in the first flush of early light when Ryder swung his legs over the parapet of the bridge. The rope was still coiled where he had left it. He was close to exhaustion, his face heavily bearded after five days on the run and it was all he could do to summon enough strength to lower himself down over the chasm.

He collapsed in a heap through the gun embrasure and tumbled onto the floor. For a while he lay there trying to assemble his thoughts and bring his eyes into focus. The past five days had honed him to the bone and what remained of his clothing hung on him like the remnants of tattered sails. Not once had he harbored a thought of giving up although he knew they were still searching for him. He had traveled only by night, eating from the discarded scraps left in bins, but always going to ground by day. Despite hunger and cold, he had stolen nothing, and had covered his tracks in the way he had been taught to do. Cork city had been his biggest obstacle, but although he had seen police roadblocks several times, it had surprised him how easy it was to evade them. He had the family to thank for that, just as he had them to thank for making him what he was.

His hunger pangs grew acute and he crawled painfully to where he had left his store of food. It was still there. The most welcoming sight of all, was the rolled up bundle of his sleeping bag. Feverishly, he ripped open a can of bully beef and wolfed it down. Then he got the chemical stove going and heated up a can of stew.

Afterwards he checked that the money was where he had left it. Although he had never counted it, he knew there was more than he would ever need. Gratefully, he zipped the sleeping bag around him and fell into a coma-like sleep.

It was evening when he awoke and although his mind pleaded for more rest he knew that he had to leave. He could not risk that rope in darkness. Once he had negotiated that he would wait for nightfall. Quickly he gathered his remaining supplies and stuffed everything into a black plastic bag. He tied it to his back with a length of cord and eased himself through the gun slit. Again came that momentary flash of fear as he gauged the distance to the rope, then he concentrated his mind and jumped.

The river was quiet just as it had been the last time he was here. He ignored the temptation of the nearby small boats at the pier, no tracks, he told himself. Slipping quietly into the water, he swam strongly towards the dark shadow of the nearest yacht.

It was more difficult than he expected to pull himself out of the water and the effort exhausted him. He lay on the side deck with his head resting on the plastic bag containing his belongings regaining his breath for a few minutes, and then crawled quietly into the cockpit. On inspection, the sliding hatch leading to the cabin was secured by a rusted padlock that probably wouldn't even open if he had the key. He searched one of the cockpit cave lockers and was rewarded instantly with a rusty screwdriver. Forcing the hasp, he slid back the hatch and eased himself down a short ladder into the cabin where he found himself standing in water that was above his ankles, dipping his fingers in it he then tasted them. Good. It was fresh, with only the slightest hint of salt. The boat had lain unused for so long, she had collected rainwater. He would find a way to pump it out later.

He felt his way around the small cabin and his fingers came to rest on a flashlight held by a spring clip over the chart table. He switched it on and got a glimmer of light from its fading batteries. It was enough to make out a heap of sails in the tiny fore cabin that also contained a toilet. The mattresses covering the two bunks in the saloon were covered in green mould from dampness. To his surprise, in the chart drawer he found charts. One was for the Western Approaches and showed the tips of the English and French coasts. His heart soared.

A locker under one of the bunks revealed a collection of rusty food tins from which the labels had long since disappeared and when he tried the hand pump over the small sink in the galley he was rewarded with a gush of water that tasted drinkable.

Turning his attention to the cooker, he fiddled with the controls until he heard the hiss of gas. Excellent. Next he took a quick look into the engine compartment. That was more disappointing. The engine was a rusted mass that only looked fit for a scrap yard but to his relief, the flywheel turned easily when he tried it, at least the engine wasn't seized up, but he didn't dare try to start it although there was a starting handle held in clips on the engine space bulkhead. That was another plus as it might enable him to start the engine later even with flat batteries. He returned to the cockpit to search for the bilge pump, and located it immediately underneath the tiller. For the next fifteen minutes he pumped steadily until the boat was empty of water, then he moved cautiously around the deck familiarizing himself with the layout of the halyards for the sails. He had plenty of time. He felt confident too, that he had chosen his boat wisely and not gone for a more modern boat that was better maintained and equipped. No one had been near this boat in months, he decided and it was unlikely to be missed and might buy him the time to make his escape. It was not yet midnight and the nearby road was still busy with cars going to and from Crosshaven. Now to his satisfaction he noticed the boat had begun to swing on her mooring and he knew that the tide had started to ebb.

As soon as the headlights of cars had begun to thin, he hoisted the foresail and cleated off the halyard. Throwing off the mooring pennant he returned to the cockpit and took the tiller as the boat started to move with a pleasant gurgle of sound rippling around her. By the time he turned the last bend in Drake's Pool, the wind had picked up into a gentle breeze from the northwest and the lights of Crosshaven lay directly ahead. Soon he was surging down river at a comfortable speed under a headsail only, leaving the black shadows of moored yachts in his wake.

He passed close to the yacht club where the voices of late night reveler's issued from the open windows and carried clearly across the water and as the harbor widened, ahead of him he saw the first twinkle of navigation buoys in the outer reaches of Cork harbor. His mood became triumphant; all the hardship of the past few days seemed irrelevant and was forgotten. The path to freedom lay out there among those winking colored lights. The risks in putting to sea in a run-down small yacht held no fear. If it meant death, that was far preferable to what he had left behind.

Under the black shadow of Fort Meagher that had sheltered him so well, he let the boat wallow while he hoisted the main sail. That done, he returned to the cockpit and bore away towards the flash of Roche's Point lighthouse. Beyond lay the open sea, France, and the far corners of the world. His heart lifted and he started to sing in French with his voice booming into the night. "Though I walk with the devil . . ."

Deep in his heart Inspector Brophy always knew they would never find him. Now, after two weeks he was sure of it. One part of him almost welcomed the fact; he couldn't find it in himself not to have a begrudging regard for Ryder. The man, in his twisted way, had done him an enormous favor and had been rewarded with a savage sentence, and Brophy was still basking in the accolades he had gathered for having broken up one of the largest drug smuggling rings in Europe, a ring that was far wider than he could ever have imagined. With Phillips on remand awaiting trial, even the British police were singing their praises of the benefits of cross border co-operation, and the Dutch were equally euphoric with the Kung brothers now in custody too.

He strode into his office jauntily, where for once, the disarray of his desk did not plunge him into despair. There were new cases to investigate, new murders to solve. It would never end, he knew, but he no longer felt daunted by it.

He set his coffee on the desk and skimmed through the morning's collection of mail and faxes and from the center he extracted a postcard showing an elephant dressed in some sort of ceremonial finery. Briefly, he wondered who he knew, that might be on holiday in some exotic place, then he turned it over and read the scrawl. "Sorry for the trouble, Inspector," it said. "You were right not to trust me - Good hunting." There was no signature. The postmark was New Delhi. Brophy started to laugh. At first it was hesitant, but soon it was turning heads in the outer office.

He picked up the phone and called O'Dwyer. "You won't believe this but I had a card from Ryder," he said when Colm answered.

"Where from?"

"New Delhi."

"You are shitting me! How do we get him back from there?"

"Colm, if you even think for one minute that the sod is in New Delhi, you're a bigger fool than I think. He's anywhere in the world but New Delhi. Perhaps one day we will read in the papers that he was killed in some godforsaken bush war somewhere, but that's all."

"I suppose you're right, Boss."

"I know I'm right, lad. Put it down to one of life's experiences and thank your lucky stars that there are few like him. I'd like to know how he slipped out of the country that's all."

"I might have an answer to that."

"If you have, I'll buy you a pint."

"Just before you called, Reynolds down in Cork called me. He said that they had received a report that a small sailing boat had been found abandoned in Morgat in Brittany. The French police think it may have come from Ireland. Our lads are trying to sort out if anything is missing from the South coast."

"That's it, Colm! That's how the bastard slipped away. I'm sure of it. Well, I have to admit he is a resourceful son of a bitch, that's for sure."

Brophy replaced the phone with a smile of satisfaction. At least, he thought, he would not be loosing any further sleep wondering how Ryder had pulled it off. With an air of renewed optimism he turned his attention to the paper work in front of him.

Later on the same morning, the postman delivering mail to Poulduff Lane in Limerick knocked on the door and handed a disheveled Helen Bell a small parcel.

Quietly she returned to her tiny kitchen and opened it. Inside the brown wrapper she found twenty thousand pounds in crisp English twenty-pound notes. There was a note written on a sheet of paper torn from an exercise book. "Dinger," it said. "Thanks for saving my life. This is to help you find your place in the country. Good Luck."

There was no signature. She sat down in total disbelief and started to cry.

EPILOGUE

The last ferry from Surat Thani carried few passengers as it powered through the muddy estuary waters at the mouth of the river before heading for the open sea. Ryder felt too tired to show any interest in the fragile fishing platforms in the shallows that excited the scattering of other European travelers. Listlessly he watched the land disappearing astern before retreating from the rain to light a cigarette and think back over his journey.

Each day had melded into one and it now seemed like a blurred half remembered dream since he had sailed out of Cork harbor. His luck had held then, and aided by a following wind that had rarely risen above force six, he had reached Morgat in Brittany in little over four days, only altering course during daylight whenever he sighted another vessel. At night he pressed on regardless, passing close to what appeared to be Spanish fishing vessels that were far too busy in what they were doing to pay him any attention, if they even saw him at all.

Successfully timing his approach to Morgat in darkness, he had tied up inside the marina in the early hours and bade farewell to the small yacht that had served him so well and by dawn on the same day he had hitched a lift on a truck carrying vegetables for the city markets and was well on his way to Paris.

His false passport served him well and a night flight to New Delhi followed. There he had rested for two days, before traveling on to Madras and Calcutta by train, breaking his journey in each place, before continuing on by air to Colombo and Bangkok. From there an overnight night train had carried him on the last leg south to Surathani. Now only his fit of bravado in sending the postcard to Brophy from New Delhi rankled in his memory. That had been a drunken mistake and he prayed that he would not live to regret it. Because of that indiscretion, he had taken no more direct flights towards his goal, and he felt comfortable that he had covered his tracks as well as he was able. The money he had sent to Dinger Bell's wife, he did not regret that at all. He owed Dinger for his freedom, it was as simple as that, and if Dinger got his place in the country that would be reward enough.

He tried not to think of what he would do if Wan was no longer in Koh Samui, but now that he was so close, the worry of that became relentless. He had been gone a long time he realized, longer than she expected. He could hardly blame her if she had tired of waiting. Perhaps he should have written to her from Mountjoy, but that had been a risk he was not prepared to take. Not once had he divulged even a hint of her existence in case it might jeopardize everything and lay bare his plans. No, he decided. She would be there, just as she had promised. No other woman in the world could have convinced him of that, but Wan was different. She had to be, he realized, otherwise his life would be meaningless again, just as it had been before. He flipped his finished cigarette into the wake of the ferry and faced resolutely into the driving rain, willing the island to show itself as darkness descended around him like a shroud.

Wan woke in an instant with an unaccustomed feeling of dread and rolled over in her bed to look at the screen door. She could hear the moist monsoon wind rattling the palms outside as though it carried a message that she could make no sense of. Water dripped steadily from the eaves turning the dust of the yard into the constituency of red porridge.

She realized that she had been dreaming just before she awoke, but couldn't recall what the dream was about, and a sense of great loneliness overcame her as she started to cry softly.

Suddenly she became tense as she realized what had awoken her. The rain had stopped. She lay perfectly still and waited for it to start again, but only a diminishing dripping sound from the palm-topped roof reached her. The rains had ended, and with that her hopes died. She screwed herself up into a tight ball with her fists clenched between her legs in an effort to halt the tears. She had waited so long. Now he was never coming back, a voice inside told her. The words revolved in her brain branding her mind with their finality. He was a farang like all of the others, she realized. A stranger who had brought lies that she had believed. She should have known better, everyone had told her so. Now she had to face those knowing faces and admit that they were right.

Slowly she forced herself into a sitting position and stared at the screen door, willing the rain to start again. When the rains end, he had promised. Now, for the first time in many weeks she could see stars twinkling in the sky as the clouds rolled away, carrying his promises with them. Instead of his presence the dry heat of summer was about to begin and soon it would bring the farangs in droves, all with new lies. Nothing had changed, she thought sadly, only the seasons.

The air was sultry but she felt inexplicably cold and as she continued to stare at the screen door, the moon showed itself above the nearest palm tree and the yard filled with soft luminescent light. She wondered if he could see it too, wherever he was, far away on his side of the world. Perhaps he was smiling up at it and laughing at her foolish beliefs. The trickery of the farangs was deep enough for that, she knew. But not he, she thought. Surely he was not the same? If she really thought that for one minute it would surely destroy her. Suddenly, a shadow crossed the doorway and she imagined the sound of a soft footfall as a momentary flash of fear replaced the doubt in her mind. She was on her feet in an instant clutching her sarong about her as the stars were blotted out and the figure of a man filled the doorway.

The door swung back revealing those familiar powerful shoulders that had plucked her from the Mekong and suddenly she hated herself for ever doubting him. She flung herself towards him as a great wave of gratitude engulfed her.

"I said I would come when the rains ended," he said in a voice that was soft, just as she remembered it.

"I doubted you," she choked. "Just now, I doubted and hated you. I should have known better." She ran her fingers over the contours of his face. "Will you stay?"

He let out a long breath that was warm on her face. "Yes," he whispered into her hair. Gently, he picked her up and laid her on the bed.